RIP TIDE

RIP TIDE

Stella Rimington

WINDSOR
PARAGON

First published 2011
by Bloomsbury Publishing
This Large Print edition published 2011
by AudioGO Ltd
by arrangement with Bloomsbury Publishing

Hardcover ISBN: 978 1 445 85906 4
Softcover   ISBN: 978 1 445 85907 1

British Library Cataloguing in Publication Data available

Printed and bound in Great Britain by
MPG Books Group Limited

To my grandson George

Liz Carlyle looked at her watch. The French Minister of the Interior was in full flow, expatiating on the new security threats facing Europe. From where Liz sat, in the back row of the seats set out in the library of the Institute for Strategic Studies in Whitehall, she could survey the whole room. At the front French and English officials, senior policemen and military officers sat alongside journalists, who were eagerly scribbling on their pads. At the back, assorted French and British spooks were grouped, well out of sight of the TV cameras. For this Friday morning was the press conference concluding the previous day's Anglo-French Ministerial Security Summit.

Liz's last posting in Northern Ireland had led to a close involvement with the French security services, and now, back in counter-terrorism, she had special responsibility for joint operations with the French. Next to her Isabelle Florian, her colleague from the DCRI—MI5's French counterpart—was shifting in her seat, looking worried that she'd miss her Eurostar back to Paris. Liz liked Isabelle, a businesslike woman in her forties with a careworn face and a good sense of humour—not at all the chic Parisienne that Liz had expected and rather dreaded.

When they'd first met they'd been able to speak to one another only through an interpreter, but since then, in preparation for this job, Liz had taken an intensive course in French and was now fairly fluent.

Out of the corner of her eye, Liz could see the tall, elegant figure of Geoffrey Fane of MI6, standing at the side of the room, leaning nonchalantly against a pillar, surveying the scene through half-closed eyes. Typical of him, she thought, to station himself where he had a bird's-eye view of the room. He prided himself on his private intelligence network, which meant knowing everyone's personal business— particularly, it seemed to Liz, her own. He would have noted that she was not sitting next to Charles Wetherby, who was now the MI5 Director of Protective Security. A few years before, she had thought herself in love with Charles and she knew her feelings were reciprocated. But at the time he had been married; his wife was a chronic invalid and a clandestine relationship had been out of the question. Geoffrey Fane had sussed this and had delighted in subtly taunting Liz about it. Now Charles was a widower, Fane would be watching to see what developed between them.

The French Minister sat down at last and the Home Secretary started her remarks. Thank goodness she will be a bit less long-winded, thought Liz, who had helped draft her speech. She listened with half an ear to the familiar phrases about the continuing serious threats Europe faced from terrorism. Traditional espionage still endangered security, she was saying, while new threats were appearing from cyber attacks on the infrastructure of countries.

The historic circular room, lined with bookshelves from floor to ceiling, was becoming warm and stuffy, overheated by the lights of the

TV cameras. The journalists' questions became desultory and at last the conference concluded. There was a scraping of chairs as the audience stood up and the Ministers and their entourages left the room. Next to Liz, Isabelle grabbed her briefcase. She gestured impatiently at someone in the row ahead of them; a man, medium height, dark-haired, and dressed in the smart casual uniform of the French—a grey turtleneck and a checked jacket.

'Martin, hurry up,' said Isabelle. 'The train's in forty minutes.'

'I wanted to say hello to Liz,' he said amiably.

'Well, be quick about it,' Isabelle ordered.

The man grinned. 'There is always another train.'

Isabelle looked at Liz and raised an eyebrow.

Liz smiled. 'Isabelle, I'll see you in Paris on Monday. Is ten o'clock okay?'

Isabelle nodded then turned to Martin, explaining, 'Liz is coming across for a follow-up meeting. This kind of conference is all very well, but it doesn't give us any time for detailed discussions.' She looked at her watch. 'We really must be going.'

'Goodbye, Martin,' said Liz. Isabelle was already heading for the exit.

'I hope you mean *au revoir*,' he said with a small smile as they shook hands.

*   *   *

Later in the day, as the train emerged from the tunnel on the French side of the Channel, Liz looked out of the window as the countryside

3

flashed past. This journey had become very familiar to her; she'd noticed that it was the appearance of the villages, particularly the shape of the church towers, that showed you were in another country, even before you noticed the road signs in French.

And then almost before she could blink they reached Paris. In the fresh sunlight of the spring evening it seemed to her the most beautiful city in the world. Not even the noisy jostling crowd on the platform of the Gare du Nord could sour things. And when the Metro slowed for Saint-Fargeau, her stop on the north-east outskirts of Paris, her pulse quickened at the prospect of the weekend ahead.

She crossed a busy road, then went down a side street. As she approached a now-familiar house, she saw the other tenant, Madame Beylion, come out of the front door. She was a stout, elderly lady with a face set in deceptively dour lines, for she was in fact the kindest of souls.

'*Bonjour*, Madame Beylion,' Liz called out, much more confident speaking in French than she had formerly been.

'Ah! *Bonsoir*, Madame.' The old lady waved and smiled. '*Monsieur est à la maison. Il vous attend.*'

Upstairs the door opened just as Liz was about to ring the bell. 'Telepathy,' she said.

'I saw you through the window,' Martin Seurat replied with a grin, and they both laughed. Then he gave her a big kiss. He'd changed out of his work clothes, and was wearing a dark blue Lacoste polo shirt and cotton trousers. With its regular features and dark deep-set eyes his face was at once handsome and a little forbidding—until he smiled, and his eyes lit up.

Martin was in the DGSE, MI6's French

4

counterpart. Liz had met him on the same Northern Irish investigation that had led to her association with Isabelle. It had turned out that her quarry was a former colleague of Martin's in the DGSE, a man called Milraud, who had become an arms dealer. As the operation had proceeded the immediate mutual attraction had strengthened between Martin and Liz, and after the operation had ended they had gone off together to a small hotel in the Provençal hills, where in the early Mediterranean spring they had unwound in each other's company.

Now, a year on, what Liz had thought of at first as a fling had turned into ... what exactly? She didn't know or care to analyse it too deeply. She was just happy with it as it was, and their arrangement certainly fitted in well with her current job. Martin's flat had become her temporary home when, as quite often happened, work took her to Paris.

On her first visit to this flat, Liz had been taken by surprise. She had been expecting a smart bachelor pad in a central district of Paris, somewhere very different from the comfortable apartment in a handsome house in the 20th *arrondissement*, which was where he actually lived. She knew him better now. The quiet, wide square shaded by plane trees, the friendly neighbours, the local shops where they seemed to have known M. Martin for years, all fitted his personality much better than the minimalist apartment she had imagined.

This evening they had a simple supper in the little alcove off his kitchen, while they caught up with each other's news. It had been almost a month

5

since they'd last seen each other apart from the brief meeting at the press conference. Martin's daughter, who lived with his ex-wife two hundred kilometres away, was taking the Baccalauréat this year and applying to the Sorbonne. He was pleased at the prospect of soon being in the same city as his daughter.

'By the way,' he said as he cleared their plates from the table, 'there's been news of our old friend from Porquerolles.'

'Milraud?' Liz asked in astonishment.

'Not Antoine,' said Martin, as he came back from the kitchen. He filled her glass with the last of the bottle of Beaune they had shared. 'His wife, Annette. She was spotted in Versailles, of all places, but by the time we heard about it, she'd disappeared.'

'I'm amazed she risked showing her face in France.'

'She has always loved the high life. Hiding out with her husband in one of the new Soviet republics would have palled for her very quickly. I am just hoping that Antoine has come with her. Then we'll get him,' Martin said with a hint of steel in his voice.

They moved into the sitting room; Liz stood by the window, holding her glass, looking out at the little square across the street. The hour's time difference with England meant dusk was starting to fall, and a small circle of old men were finishing a last game of *boules*. Small powdery explosions of dust flew up each time a player carefully tossed a heavy silver-coloured ball.

'A little Armagnac?' asked Martin.

'No, thanks. I'll just finish my wine.'

'So you're seeing Isabelle on Monday?'

'Yes. We're going to compare notes—as she said, there wasn't much time at the conference to go into detail.'

He nodded, but didn't ask any more questions. Early on in the relationship they'd established an understanding about discussing their work, which meant never enquiring in any detail about what the other was doing.

Now he got up and stood beside Liz at the window. The players were finished for the evening and were packing their *boules* away in small leather pouches. Martin put his arm round her. 'Liz,' he said tenderly, 'I've got a suggestion to make . . . and I don't want your answer right away.'

She looked up at him and smiled. 'What is it?'

'I was wondering,' he began, then paused. 'Wondering whether you'd ever think about coming to live here—in Paris, I mean, not necessarily here in this flat.' He hesitated. 'It's just that I miss you so much when you're in England.'

She drew away from him, continuing to stare out of the window. She didn't reply.

'I've said the wrong thing, haven't I?'

She turned back and reached for his hand. 'No, you haven't. You know I love being here with you. But it's just . . . it's such a big decision, Martin. I need to think about it.'

'I knew I shouldn't have said anything. Forget I did, Liz. I don't want it to spoil our weekend.'

'I don't want to forget about it, Martin. I just need to think about it.'

He put his arms round her again and kissed her. 'I want you to be here all the time, that's why I brought it up. But I know it's selfish of me. There

7

are other things in life that are important to you—believe me, I do understand that.'

She leaned her head against his chest. 'There's no other person more important to me than you are.'

He let her go and took hold of her hand. 'Come on,' he said with a laugh, 'don't let's get too serious. I think it's time for bed, don't you?'

2

As daylight broke over the Indian Ocean, spilling light the colour of chalk on the distant horizon, Captain Jean-Claude Thibault watched the outline of the huge ship emerge slowly from the darkness. He'd known she was there, just three kilometres away across the calm waters of the Indian Ocean, but now he could see her clearly. Indeed she was impossible to miss: a container vessel, probably four hundred feet long, painted a rich maroon with a yellow stripe at her plimsoll line just above the water. Fully laden, she was low in the water as she ploughed through the sea, heading south.

Standing on the bridge of his corvette, binoculars to his eyes, Thibault could see the Greek flag flying from the stern and make out the name painted in black along one side of the snub-nosed prow: *Aristides*. He'd been expecting her arrival; as part of a new international protection force, his job was to see her and other vessels safely through the dangerous waters off the Horn of Africa, on their way to port in Mombasa.

As Thibault watched her moving forward at

a good rate of knots, leaving very little wake behind, his First Officer, standing beside him on the bridge, tapped him on the shoulder and pointed. Thibault shifted his binoculars and saw a skiff, so small that it took a moment for him to focus on it. It was close in, under the overhang of the larger vessel's stern, hugging dangerously close to her side. He wondered momentarily if it were a dinghy let down by the Greek ship's crew to make some repair, but dinghies didn't look like that—a dilapidated wooden craft that couldn't have been more than fifteen feet from bow to stern, with a mast that looked like the branch of a tree. Half a dozen figures sat huddled in the little boat, one at the stern holding the rudder of a massive outboard motor, which looked heavy enough to overturn the fragile craft.

Pirates. They must have crept up on the ship in the dark, lurking alongside until dawn began to break. They couldn't have noticed the corvette waiting in the darkness and, if they saw it now, must be gambling on taking over the ship before it intervened. Captain Thibault watched with fascination as the men in the skiff began lifting a long thin metal ladder; it rose straight into the air like a construction crane, then tilted gently until it leaned against the side of the ship. It was being carefully extended, a segment at a time, aiming for the lowest point of the deck, at the stern. He could see the curved ends at the top of the rungs, designed to hook as tight as handcuffs over the deck rail.

Thibault gestured towards the tanker, and spoke tersely to the First Officer: '*En avant.*' Let's go.

Though the corvette was small compared to the

massive container ship, her engine packed a mighty punch. Within seconds she was closing in on the *Aristides* and her unwelcome visitors at maximum speed. Simultaneously the radio officer, Marceau, was trying to contact the bridge of the container ship, to warn them of the imminent attack. 'They must all be at breakfast,' he muttered after his repeated radio bursts received no reply.

When no more than two hundred yards separated the vessels, Captain Thibault gave further orders and two of his crew took up position behind the pair of .30 mm cannons mounted on the bow. Three more men armed with rifles stood by.

Ahead of them, a figure had detached itself from the huddle in the skiff and started to clamber up the ladder. He was soon halfway up, a rifle on a sling hanging from one shoulder as he climbed.

Suddenly the corvette's radio crackled into life. 'This is *M.V. Aristides*. Why are you approaching?'

The crew member did not sound alarmed; it would be evident to those on the container ship that the approaching vessel was a French patrol boat. Marceau replied sharply, 'French Warship *Tarasque*. We are not your only visitors. Pirates are climbing a ladder at your stern.'

Thibault took over the microphone. 'This is Captain Thibault, French Navy. One pirate is boarding you: stern, port side. Armed. There are others in a skiff at your stern. We'll deal with them. Keep your crew below decks and out of range. Is that understood?'

'Understood,' came the confirmation.

They were less than a hundred yards from the tanker now, and Captain Thibault ordered the engines to be slowed to idling speed. He clicked

10

a switch on a microphone, and his voice was transmitted clearly through an amplified speaker across the water.

'This is the International Protection Force. Stay where you are, and do not attempt to board the ship.'

There was an eerie silence. Looking behind him at the French patrol boat, the solitary pirate on the ladder began a rapid descent. Suddenly the outboard motor started up and the bow of the little skiff swung round. The man on the ladder jumped, clearly hoping to land amongst his colleagues. Too late: the skiff had already accelerated away, and he landed with an enormous splash in the water.

Ignoring him, Thibault tersely issued orders and at once the corvette took off after the skiff. In less than thirty seconds she was closing in, though the pirates showed no sign of slowing down.

'Two warning bursts,' the Captain ordered, then watched as his men on the bow swung the .30 mm cannons towards the skiff. They fired a line of tracer shells that sailed just ahead of the smaller boat, a few of them skimming the surface like stones thrown from a beach.

Now the skiff slowed down, and the French ship slowed too, cutting the engine and floating towards the smaller craft. The French sailors on the forward deck watched the armed men in the skiff intently. They were close enough to distinguish the individual figures, wearing jeans and T-shirts; as they drew nearer they could see details of the men's faces, some half-obscured by dark glasses. But it was the weapons they were watching most closely. Suddenly two men stood up, rocking the skiff with the abrupt movement. They raised their

11

rifles and cracking sounds rang out above the low throb of the corvette's engines.

The sailors on the bow hit the deck as it was sprayed with bullets. A second burst of gunfire rattled against the steel-plated bridge where Thibault was standing. He ducked, shouting, 'Hole that boat!'

The gunners swung their cannons round to point directly at the skiff and fired. A hole appeared above the little vessel's waterline, and the skiff began rapidly to take on water. One of the pirates stood up and jumped overboard just before the skiff tilted sharply to one side, dumping the rest of the crew into the sea. Then it sank beneath the surface.

What fools, thought Thibault, taking on an armed naval vessel. What did they think they were playing at?

*   *   *

Two hours later he was none the wiser. Below deck, in the long low room that doubled as both mess and lounge for his crew, the prisoners sat ranged on two benches. They included the hapless pirate who had jumped for it from halfway up the side of the *Aristides*. It turned out he could hardly swim; he would have drowned if a crewman from the container ship had not thrown him a lifeline.

Thibault had ordered his men to search the prisoners for weapons, but the three Kalashnikovs seemed to be the extent of their armoury—and they were now lying at the bottom of the ocean.

The pirates were uncommunicative, merely

12

shrugging when Thibault attempted to question them. From time to time they spoke to each other in short bursts of Arabic. Marceau, Algerian by origin and an Arabic speaker from childhood, spoke to them but they just ignored him. Though Arabic was one of Somalia's national languages, these men were not Somali—their appearance was Middle Eastern rather than African. Thibault was puzzled; he'd expected them to be local pirates, operating from the Somalian coast.

As he watched them, he noticed that one of the seven looked more Asian than Middle Eastern, and saw too that the other men didn't include him in their muttered exchanges. He seemed to be younger than the others: average height, lean, with the scraggly beginnings of a beard that gave away his youth. His eyes wouldn't stay still, searching anxiously around the room, and where the others looked coolly indifferent to their plight, he appeared terrified.

'Marceau,' said Thibault quietly. 'The lad at the end there . . . the one with the blue shirt. I want him searched.'

'We searched them all already,' came the reply.

'Yes, yes. Do it again—and a strip search this time. There's something different about him.'

Marceau gestured to two sailors, and together they approached the youth at the end of the bench. His eyes widened as they motioned him to get up, then led him through the bulkhead to the adjacent shower room. The other prisoners watched sullenly.

Marceau was back a few minutes later.

'Where's the prisoner?' asked Thibault.

'Still in there,' said Marceau with a shrug,

13

gesturing to the shower room. 'He's not feeling well.'

I bet, thought Thibault, knowing how brutal Marceau could be. He was about to chastise his second-in-command when Marceau held out a little square of plastic, about the size of a credit card. 'We found this in the lining of his back pocket.'

Thibault inspected the card. It was a driving licence, issued three years before and due to expire in another twenty-two. The photograph in one corner was of a young man, a boy really, clean-shaven and short-haired. But the eyes looked the same. His name, according to the licence, was Amir Khan.

Pakistani, thought Thibault. Or with Pakistani parents, perhaps, since this was a British driving licence. It gave Khan's address as 57 Farndon Street, Birmingham.

Thibault shook his head in wonder. What on earth was a British national doing here, attempting to hijack a cargo ship in the Indian Ocean?

3

It was 10.30 a.m. in Athens when the phone rang on Mitchell Berger's desk. The call was from overseas; Berger listened to it with increasing agitation.

'Are the crew all safe?' he asked finally.

He waited for the reply, then said, 'When will they reach Mombasa? . . . All right—they've only lost a day. I'll alert our people there.'

14

Berger put down the phone, trying to gather his thoughts, looking down from the window of his second-storey office at the street below. It was the Greek version of an English suburban High Street, full of small shops and restaurants. Even in spring the sun outside would be scorching by mid-afternoon, so the locals shopped in the morning.

Berger liked Athens, just as he liked virtually any part of the world—so long as it wasn't the small South Dakota town where he'd grown up, a place of such stifling dullness that he liked to pretend he'd forgotten its name. Berger had fled it at the first opportunity, enlisting in the army on the day he turned seventeen. His four-year hitch had taken him to Germany, then Korea, and given him a taste for foreign countries. He'd also discovered he wasn't as stupid as his alcoholic parents had always made out—when he'd left the army he'd gone to college on the GI Bill, and done well enough to go on and take a Masters in International Relations at Tufts University. Credentials enough for the career that had followed in the next three decades, working in four continents and a dozen countries.

It had been an eventful thirty years—too eventful, perhaps, since there had been more than one occasion when Berger had feared for his life. Reaching fifty, unmarried and feeling rootless, he had been on the lookout for a change—this time to a more peaceful existence, nothing too nerve-racking. He had found it; a pleasant billet as head of the Athens office of a UK-based charity called UCSO, the United Charities' Shipping Organisation. UCSO, as its name implied, was a co-ordinating charity. Its role was to receive

15

requests for aid from NGOs working in the field, to liaise with donors all over Europe, and to arrange for the requested aid—food, equipment, spare parts, whatever it might be—to be assembled in Athens. There Mitchell Berger and his colleagues would make up the cargoes, book the ships and despatch the aid to wherever it was needed. Much of the focus of UCSO's efforts was on crisis areas in Africa, though it had played an important role in the immediate relief operation after the 2004 tsunami. Unlike some other charities, UCSO prided itself on its efficiency rather than its public profile, and had an unsurpassed record in getting aid to wherever it was most needed.

UCSO had two hubs. The key administrative and financial headquarters were in London, as were most of the seventy-odd staff. It was from there that strings were pulled, major donors were smooched and soothed, governments were pressured. Here in Athens fewer than a dozen staff sufficed for assembling and despatching the aid shipments, and that suited Berger. He was not interested in the diplomatic stuff or the administrative problems that came with running a large office.

But it was the process of despatching the aid that had led to this morning's phone call. An UCSO aid ship, bound for Mombasa on the first leg of an operation to transport aid inland to the Republic of the Congo, had been subject to a hijacking attempt. Thanks to providence, in the form of a French Navy patrol, the attempt had been foiled. But what was agitating Mitchell Berger, as he watched a black-clad woman on the street below haggling over a bag of oranges, was that this was not the first time pirates had struck. Twice before UCSO ships had been attacked, and both times the ships had been successfully hijacked.

The first incident, a year or so before, had initially seemed to be a freakish one-off. It came during a flurry of hijackings of oil tankers off Somalia; these were the richest pickings for pirates, as the multinational oil companies which owned them were usually keen to settle quickly. From UCSO the pirates had originally demanded £1 million, but after apparently recognising that they weren't dealing with wealthy owners on this occasion, they had eventually settled with the charity's insurers for half that sum. However, when the ship was returned, the cargo, which had been unusually valuable, had gone.

The second hijacking had come six months later. Again, the ship had been carrying high-value cargo—more than the normal quantity of drugs (morphine, anaesthetic, antibiotics), which would have fetched good money in many markets. Also, lodged in the Captain's safe, there had been $200,000 in cash, intended for the UCSO people on the ground to use to grease certain palms, and thus ensure that the cargo arrived at its intended destination. Unsavoury but necessary; UCSO was effective precisely because it didn't let idealism get in the way of practicality.

The ship had been recovered after a month, though this time the ransom demanded had stayed firmly fixed at £1 million. Again most of the cargo had been removed and the bank notes were no longer in the safe.

And now there had been a third attempt. Thank God it had failed, thought Berger, since after the

17

first two, the insurance companies had raised the premium for continued cover to a near-impossible level. UCSO's donors wanted their money to go straight to helping desperate people in desperate straits, not towards paying premiums to insurance companies in glitzy City offices.

Berger, still standing looking out of the window, was no longer noticing what was going on in the street outside. He was thinking instead about this third attack. Since the last hijacking, six other UCSO shipments had sailed unmolested through the waters off the Horn of Africa, despite an overall increase in the numbers of hijackings in the region. Why had the pirates targeted the *Aristides*? A Greek-registered merchant ship, which regularly sailed those waters, was surely a far less attractive target than a tanker.

Berger wanted to believe it was pure chance that UCSO had been targeted three times, but his professional experience had taught him to be suspicious of apparent coincidence. Like the two other hijacked UCSO vessels, the *Aristides* had been carrying an exceptionally valuable cargo. The customary medical supplies were on board, in addition to food, clothing, tents and reconstruction equipment—all the staples of the charity's aid programme. But also on board was some particularly expensive kit—the equivalent of half a dozen field hospitals—which would allow surgical procedures to be undertaken miles away from the nearest city, ranging from simple amputations to open heart surgery and the complex treatment of burns victims. In addition there were a dozen of the latest all-terrain vehicles, and again the Captain's safe contained cash—this time gold coins enough to open most of the doors initially closed to the charity workers on the ground. All of this was easily saleable in a way that a cargo of oil was not.

So the pirates would have struck lucky with the *Aristides* even if UCSO could not raise their ransom. But was it pure coincidence that all three ships that had been attacked were carrying such valuable disposable cargoes? Berger didn't think so. Hadn't Goldfinger remarked memorably to James Bond that meeting him once was happenstance, twice was coincidence, but their third encounter constituted enemy action?

Lunchtime was approaching and down on the street the shoppers were beginning to head home, retreating from the mounting heat. In London it would be mid-morning, a good time to call. Berger picked up the receiver and dialled. A secretary answered.

'Hello, Val,' he said. 'Is David there?'

'Yes, Mr Berger. I'll just put you through.'

He waited patiently, thinking about the man to whom he was about to speak—David Blakey, head of UCSO and Berger's boss.

He liked Blakey, an ex-MI6 officer who had carried the professional habits of a lifetime into his new career, although by all accounts he had been around the block a bit. Blakey had the relaxed, confident style and old-fashioned manners which to Berger spoke of an English public school education. Some of his fellow Americans would regard Blakey with scorn—a typical Brit, they'd think, with extravagant, overdone courtesy overlying a snobbish conviction of superiority. But Berger had met other Englishmen cut from the same cloth and he knew better than to underestimate them. He had studied Blakey and observed how his charm and courtesy enabled him, apparently effortlessly, to extract donations from the wealthy—the female variety in particular.

He'd seen too how in dealings with the City, the corporate world and government, another side of Blakey appeared: an analytical intelligence, a command of detail and a fierce determination to succeed. With his staff he was kind and considerate, happy for them to think (especially the younger ones) that they had worked out for themselves what in fact he had taught them, but he showed no tolerance whatsoever towards incompetence or laziness. Blakey's reputation as a good boss had gone before him round the charity world so that UCSO, unlike many other similar organisations, was able to attract and keep staff of the highest quality.

Blakey's familiar voice came on the line. 'Hello, Mitchell. How are things in Athens?'

'Well, it's getting hot here, but it's hotter off the Horn of Africa.'

'Have we got another problem?'

'No, thank God, but not for lack of trying. The *Aristides* was almost boarded early this morning. Fortunately a French patrol boat intervened.'

'Any casualties?' Blakey's voice remained calm, but Berger could sense the tension in his response.

'None. Though I understand there was some shooting.'

'The French have never been slow to pull the trigger,' said Blakey with a laugh. Then, more seriously, 'Sounds like a close call.'

'It was.' And Berger knew they were both thinking how close UCSO had come to disaster.

'The thing is, David, this is not only the third attack by pirates, but also the third time they've picked an especially valuable cargo. Since the last hijacking we've had half a dozen shipments go through unmolested—and two of them were on the *Aristides*.'

'Which would suggest they're not targeting the ship in particular, but specific shipments on her?'

'Exactly. I'm beginning to wonder if they know all about our cargoes.' He paused, and the silence hung heavily between them.

'How could they know that?' asked Blakey.

'I don't know. Unless . . .' said Berger, and stopped.

Blakey filled in the dots. 'That is pretty worrying.'

'I know. But I thought I'd better raise it.'

'Quite right.' Blakey paused, then said, 'If information is getting out it needn't come from Athens, you know—we get the manifests here.'

'Of course,' said Berger.

There was a long sigh. 'Pinning this down is going to be a problem—that's if there *is* anything to pin down in the first place.' Another pause then Blakey said, 'Let me have a word with one of my old colleagues. He might be able to help—or least give us some pointers on how to get to the bottom of this quickly. I'd say speed is of the essence, wouldn't you?'

'Absolutely. Though we haven't got another shipment scheduled for the Horn until the end of next month.'

'Good. That gives us some time. Let's hope it's enough.'

Liz had been back in London less than a day when a call came in to her office from Isabelle Florian. A gang of pirates had been seized by the French Navy in the Indian Ocean, attempting to hijack a Greek merchant ship. One of them was carrying a British driving licence and, though he had said virtually nothing to his captors, did appear to be British. He had been taken to Djibouti by a French patrol boat and was being flown back to France. He should be arriving at La Santé prison in Paris within the hour. Isabelle enquired if Liz had an interest in questioning the prisoner? The details of his driving licence were being sent across by secure means as she spoke.

By the time Liz had walked along the corridor to the open-plan office, Peggy Kinsolving, the desk oficer who worked with her, was already receiving from France a copy of a British driving licence issued to an Amir Khan, aged twenty-two, at a Birmingham address.

Liz smiled at her young researcher. 'Dogged' just about summed up Peggy's way of working. A librarian by training after her Oxford degree, she had an insatiable appetite for facts, however obscure, and could trace connections between them that other people couldn't see. She stuck to the scent of a promising trail like a bloodhound, and sooner or later always came up with the goods.

'Do you think the French have really caught a Brit among a gang of African pirates?' said Peggy, pushing her glasses higher on her nose as she gazed at her computer screen. 'I bet it's just a stolen licence that's found its way out there and that the guy turns out to be another Somali.'

'I'm not so sure,' said Liz. 'Apparently the French Captain reported there was something odd about him—he wasn't really one of the gang. He looked different, and the others didn't talk to him. He seems to understand English, though he's hardly said anything. Get on to the police in Birmingham and the Border Agency and see what you can find out.'

And overnight Peggy had managed to assemble a few facts about Amir Khan. He was a British citizen, whose parents were first-generation Pakistani immigrants. This much the Border Agency had been able to report before their computer system went down, a not uncommon occurrence ever since it had been 'upgraded'. But from the police Peggy had learned that Khan had attended various local authority schools in Birmingham, then Birmingham University—where he had been a student of engineering until he'd left for unexplained reasons in the middle of his third year. He had no criminal record and had never before come to the police's attention; there was no previous trace of him in MI5's files.

So Liz was trying to keep an open mind, though she was curious about what mixture of motives, inducements, or grievances might have led young Khan, if indeed it was he, to the Indian Ocean, to enter the hijacking business that she had previously believed to be the preserve of Somalis. Some people talked about 'globalisation' in approving tones these days, but for Liz it was making her work infinitely more complex, and the challenges she faced were magnified by a world of instant communication and fast travel across international borders.

When she had first joined MI5, over a decade before, most of her work had been done in Britain. She'd started in the counter-terrorist branch where she'd had her first real success, helping to prevent an attack in East Anglia. She'd been lucky to escape serious injury in that operation and afterwards had been moved to counter-espionage where events moved rather more slowly. Of course it hadn't turned out to be a soft posting—there were no soft postings in today's MI5.

For the intelligence world 9/11 had changed everything. There was much more public focus now on 'security' of all kinds; much more government involvement; more media attention and criticism—particularly after Britain went to war in Iraq. Some of those who had joined at the same time as Liz had, now spent all their time dealing with media enquiries, writing briefs for the Director General for meetings with Ministers, or poring over spreadsheets and arguing with the Treasury. That wasn't what she wanted to do. The occasional international security conference was enough for her.

But she knew that if she were going to win serious promotion she would have to move away from the front line sooner or later; for now, though, she wanted to stay at the sharp end of things. It was the excitement of operational work that she loved; that was what got her out of bed in the morning and kept her going during the day and often far into the night. It was also, if she was honest, what had messed up her private life.

Was that in danger of happening again? she wondered, thinking of Martin and what he had said when she was staying with him at the weekend. Anyway, she thought, as she picked up her overnight bag and headed off to St Pancras International to catch a train back to Paris, there was no immediate prospect of her being put on to 'admin' work—nor of moving in with Martin permanently, she added to herself.

5

The following morning Liz and Martin left his flat together. Much to her relief, he hadn't referred again to the idea of her moving to Paris. He could see that she was focused on the conundrum of the young British man she had come to interview.

She was due at the Santé at 10 and he was on his way to his office in the DGSE Headquarters in the Boulevard Mortier. They parted at the Metro station. '*À bientôt*,' he said, kissing her on the cheek. They had arranged to meet again when he came to London for the late May Bank Holiday.

The Metro was crowded and hot. The warm weather had begun early; outside the sky was blue and cloudless and the Parisian women were bare-legged, in summer skirts and sandals. Liz felt overdressed in the black trouser suit she had thought suitable for prison visiting. She was standing up, strap hanging and trying to read the back page of *Libération* over her neighbour's shoulder when, much to her surprise, a schoolboy got up and offered her his seat. She smiled her thanks and sat down, thinking this would never happen in London. Now with nothing to read, she found her view of the carriage blocked by a young man standing facing away from her. Shoved into the back pocket of his jeans was a paperback book with the title just visible: *L'Étranger* by Albert Camus. She smiled to herself, remembering how, years ago, she'd waded through the book's relentlessly gloomy pages for GCSE. It seemed incongruous for this young man to be reading it on such a beautiful day.

Her thoughts turned to the forthcoming interview. She wished she knew a bit more about this Khan. When she was interviewing someone for the first time, she liked to be one step ahead of them, to have something up her sleeve. Maybe she should have waited until Peggy had been able to do more background research, but the French had been keen for her to come straight away. They hadn't got anything at all out of the other members of the pirate gang, so they were hoping that her interview with Khan would give them something to use to get the others to talk. From the little the French authorities had said about Khan, however, Liz wasn't very optimistic.

Emerging from the Metro at Saint-Jacques, Liz saw a missed call message on the screen of her mobile phone. It was from Peggy in London, and she hit the button to call her back.

'Hi, Liz, or should I say *bonjour*?'

'What's up? I'm just on my way to the prison.'

'Border Agency have come back—their system's up and running again. They say our Mr Khan left the UK eight months ago for Pakistan. He hasn't returned to Britain, at least not through official

26

channels.'

'Mmm.' It was strange, but not unheard of. Each year thousands of British citizens made trips to Pakistan for all kinds of reasons—to see relatives, to visit friends, to get married, to show their children where their roots lay. But for the most part they came back. In recent years a few young men had travelled to Pakistan for less innocent reasons and, if they had come back, had seemed different from before they'd left. A few hadn't returned at all, going off to fight in Afghanistan or to train in the tribal areas of Pakistan or to hang out in Peshawar. But Somalia? That was new to Liz. The interview with Khan promised to be interesting—if she could persuade him to talk.

'Anything else?' she asked Peggy.

'Yes, but not from Borders. I spoke to Special Branch in Birmingham ... Detective Inspector Fontana. He said the Khan family are well known—and well off: they own a small chain of grocery stores that serve the Asian community. Highly respectable people—he was surprised when I told him where their son's driving licence had been found. He's offered to go and talk to the parents. Shall I tell him to go ahead?'

Liz pondered this briefly. 'Not yet. Wait till I've seen the prisoner and then we can decide what to do next. If it really is their son, I'd like to talk to them myself. But I don't want to alert them until we know a bit more.'

'Okay. Anything else I should be doing on this?'

'Don't think so. I'll be back tonight. I'll ring if he says anything useful, but I'm not very hopeful that he'll talk at all. He's said nothing to the French.'

All Liz knew about the Santé prison came from the novels of Georges Simenon. *The Bar on the Seine* began with his famous detective, Inspector Maigret, going to visit a young condemned prisoner in La Santé one sunny Paris day—a day a bit like this one, in fact. Maigret's footsteps had echoed on the pavement just as hers did while she followed the high stone wall which screened the old prison buildings from the street. Strange that such a place was right in the middle of the city, just a few minutes from the Luxembourg Gardens. It was as if Wormwood Scrubs had been erected on the edge of Green Park, next-door to Buckingham Palace.

Following the instructions she'd been given Liz walked on until she arrived at a small side street, Rue Messier, where, as promised, she found a low booth set into the massive wall. Peering through a long window of bullet-proof glass, she gave her name to the dimly visible guard on the other side. He nodded curtly, then buzzed her through an unmarked steel door into a small windowless reception room.

This was all very different from Maigret's sleepy guard gazing at a little white cat playing in the sunshine. But nowadays the Santé was a high-security prison which housed some of France's most lethal prisoners, including Carlos the Jackal. And Mr Amir Khan, was he lethal? Liz wondered.

A door on the other side of the room opened.

'*Bonjour.* I am Henri Cassale of the DCRI, a colleague of Isabelle Florian.' He was not much taller than Liz. Dark-haired, dark-skinned, wearing a light suit and a bright yellow paisley tie, he looked out of place in this grim reception room. 'We have Monsieur Amir Khan ready to answer your questions. Or not . . .' He smiled with a flash of white teeth.

'Does he know I'm coming?'

'*Non*. And I wish you better luck with him than we have had.'

'He's still not talking?'

Isabelle's colleague shook his head. 'Have you and your colleagues discovered anything more about him?'

'We've learned that the owner of the driving licence, Amir Khan, went to Pakistan eight months ago. He hasn't returned to the UK since then.'

'Pakistan?' Cassale shook his head. 'I can't say I am surprised. We have sent a file of information—fingerprints, DNA, photographs—over to you this morning. That should enable you to establish the identity of the prisoner beyond doubt. Meanwhile, let's see what he says to you. Come with me, *s'il vous plaît.*'

Liz followed him through the door into a corridor, arched on one side like the cloisters of a cathedral. But unlike a cloister, these arches were secured with metal grilles, and the courtyard visible beyond was not a place for quiet contemplation—it was filled with men, standing singly or in groups, most of them smoking. At the far end a desultory game of basketball was being played.

Cassale turned a corner and they came face to face with a guard, standing in front of a heavy wooden door. He nodded to Cassale and opened the door with a jangling of keys. The smell of new

29

paint was strong as they went through—the walls had been freshly decorated, in a drab grey which seemed designed to depress. A line of closed steel doors, equally spaced, stretched along both sides of a long corridor. Liz had been in prisons before and noted the familiar small grilled window slits of the cells.

'We are in the high-security wing now. This part is where violent criminals are interned. The terror suspects are kept downstairs.' At the end of the corridor Cassale rang a bell on the wall beside a metal door. It was opened from the inside by another guard and Cassale preceded Liz down a flight of metal stairs, their shoes clanging on the steel treads.

At the bottom, he paused. They were in another wide corridor, but this one had older peeling paint on the walls. A line of fluorescent tube lights, suspended from the ceiling, gave off a dazzling, blue-ish glare that made Liz screw up her eyes.

'This is our special unit. Monsieur Khan is resident here. Your interview will take place in one of the interrogation rooms. I warn you, it is not exactly modern.'

A picture of a mediaeval dungeon flashed into Liz's mind: rings on the wall, chains, bones in the corner and rats. She was relieved when Cassale opened a door and she found herself in a high-ceilinged, white-painted room. It seemed very airy after the corridor outside. A long barred window was set high in one wall; through it a shaft of sunlight glanced, striking the polished floor. Just inside the door a policeman waited on the alert, holding an unholstered Glock sidearm. As he stood aside, Liz saw the prisoner, sitting behind a

30

metal-topped table, his hands manacled to a length of chain which was itself secured to a cast-iron stanchion on the floor.

According to his driving licence, Khan was twenty-two, but this man looked to be younger, just a boy. His face and arms and wrists were thin. A scraggly black beard barely covered his chin and the hair on his upper lip was sparse. His eyes, as he watched them come into the room, looked wary. Liz had been assured that he was being well treated, but she wondered what had happened to him before he got here.

Cassale stepped up to the table and, speaking rapidly in French, explained to the prisoner that he had a visitor who would be asking him some questions. It was obvious from the blank expression on the young man's face that he understood nothing of what was said.

Cassale turned to Liz and said in French, 'I will be next-door if you need me. Just tell the guard.' She nodded. As Cassale left, she pulled out a chair from under the table and sat down opposite the prisoner. The armed policeman remained standing by the door.

Liz looked calmly at Khan and said, 'I don't know about you, but my French stopped at GCSE.'

His eyes widened at the sound of her English voice, then he sat stiffly upright and gave her a defiant look.

Liz shrugged. 'Amir, I haven't come all this way to give you a hard time. But let's not pretend: you speak English just as well as I do. Probably with a Birmingham accent.'

Khan stared at her for a moment, as if making up his mind. The key now was to get him to say *something*—anything would do for a start. Liz had been taught this during initial training at MI5: a complete refusal to speak—even to say yes or no—was disastrous; there was no way forward from there. It reminded her of being taught to fish by her father. When she took too long setting up her rod, he would always say, 'If your fly's not on the water, you can't catch a fish.'

Fortunately Khan decided to speak, saying slowly, 'Are you from the Embassy?'

'Not exactly. But I am here to help.'

'Then get me a lawyer.'

'Well, perhaps we should first establish who you are. I take it that you are indeed the Amir Khan, of 57 Farndon Street, Birmingham, whose driving licence you were carrying when you were arrested by the French Navy?'

'I said, I want a lawyer.'

'Ah, if only it were that easy. We're in France, Amir, not England. They do things differently here. You've heard the phrase *"Habeas corpus"*?' She didn't wait for him to nod. 'Well, over here, they haven't. You can be held on a magistrate's word for as long as he likes. It could be months. Or longer, if you won't co-operate.'

Khan was gnawing his thumbnail. A good sign, thought Liz, who wanted him on edge. He said sharply, 'So why should I talk to you?'

'Because I may be able to help.'

He scoffed, 'How, if the French can hold me as long as they want?'

'If we can get a few things sorted out, we might be able to arrange your transfer to the UK.' She looked around at the room. 'I think you'd agree things would be better for you there. But that

32

would depend on your co-operating, of course.'

'With what?'

She put the battered driving licence on the table. 'Is this yours? Are you Amir Khan?'

He nodded. 'You know I am.'

'You were arrested with a group of pirates from Somalia, trying to hijack a ship in the Indian Ocean. Let's talk about how you got there from Birmingham. And why you were helping to hijack a Greek cargo ship.'

'I wasn't,' he said flatly. Seeing surprise in Liz's eyes, he said, 'They forced me to go along.'

'Who did?'

'The pirates. I don't know their names... I couldn't understand a word they said. It was some African dialect.'

'They weren't African.'

He ignored her. 'They told me to get in their boat, and I didn't argue. I was sure they were going to kill me.'

'Why did they take you along?'

'You'd have to ask them.' His tone was surly.

'Why don't we take a step back? Tell me how you ended up in Somalia in the first place.'

'I thought we were heading for Kenya.'

'Who's "we"?' She knew it was important to cut off these tangents right away, or they'd sprout like suckers at the base of a tree. Soon there'd be so many of them she wouldn't be able to see the tree, much less the forest.

'A friend. I met him in London.'

'What's your friend's name?'

'We called him Sammy, but I think his name was Samir.'

'Samir what?'

He shrugged. 'I don't know.'

'When did you meet him in London?' Seeing as you're from Birmingham, she thought.

'Last year, or maybe two years ago. I have a cousin who moved down there and I used to visit him. He has a newsagent's in Clerkenwell and—'

Liz interjected quietly, 'We know you went to Pakistan.'

For a moment Khan looked uneasy. But then he simply shifted gear, moving back into the narrative that Liz could tell he had pre-prepared. 'Of course I did. I've got relatives there. Another cousin, in fact—you can check it out. He has a shop in Islamabad—not a newsagent's, but a butcher's shop. He's done well. In fact, he's thinking of opening another shop—'

This time Liz cut in less gently. 'How did you get from Pakistan to Somalia?'

Khan looked at her as if outraged that she should interrupt him. Liz pressed, 'I said, how did you get there?'

He sighed. 'It's a long story.'

'Let's hear it. We've got all day if necessary.'

And for the next hour or so it looked as if all day was what Liz would need. For Khan launched into a lengthy, voluminously detailed, yet utterly preposterous account of his whereabouts since leaving Pakistan—involving a flight to Turkey, a boat trip to the Greek islands, another to Tunisia (where he claimed to have picked grapes for a month), three weeks of hitchhiking that included a harrowing jeep ride in the middle of the night . . . on and on he went with his story, an account so obviously fabricated that Liz could only smile.

Each time she tried to pin him down—what

34

airline had he taken to Turkey? What Greek island had he visited?—Khan's memory would suddenly falter. 'I can't be sure,' he'd say. Or, 'Maybe I've got that wrong.' And for every reluctant step towards Somalia his story took, he did his best to take two backwards.

As Khan went on—by now he was trying to reach Egypt overland from Lebanon—she interrupted less, and gradually stopped asking any questions at all. He continued talking, apparently thinking that his avalanche of words somehow made his story credible. Finally he seemed to realise that he was not convincing her, and came to a sudden halt. There was silence in the room.

'So,' said Liz eventually, 'where is your passport?'

'I lost it.'

'Then how did you get across all these borders?'

He said nothing, obviously trying to think of an answer that would not incriminate him.

It was time to up the pace. 'Come on, Amir. Why were you in Somalia?'

'I just wanted to see it.'

'Who were you with?'

'A couple of guys I met.'

'Where did you meet them?'

'In Egypt. We met in Cairo.'

'What were their names?'

'I can't remember.'

'How did you get to Somalia?'

'By car. Jeep, actually.'

'Whose car?'

'It was rented.'

'What, there's a Hertz agency in Mogadishu?'

Khan said nothing.

35

Liz went on. 'Were you in Yemen before then?'

'No.'

'Have you ever been to Yemen?'

'No,' he said crossly.

'Who in Pakistan gave you your orders?'

And before he had time to think, he snapped back, 'It wasn't in Pakis—' Then stopped, aware of his slip. He looked down at the table, mortified.

Liz smiled. 'Why don't you tell me the truth now? You must be tired of inventing.'

Khan hesitated, and for a second Liz thought his moment of carelessness might have broken down his guard. He seemed on the very edge of caving in. She waited but he said no more. Lifting his head, he looked straight at her.

'Do you have any message for your parents?' she asked.

His eyes widened with shock. 'What have they got to do with this? They don't know anything about it.' But as he looked at Liz tears started to well up. He bent his head to wipe them away with the shirt sleeve on his manacled arm.

Liz waited but something, whether determination, fear or training, reasserted itself. Having regained control of himself, Khan's features hardened and he squared his shoulders. 'I've got nothing more to say to you,' he declared.

Liz waited a moment but his gaze was steely again, determined. 'I want to go back to my cell,' he announced, and there was not even a hint of uncertainty in his voice.

Liz stood up reluctantly. 'If you change your mind, let them know and I'll come back.' She walked over to the door, and the guard opened it to let her through. Khan could have asked to go to his cell an hour ago and spared us both, she thought. But at least she'd learned one useful thing.

6

Liz and Cassale retraced their steps to the grim reception room on the Rue Messier side of the prison. 'Let's get out of this place and have some coffee,' he suggested, to Liz's relief.

Outside the prison she breathed deeply, taking in lungsful of warm air and blinking in the bright midday sun. Cassale took her elbow. 'This way,' he said, steering her along the pavement towards the Boulevard Arago, where the new leaves were unfurling on the plane trees.

They stopped at a pavement café. As the coffee arrived, Cassale lit a Gitane and asked, 'Any luck?'

'Not much,' she admitted.

'Did he talk at all?'

She waited while a young man walked past their table. He was dark—from Algeria perhaps, or equally plausibly from the Middle East. For a moment it looked as though he might sit down nearby, but he went inside the café.

Liz said with a snort, 'He certainly talked! He would have made a great storyteller in another life. He was trying to convince me that he's been swanning round Europe, apparently without a passport or any money, and ended up in Somalia by mistake. I'll send you my notes of what he said; if you believe any of it I'll be amazed.'

Cassale looked sympathetic. 'Frustrating. Still, it's good that he talked at all. Well done.'

'He did more or less acknowledge that he was acting under someone else's orders—and that he wasn't given the orders in Pakistan.'

'Really? Where did he receive them then—in England?'

'I don't know, and he wasn't saying. If you can find out anything about that it would be a big help.'

Cassale nodded. 'Do you know if you will want him back in England?'

'We've got a bit of work to do first. At least he admitted that he was Amir Khan. We've located his parents in Birmingham, and we'll see what they say, though I gather they're very respectable people and will probably be as surprised as I was to hear about their son. When I mentioned them, Khan got very upset—he just managed to stop himself from crying. You might want to try that on him again.' Liz looked at her watch. 'I'd better be going if I'm to catch my train.'

'Of course.' Cassale put some coins on the table and pushed back his chair. 'Before you do, is there is anything in particular we should try and get out of him? Assuming he will now talk to us as well.'

A big assumption, thought Liz, remembering the tight-mouthed expression on Khan's face as she'd left. 'Two things for a start: where he really was after he left Pakistan, and of course who was directing him.'

'We will do our best.' Cassale offered her his hand. 'He is a mystery man, this Khan. I think somehow you and I will be seeing each other again.'

*   *   *

Liz walked back along the prison wall, retracing her steps to the Metro station. The high wall cast a deep shadow over the pavement now, a welcome relief from the bright sun for Liz in her black suit. She'd forgotten her sunglasses too and the glare was irritating her eyes.

She thought again of Maigret in the story. The prisoner he'd visited was about the same age as Khan, not much more than a boy, but he'd been condemned to death. The old prison must have witnessed any number of gruesome events—she wondered if they'd executed people in the courtyard where the prisoners had been exercising today. When she heard the sound of someone's footsteps echoing on the pavement behind her, her back crawled and she turned round in alarm. It was only an old man a long way down the street—he must have been wearing particularly noisy shoes. But she was glad to reach the Metro station.

At Gare du Nord she had half an hour to wait before going through to the Eurostar departure area, so she stopped to buy a baguette sandwich and a bottle of water. The station was crowded and as she queued she smiled, chiding herself for letting the prison get under her skin. She'd never been quite so shaken by a visit before. Perhaps it was the contrast between the Santé's ancient history and the very modern-day events that had brought Amir Khan there.

But then, it wasn't really modern at all—piracy was one of the oldest crimes in the book. Not that Khan seemed much of a pirate. But whatever he was, he'd given nothing away to help her unravel his story. Not until he'd made that one slip. But what did it mean? If he hadn't received his orders in Pakistan, where had he got them from?

Liz paid for her sandwich and looked round for a free table. As she sat down, a young man with a dark complexion got up and walked away. Somehow he looked familiar—was it the same one who had walked into the café when she and Cassale had been having coffee? Liz watched as he walked away down the platform and noticed a book sticking out of the pocket of his jeans. Her mind flicked back to the man in the Metro that morning, standing in front of her when she had sat down, with *L'Étranger* in his pocket.

This man was too far away by now for her to see the title of the book. Could it be him again? If so, then that was too much of a coincidence. She got up and walked quickly down the platform, following the man who was now some distance ahead of her and moving fast. She managed to keep him in sight until he turned into an exit at the end of the platform. She broke into a run but when she got to the exit, she found there were three separate passages leading off in different directions and no sign of the man in any of them. She stood there panting, feeling stupid yet still uneasy, and then she slowly retraced her steps back to the café. When she got there, someone had taken her sandwich.

7

They had slaughtered the goat that afternoon. Taban had seen countless animals killed before, but he had been disgusted by the zeal with which these new men in the camp had despatched the little creature. One held the struggling animal while another slashed its neck with a knife. As blood gushed from the scrawny throat and the body twitched, cries of delight went up from the group.

Now Taban was tending the big pot, using an enormous wooden spoon to stir the cut-up chunks of meat that were bubbling together with red beans and *tamaandho*. On a brazier next to the pot, flatbreads cooked over the driftwood fire.

They were only seven miles from Mogadishu, but it could have been seven thousand. Their camp sat on a spit of sand behind a dune, overlooking the Indian Ocean. The nearest dwellings were half a mile away, the rundown shacks of an almost abandoned fishing village.

He knew the village well; he had grown up there with his father and an elder brother. He couldn't remember his mother—she had died of a wasting disease when he was just two—so he had never missed her, and his childhood had been happy. He had gone to school some of the time, but more often he'd helped his father fish; he knew the local waters inside out before he was ten. In the early morning they would cast off in their little boat, its bow stuffed with nets, and by midday, if they were lucky, they would chug back laden with anchovies, sardines and mackerel, sometimes a tuna, and very occasionally a shark. They would cart their catch to the broken-concrete highway, where the lorry bound for Mogadishu would stop and the driver get down to haggle with their father over the price of their haul.

It had been a life of hard labour and long hours, but the coast was beautiful, the waters calm, and the fish plentiful. They did not want for anything that mattered.

One day men had come, armed with automatic rifles. They had wanted to borrow the skiff but his father had said no. They went away, but a week later they were back. Again the men asked for the use of his father's boat, and again his father refused.

Then they shot his father.

For a while, Taban and his brother had struggled on, borrowing a skiff from neighbours when they could and continuing to fish, though without their father there the lorry driver cheated them when they tried to sell their catch. Precarious as their new life was, they survived. Until one day his brother went to Mogadishu, looking for a cousin of theirs who might be able to help them. He had not come back, and after three months Taban assumed he must be dead, for why else would he not have returned?

Taban had tried to make a go of it alone, but he was still too small to handle the nets himself, and he could not catch enough fish on lines to make a living. He hoped for a while to be taken on by another fisherman, but the catches were growing poorer every day, and there was no money for extra hands. Soon only a few fishermen remained in the hamlet, trying their luck in the shallow shoals that had once been fertile fishing grounds; occasionally a band of strangers would come and commandeer several of the abandoned shacks, using them as a temporary base before moving on.

When Khalid and his gang had arrived they'd built a compound of their own. They began with a high perimeter wall, built of boulders and salvaged bricks. Taban had walked over there one morning after he'd failed for the fifth successive day to catch any fish. There were roughly thirty men under Khalid's command, and none of them were fishermen. But when Khalid learned that Taban knew the coastline his eyes had lit up, and soon the boy was not only lugging water buckets to the men building the wall and serving Khalid his meals of kebabs cooked over the fire, he was also going out to sea with them. He hadn't understood at first what they were doing; they were not interested in fishing but wanted to understand the tides and currents for some purpose of their own. It was later, when they brought groups of foreigners in lorries from further down the coast, that he realised these men were pirates, carrying out raids on the big ships that sailed the shipping lanes far out to sea, and that the foreigners were their prisoners.

All the men were afraid of Khalid. He had a house they had built for him inside the compound, a bare-walled structure constructed of breeze-blocks, but inside it seemed the height of luxury to Taban, equipped with electricity from a generator, an enormous television that received hundreds of programmes through a dish on the roof, a refrigerator full of food, even alcohol stored in a rack. Khalid was not cruel to Taban, but the

43

boy worked hard merely for his food and a place to sleep, no wages. And he was never allowed to leave the compound on his own.

Now, as Taban leaned forward to stir the stew again, a large hand suddenly gripped his wrist. It was the Tall One, the name Taban had given to the leader of a new band of men who had arrived in the camp some weeks ago and taken it over. He was a massive figure, well over six feet tall, with a long ragged beard. He and his gang had come under cover of darkness, in jeeps. Their only luggage had been weapons—AK-47s, two grenade launchers, and quantities of sidearms.

Khalid had not resisted this challenge to his authority. When they insisted Taban should act as their factotum—which meant cook for the most part—Khalid had just nodded. The men kept to themselves, and treated Taban with suspicion when they were not ignoring him altogether. He noticed that they spent much of their time at prayer, kneeling or stretching out on small rugs they laid on the sand; the rest of the time they conducted classes among themselves, each of them taking turns to be the 'teacher' of the group. He had heard enough words he recognised, even when spoken in their strange dialect, to realise these men were not simple pirates. But then what were they doing here? He had wanted to ask Khalid, but fear held him back.

Now the Tall One let go of Taban's wrist and looked down at the stew, inspecting it closely. Then he stared at the boy with a penetrating gaze; the young Somali felt as if the man's eyes were boring into his brain. At last, the Tall One nodded at him with a grunt. He spoke sharply and his comrades

44

came over and began to serve themselves, while Taban stood back, waiting. At one point the Tall One gestured towards the boy, and the other men looked at him, then muttered to each other. Taban knew they were talking about him.

They were on edge—he could tell that. More than a week ago seven of them had gone out in a skiff almost as far as the shipping lanes, taking Taban with them. In sign language he had explained the tidal currents, which were notoriously tricky here, and pointed out the treacherous outcrop of rock almost a mile from shore, which had been the downfall of more than one unsuspecting craft. When, the following day, the same men had set out again, he had expected to go with them, but the Tall One had summoned him back with a threatening wave of his AK-47.

Those men had not returned and Taban was sure that something had gone wrong.

The Tall One and his men went and sat down again on the sand to eat, while Taban examined the vast iron pot. He was glad to see there was enough left to feed the prisoners, even if the visitors had eaten most of the meat. He lined up *baaquli*, rough wooden bowls, and filled them one by one, setting them on a tray he had fashioned from some short planks.

He had put the last bowl on his tray, ready to walk across the compound to the hostages' pen, when Khalid suddenly appeared. He had taken to wearing a sidearm and was dressed this evening in fatigues. He gestured towards the Tall One and his men, who were squatting down as they ate, and said to Taban, 'They want to know if you left the compound today.'

45

The boy looked at Khalid, aghast. 'Of course not. I would never do that without your permission.'

Khalid nodded grimly. 'That is what I told them. But be careful—these men don't trust anyone, and that includes you.' Then he walked off to talk with the guards he posted each night on the perimeter of the compound.

Picking up his tray, Taban headed for the makeshift jail. He was shaken by what Khalid had said to him. Taban sensed these men would happily kill him without a moment's thought, and he was very afraid. What had scared him even more was the look in Khalid's eyes. He was frightened too.

8

It was boredom Richard Luckhurst felt, far more than fear.

His best friend at school was a boy whose father had been in a German prisoner-of-war camp during World War II. A retiring man, he had only once spoken in Richard's hearing about his wartime experiences, when his son had asked, 'Dad, what was it like being a prisoner-of-war?' His taciturn father had pursed his lips, and said simply, 'Boring.'

Luckhurst now understood what the man had meant. Their hijackers had not allowed them to bring anything off the ship with them, and he craved something to read. Anything would have done. All he had was an old *Times* Saturday crossword that he had torn out of the paper and

46

put in his trouser pocket weeks ago, to do later. When the pirates had searched him before they'd taken him off the ship, they hadn't bothered with it and so he still had it. He had nothing to write with but even completing it in his head had occupied him for only a few hours. And now it was done, and he'd read the advertisements for the London theatres that were on the back of the page over and over again, and imagined himself sitting in the stalls in a cool air-conditioned theatre, wearing a clean shirt and a suit. What he would give for a book, any book, the longer the better.

Sitting here in this bizarre Somalian compound, he kept replaying the hijacking in his mind. One moment he was in charge, on the bridge of the SS *Myrmidon*, the world's seventeenth-largest oil tanker; the next moment, a young African was pointing an AK-47 at his head. Then another five pirates had swarmed in, armed to the teeth. There wasn't anything to be done: the ship's sole firearm was an old 12-bore shotgun which had belonged to Luckhurst's father, and which the crew used to shoot clay pigeons off the stern, to pass the time on long voyages.

Of course he had known that hijacking was a possibility, but he'd received no warning of any imminent attack from the naval vessels that were supposed to be patrolling the area, so he did not have his crew on alert. His instructions were not to resist if hijackers boarded and so he had followed the commands of their leader, brought his ship into the coast off Mogadishu and meekly allowed himself and his crew to be taken ashore. From then on his main responsibility had been to calm his crew and to try to make sure they did nothing to

47

excite or alarm their young captors.

The crew were a polyglot bunch from all over the world, who liked to view Captain Luckhurst as typically English. So he had played to the stereotype, adopting a stiff upper lip and a ready smile, keeping his own worries about their safety strictly to himself. It wouldn't have done to let them know how alarmed he'd been when they'd been taken off the ship at gun point, ferried ashore, and herded into this cattle pen.

He knew he could not complain about the treatment they were receiving. There would have been no point. The man Khalid, who had led the raiding party and seemed to be in charge, called their holding pen his 'Guantanamo', and like its Cuban counterpart this place was primitive: built of wooden posts with wire sheep fencing strung between them. Thank God for the fact that at one end of the pen there was a rough roof of plywood boards covered by tar paper, with a raised shelf under it for sitting and sleeping; this gave them some protection against the sun, which blazed for over ten hours a day, raising the temperature to 40 degrees Centigrade. They were let out each morning for an hour's exercise in the middle of the compound, and by the time they returned to the pen were desperate for relief from the blistering heat and the wind—a dry scorching wind which blew all day, driving sand relentlessly into their mouths and eyes.

At least the nights were cool. Then Luckhurst would sit on his bit of the wooden platform, wrapped in one of the thin blankets which the guards had grudgingly distributed, staring out at the sky. Up there, he thought, among all those

48

stars is a satellite looking at us. They know where we are. But they're not going to intervene. We just have to wait for the ransom negotiations. Get on with it, he'd implore the unknown negotiators. Get us out of here.

The biggest frustration for him lay in not knowing what was going on. The hostages had no contact with any of the men in the camp except for the young boy, Taban, who brought them their food. Luckhurst smiled at the thought of the young Somali. Even in the bleakest circumstances the kindness of an individual could stand out, and he could tell Taban was a gentle soul adrift in a situation beyond his control. The boy reminded him of his own son, George, his youngest, who despite the utterly different worlds they inhabited, had the same kind of sweetness as this African youth. At first there had been no communication between the Captain and the Somali boy, but in time Luckhurst had found that his smattering of Arabic, Taban's few words of English and a burgeoning use of sign language meant they could make their respective meanings clear.

One day, almost two weeks before, the boy had seemed very agitated. Luckhurst had gathered from him that new men had arrived in the camp, though he had not seen them himself. 'Arab,' Taban had said, lowering his voice and looking over his shoulder at the guards by the gate. 'One . . . you.' And he'd pointed at Luckhurst.

'One like me? White?' asked Luckhurst, pointing at his own face and hands.

Taban had shaken his head. 'No white. English.'

An Englishman? But not white. Someone speaking English, perhaps. Could it be another hostage? But if so, why wasn't he in the pen?

Over the next few evenings, intrigued by the idea of another Englishman living so close to him, Luckhurst had tried to learn more, but Taban was not forthcoming. Then, a week ago, when he'd brought the supper: 'Men gone. English gone,' he'd said, waving an arm towards the sea.

Now Luckhurst heard the clink of keys, and the sound of the door of the pen swinging open on its creaking hinges. Supper, he thought, visualising the guards letting Taban in with the food bowls. He wanted to learn more about the men who had gone to sea and not come back.

'OK, Taban?' asked Luckhurst now as the boy handed him his bowl of stew. Taban nodded but he looked scared.

Suddenly Khalid appeared behind him with a holstered pistol on his hip. This was new; Luckhurst hoped it didn't mean things had taken a turn for the worse. But the man was grinning as he strode up to the Captain.

'I have some news for you, Commander. Good news.'

'Yes?' This announcement had been made before, and had turned out merely to be that there was fruit with their dinner of stew.

'Your owners have seen sense at last—the ransom has been paid. You are clearly worth a lot to them.'

Luckhurst knew better—it was the ship the owners wanted back, not the crew, but there was no point in telling Khalid that. 'What happens next?' he asked cautiously.

'Next? We drive you to a collection point outside Mogadishu. A representative of your company will be there to collect you.'

It took only minutes for the Captain and his crew to get ready. They had nothing to pack. As they walked towards the dusty lorry, Luckhurst looked for Taban to say goodbye, but there was no sign of him. In the excitement of his release the Captain soon forgot about the boy.

9

Geoffrey Fane was not a generous man and he did not waste his time doing favours. But in his long career in MI6 he had developed a nose for what could be important. And when, the previous day, a call had come into his office from an old colleague who wanted some informal advice, that nose had twitched. Instead of finding some excuse, he had agreed to meet the caller. Now he was sitting in a taxi, crawling along Oxford Street in mid-morning traffic, on his way to his old colleague's office.

The caller was David Blakey, twenty years in MI6, rising to be Head of Station in Hong Kong at the time the colony was handed over to China. After Hong Kong, he had retired from MI6 and since then his and Fane's paths only rarely crossed—an occasional sighting in the bar of the Travellers Club, once bumping into each other in the Burlington Arcade. When Blakey had called, Fane had remembered that after leaving MI6 his old colleague had taken a job as director of a large international charity. In fact, it was when Blakey had mentioned the charity's name, UCSO, that he had sparked Fane's interest. It was just a week since that name had come to his attention. A young man with British documentation had been arrested by the French Navy in the Indian Ocean. He was apparently one of a group of pirates trying to hijack a Greek cargo ship, which had been chartered by the charity UCSO to carry aid supplies to Mombasa.

The case had been handed to MI5 to pursue; Elizabeth Carlyle—or Liz as she preferred to call herself, thought Fane with a grimace—had gone to Paris to interview the prisoner. And now the head of that same charity had suddenly popped up, asking for advice and refusing to say on the telephone what it was that concerned him.

Although they had lost touch in recent years, Fane had once known Blakey well. They had been at the same Oxford college before going their separate ways. Blakey had spent a year or so doing research for a thesis he never finished, while Fane had worked as a trainee on the Middle East desk of an investment bank. Then, to their mutual surprise, they had met up again on the initial MI6 training course. Together they had filled and emptied dead letter boxes, practised brush contacts and covert agent meetings all over Hampshire; they'd been arrested by the local police, and had survived rough interrogations by the SAS. They had dozed through lectures by retired officers reliving the glories of their Cold War agent-running triumphs, and at the end of it all, both had passed with honours and been marked out as high fliers.

Their careers had run in parallel for a while, then gradually Fane had pulled away and by the time Blakey had retired, his old college friend was several ranks above him. But Fane had always respected Blakey and knew that he would not have rung unless there was something important to talk about.

Fane had called up the file on UCSO but had found it pretty uninformative. He was interested in all large international charities; they operated in trouble spots all over the world—places from which he needed information, but from which information was difficult to obtain. But most charities kept intelligence services at arm's length; if they supped with them at all, they supped with a very long spoon, since they couldn't afford to have their people suspected of being spies. So the file on UCSO was very thin. From what he could gather, it was mainly a co-ordinating and shipping organisation, not one with teams of aid workers in the field, so not on the face of it of particular interest to Fane. But if Blakey had something to say about the hijacking attempt, some information about the gangs of pirates operating out of Somalia, then Fane wanted to hear it.

Somalia was a worry. It wasn't a country any more, not in any real sense. Rebel groups proliferated, fighting with each other or with any new government that emerged. The native population kept its head down amidst the warring factions, and scraped a living by subsistence farming. Or fishing, though Somalia's inability to patrol its own waters meant foreign fishing fleets had depleted the fish stocks to the point of disappearance. With no legitimate living to be made, small wonder many fishermen had turned to piracy.

All of which was worrying enough, but Fane

53

knew that such chaos created just the sort of situation that attracted people even more sinister than pirates. Al Qaeda, under pressure in Pakistan and Afghanistan, was looking for safer bases from which to launch their attacks against the West. Yemen was already on their list—was Somalia following? Fane thought of the young boy sitting in a Paris jail cell, arrested helping hijack UCSO's ship and carrying a British driving licence.

He paid off the taxi, still stuck in traffic, and walked north, leaving the hubbub of Oxford Street for the quieter byways of Fitzrovia. He passed the crumbling brick pile of the former Middlesex Hospital. Further along, dark brick mansion blocks lined the narrow street. It was not a part of the city he often visited. It was too full of students drinking on the pavements outside the pubs, and media and fashion types in their bright, flashy clothes. Fane, in his dark suit and polished leather shoes, didn't fit in here; he felt uncomfortable.

There had been a time when he had been able to blend into surroundings many times more exotic than these. He had spent several years in Delhi where he'd met his agents in the bazaars around the Red Fort with barely a second thought, and he'd served in Moscow in the Cold War with the KGB hot on his heels every time he left the Embassy. He certainly hadn't worn a three-piece suit in those days.

But this was London, and nowadays his heron-like figure was invariably clothed in a well-cut suit, and he was most at ease in Whitehall or walking through St James's Square and turning left along Pall Mall for the Travellers Club.

To his surprise the address Blakey had given

turned out to be a handsome modern building, six storeys of glass and steel set beyond a courtyard leading off the street. A directory on the wall behind the security desk showed the names of a dozen enterprises. One of these was UCSO.

10

On the third floor Fane found Blakey waiting for him, looking little changed from when they had worked together.

'Geoffrey. How very good to see you,' Blakey said, offering his hand. 'Let's go into my office and I'll tell you what it's all about.'

They walked through a large, brightly lit open-plan floor where young people dressed in jeans and T-shirts sat working at computers or stood talking together. The atmosphere seemed busy and cheerful.

Blakey led the way into a small ante-room in one corner of the floor. 'My PA's off ill,' he explained, as they passed the empty desk. He shut the door behind them and led Fane into his own office, a large room with a view over the little courtyard below. The walls were decorated with Chinese prints, and a carved African mask hung behind the large glass desk. Another door leading straight out to the open-plan area was already closed.

'This is all very smart,' said Fane as Blakey gestured to a leather armchair in front of his desk.

'Yes. We're lucky. The rent's not too bad, actually,' he said, sitting down. 'We managed to negotiate a long lease when the building first opened. But it's always a delicate balance,' he added with a smile that seemed slightly defensive. 'Too poor an appearance and you look amateurish; anything too smart, and people think you're spending their donations on overheads.'

Then he got down to business. 'Thanks for coming over so promptly, Geoffrey, and I hope I'm not wasting your time. But I really feel I need some advice and I couldn't think of anyone better to give me it than you.'

Fane sat back in his chair, crossed one long leg over the other and watched and waited. Blakey had always had a certain charm, he reflected, which had served him well as an agent runner and no doubt helped a lot in the charity world. Fane had no objection to its being exercised on him. It would have no effect whatsoever on what he decided to do.

Blakey went on: 'You'll have to judge what it means for yourself—all I can say is, it worries me. I'm sure you know what we do in UCSO?' Fane nodded. 'Our cargoes are assembled and shipped by our office in Athens. In the last nine months two shipments we've made have been hijacked off the Somalian coast. The shipping line's insurers and our own broker negotiated, and the ship's crew were returned. Last week a third attempt was made, but fortunately this time it was foiled by the French Navy.'

Fane nodded. 'Yes, I heard something about it,' he said. 'Dangerous sailing through those seas.'

'Unfortunately, we haven't got any choice. Kenya is our major destination. We use it as a safe base from which to supply the Congo, and Rwanda, and Burundi. Air cargo rates are prohibitively high, and any other route by sea would be out of the question.'

That checked out, thought Fane. The alternative would be to sail west the length of the Mediterranean to the Straits of Gibraltar, then down to the Cape, and up past Madagascar to Kenya. Four, maybe five times as long, and probably four or five times more expensive.

Blakey went on, 'To make things worse, the two shipments that were hijacked were unusually valuable. As was the third.'

'Valuable? What does that mean? And why should one aid shipment be more valuable than another?'

'I mean the black-market value of the drugs and equipment on board was unusually high. And what's more, the last two cargoes included a good deal of cash—for emergencies.' He avoided Fane's questioning look. 'We've had half a dozen other shipments go right through the same shipping lanes unscathed, but none of them was worth nearly as much.'

'Hmm,' said Fane. 'What are you saying? That you think the pirates know which ships to target?'

Blakey didn't hesitate. 'I'm beginning to think they must. It beggars belief that it's simply coincidence that the three ships with the richest pickings were the only ones they've gone for.'

Fane uncrossed his legs and leaned forward. 'What about the cash?' he asked. 'What sort of sums are we talking about?'

'High thousands, not millions. In dollar bills usually, but this last time it was gold.'

'I see what you're getting at,' said Fane. 'But how could the pirates know what's on board?

Are the manifests published? Is there some way they could tell from the appearance of the ships?' Fane's maritime experience was confined to a day's sailing with friends each year during Cowes Week.

Blakey shook his head. 'We keep the detailed manifests in our Athens office. And for published accounts the cargo is described in broad terms as "aid supplies"; there's no mention anywhere of the cash, and nothing to distinguish one of our shipments from another. No more than I could tell whether the wallet in your jacket held fifty pounds or five thousand.'

'So therefore . . . ?'

Blakey shifted uncomfortably in his seat. 'This is where it seems to be getting ridiculous. I'm almost embarrassed to say this, but I'm wondering if information about the cargoes could be getting to the pirates from inside UCSO.'

He looked straight at Fane, who said nothing for a moment. He was surprised; this was more interesting than he'd expected. His mind was working rapidly. If what Blakey was thinking was true and there was a thread leading from UCSO into a pirate group, it was a thread well worth tugging.

'Let me be quite clear what you're saying. You think there might be some connection between UCSO and Somalia.'

'I know it sounds ridiculous when you put it like that. But, yes, that's what I'm worried about. It's not necessarily from here,' said Blakey, waving his arm vaguely at the office outside. 'The Athens office handles all the logistics, and leases the ships. The cargo is assembled and loaded in Greece as well.'

'Who runs your Athens office?'

'Chap named Berger. He's American.'

'What's his background?'

'A bit of this, a bit of that—journalism, import/export. He's worked all over the world. It was his idea that there might be a leak.'

'And the staff?'

Blakey shrugged. 'Usual mix of local recruits—an accountant, secretaries—and a couple of people from other countries. Ten or eleven employees in all. Berger runs a tight operation; I'm sure he keeps a pretty sharp eye on what goes on.'

Even if he does, thought Fane, you'd need a professional to unravel something as sophisticated as the connection Blakey was proposing. He started to say, 'I have a thought—' when suddenly the door to the open-plan floor opened, and a voice said excitedly, 'David, the bastards have done it again! I can't believe those wretched people —'

The door was now fully open, revealing a woman standing in the doorway, clutching some papers. The look on her face showed she was as startled to find Fane sitting there as he was by her interruption. She was forty-ish, elegantly dressed in a smart, dark grey suit, sheer tights and shiny maroon high-heeled shoes. This was not Blakey's PA, Fane concluded without much difficulty.

'I'm so sorry, David,' she said. 'I thought you were alone.'

'Let me introduce you. This is Geoffrey Fane,' said Blakey. 'An old friend.'

'Katherine Ball,' the woman said, offering her hand.

'Katherine's my deputy,' said Blakey. 'The place wouldn't function without her. She's got a desk in Athens too—I know they'd say the same about her.'

'It's kind of you to say so,' she said with a laugh. 'But I'm not sure it's true.' She had a deep smoky voice. 'But don't let me interrupt,' she continued.

'Anything urgent?' asked Blakey.

'More annoying than urgent,' she said. 'I'll catch you later.' She looked at Fane appraisingly. 'Nice to meet you,' she said, and left the room.

'You were saying?' Blakey reminded him.

'I was wondering how we could help you. I might ask the Athens Station if they have anyone on their books that we could put into your office there to do a bit of quiet investigation. We have a new Head of Station and I could ring him this afternoon. What do you think?'

'I think it's an excellent idea,' Blakey said, looking relieved that Fane was willing to help.

'I take it this man Berger can be trusted? An American, you say?'

'I trust him absolutely. As I said, he's the one who first pointed out that we might have a problem.'

'Good. Tell him someone will be in touch. They can talk over a cover story.'

'What should I do about the London end?'

Fane smiled benignly. 'Why don't we focus on Athens for now? I'd say that's a much more likely source of any leak. But keep an eye out here; if anything strikes you, let me know and we'll take it from there. What about your deputy—Katherine, was it? Is she in on the picture?'

'No, not at present.'

'I'd keep it that way,' said Fane. '"Need to know" is always best in this sort of operation. We

60

can widen the net later if we have to. There's one other thing: when is your next big shipment going past the Horn?'

'Berger and I discussed that. It's not due for six weeks.'

'I might suggest that we put someone on board, but I'll discuss it with Athens Station. Tempting though it is, I'm not going to run this operation myself.'

'You see it as worthwhile then?' asked Blakey. 'You don't think I'm wasting your time.'

'Oh, no, old chap,' said Fane, standing up. 'This could give us a much-needed lead into these pirate gangs.' And that would be a great coup for the Service, he thought. It would also provide good bargaining chips to use with the allies.

He looked at his watch. 'I've got a meeting back at Vauxhall. Let me ring you after I've talked things through with the Athens Head.'

The two men rose, and Blakey ushered Fane out through his own door into the corridor. As they headed towards the lift, Fane noticed that the door to the ante-room, where Blakey's PA normally sat, was ajar, even though Blakey had closed it firmly when they'd first come through.

It was going to be difficult to keep anything secret in an environment where most work was done in an open-plan floor and people wandered in and out of offices without knocking. Of course, it only mattered if Blakey was right to think there was a link between UCSO and a group of pirates. It would have seemed improbable a week ago, but so would the presence of a British Pakistani in a pirate's skiff.

Returning to Vauxhall Cross, Fane's mind was

61

pulling together the strands of information that all seemed connected to UCSO. He decided the next thing was to find out what Liz Carlyle had discovered in Paris.

As he walked into his outer office, his PA said, 'Liz Carlyle rang. She'd like a word ASAP.'

Great minds think alike, thought Fane. He admired Liz Carlyle. Pity she didn't reciprocate.

11

Liz sat in her office in Thames House, gazing out through a steady drizzle at the river, mud-brown at low tide and sloshing against a litter-festooned strip of sand on the far bank. She thought of Paris, the warm sun as she had left Martin's flat, the bistro in the square where they'd eaten supper at a pavement table under the plane trees. And Martin himself—when they'd said goodbye the following morning he hadn't returned to the subject of her moving to Paris, but there'd been a questioning look in his eye that suggested the topic wasn't going to stay buried for long. Paris . . . how tempting it seemed on this gloomy London morning.

But then she thought of the young man in the Santé prison. Why was he there? What had pulled him away from a respectable Birmingham family to a pirate boat in the Indian Ocean? She turned with a sigh as Peggy Kinsolving came into her office, looking eager, a file clutched in her hand and her spectacles firmly in place. Peggy smiled and said, 'Don't tell me—it was sunny in Paris.'

'Naturally.' Liz waved her to a chair. 'Did this DI Fontana have anything more to say?'

'No. I told him not to go near the Khan family until you were back.'

'Good. I'll ring him. I want to talk to the Khans myself, but if he knows them, it might be best if he came with me.'

Peggy nodded then said, 'There's one more thing. One of our agent runners has a source in the part of Birmingham where the Khans live. It's a young Asian who's a member of one of the radical mosques there. I thought he could be useful.'

'He might . . . we need all the information we can get. The Khan family won't necessarily tell us everything they know about their son—that's if they know anything themselves. Who's the agent runner? I'd like to have a word.'

'It's Kanaan Shah. He's in the office today; I saw him earlier. Let me see if I can find him.'

Peggy bustled out and returned a few minutes later escorting a tall, dark, good-looking young man, wearing chinos and a blue open-necked shirt.

'Have a seat, Kanaan,' Liz began.

'You've pronounced it correctly,' he said with a smile. 'Most people don't. That's why I'm called "K" around here.'

'How long have you been in the Service?'

'Three years. But I've only been running agents for a few months. I was in protective security before. "Agent", I should say,' he added with a grin. 'I've only got the one.'

'That'll change once you get the hang of it. You'll soon find you've got a whole stable of them.' She remembered her own first days as an agent runner—and one particular agent, the boy in the

63

Muslim bookshop, codenamed Marzipan. He had helped to prevent a serious terrorist incident, but had later been killed—his identity blown to the extremists by a mole in the Service. That had been the worst period of Liz's career. She'd almost resigned over it, even though none of it had been her fault. Now here was young Kanaan, starting out on his career as an agent runner. He'd be asking people to put their lives in his hands in the national interest; making the compact with them that he would look after them in return for their information. It was a compact made in good faith but one, as Liz knew only too well, that was never without risk.

She asked Kanaan about his background; there were still comparatively few Asians at the operational end of the Service. He told her he was from a Ugandan Asian family. His grandparents had been forced to leave when Idi Amin drove out the Asian community. London-born, Kanaan had grown up in Herne Hill and gone to Alleyn's School for Boys, then he'd read Politics and Economics at LSE. Personable, obviously intelligent, he could have had any number of jobs; Liz asked him what had attracted him to the Security Service.

'Adventure,' he said with a boyish grin that was infectious—she found herself smiling back. 'And,' he added, the grin disappearing, 'I wanted to give something back. My grandparents came to Britain with nothing but a single suitcase, but my family has done very well here. My father became a GP, then he changed direction and now he's a partner at Morgan Stanley. And he's made sure I've had every opportunity to do what I want to do.'

Liz nodded. She was charmed by Kanaan's willingness to express sentiments that many would find old-fashioned. Her own father had had a very strong sense of duty, of service to his country. He'd carried it through into civilian life from his days in the army, and it had rubbed off on her. That, she thought ruefully, was why she couldn't just pack it all in and go off to live in Paris. Not yet anyway.

'Tell me about your agent,' she said. 'Peggy says he's in Birmingham.'

'That's right.' And Liz listened carefully as K began to tell her about a young man in Birmingham called Salim Alavi, codename 'Boatman'. He was the son of first-generation immigrants from Pakistan. His mother worked as a cleaner; his father was a mechanic in a local garage. Salim had done well at school, getting three good A-levels; he didn't go to university but instead applied to join the West Midlands Police. His application had been unsuccessful: he'd passed his written tests with flying colours, but he'd failed the medical exam—there was some problem with his eyesight. Yet he was so obviously keen and bright that one of the recruiters had mentioned him to Special Branch and in time he'd been drawn to MI5's attention.

After his application was rejected, Salim took a job in a hardware store run by his uncle. He seemed to have become embittered by his experience with the police and, for the first time in his life, became extremely religious. He joined a small, recently founded mosque, the New Springfield, and went there daily to pray; he also spent his free time listening to clerics preach and began to participate in discussion groups. If you had asked him why he had previously wanted to become a policeman, Salim would have told you it had been a mistake, a youthful error committed when he hadn't realised he would be doing the Infidel's bidding by becoming a copper. He would not have told you about his monthly meetings with an officer of MI5.

After almost two years of faithful attendance at the mosque, 'Boatman' was asked to join a small study group, under the tutelage of a cleric named Abdi Bakri who had recently arrived from Pakistan. He agreed at once. At first the sessions were merely versions of the larger discussion groups he still attended. Islam was always on the agenda, and the overriding theme of the talks was how to follow the faith while living in the secular and corrupt society of the West.

But gradually the tenor of the cleric's study sessions became more political—and Abdi Bakri shifted emphasis from adhering faithfully to Islam to defeating its enemies. This transition was noted by Boatman—and reported to his new MI5 controller, Kanaan Shah.

'How did Boatman take your arrival on the scene?' asked Liz. Agents usually hated any change to their controller—such relationships were of necessity close ones, and made closer by their clandestine nature.

'I think he was a bit surprised. He was recruited by Dave Armstrong and I took him on when Dave was posted to Northern Ireland. I'm sure he was expecting another white man, and at first he was suspicious of me. But the fact we were both Asians helped—even though I'm Indian and a Hindu, not Muslim.' He added with a little laugh,

'Boatman was willing to overlook this flaw when he discovered that I hated cricket too.'

Kanaan continued with his account. In this new elite group, Boatman slowly felt his way; it took him over a month even to learn the names of his fellow members. But his patience paid off, and one of them in particular, an old hand named Malik, seemed to trust him. It was from him that Boatman learned that there had been earlier incarnations of this little group, taught by another cleric now thought to be in Yemen, and that some of his disciples had travelled to Pakistan.

'And what happened to them after that?' asked Liz.

'Most came back. I got three names from Boatman and they're under surveillance. But the interesting thing is that at least two others don't seem to have returned.'

And now those in the present group were being offered the chance to travel to Pakistan as well, to 'study', they were told, with a renowned imam near the Afghan border.

Kanaan said, 'Boatman is asking me what he should do. We're stalling for the moment, but they've started to put him under pressure. Boatman told Abdi Bakri he couldn't afford to leave his job for long—they've said he'd be gone at least two months. But now the imam has explained that all his costs would be met, and that if he lost his job they would help find him another one when he returned.'

If he returned, thought Liz. 'Who's they?' she asked.

'The imam and his associates at the New Springfield Mosque.'

Liz thought hard for a minute. If Boatman went to Pakistan, he might be able to discover what had happened to those who didn't come back. But the pressing requirement was for information about people in England, particularly Amir Khan. 'When has he got to give them a definite yes or no?'

'Pretty soon, I think. As I say, they're beginning to put the pressure on and if he doesn't either agree to go or come up with a convincing reason why he can't, they're going to get suspicious. I'm afraid he may be frozen out and then we'll lose our access.'

Liz told Kanaan about Amir Khan and how he had come into the hands of the French Navy off the Somalian coast.

'That's not a name that rings any bells,' Kanaan said with a shake of his head. 'But I'll look back at my reports to see if it's been mentioned. There'd be a trace in the files if Boatman ever said anything significant about him.'

'There isn't. Peggy has looked him up.'

'I'll ask if he can find out anything.'

'Tell him to go easy,' Liz cautioned. 'I'd sooner he did nothing than have his cover blown.'

'I'm sure he'll be careful. He's pretty sensible. But what do you think about Pakistan? Should he go? He doesn't want to, but he'll do it if I tell him it's important.'

'I'm going up to talk to Khan's parents tomorrow with the local DI. Let's wait till we hear what they have to say. Who's your group leader?'

'Nicholas Carraway.'

Liz nodded. She didn't know him well, but he had a good reputation. 'OK. Let's all get together when I come back from Birmingham and we'll make a decision then. If anything comes up in the meantime, let Peggy know.'

12

Liz had half an hour before she needed to leave to catch the train for Birmingham. She closed her office door and started to type a note for the file about her conversation with Amir Khan. She hadn't completed more than a few words when the door opened a crack and a familiar face peered in. Her heart sank.

'Good afternoon, Elizabeth,' said Geoffrey Fane. She was convinced he used her full name just to annoy her.

'Geoffrey,' she said through gritted teeth. 'To what do I owe the honour?'

'Just passing through. Had to see Charles on a minor matter, and my secretary said you'd rung.'

At the mention of Charles Wetherby, Liz's eyes narrowed. She suspected Fane had brought his name up on purpose. She saw very little of Charles these days, and Fane, who prided himself on knowing everyone's business, would be aware of that.

Fane himself was divorced and never seemed to have any close female companion. Peggy was convinced that he was keen on Liz and had been jealous when her relationship with Charles Wetherby had grown close. Now that it no longer was, perhaps he fancied his chances.

Liz's professional dealings with Fane had always been edgy, but they'd hit rock bottom a few years ago at the time of an investigation into a Russian illegal in Britain. That case had ended badly, with an unnecessary death—tragic by any measure. Fane had been deeply shaken, and for a time it seemed to Liz that he'd been humanised by his role in the débâcle. But in the last year he had gone back to his former ways: arrogant, patronising and manipulative.

Now he said, 'So how are things across the Channel?'

'Where precisely?'

'In Paris, of course,' Fane said cheerfully. 'I gather you're there quite often these days. Our mutual friend Bruno Mackay says he's run across you several times.'

Liz face was expressionless as she looked at him How dare you? she was thinking. Standing here in my office, in your beautifully cut suit, with your arrogant expression, poking around in my private life. But all she said was, 'Yes, my work does take me to Paris from time to time. As you know I'm our main liaison with the French services on counter-terrorism.'

'I know there's one French service you are very involved with,' he replied, and she could see he was struggling to keep a smile off his face.

'I wouldn't believe everything Bruno Mackay tells you.' Mackay was number two at MI6's station in Paris, and an old sparring partner of Liz's. Clever, self-confident (over-confident Liz would have said), charming if he wished to be, yet often simply arrogant, Bruno had always enjoyed teasing her. So he knew about Martin Seurat, she thought crossly. She was perfectly happy for people to know she

70

was seeing Martin, but she disliked the thought of being gossiped about, especially by Bruno Mackay and Fane.

'Sadly I'm going to have to find a new source of information from Paris.'

'Why's that?' asked Liz. She had seen Bruno at the embassy only last month.

'We're posting Bruno.' And before Liz could ask where, Fane leaned over her desk and said teasingly, 'Will you be my source of Paris social news then, Elizabeth?'

She gave a thin-lipped smile and shook her head, hoping he'd had his fun and would now get to the point. She said, 'I have a train to catch—and before you ask, no, it's not to Paris.'

'What I was wondering,' said Fane, sitting down in her visitor's chair, 'was how it went with this Amir Khan character. I heard that the French had asked for your help. Did you get anything out of him?'

'I was just writing up my report when you came in. Khan hasn't opened up at all to the French and he wasn't much more forthcoming with me. I was going to come and tell you about it.'

'He wouldn't talk at all?'

'Silence wasn't the problem.' She told him about Khan's long-winded monologue, and how he'd obviously decided to try and bury her in words. 'We've learned he went to Pakistan eight months ago and didn't come back. I tried to get him to say how he'd got to Somalia, but he just fed me a cock-and-bull story. He even claimed the pirates had taken *him* prisoner.'

'That's disappointing,' said Fane, with a note of mild reproof.

71

'I thought so too,' admitted Liz cheerfully. 'But then he slipped up.' She waited while Fane looked at her with undisguised curiosity. 'I asked him who had given him his orders in Pakistan, and before he thought, he said that it hadn't been in Pakistan.'

'Ah-ha,' said Fane approvingly.

Liz felt as if she'd been awarded a gold star by the headmaster. 'Frankly, he's pretty green. I think his defiance is a big act and underneath he's scared stiff. Though if he's scared of us, I think he's even more scared of whoever got to him in the first place.'

'Well, he's got that right. We might keep him in prison but we're not going to kill him.'

'He claimed the French Navy chaps roughed him up.'

'They probably did,' said Fane dismissively. 'The *Marine Nationale* can be a little over-zealous. But if he didn't get his instructions in Pakistan, where did he get them? Here?'

'Possibly. Or in some other country he went to after Pakistan. That's why I rang you when I got back; I thought you might be able to help.'

The trace of a smile touched Fane's lips. Liz knew he was pleased. He liked nothing better than to be asked for help, particularly by her. At heart he was an old-fashioned chauvinist, instinctively assuming superiority over all women. There were still a few of that breed left in Liz's own service. She thought particularly of Michael Binding, most recently her boss in Northern Ireland. He could not take any advice from a woman, but expected only to issue orders and receive slavish agreement; if that wasn't forthcoming, he got angry and shouted.

But Geoffrey Fane was a much more complex

character. Fane positively enjoyed disputes, though he was always sure he was right. He liked to watch Liz getting angry when he did something to annoy her. She knew that and therefore tried always to keep her temper. But it was difficult to do when she found him out, as had often happened, in some outrageous piece of double-dealing or concealment. He would show enough grace to apologise, though she always felt that even then he was secretly enjoying his own cleverness.

Fane leaned back in his chair and crossed one flannelled leg over the other. 'Do you know anything about the ship the pirates tried to hijack?' he asked.

'No.' Liz immediately felt cross with herself, since she hadn't pursued that angle of the investigation at all. She made a mental note to ask Peggy to look into it. 'I know the ship is called the *Aristides*.'

'That's right,' said Fane approvingly. Again, she felt as if she were being patted on the head. 'It was leased by a charity called UCSO. Quite coincidentally, I had a call from the charity's director, a chap named Blakey. Used to be one of us—Head of Station in Hong Kong for a good while. He's based here in London, though UCSO also have an office in Athens.'

Liz's antennae were vibrating now. 'Did he say anything about the hijack attempt?'

'He mentioned it,' said Fane airily. Something in the tone of his voice struck her as suspicious. She knew he was holding something back. Then he said, 'Tell you what: let me have another word with him. It could be that the hijack attempt and the fact the ship was an UCSO one are connected. If they are, we'll need to liaise closely.' He looked at her and smiled. 'You'll enjoy that, Elizabeth. We work well together.'

13

There was no need for introductions. Liz could recognise a Special Branch officer in the dark. DI Fontana clearly felt the same about MI5 officers; he strode up to her as she walked towards the end of the platform at Birmingham New Street station and greeted her with a handshake. 'Liz Carlyle,' he said. 'Pleased to meet you.'

He was tall, lean, athletic-looking—and disconcertingly blond, thought Liz, given his Italian surname. They walked towards his car, which was parked on a double yellow line outside the station.

'You sound as if you've lived here all your life.'

'I'm third-generation Brummie. My grandfather came over from Italy in the thirties; he couldn't be doing with Mussolini. He made his living selling ice cream from a van—a real Eyetie,' the DI said with a grin. 'Then he married an English woman.' He raked a hand through his blond hair. 'That's how I got this.'

'Tell me about the Khans.'

'I started as a beat policeman, and for a few years I was stationed in Sparkhill. That's when I got to know them. I used to stop in at one of their shops sometimes—you know, for a chat and a quick cup of tea. Shopkeepers like to keep in touch with the local bobby and they always seem to know what's going on in their neighbourhood. It's a two-way process. Not that I'd say I know them well . . . not nowadays anyway.'

'Do they have other children?'

'Lots. Amir must have six or seven brothers and sisters. I could never keep track of them all, though I do remember him as a little boy. He's the youngest—unless his mum's had any more since then, but she's getting a bit long in the tooth now. She doted on Amir. Mr Khan was very strict with all the kids; too strict, I'd say.'

Not a good combination, thought Liz. It would have made the boy keen to cut his mother's apron strings as well as want to rebel against his father.

Fontana went on, 'When I first knew them the family had two corner shops; now they must own a dozen. One of them's a small supermarket.'

'So Mr Khan's done well.'

'The whole family has,' Fontana said. 'It's a team effort. The kids are put to work in the shops pretty much when they start school. God knows how many child labour laws their father's broken. Still, he's a classic Asian success story. It's a pity it hasn't rubbed off on the next generation.'

'What do you think happened?'

'With Amir?' said Fontana, glancing over at her as he stopped at traffic lights. They'd reached the Stratford Road, an urban High Street with residential streets running off it like spokes.

The lights changed. Fontana pointed ahead towards a park on their right: acres of grass ringed by tall weeping birches, only now fully leafing. 'That's Springfield Park,' he said, and Liz wondered why he wasn't answering her question. 'In a way, it's a symbol of what's happened to parts of the Asian community here. One of the

75

Royals is supposed to come at the end of the summer to dedicate a new playground. Yet the older generation—Mr Khan, for example—never set foot in the place. They're too busy running and expanding their businesses, completely focused on financial success.

'They want success for their kids too, but they want them to become professionals. They drive them hard to do well at school; they've got to be top of the class, go to uni, become doctors or lawyers. But at home the likes of Mr Khan still cling to the more traditional Pakistani way of life: his wife stays in the house; he arranges marriages for his daughters; socially they only mix within the Pakistani community. It's not surprising that some of the next generation rebel. They meet people at school who have a very different way of life, and they want some of it too. So they conform at home, but when they get the chance they'll be hanging out in the park, smoking and drinking, and going to watch American films.'

'So how does someone like Amir end up in Somalia?'

Fontana had clearly thought about this before. He said, 'I think they go through a sort of identity crisis. All this Western culture is only skin-deep with them; a lot of these kids don't feel they can ever truly be English, and once they realise that, they feel alienated both from their parents and from this country and Western culture as a whole. Most of them don't share the same work ethic as their parents; without that, they're very vulnerable to the concept of a cause. Enter the extremist imams.'

They turned off the Stratford Road, on to a

76

residential avenue that led gently uphill. 'This used to be all Irish a century ago,' said Fontana. 'Then after the war immigrants from the Caribbean lived here. But for the last thirty years it's been Asian. Lots of small businesses—people like the Khans, just trying to get ahead.'

He turned the car again, and they drove up a street of small Victorian terraced houses with little front gardens behind low walls. The street looked to be in good order—the houses freshly painted, the windows clean, dustbins neatly lined up in the front gardens—but when Fontana pulled over to park outside a house in the middle of the terrace, Liz was surprised.

He saw her expression and laughed. 'Don't be fooled. Mr Khan could buy half this street, but it's not his style. He'd never want to leave this neighbourhood—most of his extended family live within a quarter of a mile of here, and all his friends. You'll never find him in a mock-Tudor villa out in the suburbs.'

Fontana's knock on the half-glazed front door was answered by a small fierce-looking man, who seemed to be in his sixties. His hair was white, and his black, sharply trimmed moustache was speckled with grey. His self-important demeanour made it clear that he was the lord of this particular manor.

'Hello, Mr Khan, very nice to see you again. This is Miss Forrester from the Home Office. I told you she'd be coming along.'

Khan nodded curtly, and led them into the front room. The heavy gold curtains were pulled back, but the windows facing the street were covered by dense lace nets. A small woman was sitting, slightly hunched, on a maroon sofa. 'My wife,' said Khan,

77

waving a hand towards her. She nodded but did not get up. Mrs Khan was wearing a brown *salwar kameez* and a woollen cardigan; her head was almost covered by an embroidered shawl.

Liz and Fontana sat down in the pair of armchairs that faced the sofa. Mr Khan remained standing, and said to Fontana, 'Now, officer, what is all this about?'

Liz replied, 'I've come to see you about your son.'

'Which son?' asked Khan sharply.

'Amir,' said Liz. 'I want to talk to you about Amir.'

Mrs Khan lifted up her head and looked at Liz, her face a mask of concern. 'Is Amir . . . ?'

'He's fine,' said Liz soothingly. 'I've seen him myself. He's in good health.'

Mr Khan was now sitting on the sofa beside his wife. 'Where is he?' he demanded, looking pointedly at Fontana. This is a man constantly on the brink of losing his temper, thought Liz. And he's not used to being questioned by a woman.

She continued, 'I am afraid that he is being held by the French authorities in a prison in Paris. He may be extradited to the UK—or possibly not. That's still up in the air.'

'What has he done?'

'He was part of an attempt to hijack a cargo ship off the Horn of Africa. We believe he had been living in Somalia.'

For the first time Mr Khan seemed at a loss for words. He sank back against the sofa cushions and exhaled noisily. Liz said, 'When I talked to him, he said that he'd ended up there by accident, that he'd been press-ganged into helping a crew of pirates.

He's being held in France because the French Navy arrested him—they stopped the pirates from seizing the ship.'

Mr Khan latched on to his son's explanation greedily. 'He's a good boy. I would believe him if I were you.'

'We're not sure what to think, Mr Khan. The first thing we'd like to establish is how your son got to Somalia.'

Mr Khan was silent. Liz noticed he didn't look at his wife.

'When did you last hear from Amir, Mr Khan?' Fontana interjected gently.

He said stiffly, 'Amir went to Pakistan last year. He was working for a relation of my wife's. The last letter we had from him was in . . .' He paused, and for the first time looked over at his wife, as if asking for confirmation. He's lying, Liz suddenly sensed.

The door to the sitting room opened then and a young woman appeared. She looked to be about twenty or so and was strikingly beautiful, with thick black hair that flowed over the shoulders of the rose-pink embroidered *kameez* she wore over wide white trousers.

Mr Khan looked up angrily. 'Tahira, why aren't you at the shop?'

'You know we close early on Tuesdays, Papa,' she said. 'Besides, when Mama said the police were coming, I wanted to hear if there was news of Amir.' Seeing her mother's expression, she hesitated. 'Is he . . . ?'

'He's alive and well,' Liz said firmly. She wanted to keep Mr Khan from dismissing his daughter, who seemed more likely to speak her mind than his

79

submissive wife.

The girl's eyes lit up. 'Where is he? Is he coming home?'

'Tahira, go to your room—' Mr Khan started to command her, but Liz interrupted. 'He's in France.' She explained again about Amir's arrest in the Indian Ocean, adding,'We're trying to understand how he got from Pakistan to Somalia. To be honest, what your brother's told us doesn't make sense. We don't know how he got to Africa.'

'I thought he was in Athens,' said Tahira.

'Athens?' Fontana and Liz said simultaneously.

Tahira looked at her father, who seemed to have given up any attempt to send her away. He shrugged, stony-faced. Tahira said, 'Father, didn't you tell them?'

'Tel them what?' Fontana asked firmly.

Liz almost felt sorry for the girl, who seemed bewildered. Tahira looked at Liz and, finding sympathy in her expression, said, 'He sent us a postcard from Athens. Said he was working there.' She looked again at her father, but his face remained blank. It was as if he had wiped his hands of any responsibility for his son, having made the obligatory attempt to protect him. Doubtless, if sufficiently provoked, he would wipe his hands of Tahira too.

'Did he say where he was going next?' Liz pressed her.

'He said he was working until he had saved enough money to come home.' Realising suddenly this must have been the last thing Amir had in mind, his sister faltered and stopped talking, on the verge of tears.

Mr Khan suddenly erupted. 'Tahira, that's

enough! Go to your room.'

Shaking her head, she said, 'I knew Amir should not have changed mosques.'

'Tahira . . .' her father said warningly.

Liz held up a hand to silence him. 'Which mosque did he attend?' she asked the girl.

'The New Springfield,' Tahira managed to say, and then broke down, sobbing. Her mother stood up and put her arms round her. Mr Khan sat mute on the sofa with his arms crossed. It was obvious to Liz that she wasn't going to get anything more out of the family on this visit.

*　　　*　　　*

Outside, Fontana sighed. 'I should have warned you about Mr Khan.'

'Don't worry. I'm just glad Tahira showed up.'

'What would you like me to do?' The DI seemed younger now, not quite so confident.

'Stay in touch with the Khans and keep your ear to the ground. If you hear anything about Amir, let me know. I'll keep you posted with any news of what the French do with him so you can keep the Khans informed.

'If you can find out who Amir's friends are, that would be helpful. But stay clear of the New Springfield Mosque. We've got a source there and we don't want to queer his pitch.'

'OK. It's not far from here, you know. In fact, it's just two streets away,' Fontana added. 'Would you like to see it?'

'Yes, I would,' said Liz. 'I think everything that's happened to Amir is going to turn out to have links back to that place.'

The mosque stood on the intersection of a residential street and a wider thoroughfare of shops. It was a large, squat, two-storey building of red brick that must have been built in the thirties. It had a row of small-paned windows along its façade and, above an ugly flight of concrete steps, an entrance comprising two sets of double swing doors.

As they passed the building the doors suddenly burst open and a stream of Asian men emerged, obviously having just finished prayers. A few wore T-shirts and jeans, but most of them were in robes or white shirts and cotton trousers and with embroidered skullcaps on their heads. Several stopped to smoke and chat on the front steps.

Liz and Fontana walked on, and at the next corner the policeman looked at his watch. 'I've got an appointment back in the centre of town. I'll drop you at New Street on the way.'

'Birmingham International station is closer, isn't it? I can take a taxi there.'

'Would you mind?' He pointed in the direction of where he had parked, a couple of streets away. 'Let's go back to the car and I'll drop you on the Stratford Road.'

But Liz wanted to get the feel of the neighbourhood. 'I'll walk down—the fresh air will do me good.'

'You sure?' When she nodded, Fontana said, 'If you have any problem finding a taxi, there's a minicab office on the corner.'

'Great. Thanks for all your help. I may need to

come and see the Khans again. And if I do,' she added with a grin, 'I'll want you to come with me.'

Fontana laughed. 'Old Khan hasn't much time for women. Not those in authority anyway.'

'It's Tahira I'd really like to talk to. If you can, find out how I could meet her alone. I don't get the feeling Mr Khan knows much about the company his son was keeping before he left—but I bet she does.'

14

Liz turned left at the corner and started to walk down the gently sloping street towards the Stratford Road. Hearing footsteps behind her, she turned and saw two young Asian men about thirty feet away, walking fast so as to catch up with her. They were both bearded, and neatly dressed in pressed jeans and T-shirts. One of them, the taller of the pair, was wearing a New York Yankees baseball cap. He grinned at her, and Liz smiled back then continued walking.

'Are you Fontana's girlfriend?' one of them called out.

Liz stopped and turned around to face the two men. The taller one was grinning again; his sidekick, short but stocky, wasn't smiling at all—his expression was grim and tight-lipped.

'Or are you a cop too?' the tall one in the cap said. They were only a few feet away now, and both stood still, watching Liz.

'What do you want?' she asked sharply. She gave a quick look round, but the street was empty.

'What do *you* want is more like it. What are you and the cop doing checking out the mosque?'

'What I'm doing is none of your business.' Liz turned on her heel and started walking again. Ahead she could see the traffic on the Stratford Road, but it was several hundred yards away. There was still no one else on the street, and no passing cars.

She sensed the men move behind her, and then suddenly there was one on either side of her. Keep calm, she told herself as she kept walking.

'I don't think you're a cop,' offered the tall one, only now he wasn't smiling. 'I think you're from MI5. Am I right?'

'Don't be ridiculous,' said Liz, hoping that by answering she could buy herself some time. There was an unmistakable sense of menace in the way the men were crowding in on either side of her. Then the shorter, heavy-set man on the street side of the pavement put his hand around her left wrist.

'Don't touch me,' she said, her voice rising sharply. She twisted out of his grasp, but suddenly the man in the baseball cap man grabbed her other arm and twisted it sharply up behind her back. His grip was like steel.

To slow the men down she stumbled deliberately, hoping to break the iron grip on her arm. She tilted her head up to one side, and shouted as loud as she could: 'Help!'

The shorter man grabbed her hair and jerked hard, pulling her head back. The pain was excruciating. She tried to dig her heels in, but now they were half-pushing, half-towing her by both arms. Ahead, a narrow alley led off the street and she suddenly felt sure they were planning to force

84

her up it, out of sight of any passersby, and then she'd be completely at their mercy. They reached the entrance to the alley, the men still holding tightly on to her, and as they turned, pulling her with them, Liz suddenly tripped over a pile of rubble and fell to one side, dragging the man in the cap down with her. He let go of her wrist for a moment but the shorter man crowded in from her left, reaching for her arm to pull her up.

It was then Liz made her move. Standing up, she spread the first two fingers of her freed right hand and jabbed them viciously into the eyes of the smaller man. As he began to howl in pain she swung her elbow back ferociously into the groin of the tall man in the Yankees cap, who was still off balance. Then she turned away and ran into the street, where a car was driving slowly along from the direction of the Stratford Road. She stood in front of the oncoming vehicle, hands held up to force it to stop. She saw the startled face of the driver, a middle-aged Sikh in a turban, as he hit the brakes. His little car skidded once, twice, then stopped with a squeal of its tyres about three inches from Liz.

'Help!' she shouted, running round to the driver's window. 'I've been attacked by those two men. Call the police! Quick . . . before they get away.'

The Sikh held up both hands and his expression of concern turned to one of bafflement. 'If you wish I will call, young lady. But what two men?'

And when Liz looked around, breathing hard, she saw that her attackers had disappeared. The alley was empty. At the end of it the green-painted door of a garage hung open, gently swinging.

15

This Monday morning Arthur Goldsmith was looking forward to retiring. He could have gone several years earlier, with a decent pension too, but the last Head of Station, Danny Molyneux, had persuaded him to stay on. Arthur had liked Molyneux, a friendly chap who'd run a good station. He and his wife Annie had created a real family atmosphere. They'd organised swimming parties for the kids in their pool and picnics in the garden, and the station had run some excellent operations too. The whole station had been commended for the way they'd handled a Libyan diplomat who'd defected from the embassy. He'd been in their London embassy in the eighties and knew all about what had gone on when that policewoman was killed in St James's Square. He knew quite a bit about Pan Am 103 too. They'd all got involved in that case, even the secretaries and some of the wives, though Arthur's own wife had left by then. Gone off with a Greek lawyer. She still lived in Athens, though they never met.

But Danny Molyneux had gone back to London and now a new Head of Station had arrived and Arthur was not at all sure he was going to enjoy working with Bruno Mackay. He was an Arabist; he'd worked in Pakistan, and most recently been Deputy Head of Station in Paris. Mackay's reputation had preceded him on the grapevine. He was an Old Harrovian and a bit of an arrogant shit, it was said, a protégé of Geoffrey Fane, who could be an arrogant shit too though he had many a brilliant operation under his belt. Mackay was still in his thirties, young for a Head of Station, but that was par for the course nowadays.

Arthur wasn't public school and Oxbridge—not a graduate at all. He'd joined MI6 from the army; had come in to the General Service Branch, not Intelligence. Communications was his forte. He'd had a good career and done very well to get as far as he had: Deputy Head of Station in Athens was an important post. But it looked as though the station might be about to change, and probably not for the better.

His thoughts about his new colleague were rudely interrupted by the sharp buzz of his internal line. He picked up the phone. 'Yes,' he said quietly. It was a point of principle with Arthur Goldsmith never to show his feelings at work. He reserved emotions for Tia, the only other resident of his small, comfortable flat near the Parthenon. People might wonder how anyone could care so much about a cat, but Goldsmith felt no need to explain the depth of his affection. Tia was special.

'Arthur? It's Bruno. Can you pop along for a minute?'

Goldsmith went along to Mackay's office cautiously. You never knew what might be going on in there. Once he'd discovered the new Station Head showing a secretary (a pretty young thing called Veronica) a new fishing rod he'd had sent out from Hardy's in Pall Mall. What would he find in progress now? he thought sourly. A practical tutorial on Greek cuisine? Or a troupe of belly dancers brought in from Egypt?

'Ah, Arthur,' said Mackay, who was for once sitting at a desk covered in papers. 'I was hoping you could help me. Have a seat.'

Goldsmith grunted, then sat down in the chair opposite the desk. Mackay looked as though he'd had a good weekend. He was ridiculously handsome, with his deeply tanned face, sculpted nose and mouth and grey-blue eyes. No wonder all the girls were in a flutter. This morning he was wearing a dark red shirt, the sleeves rolled up to his elbows revealing tanned arms downed with fine blond hair and a heavy, expensive-looking watch. It wouldn't have been so annoying, Arthur thought, if Mackay hadn't also been very clever.

'There's a job come in for us from Head Office. They've got a bit of a situation. The French have managed to catch some pirates trying to board a cargo ship in the Indian Ocean, off Somalia. It turns out the ship sailed from here; it was leased by a London-based charity with an office in Athens.'

'UCSO,' Goldsmith murmured.

'That's right,' said Mackay, looking up in surprise. 'How'd you know that?'

'It's the only major international charity with a base in Greece.'

'Do we have a contact in their office?'

'Danny knew the boss, an American called Berger, but I've never met him. Danny didn't hand him on when he left; I think he was more of a friend than an official station contact. You know the rules about not getting too close to charities.'

'Yes. Well, Geoffrey Fane's in touch with their boss in London and it seems they've been having a bit of a hijacking problem for some time. Not alone in that, of course, but this time the French Navy nabbed the pirates and one of them turns out to be a British citizen. Hails from Birmingham, would

88

you believe?' Mackay leaned back in his chair, stretched out his long legs and laughed.

'Anyway, that's one aspect. The other is that the UCSO people are worried that someone's been leaking information about their shipments. The only ships hijacked have had especially valuable cargo—cash in particular. Those with just the routine stuff have been left alone.'

Arthur Goldsmith pondered this for a moment. 'Don't tell me Head Office believes that Somalian pirates have a source inside UCSO?'

Mackay grinned. 'Who knows what Geoffrey believes or what he's really up to? He plays his cards close to his chest. But he's agreed with the London UCSO boss that we'll put someone in at the Athens end to try and find out what's going on. Berger's in on it and we're going to do it straight away.

'Apparently there's a vacancy for an assistant accountant at the moment, and Geoffrey wants us to find someone with the right credentials to apply. Then Berger will fix it for them to get the job and we'll run them from here.

'So what I'd like you to do, Arthur,' said Mackay, standing up, 'is to look through the station assets and see if we've got anyone on the books who fits the bill. It'll be so much quicker if someone's already recruited than starting from scratch. I gather there's some urgency about this.'

Bloody Fane, thought Arthur to himself, as he walked back down the corridor, he must be short of things to do. Back in his office, he took out a dozen files from a combination-locked filing cabinet. After about half an hour he picked up three of them and walked back to Bruno's room.

The door was open and Bruno, feet propped up on the desk and hands locked together behind his head, was listening to the radio. 'Just polishing up my Greek,' he said as Arthur walked in. 'What have you dredged up?'

There were three candidates who had the necessary credentials.

George Arbuthnot had been on the books for ten years. His track record was sound if not inspiring; he was a chartered accountant who had retired to the island of Naxos. He'd worked as a civilian employee for the British Military delegation in Berlin during the Cold War, had married a German and stayed on after the Wall came down. He had been an occasional but useful source of information since then, as his auditing responsibilities had included some of the businesses set up in the former East Berlin by retired officers of the KGB and the Stasi. Then he'd retired, but after three months of Naxos narcolepsy, as he was fond of calling it, he'd moved to Athens, where he and his German wife found life more lively if more expensive. He still did occasional auditing when one of the big firms needed reinforcement; he found the money useful. Arthur had always found him very reliable.

Then there was Pappas. A Greek native but bilingual, or actually trilingual since his Arabic too was fluent after a decade spent in the Gulf working for a sheikh in the Emirates. It was there he had first come under MI6's wing, passed on by the CIA during a time of co-operative swaps; he'd been recruited by Langley easily enough, since he loathed the corruption in the regime he worked for. Back in Greece, he'd set up his own accountancy firm, hiring and firing staff as the economy waxed and waned.

But there was a small problem with the Greek. He drank. Arthur remembered a catastrophic dinner he'd had with Pappas and Danny Molyneux; by the time the dessert had arrived, Pappas was stupefied with *ouzo*. They'd had difficulty persuading a taxi driver to take him home.

The third candidate was new to Goldsmith. Maria Galanos had been passed on from Head Office and signed up by one of the more junior members of the station. Greek father, English mother. Educated at a girls' boarding school in England; economics degree from Manchester, followed by an MBA at INSEAD. A job with Price Waterhouse in London, where she was first contacted by MI6, was followed by a post in a Saudi bank in Frankfurt; the file didn't make clear if that was at the Service's instigation. But whether it was or not, she'd helped the Service and their German counterparts expose an Al Qaeda money-laundering scheme. She'd come to live in Athens six months earlier, for 'personal reasons' the file said, and was not currently working. The photograph in the file showed a dark, attractive young woman with a pleasant smile.

Mackay read the summaries that Arthur had prepared and flicked through the files. 'So tell me your thoughts, Arthur. Who's it going to be?'

Goldsmith made a show of thinking about it; there was no point in offering an immediate opinion—he'd already formed the view that Mackay was the sort who would always plump for the opposite.

Mackay said, 'What do you think of Pappas?'

Goldsmith made a drinking motion.

'I see. Well, we all have our failings, but I don't think we can live with that one in this instance. What about young Maria then?' He glanced down at her photograph. 'Pretty girl, don't you think?' When Goldsmith said nothing, Mackay shrugged. 'Perhaps not. But what's your view?'

'Excellent credentials.' Best to begin with the positive, then move in for the kill. 'But awfully young. If you think about it, she's only really had the one mission in Frankfurt.'

Mackay nodded. 'So you think Arbuthnot's our man for the job?'

'I think so. Sound pair of hands.'

Mackay nodded. Arthur was surprised. Perhaps this was going to be easier than he'd expected.

Mackay went on nodding in an absent-minded sort of way. But then he said firmly, 'Can't see Arbuthnot myself. Too conventional in my view, and he's just not going to have the radar for office gossip that we need. My vote's for Maria— her credentials are just as good, and she's shown initiative in the past. Yes. I think Maria's the one for this job.'

16

The old Sikh had driven Liz all the way to Birmingham International Station, though he obviously suspected she was a hysterical woman who had overreacted to some harmless game played by a pair of boys. She had decided not to call the police, as her attackers were long gone into the maze of streets around the Khans' house and she did not want to draw the attention of the local constabulary to her interest in the family. She would tell Fontana about it in the morning. He might know the boys—they obviously knew him—and be able to find out what their connection was with Amir Khan, and why they had attacked her.

The train from Birmingham to King's Cross had been packed and with no seat reservation she'd had to stand all the way, which had not helped her to calm down. So when she got inside her Kentish Town flat, Liz headed straight for the fridge and poured herself a glass of Sauvignon Blanc from the half-full bottle there.

She had moved into this flat six months ago, after she'd got back from the operation where she had first met Martin. The flat was on the ground floor of a large Victorian house; she'd previously owned the basement flat in the same building. When she first bought that, it had been dark and gloomy, but it was all she could afford at the time and, as the first property she had ever owned, she had loved it. Gradually, over several years, she had brightened it up and improved it. The whole place had been painted white, and the wallpaper, which had hung off the wall in a strip over the bath where the steam had detached it, had been removed and the bathroom tiled. She'd bought a new washing machine to replace the one she'd inherited when she moved in, which had had a habit of stopping in the middle of its cycle, leaving her underwear in a puddle of grey scummy water.

But when she'd returned from her posting in Belfast, the flat, even in its improved state, had no longer seemed so welcoming. It had been empty while she'd been away and she seemed to have grown out of it. So when the flat above had come up for sale she'd gone to look at it, even though she knew she couldn't afford it, and as soon as she saw the high airy living room with its corniced ceiling and Victorian fireplace, and the big sash windows overlooking the garden, she fell in love all over again. Her mother's close friend Edward had lent her some money, and that, together with a breathtakingly huge mortgage and the surprisingly large profit she'd made selling the basement, had been enough to secure the flat.

She took her glass of wine into the bedroom, still feeling rattled by her experiences in Birmingham. She looked at the phone, hesitating, then picked up and dialled.

Martin answered at once.

'Hello. It's Liz.'

He laughed. 'I was sitting here, thinking about you. I was just about to ring you.'

'Is everything all right?' she asked.

'Yes, of course. Though the lady I was after seems to have given us the slip this time.'

'You'll find her,' Liz said confidently. Just talking to Martin was a relief.

'What about you? What is your news?'

'I've been in Birmingham all day, looking into the background of our friend in the Santé.'

'Ah. How did it go?'

'Okay, though some of his friends were not very pleased to see me.'

Martin could read between the lines. 'I don't like the sound of that. Are you sure you're all right? You're not hurt, are you?'

'No. Not hurt, just a bit shaken up. But I'm fine

94

now,' she said, and it was true. Just hearing his voice had made her feel better. They talked for a few minutes more, planning their next meeting, then they said good night and rang off.

Liz lay down on the big double bed. She'd bought it when she moved into the new flat where the large rooms had seemed to swallow up the furniture she'd had in the cramped basement accommodation. She snuggled under the goose-feather duvet, wishing Martin were snuggling with her. The duvet dated from the time of Piet, the Dutch investment banker she'd met at a colleague's party. He had stayed with her when he came to London every third Friday for meetings at Canary Wharf. It was an arrangement which suited them both perfectly: warm, happy and undemanding. Until he'd telephoned one day to tell her that there would no longer be London meetings, and in any case he had met someone else.

She hadn't had a man in her life since she broke up with Piet until she met Martin last year. It was the first time she'd been involved with someone she worked with. Was it a good idea to mix private life with work? Probably not, but the nature of the work, its secrecy and irregular hours, meant that most of the people she met were in the same business. She had had relationships in the past with people outside 'the ring of secrecy', as it was called, but it had never worked out. She'd not been able to be frank about what she did for a living. Piet had never enquired—it wasn't that sort of relationship. Before him there was Mark Callendar, the *Guardian* journalist, who'd wanted to leave his wife for her. She had been tempted, just for a moment,

95

but had known that, realistically, it wasn't possible. If she'd got involved in Mark's domestic upheaval, she'd have become a sort of *Guardian* pet spook— he and his friends had worked out without much difficulty what she did. Her career in the Service would not have prospered. The powers that be would have parked her somewhere safe, until they saw how her private life worked out.

Before Mark there was the photographer, Ed. She'd met him at the private view of an exhibition of photographs taken by a woman she'd known at university. Ed had been putting together a film about New Age travellers and had been living with them on and off. He viewed the world from a fascinatingly oblique perspective, and her part-time membership of his arty, kaleidoscopic world had provided a welcome escape for Liz from the grim world of organised crime, which she was working on at the time. She'd told Ed that her job was in a government personnel office, but the vagueness of her account must have aroused his suspicions. For one day he'd rung various departments, trying to find out exactly where she worked, and it was then she decided to end the relationship.

It was Charles Wetherby, her boss, who had held her heart for the longest. It had been strange, almost a non-relationship in fact, since Charles was married to a woman who was slowly dying. Liz knew instinctively that he returned her feelings, but he never spoke about it and while Joanne was alive Liz knew that he never would. It was as though they saw each other through a swirling mist, reaching out but never quite able to touch.

Then Joanne had died and Liz had waited for Charles to make a move. Instead he'd seemed to draw back from her and take comfort instead from his next-door neighbour, a widow whom he'd known for a long time. She helped him to look after his two boys. Liz was never sure whether this was any more than a relationship of convenience, but was hurt by his hesitation over contacting her. By the time Charles finally did make a move towards her, she had met Martin Seurat.

And now Martin was talking about her moving to Paris. Liz rolled on to her side and fell into a light sleep, troubled by confused impressions of the Santé prison, the Khans' house in Birmingham and Martin's flat in Paris. But as she dozed she could still feel around her wrist the iron grip of the young man who had tried to pull her down the lonely alley.

17

A welcome blast of air-conditioning greeted Maria Galanos as she got out of the lift on the second floor of the office block in suburban Athens. Waiting for her was a tall, middle-aged American who introduced himself as Mitchell Berger, Athens Director of UCSO. 'I bet you could do with a cold drink,' he said. 'It's hotter than ever today.'

'They say it's going to be worse at the weekend,' replied Maria. The heat was one thing about her homeland that she had never missed when she'd worked abroad.

She followed Berger along a corridor to his office and sat down while he poured her some iced water from a small fridge in the corner. 'We all look after ourselves here,' he explained. 'There are only eleven of us in this office. I share a secretary with my deputy, Katherine Ball. She's on her way back from London. Should've been here by now but I gather there's some trouble with the airlines.'

'What's new?' said Maria, smiling in response to his grin.

'Well,' he said, sitting down opposite her behind his desk, 'we both know why you're here. I understand they explained the situation to you pretty fully at the embassy. I've prepared a list of the staff here, with background details on each one, so you can see who we've got. I think you'd better read it here and not take it away with you. We don't want to raise anyone's suspicions at this stage.' He pushed a sheet of paper across the table to her.

'Thank you.' She read through the short CVs of the eleven staff, noticing with surprise that he had included himself, and with interest that his foreign experience was extensive. 'Is there anyone you think I should be focusing on?'

'No, not at this stage. As far as I can see everyone here is completely above board. Of course, you wouldn't be here if I didn't have some suspicions but they aren't directed towards anyone in particular. If there is some sort of a leak here, someone must be monitoring the precise make-up of each of our cargoes and passing it on.'

'Who has access to that information?'

'In theory, just the accountant and myself. But in practice, who knows? We don't exactly have top-level security here. We are a fairly friendly team—just the eleven of us. Let's hope you'll make it a Lucky Dozen.'

He paused, looking thoughtful, then said, 'I'm sure you know your business, Maria. I gather you've done undercover work before. But the fact that we are so small here means you're going to have to go carefully if you are not to draw unwanted attention to yourself. You're vastly overqualified for this job so you'll need to downplay your credentials. Otherwise people are going to wonder why you're here.'

Maria nodded and said, 'My cover story is that I've been living and working in England for some years. I wanted to come back home to Athens because a long relationship in London suddenly broke up. And I was getting sick of the ethics of the commercial world—or lack of ethics—and now want to do something more worthwhile.'

'That will do fine.' Berger smiled and got up. 'I'll walk you round the office and introduce you. Then we'll go and have some lunch.'

They walked back down the floor's one corridor, passing an empty office on the left. Berger pointed through the doorway. 'That's where Katherine sits. She'll come to lunch with us if she's back in time. She's not in on your real purpose here—I decided to keep that between the two of us.'

Further along they came into a high-ceilinged room where two Greek girls were sitting at desks in front of computer screens. Berger introduced them as Anastasia and Falana, general assistants who did everything from typing to wrapping parcels. They were little more than teenagers, and could have been sisters with their long, dark hair and big doe eyes. When Berger left to take a phone call, the girls started giggling.

'What's so funny?' asked Maria.

Falana giggled even more while Anastasia explained, 'We were admiring your dress. But Falana's too shy to ask where you bought it.'

Maria glanced down at the cherry-coloured cotton frock, which she'd found in a little Covent Garden boutique the previous year. 'I bought it in London.'

'London?' exclaimed Falana, her eyes widening. 'You have been to London?' For all the wonder in her voice, Maria might have said she'd been to Mars.

Anastasia explained, 'We both love London. I mean, the idea of London. Neither of us has been.'

'I used to live there. My mother is English.'

The girls were very impressed by this and soon Maria found herself chatting with them about Topshop and fashion, and clubbing, and Athens nightlife—all as if she were nineteen again. When Berger returned, the Greek girls looked disappointed, though both of them brightened when he explained Maria would be starting work the following day.

'You've made a hit with them, I see,' he said, as they walked down the corridor.

'They've forgotten more about pop culture than I ever knew.'

Berger introduced her to the rest of the staff, including a Frenchwoman in her forties called Claude, who travelled much of the time to the crisis-stricken areas where UCSO aid was sent. They walked into another room that led off the large central office. Here Berger left her with the chief accountant, Alex Limonides.

Limonides must have been at least sixty. He was gaunt, with wrinkled walnut skin and receding hair, its thin strands carefully brushed over his balding scalp. His pale grey suit, far too big for him, was almost falling off his thin shoulders. His breath smelled of sweet tobacco. As they sat down together to look at the books, he offered Maria a filterless cigarette the colour of dried corn; when she refused, he politely put the packet away without taking one for himself.

There was nothing very complicated in the UCSO accounting systems: the overheads of the office itself were straightforward, mainly rent and salaries; the details of the cash in from various sources, and the outgoings including any purchases of aid made locally and payments to the shipping brokers, were all recorded in the ledgers. Any accruals of cash were transferred to the London office when they hit £25,000. It was all very easy to understand and there seemed little opportunity for petty theft, much less big-time larceny. But Maria reminded herself that it was information, not money, which someone was stealing.

Limonides showed her how the cargo manifests were compiled, then confirmed by the shipping agency they used. Interestingly, this was still done on paper—long foolscap sheets more suggestive of a Dickensian counting office than a modern international charity. The lists were kept under lock and key in the drawer of Limonides' wooden desk. About as secure as an ice-cream wrapper, Maria thought to herself. Besides Limonides, only Berger and an accountant in the London office would have known the full contents of a shipment. No new ones were scheduled for the next six weeks; that should give her ample time to familiarise herself with office procedures and discover if anyone had been snooping around.

At one point they were interrupted by a phone call. The elderly Greek picked up the receiver and listened impatiently. Then he replied, in disapproving tones, saying that he would certainly pay the invoice in question, as always, but only within the thirty days of their standard terms. Xenides, he declared, must know this by now, and it was not the business of UCSO to advance funds to other organisations. With a terse goodbye, he put the phone down and gave a weary sigh, then resumed his briefing of Maria.

After twenty minutes more, she felt that there was nothing she didn't know about UCSO's financial systems, and was grateful to be rescued by Berger and taken for lunch. They walked a short distance down the baking hot street to a taverna, where they sat under an enormous mahogany ceiling fan that revolved like a slow helicopter, just stirring the air.

'First impressions?' he asked as the waiter brought a basket of pitta bread and large glasses of ice-cold water with lemon.

'Everyone was very welcoming. It's a friendly atmosphere.'

'It needs to be—the office is too small to allow for any friction. The only politics are about the venue for the Christmas lunch. Falana always wants to go somewhere trendy.'

'They're funny girls.'

Berger nodded with a smile. 'What did you make of Mr Limonides?'

Maria laughed. 'He's very old school, and quite charming. When I said I didn't smoke, he wouldn't have one himself.'

'But as an accountant . . . ?'

'He's cautious and precise—just what you want. I didn't see anything that any auditor could even begin to query. The only unusual item I noticed was Sundries in the P&L. Usually, it's a trivial amount—we used to call it "toothpaste money". But yours is very large—over ten thousand sterling. Why?'

For the first time, Berger hesitated; he seemed almost embarrassed. Then he explained: in some of the countries receiving UCSO aid, it was necessary to make informal payments (he neatly avoided the word 'bribe') to ensure that the aid was delivered to the people who needed it. Otherwise, he went on, anything from Range Rovers to one-hundred-pound bags of flour could find their way on to the black market, or into the garages and larders of Government Ministers. 'It's not admirable, or ethical, or something I'd want to appear in the press. But ultimately, it's *necessary*.'

Maria nodded and they concentrated on their lunch for a while. Then she asked, 'When I was talking to Mr Limonides he had a phone call complaining about an unpaid invoice. I think the company was called Xenides.'

'Ah, that would have been Mo Miandad—he's the shipping agent for the company that leases the ships and hires the crew. Mo's a bit of a rogue, not quite upright enough for the likes of our Mr Limonides. His family emigrated here in 1947 at the time of Partition in India. Mo was born here. The family are now very well off but it's said that they disowned him because of his behaviour—apparently he became involved with a married woman and got her pregnant. He's certainly a bit

103

of an acquired taste, particularly if you're female. Asia's answer to Casanova.'

As they walked the short distance back to the office, the shops were reopening after the midday break. Maria was about to thank Berger and head off home when a taxi drew up beside them. A blonde woman got out and thrust some money at the driver.

'You made it,' Berger said, as the woman stepped on to the pavement, pulling a small suitcase.

'What a nightmare,' she replied. 'The French air controllers had a wildcat strike, bless them. For a while, I thought we were going to fly to Athens via the North Pole.'

'Let me introduce Maria Galanos,' said Berger. 'She's joining us tomorrow. Working with Mr Limonides.'

The woman stepped forward to shake hands. 'I'm Katherine Ball. I heard you were starting. Welcome to UCSO.' She gave Maria a warm smile.

'You'll see each other tomorrow,' Berger said.

'Yes, see you then,' said Maria. She turned to Berger. 'Thanks for lunch. I'll be in the office first thing.' And as she walked away, she wondered if there really could be anything sinister about the Athens office of UCSO. Everyone seemed so charming and straightforward.

Bruno Mackay at the embassy had seemed confident there was something wrong there, but then Bruno Mackay had struck her as confident about everything.

18

Richard Luckhurst had always liked the idea of 'gardening leave'. But confronted with it, he realised that there was only so much gardening he wanted to do. When in quiet moments at sea he'd thought about retirement, he'd seen himself tending his roses, edging the lawn and erecting the big greenhouse he had always wanted. But faced with the opportunity to do all that, he couldn't even find the enthusiasm to cut the grass.

His employers had been firm: he couldn't sail for another four weeks, and even that was contingent on a doctor's certificate. Not from his own GP, a nice old buffer who Richard knew would say he was fit as a fiddle, but from the company's medic—a pompous ass who'd ask him how he was feeling 'in himself'.

Luckhurst felt fine. Not for him this post-traumatic stress nonsense. He'd been well treated by the kidnappers in Somalia, and his only worry had been about the welfare of his crew. But they had been all right too. None of them had been hurt or seriously threatened, just a bit scared and very bored. The food had been disgusting, it was true, but that was all he could really complain about, and even that had had a side benefit— he had lost half a stone, something which he'd struggled unsuccessfully to do for years.

But he'd be putting it all on again if he couldn't get back to work soon. The company had him down provisionally to take command of an oil tanker sailing from the Gulf of Aden to the east coast of

America. But that was a month away, and just now a month seemed an eternity to him.

He was sitting outside on the patio, trying not to notice how long the grass had grown, while his wife Sue was inside, vacuuming. They'd settled in this pleasant Birmingham suburb twenty years before. Their children had grown up here—largely without their father, he thought ruefully. Sue was such an old hand at running the place that he felt he'd only get in her way if he offered to help. She must find it strange having him around so much. In any normal year, he was away at sea ten months out of twelve.

He was listening with half an ear to the radio as he dozed in his deckchair. On Radio 4 a presenter was leading a discussion about the threat posed by home-grown terrorists. What a world we live in, thought Luckhurst. He'd grown up during the Cold War, and like many children of that era had felt scared by the idea of nuclear missiles pointing at his town. When the Soviet Union had collapsed at the end of the eighties, he'd felt a profound sense of relief. But now the Cold War seemed to have been replaced by something just as frightening and more difficult to understand. You couldn't blame it all on Osama Bin Laden, thought Luckhurst. Even if that sinister character died tomorrow, there seemed to be countless followers around to carry on where he'd left off.

They were saying on the radio that the danger zone was shifting—not everything was coming out of Afghanistan or Pakistan now. Some security expert from an institute somewhere was saying that many of the hardliners were moving away from their traditional hideouts and setting themselves up in lawless places in other parts of the world, where there were no effective governments and they could live and operate without interference. A Middle East correspondent from Reuters added that he'd learned that training camps were being set up in some of these places and new recruits from Britain were being sent there instead of Pakistan. Al Qaeda were planning to use these places as bases from which to hit new targets, he said.

They're everywhere, thought Luckhurst, only partly reassured when a man identified as 'a security consultant' paid tribute to the excellent job the intelligence services were doing in tracking down these new threats. Then the Reuters man piped up again, pointing out how hard it was to track anyone in Yemen where, he said, Al Qaeda had a growing foothold. And if Yemen got too hot for the terrorists, there was always near-neighbour Somalia.

At this mention of the country where he'd been so recently a prisoner, Luckhurst opened his eyes and sat up. Memories came flooding back. He was in the cage again, in the camp somewhere near the Somalian coast. He could visualise dinner coming, carried by Taban—yes, that had been his name, the young boy he'd befriended. Luckhurst wondered what had become of him, remembering that last evening, just before the hostages were freed, when Taban had seemed so alarmed. The boy had said there had been Westerners visiting the camp—not hostages, but associates of the pirates. He'd said one had spoken English—a brown Englishman. Could this be one of the British Pakistanis the man on the radio was talking about?

It took a few minutes for the connection to take

root in Richard Luckhurst's mind, and another hour before he picked up the telephone. But after that things moved fast: just as Sue put the kettle on for tea, Detective Inspector Fontana drove his car into the Luckhursts' drive and rang the doorbell.

19

For three weeks, Maria went conscientiously into the UCSO office every morning and spent the day helping Mr Limonides with the accounts, keeping her eyes open for anything out of the ordinary. She wasn't at all sure what she was looking for. Neither her handsome contact at the British Embassy nor her new boss Berger had been at all precise about what they thought might be going on in the office. 'Someone taking a nosey interest in the manifests of aid shipments sailing from Athens' seemed to sum it up, but at the moment there were no shipments being assembled. In fact, not much was going on in the office at all as far as she could see. The only member of staff who seemed to be doing anything interesting or out of the ordinary was Claude, the Frenchwoman, who had just returned from a short visit to Kinshasa. Maria was interested to hear about her trip but Claude was such a dour soul that she made even the most exotic parts of the Third World sound dull.

Mr Limonides was proving difficult to get to know. He was a model of courtesy, but volunteered no information about himself or his private life. He was a widower, according to Falana, but she didn't know if he had any family or children; there were no photographs on his desk, and any questions Maria asked that got close to the personal were politely rebuffed. One evening as she was walking to the bus stop near the office after doing some shopping, she caught sight of him in a little taverna, eating a solitary supper, his eyes focused on his plate. Maria thought there was something ineffably sad about the scene and she hurried past before he could look up and see her.

She saw little of Berger, who seemed busy enough in his office. He didn't ask to see her and she didn't want to bother him as she had nothing to report. She had no contact with the British Embassy; she'd been told to report in the first instance to Berger.

Of the rest of the staff, Katherine Ball was her favourite and the closest to her in age and style. Katherine worked mainly in London as deputy to the charity's overall director, but she kept a desk in UCSO Athens and visited several times a year for a few days or weeks, depending on what was going on. She was often closeted with Berger, presumably discussing policy matters, but occasionally she walked round the general office, chatting to the staff. When she put her head round the door of the room where Mr Limonides and Maria worked, it was as if a breath of fresh air had blown in.

For Anastasia and Falana, Katherine's elegant clothes and easy cosmopolitan chic provided hours of conversation and debate. When from time to time Maria drank her morning cup of coffee with them, she was required to join them in speculating on such important matters as whether Katherine's shoes could be real Jimmy Choos. Both girls loved to ask Maria questions about London, which she was happy to answer, and about herself, which she was not. But she had no difficulty at all in diverting their interest in her life by questioning them about theirs, which led to lengthy accounts of their favourite clubs, their favourite music, and their favourite boyfriends. Anastasia was the more outgoing of the two and she was insistent that Maria should join them and some friends for a night out, an invitation that Maria had managed so far to find an excuse not to accept. But she had a sinking feeling that in the interests of politeness and good relations, she wouldn't be able to duck the invitation for ever.

*   *   *

The only thing at all out of the ordinary happened one evening in her third week when Maria got back to her apartment block after her day at UCSO. Madame Coco was standing in the foyer, sucking on a hand-rolled cigarette not much thicker than a toothpick. A small woman of indeterminate age—probably in her seventies—Coco looked after the building with the gossipy vigilance of a Parisian *concierge*; she also cleaned some of the residents' flats, including Maria's.

'You had visitors,' she said. 'A couple.'

'When was that, Coco?' asked Maria, wondering if her parents had come round. They'd only been here once, when she'd first moved in, and Coco had never met them.

'After lunch.'

'Really?' That seemed odd; her parents knew she was usually out at that time of day. The faintest suspicion flickered through her mind.

'What did they look like?'

Cocoa shrugged. 'I didn't see them. Mr Pharmakes told me they'd been here.' He was a retired gentleman who lived on the top floor of the building. 'He came across them in the hall outside your flat.'

This was odder still. The door to the foyer was kept locked, so non-residents couldn't simply wander in and out of the building.

'Did he describe them?'

Cocoa laughed, and stubbed out her cigarette end with a carpet-slippered toe. 'All he said was that one was pale and the other dark.'

'Which was which?' Maria asked instinctively.

Coco shrugged her shoulders. 'Don't ask me. And I wouldn't bother asking Pharmakes. He has cataracts in both eyes.'

Maria thanked Coco and went up to her flat. The visitors probably had been her parents after all. Her mother was an English rose, with pink skin that easily burned in the sun, while her father was a typical Greek with nutmeg-coloured skin and dark hair.

But as she let herself into her flat, she still wasn't satisfied. Why would her parents come here in the middle of the day? It would have to be about something urgent ... her mother's sister had been very ill. Maybe it was something to do with that. But surely they would have left a message. Maybe she should ring Bruno Mackay and report this. But he'd probably think she was very green, getting jumpy for no good reason. Don't be silly, she told herself, even though, when she rang her parents, her mother told her they hadn't been out all day.

By the end of the third week, Maria was

111

beginning to wonder how long she would be able to put up with the boredom of this new assignment. The extra money she was being paid by the British Embassy was nice to have, but she didn't feel that she was doing anything to earn it. Then on the third Tuesday morning, as she was leaning on Falana's desk drinking her morning coffee and chatting, Berger came out of his office and asked to see her.

'How's it going?' he asked as she sat down.

'The job's fine. But I'm afraid I haven't uncovered anything.'

'Don't apologise,' he said with a laugh. 'I'd much prefer to be wrong about all this.'

'I can't say if anything's going on or not. I certainly haven't noticed anything. And, to tell you the truth, I don't know if I ever will.'

'Well, that brings me to what I was going to tell you ... we've got a good chance now to find out, one way or another. Our next shipment is due out in three weeks. I want you to start to build up the manifest.'

'Doesn't Mr Limonides usually do that?'

'He does, but I've got a special project I want him to work on.' Berger raised one eyebrow. 'Now, let me give you an idea about this cargo. It's going to be rather special ...'

*　　　*　　　*

For the next few days Maria immersed herself in putting together the manifest, and by late Thursday evening she was glad to be finished with it. She had been so busy working that she hadn't even realised Katherine Ball had gone back to London.

Maria and Berger had agreed that she would be careful to keep the details of the new shipment secret. She wouldn't talk about it and she would make sure that all paperwork concerning it was carefully locked up. Manifests should always have been handled in that way but it seemed very likely, given the relaxed atmosphere in the office, that these rules had not been followed.

This shipment was as special as Berger had indicated. The drugs alone were worth a fortune and included large amounts of liquid morphine and a pharmacist's range of codeine-based painkillers. More field-hospital kit was going out as well, with surgical apparatus enough to equip a decent-sized hospital. There were three high-end Range Rovers, and, most temptingly, $100,000 in cash. Maria carefully noted and valued all of this. None of it was being documented in UCSO's London office, so that if any information leaked out, it would be clear that it had come from Athens.

The most important fact about the cargo which Maria had spent the week working on was that it did not actually exist. The details had been planned purely to tempt any spy inside the organisation. The actual cargo of the next UCSO shipment to pass the Horn of Africa would be much less attractive, consisting as it would of foodstuffs—powdered milk, sacks of grain—and vitamins by the gross. Desperately needed by its eventual recipients, but of only of modest resale value and thus not worth the attention of Somali pirates—unless they had been told the cargo was something else altogether.

Maria picked up her working sheets and the finalised manifest and put them in the top right-hand drawer of her desk. Then she locked it carefully, with the key that she always kept safely in her bag; Berger had had a new lock installed, and the only other key was with him.

*   *   *

On Friday morning Maria was late into the office—her bus had hit a dog (which, miraculously, had survived); the dog's owner had threatened the bus driver; the driver had blamed the owner; a crowd had formed; someone had called the police, who took twenty minutes to arrive and then insisted on interviewing the passengers. It all seemed very Greek to Maria, and it was almost ten o'clock when she got to work.

There was no sign of Mr Limonides. He was probably outside having a fag, thought Maria as she sat down at her desk and checked the drawer. It was still securely locked. She opened it with her keys and checked the pages of the manifest. All present and correct.

Hers was a new desk, a modern one made of wood laminate and metal, its top a single sheet of laminate supported by the two upright sides. As she unlocked the drawer, the desktop rocked very slightly and slid a little to one side. Puzzled, she pushed one end of the desktop with both hands. It gave again, almost imperceptibly. Odd.

Maria got up, walked to the door and looked down the corridor. No one in sight. Out on the rear fire escape Mr Limonides stood by himself, mournfully smoking an Egyptian cigarette.

She returned quickly to her desk. Down on all fours, she peered up at the overhanging desktop. It

114

was attached to the sides at each corner by metal brackets, held in place by two screws. One screw in the corner nearest her was loose and hanging halfway out of its hole; looking more closely, Maria could see fresh scratches in the laminate. Someone had been fiddling with the screws.

Then she understood. Removing the brackets had freed the desktop; removing the desktop left the top drawer exposed from above. The intruder could have read the papers in the drawer, put them back safely, apparently untouched, and then replaced the desktop. No one would have been any the wiser—if the screws had been put back properly.

How clever, thought Maria, then felt suddenly chilled as she realised that this must mean there really was a spy here in the Athens office of UCSO.

Maria went straight away to Berger's office to tell him about her discovery. But to her dismay she found that the American was taking the day off—he had gone on a long weekend to one of the islands. So, with some hesitation, she rang Bruno Mackay at the embassy, but was answered by his secretary, who explained that Bruno, too, was away for a long weekend. The secretary offered to get Mr Mackay to telephone Maria back but she didn't want to seem panicky, so she said no, it could wait till Monday.

Then Mr Limonides returned, and began quietly working on the special report about UCSO's overheads that Berger had commissioned, while Maria wondered what to do next. There seemed no point in moving the papers in her drawer to a safer place. In one sense the damage had been done; in another, of course, the bait had been taken.

But what was supposed to happen next? And how was she meant to narrow down the list of possible suspects?

20

Anastasia and Falana were waiting for her at a table in the bar. They'd already acquired a pitcher of sangria, and Falana poured out a large glass for Maria as soon as she sat down. The place was noisy, filling up quickly with young people celebrating the start of the weekend. In the background techno dance music throbbed. Not much chance of serious conversation here, thought Maria.

She had agreed to meet the two girls after Anastasia had bumped into her at lunchtime and asked if she'd join them that evening; caught on the hop, and distracted by the discovery that her desk had been tampered with, Maria had said yes. All afternoon she had kicked herself for agreeing, but having said yes, she didn't see how she could get out of it without being gratuitously rude.

She had gone home first, showered and changed into tight jeans and a sparkly top—she was expecting to find the girls done up in their latest finery. She swapped her office shoes for strappy sandals, and her handbag for a little shoulder bag, then she closed the windows, put down the blinds and left her flat.

'Do you always come here?' Maria now asked.

Anastasia nodded. 'We usually have something to eat in this place, then go on to the clubs nearby.'

They stayed in the bar for an hour or so, sharing various small plates of *meze*, which were plonked on the table from time to time by passing waiters. The sangria jug gradually emptied and another was acquired. Maria tried to steer the conversation towards their office colleagues but UCSO Athens was devoid of eligible men and the girls had little interest in talking about anything in it beyond Katherine's clothes. They shared a gentle laugh at the old-fashioned ways of Mr Limonides and they all spoke with envy of Claude's travels, but beyond that neither of the Greek girls said anything to provide Maria with additional insights into the staff of UCSO.

After one false start in a new nightclub, which turned out to be for men looking for other men, they moved on to a place called Broadway, which had an enormous dance floor. By the bar, girls gathered in small packs, eyeing groups of young men who were eying them. Maria had been brought up rather traditionally and found all this a bit unnerving. Anastasia and Falana met some friends in the club, most of them young enough to make Maria feel ancient. She nursed a glass of wine while Falana talked with a succession of youths who seemed barely old enough to shave. Anastasia turned out to have a steady boyfriend, and stayed clinched with him on the dance floor. When a small pimply youth offered to buy Maria a drink, she decided it was time to go home.

Outside the club there was no sign of a taxi, but the doorman pointed out a bus stop a little way down the street and, though it was almost one o'clock, assured her the buses were still running. Before long a half-full bus arrived and she climbed

117

on and sat down in the comparative peace and quiet with a sigh. What a waste of an evening, she thought. Nothing new learned and only a raging thirst and a headache to show for it. At least she had done her bit for good relations with the girls. They had been happy that she'd joined them. Hopefully a repeat performance would not be expected.

Maria was the only one to get off the bus at her stop. The small shops in the street were closed up and deserted. The night was still, the air heavy. All she could hear was the occasional distant whoosh of a passing car, and the slapping of her sandals against the pavement. Then she heard another sound behind her. It took her a minute to realise it was someone else's footsteps.

She was still a good ten minutes' walk from her flat. As she went on she continued to hear the steps. She turned round once, but couldn't see anyone. Perhaps they were too far back. But when she stopped to listen, the footsteps stopped as well. Could it have been an echo? No. When she started to walk again, the other footsteps were not in synch with hers.

Tock tock tock. Still the other steps rang out, but no one caught her up. Maria tried to find this reassuring; if someone were following her, wouldn't they be drawing closer? Yet she found herself growing alarmed.

This was not a neighbourhood for late-night revels; the surrounding apartment buildings were all dark. The streetlamps threw out only a weak, watery light. She could always scream for help— that would certainly wake people up. But doubtless the mysterious stranger behind her would turn out

118

to be some teenager, walking home after a party. How embarrassing that would be.

She was now just a minute or two from the safety of her flat, but the footsteps were still echoing hers. Was the noise drawing any closer? She couldn't tell. What should she do? She turned the final corner on to her own street, then quickly reached down and took off her sandals.

Then she ran, holding the shoes in one hand, barefoot along the pavement. At last she reached her building and stopped, breathless, at the front door to tap in the entry code. As she did so her back crawled and she tried to listen for the sounds of someone else on the street, but all she could hear was the drum-like thumping of her heart.

Inside the building at last, she closed the outside door firmly behind her. The light to the stairwell was on, which comforted her as she climbed the flight of stairs. She opened her door slowly, still listening.

Her flat felt stuffy and warm, and she remembered she had closed the windows and the blinds earlier. She went to the fridge to get some cold water, feeling rather silly about the fear she'd felt in the street, now that she was safe. Whoever had been behind her was probably sitting in their own flat around the corner now, blissfully unaware of the scare they'd given her.

Crossing the sitting room, she went to run a bath. When she flicked the switch just inside the bathroom door, the bulb popped and the room stayed dark. She turned to get another bulb from the kitchen, but the light in the sitting room had gone out as well, leaving the entire flat in darkness. Damn, Maria thought, the fuse must have blown.

She edged back out of the bathroom to get the torch she kept in the sitting-room cupboard.

It was then that she heard a noise behind her. 'Who's there?' she demanded, her stomach suddenly contracting with ice-cold fear.

Something moved in the darkness. She felt an arm encircling her throat. She choked, and found she couldn't scream.

Or breathe.

21

After five years, Peggy Kinsolving felt so much a part of Thames House that she often forgot she had begun her career in the other Service. She had applied for a transfer after being seconded to MI5 to work with Liz Carlyle on an investigation into a mole in one of the intelligence services. Peggy admired Liz; she liked her straightforward manner, which was such a contrast to the deviousness of some of the people she had worked with in the other Service. She'd felt from the start of working with Liz that they were a team: that Liz would take Peggy into her confidence, and give her credit for what she did.

And Peggy enjoyed her work. She was never happier than when she was following a paper trail, supporting Liz as she made her investigations. Peggy had started her working life as a librarian and loved the cataloguing, classification and retrieval of facts. That was her métier. She could sniff out information and make sense of what others saw as a meaningless jumble of unrelated facts.

Every three months or so, she was reminded of her original employers when she had lunch with her one remaining link to Vauxhall Cross, Millie Warmington. After Peggy's secondment to MI5 and subsequent decision to join for good, the two women had kept in touch. They had been young trainees together and had got along from the start. Millie had a sweet nature and was a loyal friend. But she was also one of life's complainers; Peggy privately called her 'Millie the Moaner'. Today Peggy could have done without their long-standing lunch date, because she was busy trying to find out more about the *Aristides* and her crew while also investigating Amir Khan's past in Birmingham. There was the further drawback that Millie liked to take her time over lunch. However simple the meal—they usually met in an Italian pasta place on the South Bank—she always managed to spin it out for at least an hour. Peggy's efforts to move things along were never successful.

Today proved no exception. At first, they chatted for a while about their social lives. Millie had no steady boyfriend but seemed genuinely pleased that Peggy's Tim, a lecturer in English, was still very much in the picture. Then the conversation moved on to work and their respective jobs. Peggy was always fairly discreet since she knew that Millie was a bit of a gossip. She also knew that her boss, Liz Carlyle, was the object of much interest on the other side of the river, and that plenty of MI6 officers would love to know more about her—both what she was working on and, in particular, her private life. Peggy was fiercely loyal to Liz and so diverted Millie's probing

121

remarks by asking her about her own work.

This gave Millie just the opening she wanted and there followed the usual litany of complaint, especially about her boss. When they had joined up, both Peggy and Millie had worked under Henry Boswell, an old-fashioned but thoroughly decent man. Then Millie had switched departments and now worked for a female tyrant she called The Dragon. After ten minutes ranting about The Dragon's latest misdemeanours, Millie had barely hit her stride, but by then Peggy had tuned out, her thoughts turning to the work she needed to do that afternoon.

It was only when they finally left the restaurant and walked towards Vauxhall Bridge for Millie to go back to Vauxhall Cross and Peggy to cross the river to Thames House, that something her friend was saying caused Peggy to tune in again. Afterwards, she was very glad that she had.

*   *   *

'Good lunch?' asked Liz. She was in her office, the remains of a salad from the canteen in a take-out container on her desk.

'I saw my friend from Six.'

' "Moaning Millie?" ' asked Liz with a laugh. Peggy had described her friend's habitual complaining often enough

'The same,' said Peggy. 'And still moaning. But she did tell me one thing I thought you'd want to know. Bruno Mackay's been moved from Paris.'

'Fane mentioned it but he didn't say where.'

'Athens. He's been made Head of Station there.'

'Golly. Good for old Bruno,' said Liz, which

122

seemed a generous thing for her to say. Peggy knew there was no love lost there.

'Yes, but he's come a bit of a cropper, I'm afraid. One of his agents has been killed. Murdered actually—she was strangled.'

Liz's face showed her astonishment. 'How dreadful. What happened?'

'They're not sure. She was found dead in her flat.'

'Do they know who did it?'

'I don't think so.'

'Was it connected with work?'

Peggy shrugged. 'I don't think they know that either. She was a long-standing asset of Six, doing some undercover investigation for the Athens Station. I gather Bruno selected her himself.' Which made it even worse for him, thought Peggy. Hard though it was—because he was so insufferable—you nonetheless had to feel sorry for Bruno Mackay. One month in his new job and an agent dead.

Liz seemed to share her feelings. She asked, almost as an afterthought, 'What was the undercover investigation?'

Peggy looked expressionlessly at her as she said, 'Working in some charity, I believe.'

'Not UCSO?'

Peggy nodded.

Liz was shaking her head angrily. 'They say a leopard doesn't change its spots . . . but I thought, just for a moment, Geoffrey Fane might have changed his and gone straight. I see I was wrong.'

22

Liz was sitting at her desk, still fuming that Geoffrey Fane had put an agent into UCSO without telling her, when the phone rang. It was Fane's secretary.

'Hello, Liz. You wanted to see Geoffrey. He's suggesting lunch. Can you do tomorrow?'

Liz groaned to herself. She'd originally wanted a short meeting in his office, so they could bring each other up to date. Now she wanted to make a formal complaint about his duplicity. She certainly didn't want to sit exchanging pleasantries in a public place. But, in typical Fane fashion, he had forestalled her.

She sighed. 'OK. Where does he want to meet?'

'The Athenaeum. Twelve-thirty.'

'The Athenaeum? I thought his club was the Travellers.'

'It is. But he's just joined the Athenaeum as well and he's doing most of his lunching there at present.'

'How grand,' said Liz sardonically. Fane's secretary laughed and rang off.

The following morning Liz dressed with more care than usual for a working day, since she wasn't going to be outfaced by Geoffrey Fane with his two smart clubs. The idea was to look charming and demure.

There had been a time, several years ago, when Liz had been afflicted by wardrobe chaos. In those days, not long after she'd acquired her first flat in the basement, she'd found it impossible to keep both her domestic life and her busy working life in order. On a morning like this she might well have found all suitable garments either stuck in a non-functioning washing machine or waiting in a pile to go to the cleaner's.

But, along with her rather larger apartment, she had inherited a helpful lady, who not only cleaned the flat but also took her clothes to the cleaner's and managed the washing machine. So today when she opened her wardrobe she actually had a choice. It was a lovely sunny day and after a moment's thought she selected a pretty silk skirt, a pink linen jacket and a pair of kitten-heeled shoes that she'd bought for a friend's wedding.

That should do, she decided, hoping to lull Geoffrey Fane, so that when she revealed that she knew about the agent he'd put into UCSO without telling her, he'd be caught completely off guard. She was looking forward to seeing his face then.

Not even the prospect of Fane could dampen Liz's spirits this morning. Martin was coming to London for the long Bank Holiday weekend. He had an early-afternoon meeting, coincidentally with MI6, but they planned to meet up later in a Pimlico wine bar near the headquarters of both Services. Then home to Liz's flat. If the weather stayed fine on Saturday, they might drive down to Wiltshire where Liz's mother still lived in the gatehouse of the former estate where Liz's father had been estate manager and where Liz had grown up.

By mid-morning the sky was overcast but the cloud looked unthreatening. Liz decided to walk to the Athenaeum. The deckchairs in St James's Park were occupied by optimistic lunch-hour sunbathers, waiting for the cloud to clear. She crossed the Mall and climbed the long flight of stairs, her light skirt fluttering in the sharp breeze that had sprung up, and emerged on to Waterloo Place, where the Athenaeum Club stood four-square and confident, a pristine white stucco Georgian building with classical columns and a blue and white frieze set high up along its façade.

As she climbed the steps to the entrance, Liz realised with some annoyance that she felt nervous. She was not an habituée of the Pall Mall clubs, which she found dauntingly grand, and this one seemed grander than most. As she pushed open the tall semi-glazed door, Liz combed her hair into some sort of order with her fingers. Inside, was a tall pillared hall leading to a magnificent double staircase. Moonlike, high on the wall, a large round clock dominated the space below. Classical statues loomed to right and left of her.

Inside, a green-suited, brass-buttoned porter looked at Liz with polite enquiry. After a moment's hesitation, she asked for Geoffrey Fane. The porter nodded and indicated a familiar figure rising from a leather bench to greet her. Somewhere in a room to the right there was a deep masculine hum of conversation—some kind of a bar presumably. But to Liz's relief Fane pointed a long finger in the opposite direction and said, 'Shall we go straight in?'

'Please,' she said. Lunch would be long enough spent in his company without wasting further time on a drink beforehand.

She followed Fane's tall lean figure, smart in a dark pin-stripe suit, into the almost empty dining room; most people were evidently still in the bar. The head waiter seated them at a small,

126

highly polished darkwood table, beside one of the huge floor-to-ceiling windows, looking out over a balustrade on to a garden. The room seemed enormous and oddly bare. No pictures hung on its high cream-coloured walls and the only decoration came from the huge pendant ceiling lights.

Liz said, 'I didn't know this was one of your clubs.'

Fane looked flattered. 'I've only just become a member,' he said, with a trace of satisfaction. 'You're one of my first guests.'

She watched as he wrote down their choice of food with a pencil on a little pad and handed it to the waitress. She'd seen this routine before when she'd lunched with her mother and her friend Edward at his military club further along Pall Mall. It had struck her as odd then; some sort of hangover from the past, she supposed.

'Well, Elizabeth,' said Fane, leaning back comfortably, 'how goes it? Have you managed to find out anything more about this Khan chap?'

'A bit. I went to Birmingham and saw his parents. They seemed astonished to learn where their son had been. The father was a traditional head of the household. He didn't let his wife get a word in, and he certainly didn't approve of female authority figures—namely me. At first he claimed that the last time they'd heard from Amir, he was in Pakistan. But then one of Amir's sisters showed up: before he could stop her, she said they'd had a postcard from Amir recently—from Athens.'

'Athens?' Fane's fork stopped in mid-air on its way to his mouth. 'What on earth was he doing there?' There was a studied nonchalance to his tone.

127

'I was hoping you might be able to tell me that, Geoffrey.'

'Me?' Fane's eyes opened wide in a show of innocence.

'Yes. I gather you've just lost an agent there.'

He put down his knife and fork. 'You seem to hear the Service's news almost before I do.'

'When it concerns my business, I do,' Liz said crisply. 'I gather the agent was working in UCSO. I hope you're not going to tell me it had nothing to do with the Amir Khan investigation.'

'Of course not, Elizabeth. I was going to tell you this week in fact, only news of this death . . .' He faltered expertly. 'It rather knocked me for six.'

'I don't know why you didn't tell me before you put her in. You were the one who suggested there might be a link between UCSO and Amir Khan; you were the one who said, and I quote, "We'll need to liaise closely."' Liz's voice was rising in anger but the neighbouring tables were unoccupied and no one could overhear their conversation.

Fane's jaw clenched, his face flushed. For a moment Liz thought he would lose his temper. Then, as she watched, he got a grip of himself and his face returned to its usual pallor. 'Reproof accepted, Elizabeth,' he said stonily.

This was as close to an apology as he was ever likely to offer, so Liz sighed pointedly and said, 'Why was this woman planted in UCSO?'

Fane jumped at the question like a lifeline. 'When I saw you last, I mentioned Blakey had been in touch—he's the USCO director in London, you remember. He was concerned someone in the organisation was leaking information about their shipments. I offered to help and had a word with

128

Bruno.'

He added tartly, 'I imagine with your intelligence network you already know that he's become Head of Station in Athens.'

Liz nodded. 'So are you saying this was all Bruno's doing?'

'Well, not exactly.' Fane paused; Liz could see he was caught between a desire to be seen as in charge and a wish to avoid assuming any blame for the disaster. 'I decided to put someone in, but the selection was left to Bruno. He chose a young woman, half-Greek, with an English mother. Possibly not the wisest selection as it's turned out.'

'Was her murder linked to her agent work in USCO?'

'Unlikely, we think. She was just told to keep her eyes open and, as far as we know, hadn't reported anything at all. No, it seems she was young and fancy-free. Perhaps something of a goer, as we used to say.' Fane's lips creased briefly into a smile until he noticed Liz didn't smile back. 'A good reason not to choose her, I'd have thought.' He shrugged as if to imply it had had nothing to do with him, it was all very regrettable, but there you had it.

'So what happens next?' asked Liz. She wasn't going to let Fane wriggle out of this.

'Well, nothing for the moment. There's an investigation into her murder underway, and the Greek police are already a little suspicious about why the girl was working for UCSO. It seems she was wildly over-qualified for the job she was doing. Another reason not to have picked her, I'd have thought. Bruno's keeping his head down.'

Liz said, 'If we assume Blakey's suspicions were

129

correct and there is a leak, the question I have is: why? Why would anyone go to so much trouble? I know the UCSO shipments were very valuable, but surely an oil tanker has to be a better bet. If I were a pirate, I'd rather demand a ransom from the likes of Exxon or Shell than from a charity.'

Fane considered this. 'I agree,' he said finally, as if conferring a blessing. 'There must be another agenda being pursued.'

'And if it turns out that your agent's death was connected with UCSO, then it's something important. If it's worth killing for.'

Fane nodded. 'The problem is, my hands are tied in Athens right now. At least until the local police are out of the way.'

But I don't have that difficulty, thought Liz. She said, 'We have a few leads in Birmingham to follow up. It would be useful to check the UCSO side of things over here as well. If there is a connection between Amir Khan and UCSO, it might not be confined to their Athens office.'

Fane nodded. 'I'll ring Blakey and tell him to expect a call from you.'

Honours even, thought Liz.

When Fane suggested having coffee upstairs, she shook her head. She'd got what she'd wanted out of the lunch and had no desire for more of Geoffrey Fane's company.

'Oh, come on, Elizabeth,' he said in his most charming manner. 'I've apologised, so let's raise a cup of coffee to our further close co-operation.'

Liz relented; it would have been churlish not to. As they climbed the broad staircase up to the library, Fane pointed to the clock. 'Do you see anything odd about that?'

Liz stared for a moment at the round face with its roman numerals. 'Yes. There are two sevens and no eight.'

'Clever girl', he said approvingly. 'Not many people notice that.'

'Why don't they change it?'

'It's been like that since the clock was made. It's kept that way, perhaps as a reminder that nothing is perfect.'

Was this a further apology? 'Well,' Liz said, as she climbed the staircase, 'perhaps all intelligence services should have a clock like that. To remind us that what we see is not necessarily the truth.' Their eyes met for an instant and they both smiled. For different reasons, she thought.

23

In the library, Liz sat down in a button-backed leather chair while Fane collected coffee from a table by the door. He brought the cups over and sat down next to her, facing the door, stretching out his long legs and leaning back. Given the rather fraught conversation downstairs, he looked surprisingly pleased with himself. He looks like a cat, thought Liz. If he had a tail he'd be swishing it.

One of the porters came in through the open door of the library, followed by another man. The porter pointed to Liz and Fane, and to her astonishment she saw that the newcomer was Martin Seurat. From the expression on his face, Martin seemed as surprised to see Liz as she was to see him.

'Ah,' said Fane, 'Monsieur Seurat is here.' He looked at Liz archly. 'I forgot to say that I'd asked him to join us. I thought it could be useful for us to compare notes on Amir Khan.'

As Seurat came across the room towards them, Fane stood up. 'Martin, how good to see you,' he said, sounding uncharacteristically warm. 'You know Elizabeth Carlyle, don't you?'

Martin had recovered from his initial surprise. 'Of course—though I know her as Liz. She is Thames House's liaison with our other Service.'

As the two men sat down, Liz wanted to box Geoffrey Fane around the ears. He had set this up, and was clearly determined to enjoy a joke at their expense—since the Frenchman would have no idea that Fane knew he and Liz were seeing each other.

He said to Martin, 'Kind of you to come over on a Friday. I hope it won't spoil your weekend.'

'I am sure it won't,' said Martin, and left it at that. As Fane glanced at his watch Martin winked at Liz.

Fane said, 'Elizabeth and I have been discussing the prisoner you're holding . . . Amir Khan. We were wondering if you've got any further with him.'

Martin shook his head. 'He has continued to be unco-operative. I am due to see him myself next week, and will certainly let you know then if this particular bird begins to sing.'

Liz decided to cut into the conversation. 'We're trying to find out more about Khan's activities here in the UK and how he might have been recruited. As you know, we think he went to Pakistan for training. His parents emigrated from there before he was born. He went supposedly to visit relatives, but we think he attended some sort of training camp.'

Martin nodded knowingly. 'We have similar problems. We find the recruitment takes place in France, usually in one of the new radical mosques, but the instruction in terrorist tactics occurs elsewhere. We have many second- and third-generation French Algerians, for example, who have become disaffected with the West. They return to Algeria under the cover of a family visit, but come back knowing how to blow up a train.' He exhaled wearily. 'There is no easy answer to the problem.'

Liz said, 'We've learned one thing just recently from his family: we think he went to Athens sometime between his stay in Pakistan and Somalia.'

'Athens?' Martin digested this for a moment.

'Ring any bells?' asked Fane.

'I'm afraid it does not. The links we've uncovered recently with our own Al Qaeda sympathisers have been with Yemen and North Africa. That's why I was intrigued when I heard Khan had been picked up off the Somalian coast. Still, it will be useful when I see him to know that he was in Greece—especially since Khan doesn't know that we know he went there.'

'It's the best position to be in, don't you think?' demanded Fane. He looked sharply at Martin, and spoke with the faintest hint of a sneer. 'I mean, when you know something and the other chap doesn't know you know.' He looked at Liz then. It was quite clear to her that he was no longer talking about Amir Khan.

*   *   *

That evening Liz and Martin met up in Gaylord's, a wine bar halfway between Victoria and the river, just off the Vauxhall Bridge Road. It was slowly filling up with professionals who worked in the area, having a drink before the long weekend.

Martin was in a good mood. He had left the Athenaeum with Fane and they'd gone together by taxi to Vauxhall Cross. Still fuming over Fane's antics, Liz had declined their offer of a lift and had walked back to Thames House on her own. She found Fane's breezy lack of concern for the death of the undercover agent, and the absence of any sense of personal responsibility for what had happened, quite astonishing. As a rule she had little sympathy for Bruno Mackay, whom she found self-satisfied and patronising, but she couldn't help feeling sorry for him when she saw how his boss was subtly shifting blame for an agent's death on to his shoulders.

'You know,' said Martin, sipping his glass of Chablis, 'I found Geoffrey Fane rather strange today.'

'Oh, yes?' asked Liz a little warily. Now did not seem the right moment to tell Martin that Fane knew about their relationship.

Martin shrugged. 'As a Frenchman, one knows that there are always Englishmen who think we are buffoons, and that there are others who simply dislike us. But many Englishmen seem to like the French, even admire our culture. I always thought Fane was one of them.'

'And you no longer do?

Martin lifted his hands, perplexed. 'I found him different this afternoon. He seemed to become

134

competitive, sparring with me if you like.' He gave a small smile. 'But I think I know the reason.'

'What do you think it is?'

'The presence of Mademoiselle Carlyle! He is quite keen on you, I believe, and not very happy that you should be associated with the likes of me—a foreigner. However good the relations between our *bureaux*, he sees me as a competitor nonetheless.'

So Martin realised Fane knew about them, thought Liz, impressed that he had sussed that out for himself. Before she could say anything he went on, 'I don't take it personally. He would feel that way about any man you were with, I sense.'

He took an appreciative sip of his wine, then said cheerfully, 'Anyway, it is of no real consequence. Geoffrey Fane remains *formidable* in many respects, and he will continue to have my respect. But I will soon encounter someone who to me is far more daunting.'

'You will?' asked Liz. Did Martin have another meeting he hadn't told her about?

He looked at her with a sly smile. 'The weather is supposed to be very fine tomorrow. I expect I will be meeting your mother.'

24

Sound chap, Blakey. Fane's words were in the back of Liz's mind as she sat in the office of the Director of UCSO. David Blakey had the characteristic poise of an MI6 officer, but seemed a good deal more relaxed than the version Liz usually found herself working with. True, Blakey's suit was beautifully cut, but she noted with relief that there were none of the flamboyant extras that Geoffrey Fane and Bruno McKay liked to affect—no paisley silk handkerchief peeping out of the top pocket, no obvious shirt cuffs with gold cufflinks, no regimental tie.

Blakey had calmly explained the history of UCSO's concerns: how his original call to Fane had come after the head of UCSO's Athens office, Mitchell Berger, had become suspicious about the recent spate of hijack attempts on valuable shipments. Now, as Liz moved the discussion on to the murder of Maria Galanos, David Blakey begin to look uneasy.

She said, 'We're still waiting for the Greek police report, but we know Maria Galanos was strangled.'

'Yes, I'd heard that. Do they think she knew the person who killed her?'

'It doesn't sound like it—apparently her electricity had been tampered with, presumably to make the flat dark when her attacker struck. Which means it wasn't some sort of argument that suddenly escalated. It was planned—someone must have got into the flat beforehand. Do you know if she had a boyfriend?'

Blakey shrugged. 'I've no idea. The thing is, I never met the girl. I would have thought Geoffrey's colleagues in Athens would know all that sort of thing. They chose her for the job,' he added with a note of weariness. He seems more disturbed by her death than Fane was, thought Liz, even though he'd never met her. It must be causing a big upset in the Athens office.

She said, 'Berger met her, of course, so he probably knows more about her. When's he coming to London next?'

But Blakey didn't answer. Instead he reached for his phone and dialled two numbers—an internal extension. 'Could you pop in?' he said without preamble.

Moments later, the door to his office opened and a tall, slim woman walked in. She wore a smart linen shirtdress and plain but expensive-looking jewellery—a necklace of gold coins and a bracelet of fine gold wires. No wedding ring, observed Liz. The new arrival was about forty, with a mature, lightly sunburned face, blonde hair tied back, revealing a high forehead, bright blue eyes, and a sharp chin. The effect was smart and attractive rather than beautiful. It was a look that Liz would love to be able to achieve, though she had long ago accepted that she never would.

Blakey stood up and pulled out a chair for the woman. 'This is Liz Carlyle. She works with the friend I mentioned,' he told her.

Liz looked at him in surprise; her understanding from Fane was that only Berger in Athens (as well as Blakey himself) knew about the involvement of Fane and his colleagues in tracing the possible UCSO leak. Just how much had Blakey told this woman? She decided to ask Fane at the earliest opportunity what the agreement with Blakey had been.

'Katherine Ball,' said the blonde woman, stretching out her hand to Liz.

'We were talking about the problem in Athens,' said Blakey.

'Yes,' said Katherine, non-committally.

137

'Liz was asking about Maria, and I said I'd never met her. I think you did, though.'

'Yes, though I can't say I got to know her particularly well. Mitchell and I are usually pretty busy when I'm there,' she said, looking at Liz and smiling. 'I'm never in Athens very long, so my days are full—I don't have much time to chat to the staff.'

Liz nodded. 'I understand. Do you know if Maria was friendly with anyone in particular?'

While Katherine thought about this, Blakey interjected, 'She hadn't worked in the office very long . . .'

Katherine interrupted. 'The twins,' she said. Liz looked at her and she explained. 'Two Greek girls who work in the office. Anastasia and Falana. They're not related, actually, but I always call them the twins because they're inseparable.'

'And Maria knew them?'

'Everybody knows them. They're the dogsbodies in the office. I don't mean that unkindly—it's just that if you need anything, from a photocopy to coffee for a visitor, one of them gets it.'

'And Maria and these two?' asked Liz, trying to move the woman on.

'I think they were intrigued by her. Another Greek girl—slightly older but roughly the same generation. Yet half-English, educated—she'd travelled.' She glanced over at Blakey as she said this. 'Anyway, I think they got quite friendly. Even went out together.'

This was not surprising, given Maria's brief from the Athens MI6 Station. It would have been a good way for her to learn the office gossip. The 'twins' would have known far more than Berger about the personalities in the office, all their foibles and little habits, which when added up could provide the lead she'd been asked to look out for.

Katherine went on, 'I have to say, I was a little surprised. Not to be snooty about it, but Maria came from a different background—I don't think either of the twins has much education, and they both come from fairly humble families. I wouldn't have thought they had much to offer someone like Maria. All they ever talk about is pop music, clubbing and boys.'

'Well, they're young after all,' said Blakey mildly. 'That's understandable.'

But Katherine shook her head. 'There was more to it than that. I have the feeling they've got some pretty ropey friends in the clubs they go to. The girls are often the worse for wear when they come to work; I was going to speak to Mitchell about it, in fact. I think sometimes he's too tolerant.'

'Was Maria like that?' asked Liz. It sounded unlikely. Surely she wouldn't have been on the books of the Athens Station if she had been a committed party girl.

Katherine shrugged. 'I don't know. But she was young and single—and pretty.'

'But wouldn't the boys she met through the "twins" have been a bit young for her?' asked Blakey. 'Or was she a . . . what do they call it these days . . . a cougar?'

'I'm surprised you know that expression, David.' Katherine smiled at him. 'Maria wasn't anything like old enough.'

Liz nodded. 'Anything else we should know about Maria?'

'I don't think so. She was very professional,

and very good at her work.' Katherine seemed to be backtracking. 'I had the feeling everybody liked her.' She paused and Liz could see from her expression that there was something she wasn't saying.

This slant on Maria was rather different from the picture that had emerged from the thin file which the Athens Station had copied to Geoffrey Fane. That gave the impression of a serious professional young woman, soon to become thirty. Someone who was most unlikely to go clubbing—unless it was in the line of duty. But maybe the file was out of date. When Bruno Mackay had chosen Maria for this job, he didn't seem to have bothered to update it. Most people had some sort of hidden self—why should Maria Galanos be any different? She might have had a whole web of emotional entanglements, one of which could have gone disastrously wrong. With the bare facts Liz had, it was impossible to tell.

She wanted to talk further about all this to Blakey, though not in front of Katherine. But the woman continued to sit there, as if expecting to be included in the rest of the conversation. Then Liz noticed Blakey give her a look and Katherine stood up. 'I'd better get back to my office. Mitchell is supposed to be ringing me from Athens. Is there anything you'd like me to ask him?'

'No, thank you,' said Liz, and Katherine Ball left the office, closing the door firmly behind her.

After she'd left, Liz and Blakey sat in silence for a minute; Liz sensed he was uncomfortable. 'I hope that was helpful,' he said at last.

'Thank you,' she said. 'Has Katherine been working here long?'

140

'Two years.'

'And before that?'

'Before that she'd had a bit of a hiatus.' He gave a small smile. 'She trained as a lawyer originally, and worked for a few years in one of the big City firms. Very good at it too, I gather. Then she married a businessman, quite a wealthy one; he had business interests in the Middle East and they lived out there in various places for over ten years. Then one day out of the blue the poor chap dropped dead—a heart attack. They didn't have children, and Katherine didn't want to stay out there on her own, so she came back to London and started looking for work. Someone suggested she come in for a chat, we hit it off, and I took her on as my deputy. Within six months she was irreplaceable.'

'You're obviously lucky to have her,' said Liz.

They spoke for a few minutes more, and Blakey arranged for Liz to have copies of the CVs of the staff in both UCSO offices. As she left, she wondered again how much he had told Katherine Ball about the investigation. Had he told her of the suspicions about leaked information and why Maria had been taken on in the Athens office? Just how indiscreet was he?

25

'I hope you know the way,' said Liz to Kanaan Shah as they emerged from Birmingham New Street station. 'I've never been to this place.'

'Yeah, I know it well. Our best bet is to get a

141

bus.'

The MI5 office in Birmingham was a comparatively new development, set up after the invasion of Iraq had generated a burst of extremist activity in the area. Rather than send teams of people up from London, only to have to feed and water them and provide them with accommodation, it had been decided to open a regional office and post staff there or recruit them locally.

The bus stopped outside a rundown-looking Odeon cinema in an otherwise well-kept street in an inner suburb of the city. The building appeared to be undergoing restoration; its 1920s exterior was covered with scaffolding, and razor wire topped the two solid metal gates securing the site. Little more of the building could be seen through the security gates.

The entrance to the building itself was through a side door, which had obviously once been one of the exits from the cinema. Kanaan tapped a number into a pad on the wall beside the left-hand gate, and a small door clicked open. Liz followed Shah and they walked together into an extensive car park where a variety of cars and vans were parked.

In spite of its scruffy exterior, the inside of the building was clean and brightly painted. A number of small offices had been made out of what was once the entrance concourse of the cinema. Most of the doors were open but only a few of the rooms were occupied. As they walked past one door, a familiar, cheerful-sounding voice shouted out, 'Hello, stranger.'

Liz stopped, took a few steps back and saw Dave

Armstrong, her long-time colleague and friend, getting up from behind a desk. 'What are you doing here?' she asked in surprise. 'I hadn't heard you'd left Northern Ireland.'

'Your spies have let you down again,' said Dave with a huge grin. 'They moved me after I came out of hospital. I can't say I was sorry to leave beautiful Belfast.'

'I don't expect you were.'

Liz and Dave had last worked together on an investigation into a renegade group of Republican terrorists who were trying to kill police and intelligence officers in Northern Ireland. They had had some hair-raising experiences during the operation, and Dave had ended up badly hurt.

He looked at his watch. 'I'm coming to the briefing for your meet,' he said, following Liz out into the corridor and nodding at Kanaan Shah, who was waiting for her.

*   *   *

The briefing room had once been the auditorium of the cinema and not a great deal had changed. A few of the rows of red plush seats had been removed, but most were still in place. Now they were occupied by twenty or so casually dressed men and women, some white, some Asian, some young, some middle-aged. Most of them were new faces to Liz, but she recognised a few from Thames House and gave them a wave before sitting down at the end of a row near the back with Dave and Kanaan Shah.

The briefing was for the A4 surveillance operation that was going to cover their meeting

143

that evening with Kanaan Shah's agent, Boatman. Liz wanted to meet Boatman herself; it was crucial to find out if he knew anything about Amir Shah and how he came to be involved in hijacking an UCSO ship off Somalia.

The room fell silent as the A4 controller, Larry Lincoln, climbed on to the stage. Behind him was the screen on which the faces of Errol Flynn and Clark Gable had once appeared, to the delight of Birmingham audiences. Now it showed a collage of photographs of a young, thin, lightly bearded Asian man. In some he was wearing skullcap and robes, in others a suit or jeans. Liz looked with interest at the images of Boatman.

Lincoln, known to his teams as 'Lamb', began by welcoming Liz, then he turned to the A4 teams. 'Tonight it's the usual routine for Boa tman meetings. The only difference is that Liz Carlyle will be with us. The meeting will be held in "Pie Crust".' A picture of a red-brick Victorian villa came up on the screen. It had a green- painted wooden gate that led to a small overgrown garden; the villa's front door was obscured by a tall, unkempt privet hedge.

'Most of you know that there's a primary school along the road from Pie Crust and it gets very parked up from fifteen hundred. Then when the Mums leave, the commuters start coming back into the area. So we need to get all cars in place considerably before then. That includes comms and photographers. Comms will be tested as soon as teams are in situ. After receiving the all clear by bleep, Liz Carlyle and K will each go, but separately, to Pie Crust. K to enter at sixteen hundred; Liz at sixteen thirty.

'Two foot teams with drivers in cars will be in Boatman's street from seventeen hundred to carry out anti-surveillance. Foot teams will follow Boatman when he leaves his house at seventeen-thirty. Can you confirm, K, that Boatman knows what to do?'

Kanaan nodded. Lincoln went on: 'Boatman will walk with anti-surveillance cover, by the route he's been given—' he cocked an eye at Shah, who nodded again '—to Pie Crust, where he'll knock and enter at about eighteen hundred hours. We'll give a heads up to you in Pie Crust when he's a couple of minutes away. If any surveillance is detected, he'll be approached by an officer standing outside the primary school and asked the time. He will then abort the meeting. All OK with you, K?'

'Yes. He has his instructions.'

'While the meeting takes place any untoward activity in the surrounding streets will be assessed in the Control Room by Dave Armstrong, who will decide on any further action. OK Dave?' A nod from Dave Armstrong.

'When the meeting is over, Liz or K will ring to alert Control who will check round and confirm all clear. Anti-surveillance will follow him home. All A4 please stay behind now to get your positions. Any questions from anybody?'

A few hands shot up and some details were thrashed out, then Liz, Dave and Kanaan Shah left the auditorium.

'That's pretty thorough,' Liz said to Dave. 'I see Birmingham is now hostile territory.'

'Hostile enough,' he replied. 'I wouldn't give a lot for Boatman's chances if his pals at the New

145

Springfield Mosque knew he was talking to MI5.'

* * *

At 4.30 that afternoon Liz rang the doorbell at Pie Crust; it was opened straight away by Kanaan, who must have been standing behind the door waiting for her.

Liz had been in many safe houses in her career. This one was larger than normal—a detached house unlike most of them, particularly those in London, which were usually flats of various kinds. But in every other way it was familiar. Off the square hall was a sitting room containing two well-used sofas covered in a familiar flowery fabric which Liz had seen before. It made its appearance in many MI5 safe houses and was known to the agent runners who used these places as 'Ministry of Works chintz'. A couple of chairs with wooden arms, dating from the eighties, and a coffee table of light veneer, marked by white rings where hot mugs had rested, completed the furnishing of the sitting room. Poking her head round the door of the dining room next door, Liz found it similarly spartan. Safe houses were one of civilisation's dead ends. Strictly utilitarian, they were kept stocked with essentials for making coffee and tea, but there was never any food in their kitchen fridges, which contained nothing but milk.

Liz had once had to live in a safe house for almost a week in order to keep up a cover story. They had been some of the gloomiest, most uncomfortable days of her life.

On the dining-room table, K had put a small pile of photographs; there was also a new notebook in

146

the sitting room, and a bottle of mineral water and three glasses stood on the coffee table. 'Boatman will only take water,' he said, seeing Liz looking at his preparations. 'He doesn't drink tea or coffee.'

Liz spent some time looking through the photographs in the dining room before going to join Kanaan in the sitting room. He was sitting on one of the flowery sofas, scanning the *Guardian*. She sat down opposite him on the other sofa and they made desultory conversation. But as the time for the meeting drew nearer, they fell silent. Even after years doing this sort of work, Liz still felt a tension in her stomach, a quickened beating of the heart, as she waited for the phone to ring. Kanaan must be much more nervous, she thought, though to do him credit he didn't show any sign of it.

The phone rang, breaking the silence; one ring and then nothing. Kanaan went to the front door and looked through the peephole; then, just as Boatman walked up the path, he opened the door and closed it again as soon as the young man was inside.

Liz heard them in the hall exchanging greetings. '*Salaam alaikum*,' Boatman said to Kanaan.

'*Wa Alaikum as-Salaam*,' Kanaan replied. 'I have brought someone to meet you like I told you,' he said, as they walked into the sitting room. 'This is Jane. I work with her. She can be trusted.'

Boatman peered at Liz, then nodded. She smiled and nodded in reply. The young Asian was wearing a white embroidered skullcap and the traditional white *shalwar kameez*; his feet were in sandals. His face was young but his expression very serious. He looked, Liz thought, as though he had considered the follies most young men opt for and rejected

147

them. If the weight of the world was not yet on his shoulders, his expression seemed to say, it was only a matter of time. Liz was used to agents being scared, even sometimes cracking jokes to allay their nerves. But Boatman seemed entirely composed and serious—almost forbiddingly so. There was a rather chilly air of religious probity about him.

Kanaan said brightly, 'How is married life treating you?'

'Very well, thank you,' Boatman answered gravely, like a potentate accepting a subject's best wishes.

'How long have you been married?' Liz asked, though she knew from her briefing that his wedding was four months ago.

'Not long,' he said, then his voice brightened. 'But I find I like my wife more and more each day. She is very kind, and more intelligent than I expected.'

Liz was startled, then realised that it would have been an arranged marriage. It was not a practice she approved of, but at least Boatman seemed pleased to have discovered unexpected virtues in his bride.

'How are things at the mosque?' asked Kanaan, getting down to business.

Boatman shrugged. 'They have stopped pressing me to go to Pakistan—they accept that with a new bride, I don't wish to go away. Especially . . .' he said, and Liz understood at once—especially since he might then never see his wife again.

Boatman went on, 'The others are going. We still meet together once a week, but there are meetings to which I am not invited.'

'At the mosque?' asked Liz.

'Yes, but elsewhere also. Malik says they have been to London.'

'Did he say where?' asked Kanaan.

'Only that it was in North London. They went for a briefing about what they should expect when they arrive in Pakistan.'

'And what was that?' asked Liz.

'He didn't say, and I didn't feel I could press him.'

'No, that's quite right. Let him tell you what he wants to. You mustn't push him too hard for information.'

'He did say something about the meeting though. He said they were addressed at one point by a Westerner. Not an Asian.'

Kanaan interjected, sounding excited. 'Wasn't Malik surprised?'

Boatmen put a hand on his chin contemplatively, stroking his wispy beard. 'I didn't get the feeling he disapproved. I think if anything he was proud that a convert to Islam was helping him and the others.'

'Did he describe this Westerner?' asked Liz.

Boatman shook his head. 'No. But I am seeing Malik tomorrow.'

'Ask him then,' said Kanaan.

'Steady on,' said Liz a little sharply. 'Go carefully.' She looked at Boatman, but was dismayed to see that all his attention was focused on Kanaan. He clearly saw the male figure as naturally in charge, and looked to his handler to tell him what he should do. It wasn't surprising, and Kanaan was his controller, but she was alarmed that her youthful colleague's enthusiasm was getting the better of his judgement. She said to Boatman firmly, 'Find out what you can, but don't

149

press Malik too hard. If he wants to talk, encourage him. But I don't want you to give out any signal that you're any more than casually curious—particularly about this Westerner.'

She couldn't tell if Boatman was listening to her, as he was still looking at Kanaan, but short of grabbing him by the ears and shouting, there wasn't much more she could say. And the last thing she wanted to do was to undermine Kanaan in front of his agent.

Kanaan stood up. 'I've got some photographs for you to look at, Salim. They're in the other room. I'll just get them.'

In the brief time they were alone together Boatman did not look at Liz. He poured himself a glass of water and drank it slowly, without asking her if she would like one too.

Kanaan came back and put the pile of photographs on the coffee table. 'Would you have a look through these to see if you recognise anyone?'

For the next few minutes Boatman leafed through the pictures. They were mainly of young Asian men in a variety of Western and traditional clothes, with a few older men and even fewer young women. He took the task seriously, examining each photograph with care, only to shake his head. In the middle of the pile he paused and looked hard at a photograph of a young man in traditional costume. 'I have seen this man before. I don't know his name but he used to go to the mosque. I have not seen him for a long time, though, and he certainly doesn't go to the mosque now.'

He pushed the photograph across the table

and Liz picked it up. No, he certainly doesn't, she thought. It was a picture of Amir Khan, at present in the Santé prison. 'Can you remember when you last saw him?' she asked.

Boatman screwed up his eyes in thought. 'It must be well over a year ago. I have been going to this mosque for just over two years now and I saw him only at the beginning.'

'Do you know anything about his friends?'

'No. I never knew him. I don't even know his name. I just recognise his face.'

He went on looking through the photographs. Then, as he neared the bottom of the stack, he suddenly did a double take. 'That is Malik.'

He pushed the photo across the table, and Liz reached out and turned it around. It had been taken from across a street and showed a young man coming out of a newsagent's. He wore jeans and a T-shirt and was short and stocky, with a stolid slab-like face.

Boatman pursed his lips, and for the first time seemed agitated. 'He is not a bad fellow, I believe, not deep in his heart. I would say he is simply misguided. He has never advocated violence to me.'

'Oh, really?' asked Liz mildly, and if there was scepticism in her voice, Boatman didn't seem to notice. But she remembered the stubby hand which had gripped her wrist so hard, twisting her arm behind her back. It had belonged to the man pictured in the photograph. So one of her attackers had been Malik.

26

In another Birmingham suburb Peggy Kinsolving parked her car outside a very different kind of house. A black wrought-iron gate opened on to a neat front garden; a York stone path led through low shrubs to a solid oak front door with two stained glass panels.

Arts and Crafts, Peggy said to herself. She and her boyfriend Tim had recently been on an evening course on English domestic architecture, and she was glad some of it had stuck.

A pretty middle-aged woman answered the door. She smiled at Peggy and said, 'You must be Miss Donovan, come to see my husband. I'm Felicity Luckhurst.'

Mrs Luckhurst led Peggy into a square entrance hall with a colourful tiled floor. Peggy was interested to see the shoulder-high oak panelling on the walls of the hall. It was just as it should be, she thought. She followed Mrs Luckhurst through a modern, spick-and-span kitchen and into a conservatory, from which she could see a freshly mown lawn, neatly edged beds of shrubs, pots of flowers and a little pond with a fountain. At the bottom of the garden there seemed to be a greenhouse under construction.

'Good afternoon, Miss Donovan,' said a loud masculine voice, and Peggy turned to see a tall, upright, middle-aged man with friendly eyes. He was dressed casually—fawn trousers, an open-necked shirt and pullover. 'I've just been tidying myself up a bit. I've been working on that greenhouse all morning.'

'Yes,' said Felicity Luckhurst. 'I've told him he's got to finish it before he goes back to work.'

'When will that be?' asked Peggy.

'I'm not sure yet. In a month, I hope, but I've got to get the medic to sign me off. Lot of nonsense.'

'Now, now,' said his wife. 'Miss Donovan doesn't want to hear you grousing. Go and sit down and I'll bring you some tea.'

They sat down in the wicker chairs in the conservatory and talked about the garden and the design of the house until Mrs Luckhurst brought the tea tray and left them to it.

'So,' Luckhurst said, 'tell me what I can do to help the Home Office.' He raised a sceptical eyebrow.

'I've come to follow up your conversation with DI Fontana. You gave him some information about where you were held in Somalia.' Peggy was trying not to lead him in any particular direction.

Luckhurst nodded. 'I take it you know broadly what happened to us?'

'I think so—your ship was seized, and you and your crew were held captive until a ransom was paid. DI Fontana said you had something to tell us about the camp.'

'Well, not so much about the camp itself, but rather what one of the people guarding us said to me.' Luckhurst told Peggy about the young boy, Taban, who had brought them their supper each evening. On the last occasion that he'd seen him, he explained, Taban seemed really nervous. 'Quite different from his usual self. I'd managed to establish quite a rapport with him—thought it might come in useful somehow. We talked in a

153

kind of pidgin English. That evening he said—
well, he didn't exactly say this but it's what I think
he meant—that an Englishman had come to the
camp. Not English like me, but like Taban; I think
he was trying to say he was dark-skinned. He wasn't
a hostage, according to Taban; this "Englishman"
had come to the camp with a bunch of Arabs.'

'Arabs?' asked Peggy. 'Not Somalis?'

'No, that's why it stuck in my mind—that and the
fact that he was a dark Englishman, whatever that
means.'

Peggy had a very clear sense of what it meant.
'Did he say what these Arabs were doing there?'

Luckhurst shook his head. 'No, and I never saw
them myself. You see, we never got a look at the
whole camp. They brought us there in the dark,
and we were kept in a pen. We were let out each
day for exercise, in a kind of dusty open courtyard,
but all I could see were dunes on one side, and a
wall on the other.'

'You said "dunes"—were you right by the sea?'

'I assume so. Though to tell you the truth, I
don't know exactly where we were.'

Peggy reached down for the case holding her
laptop. 'Why don't we try and find out?'

*   *   *

Five minutes later Peggy sat at the dining-room
table, with an attentive Captain Luckhurst by
her side. Thanks to Mrs Luckhurst's attachment
to online shopping, the household had fast
Broadband access, and on the screen of Peggy's
laptop a picture of the United Kingdom suddenly
appeared, viewed from hundreds of miles above.

154

'Google Earth,' said Luckhurst knowingly. 'My son was showing it to me the other day.'

'Something like that,' said Peggy cryptically. In fact, they were looking at Ministry of Defence satellite photographs—unlike Google Earth, these pictures were constantly updated, so that instead of patches of cloud obscuring a given location on the day the Google satellite was at work, these were all razor-sharp.

'You said your ship was boarded almost dead east of Mogadishu.'

'That's right. We were about thirty miles offshore.'

'Did you have a sense of where you went next?'

'Not really. It was south of Mogadishu—though I couldn't see the city. Frankly I was too busy following the pirates' orders to check the final co-ordinates.'

Meaning he'd had a gun to his head, thought Peggy, admiring Luckhurst's understatement.

He pressed a finger to his lips, thinking hard. At last he said, 'In the old days we'd have had a log—it would probably still be there in the pilot house. But nowadays it's all electronic. That means HQ have a constant fix on the ship's whereabouts.' He looked at Peggy. 'Let me go and make a call.'

When he returned he held a piece of paper. 'Hope this means something to you.'

And when Peggy looked at the sequence of numbers it did. Opening a small box in one corner of the screen, she entered the precise latitude and longitude co-ordinates he had given her. Seconds later, the screen cleared and they were staring at a topographical view of ocean, with a superimposed X in the middle of the laptop's display.

'What's that?' asked Luckhurst.

'The place where you were last anchored.' She clicked a sequence of keys and suddenly the focus pulled back, exposing the nearby coastline. 'Now, you were anchored only a mile or so offshore. Do you think you went straight in?'

Luckhurst replied without hesitation, 'No. It took maybe twenty minutes before we got to the beach. Admittedly the boats they took us in were pretty small, but they had reasonable outboards on them. We must have gone south, or else I would have seen Mogadishu. It's quite a large city.'

Peggy zeroed in on the coastline, starting on the southern fringes of the capital city, which was laid out in visible rectangles, then moving slowly south, past the long strip of the international airport and further down the coast. Here the white tops of breakers could be made out, the flat sand of the beach, and dunes pockmarked by the few trees hardy enough to grow there. There seemed to be little or no signs of habitation, and no obvious dwellings; where the city ended, the desert took over.

'Can't say anything looks familiar . . .'

Peggy understood, since even at close range, from a height of less than a mile, it was hard to make sense of a terrain of water, sand, and more sand. 'Was there any specific feature in the camp you can recall?'

'I can't give you an account of the whole camp, as I said. But there was a big block house behind the compound wall which I once got a glimpse of—Khalid lived there. He was the leader of the pirates. And the pen we were held in was very long—fifty, maybe sixty feet, and seven or eight

156

feet wide. It must once have been used to hold animals—chickens, maybe.'

'Would it be visible to an aerial shot?'

'Absolutely. If there'd been any shade—even a baobab tree or whatever—we'd have been delighted. But there was nothing—just the sun above.'

Then Peggy clicked for another pop-up box, which listed categories of search items: *elevated contours, elevated installations, bodies of water, moving water, vegetation, dwellings, vehicles, humans, animal life*. She ticked *dwellings* and hit return.

'What's this?'

'It ties intelligent search to the satellite photos,' she said, and left it at that. Not that I could explain much further, she thought, since she was just parroting the explanation of Technical Ted, from A2, who had loaded the special software on to her laptop the day before, and briefed her on how to use it.

The screen view was from a higher vantage point again, but this time a series of highlighted dots, labelled A, B, C, etc., also appeared onscreen, scattered along the shoreline for a range of roughly twenty miles.

They worked their way through the dots carefully. Several were false positives—large boulders detected as buildings, or else abandoned sites, including a tiny village perched right on the shore, now full of deserted crumbling shacks.

Then, just half a mile down from the former village, they examined a number of shapes bunched closely together. They sat under a high rolling dune which half-disguised them from the

157

normal perspective of the MOD aerial cameras. But zoomed in on and looked at carefully, they revealed a suspiciously orderly arrangement, with a central blob that could have been the block house Luckhurst had mentioned, surrounded by a thin line that might have been a wall. A dusty square sat next to it, and at its far end was a long dark rectangle.

'The pen you were kept in,' asked Peggy, 'was it roofed?'

'Part of it was. With plywood covered by tar paper—to keep us warm,' Luckhurst said ironically.

Peggy laughed and increased the magnification by a notch. The blob sharpened slightly, and she could see that, yes, it was a structure—nature didn't like straight lines. 'What about this? Have we found it?'

Luckhurst peered closely at the scene. Finally he nodded. 'It must be. There's the wall, and the compound, and the pen next to the patch of ground where they let us out to exercise and where the food was cooked. There's something else inside the compound wall . . .'

'They look like huts,' said Peggy.

'Probably—that's where Khalid's men would stay, I suppose. But what are those?'

He pointed to some small triangular shapes that sat at the bottom of the square. 'Can we look at them from a different angle?' he asked hopefully.

'You mean, like Google View?' Peggy said, referring to the perspective showing scenes at street level. 'Not very likely,' she said, and laughed at the thought of a Google representative venturing out to the camp with a video camera. She looked back at the screen and suddenly said, 'I know—

they're tents. Lots of tents. There must be a dozen of them.'

'Taban said there had been visitors.'

'And now we know exactly where they were staying.' The next step, thought Peggy, was finding out who they were.

27

It had taken Tahira six months to persuade her father that the shop needed more than one till. Always cautious, always suspicious even of his own family, Mr Khan had resisted all her efforts to install another cash register, ignoring the queues that formed as a result, sometimes halfway to the shop's front doors. It was only when he had seen with his own eyes two customers leave one evening in disgust, not prepared to wait ten minutes to pay for a bag of crisps and a bottle of Sprite, that he had relented.

In the same way, Tahira had managed to change the stock—gradually adding more staples for people who'd run out and didn't want to make the journey to the big supermarkets; and more high-end items, like ready-made curries and sauces, for the increasing number of young singles living in the area. It seemed to be working. Not that her father gave her any credit for the way sales and profits were holding up, even in the middle of a recession.

She sighed, hearing yet again in her head the constant paternal reminders that she wouldn't be working in the shop for long, that marriage was the next step in life for her—as far as she was concerned, marriage would be the grim last step, the end of everything she enjoyed. She liked business and working; getting married could wait . . . and wait some more. But she saw trouble ahead, for she knew her father was in touch with the extended family in Pakistan to find her a suitable husband. A plan she was determined to resist.

Now she was getting ready to cash up, just waiting for her cousin Nazir to flip the sign on the front door to CLOSED. There was a solitary customer still in the shop, someone moseying around the magazines at the far end. She heard him moving down the aisle and, peering at the monitor which showed the images from the video camera set in the corner above the ice-cream cabinet, she could make him out clearly. A man in a parka—a white man, unusual in this neighbourhood in the evening. He looked to be in his mid-thirties, dressed in smart jeans and trainers—clearly not a builder. During the day this was quite a mixed area—many of the people working nearby, in other shops and in offices, were white—but those who shopped in the evening, the residents, were almost all Asians.

There was something familiar about his figure, and she wondered if he'd been in earlier in the day. Her mild suspicions went away when he came up to the counter and put down a copy of the *Birmingham News,* paying for it with a pound coin. When she gave him his change, he said thank you very politely and smiled at Tahira—a nice smile, and he had a pleasant face. Good-looking, she thought, if a little old for her. Not that it would

160

ever be a possibility—her father wouldn't dream of letting her go out with a white boy, and while she continued to live under his roof she was obliged to obey. The man in the parka left the shop and Nazir flipped the sign and turned the key.

Silly to distrust the man, she thought. Though you couldn't be too careful. They hadn't been robbed recently, not since the nasty incident three years before when two young men wearing balaclavas had rushed in, one brandishing a knife, the other a hammer. Thank God her father hadn't been there; with his hot temper, he might have tried to resist. Tahira had just held up both hands and let them empty the till—no life, much less her own, was worth £74, the amount the robbers had gone off with. They didn't realise that the register was checked every hour, so that only relatively few takings were ever held inside.

It was now that she saw the piece of paper. It was lying on the counter, folded in two. It must have been left by the man in the parka—otherwise she would have noticed it before. She looked around but of course the shop was closed, and Nazir was busy pulling down the window grilles. She unfolded the paper quickly and her eyes widened as she read:

Could we have a word, please? It's about your brother Amir. If you walk home via Slocombe Avenue we could talk in private.

Her hands were shaking. She took the note and ripped it in two, then four, then eight. Pushing the strips deep down into the rubbish bin that stood behind the counter, she tried to concentrate on the

161

closing up routine. Methodically she emptied the two tills and rang up the day's takings. Good, better than the day before; better than she would have expected twelve months before as the recession took hold.

She wondered what to do. Should she walk home by Slocombe Avenue and see what this man wanted? But what if he was luring her there, by the lime trees and the small park, because he had something else in mind? How could a white man know anything about her brother Amir? Unless . . .

Nazir called goodnight and she followed him out a few minutes later, turning out the lights by the shop's entrance, then tapping in the numbers to activate the alarm before closing the heavy door behind her. She set off along the street, noting that Kassim's newsagent's was still open as usual. I work hard, she thought, but Kassim seems never to sleep.

She turned on to a side street and began the long uphill walk that would take her to her father's house. Funny, she realised, she never thought of it as her mother's. Whatever happened to her, she was determined not to follow her mother's path; Tahira vowed to have a life of her own.

At Slocombe Avenue she hesitated, realising she had been putting off the decision. She turned round abruptly to see if she was being followed. No one. Then she turned into the street.

*　　　*　　　*

'She's on her way. All clear,' said a voice in Dave's ear as he waited under cover of a line of tall trees outside the gate of the small park further up the street. The A4 surveillance van parked in Slocombe

162

Avenue was monitoring Tahira's walk from the shop and Dave was ready to abort the meeting if any sign of danger was observed.

Tahira walked on, passing a line of semi-detached houses, lights on in their sitting rooms, the noise of televisions plainly heard in the street, until the houses gave way to the park, a favourite of mothers with toddlers, now gloomy and deserted, its gate shadowed by the line of trees set back from the street. At the gate she hesitated.

'Tahira.' The voice was soft and English. It startled her. She turned and there was the man in the parka again, standing ten feet in from the pavement, under the branches of one of the lime trees. He was still smiling and looked entirely unthreatening, but she felt frightened nonetheless. How did he know her name? What did he want? She looked around, but there was no one nearby, and the light was fading now that the sun had set.

'Can I have a word, please?' the man said.

'Who are you?' Tahira demanded, trying to project an air of confidence she didn't feel. Then a woman emerged from the shadows behind the man. Tahira recognised her at once—it was the same woman who'd come to her father's house to tell them about Amir. Tahira had liked her directness. She relaxed slightly, though she still wondered what they wanted from her.

The Englishwoman said, 'Tahira, there's a bench over here, behind me. If you go in and sit there, I'll join you in a minute.' When Tahira didn't respond, she added, 'My friend here will keep watch. No one will see us, I promise you.'

Tahira thought hard. It was all very well to say there was no danger, but she knew that was nonsense. If she were spotted talking to this woman, word would get around right away—if not to the young men from the mosque, then to her father, who would be furious that she'd met the officials who had come to see him, off on her own. There would be no explanation for it that he would accept.

But the note had said they wanted to talk about Amir. Her adored younger brother Amir. She realised now how worried she had been about him, how much she had wanted to know where he was, how fearful she had grown that something had happened to him. It had been a relief to learn he was being held in Paris—at least he was alive— but a new wave of worries had set in then. He was alive, but she had no confidence she would see him again soon.

Concern and plain curiosity won over caution. Tahira took a deep breath and turned into the park through the open gate. She went to sit on the bench, trying to slow down her breathing.

She heard a step behind her, then the woman was sitting on the bench beside her. 'It's quite safe, Tahira,' she said soothingly. 'There's no one else around.'

'What has happened to Amir?'

'He's fine. Still in Paris, but there's a good chance he will be coming back to this country. Then it might be possible for you to visit him.'

'Really?' she asked, hope overcoming the suspicion in her voice. 'When?'

'Soon. I can't tell you an exact date. Weeks rather than months. But you can help him before then.'

'Me? How?'

164

'We need to know what happened to your brother. Someone got to him; someone persuaded him to leave home. We think it might have been at the mosque.'

'Of course it was at the mosque,' hissed Tahira crossly. There wasn't any doubt in her mind. 'He should never have switched.'

'To the New Springfield Mosque?'

'Yes.'

'Did some of his friends switch as well?'

'Not that I know of. But he made new friends there. That was part of the problem—none of us knew any of them, or their families. Suddenly he was with a different set.'

'Did they go to Pakistan as well?'

'Yes.' She had learned two names and said them aloud now.

'What happened to them?'

'I don't know for sure. But neither has come back to Birmingham.'

'Were they students of the same imam?' The woman's voice was calm but insistent.

'There is only one imam at that mosque. Abdi Bakri. He sent them all to Pakistan. My father doesn't realise that—he still thinks Amir went to see the family there and work for our cousin.' She frowned, thinking of her father's naiveté.

'Do you know anything about this Abdi Bakri?'

Tahira shook her head. 'Only that he hasn't been in Birmingham more than a few years.'

'Was he in Pakistan before that?'

'Pakistan? I don't think so. He's North African. But why, is that important?'

'It could be very important.'

'I suppose I could try and find out.'

165

And as Tahira spoke the words, Liz knew she had a new agent. Did Tahira realise what she'd volunteered for? She would soon find out.

28

Berger was on edge, though he did his best not to show it in the office. It had been a shock for everyone when the police had arrived on Monday afternoon and told them that Maria Galanos had been found murdered in her flat. Apparently her parents had spent the weekend trying to reach her on the telephone; the concierge had finally relented on Monday morning and used her key to open the poor girl's door. With Greek efficiency, it had taken the police most of the day to contact her employers.

Falana had fainted when she'd heard the news, and Berger had sent her home right away. But he knew that her alarm was felt by everyone else in the office, and even now, three weeks later, the atmosphere remained tense as well as mournful. In his experience, sudden deaths were upsetting; a murder had the added effect of being frightening.

Katherine Ball was due out in a couple of days, and Berger was looking forward to her arrival—her imperturbable confidence might rub off on his edgy staff. He wished it could rub off on him as well. Unlike the staff, he didn't think Maria's murder had anything to do with her personal life, or was the random act of some homicidal psychopath. He was sure that her real role in the office had been discovered, either because she had asked too many questions or because she had found something out which she hadn't been able to tell anyone in time—Berger's secretary said that Maria had been looking for him on the day he had gone away for a long weekend.

So perhaps there was a spy in the office after all, one prepared to kill to keep their identity secret. Which meant they might kill again. Berger had not felt so exposed for several years, not since moving out of his risky former life and joining the calm backwaters of charitable work. Or rather, calm no longer; he kept wondering if Maria's death was not an end but a beginning, and if the killer would continue to kill anyone who might get in the way. In the way of what, though? Berger didn't know, but it had to include the hijacking of the UCSO shipments.

He wanted back-up—protection, yes, but also someone with a fresh perspective who might see what was going on here in a way that Berger couldn't. The people from the British Embassy who'd sent Maria had been no help at all. They'd just told him to keep his head down and say nothing about them to the Greek police while they awaited instructions from London. He'd heard no more from them. That wasn't good enough for him. He hated returning to his former way of life, but he hated being in danger again even more.

The switchboard put him through right away. 'Trade Affairs,' a flat Midwestern voice announced. 'This is Hal Stimkin.'

'My name is Mitchell Berger. I run the UCSO office here in Athens. I'm Brown Book status.' This was the register of former employees. 'I need a meet—ASAP.'

There was a pregnant pause. 'Well, Mitch. Give me a minute or two and I'll get back to you. What's your number?'

Berger gave him a number and the phone went dead. He could imagine the process now put in train—the encrypted email to Virginia, the internal call, the email back. Three hours later he was still musing on how long it would take when his phone rang. It was Stimkin. 'OK, Mitchell. Now here's what we're gonna do . . .'

He was preoccupied for the rest of the day—even Elena, his normally timid secretary, commented on it when she brought him coffee at four that afternoon. He did his best to focus on work affairs—after Maria's death he had postponed the planned shipment but needed now to reschedule it—but he was glad when the clock showed six o'clock. By then the office had emptied and he had the lift to himself as he left the building.

He had an hour to kill so he walked. Spotting any surveillance in Athens at that time of night was well-nigh impossible, though he felt pretty sure that if anyone were watching him it would be an individual rather than an organisation, and would therefore be easier to shake off.

Fifty minutes later, as he circled around his destination, he was confident he wasn't being followed. He was heading for the Venus de Milo, a luxury hotel situated only a few hundred yards from the Parthenon. He'd checked the pavements behind him carefully as he'd walked, and been alert for a front tail as well; he'd detoured through a large department store that stayed open late, taking the lift up and the stairs down, then had a quick espresso in a coffee bar with a good vantage point towards the street. He'd even searched himself, against the remote possibility that a tracking device had been planted on his clothes. Nothing, and no one.

The bar in the Venus de Milo was humming, full of tourists staying at the hotel and locals from the offices nearby, willing to pay over the odds for a cocktail in order to enjoy the air-conditioning. A long mahogany bar hugged one side of the low room on the hotel's ground floor. Berger spotted a tall frosted glass of beer sitting on the bar top in front of two empty stools. He sat down on one of them, and as the barman approached pointed to the full glass. The barman drew another beer from the tap and, as he put it down in front of Berger, a tall, heavy-set man sat down next to him.

'I'm Stimkin,' the big man said, taking a long pull from his waiting glass of beer. He didn't shake hands. 'You checked out fine, Mitch, but this is your first contact in five years. So what's the big emergency?'

Inwardly Berger sighed. He'd seen enough of the world not to stereotype people, but he'd seen an awful lot of versions of Hal Stimkin before, especially in the Agency. He would be a former jock, probably a former football player, possibly ex-military; he'd have joined the Agency on the heavy rather than the cerebral side, but shown enough polish to rise in the ranks and become a Head of Station. He'd be a self-proclaimed 'straight shooter', which really just meant he not only lacked sophistication but was proud of the deficit. All in all he was about as far as you could get from the Ivy League WASP who, both in the old days and in the popular imagination, staffed the

169

higher ranks of the CIA.

Berger gave a terse account of recent events to Stimkin, ending in the death of the planted MI6 agent.

'Why didn't you flag Six's involvement to us?'

Berger shrugged. 'To be honest, it didn't seem relevant. They were just helping sort out a criminal situation. Nothing of interest to Langley.'

'Let Langley be the judge of that, pal. Six must have thought it was more than that or they wouldn't have bothered.'

'My boss is ex-Six. They were doing him a favour.'

'Oh, really?' asked Stimkin, gesturing to the barman for two more beers. 'That would imply they're a lot nicer than we are. And they're not.' The second implication was clear: Stimkin thought there was more to this than met the eye. Perhaps he wasn't so stupid after all.

Their beers came and they waited for the barman to move away. Stimkin said, 'So, what do you want from us?'

'Help,' said Berger bluntly. 'I need my back watched.'

'And in return?'

'You know everything that happens.'

Stimkin grimaced. 'A bunch of hoods are ripping off your ships. Do we care who they are?'

'Not if it's that simple. I'm not sure it is.'

Stimkin nodded. 'You could be right, bud.' The big man would have seen Berger's Agency CV, or at least a précis of it. He'd know Berger wouldn't have spent twenty years doing the things he had done for the Agency if he were some sort of crank. 'OK, so let's keep in touch. I'll brief Langley.'

'And I get back-up?'

'Let's see. For now, sit tight.'

Stimkin looked at the bill the barman had placed next to their beers. 'I don't believe the Brits are just going to give up because one of their people got iced. They'll be back as soon as the Greek cops get out of the way. I want to know when they are, understood?'

Berger had had enough. He'd left the Agency after all, he hadn't been pushed out. And now Stimkin was acting as if he were some sort of underling or, even worse, a dubious source. He decided to beat Stimkin to the punch, and got down off his stool before the big man did. He said, 'Don't worry, I've got it, Hal.' And he didn't mean the bill; he figured Langley owed him that at least.

29

This was weird. Peggy sighed and looked again at the CV in front of her. It was the third day she'd spent checking the credentials of the UCSO staff in London and Athens. She wasn't entirely sure what she was looking for—just anything that might mean someone was not who they appeared to be, and had joined the charity with an ulterior motive. It was as vague as that, but she hoped she'd recognise it when she saw it. So far all she had found were the sort of discrepancies that you might find in any organisation of fifty-five employees that wasn't too careful about its recruitment processes.

And it looked as though UCSO was just such a one. Maybe charities didn't bother too much, she thought. Maybe they were glad to get anyone to work for the modest salaries they paid.

A young woman called Wainwright had claimed an Honours degree in Anthropology from Cambridge, though a few simple enquiries produced the information that she had never completed a university course and had no formal qualifications at all. Cathy Etherington, a fund-raising assistant, claimed to have spent two years working for the Red Cross, but a phone call found no record of her employment there, and a check with a previous employer uncovered the fact that she had been fired for chronic absenteeism. Finally, the business analyst Sandy Warlock's proud claim to have been a finalist in the Olympic trials in judo turned out to be complete phooey.

Though all this had revealed that UCSO was pretty careless, it had not set Peggy's antennae vibrating. But what she was looking at now certainly did. It was the CV of Mitchell Berger, Head of the Athens office, that had made her sit up. It wasn't that she had any reason to doubt the accuracy of the impressive list of previous posts he'd held—and it was impressive: as he'd said in his covering letter when he applied for the job in Athens, '*My background is a mix of military, diplomatic, journalism and NGO, and it has taken me to many parts of the world . . .*' It was something about the location of those posts and the dates that had sparked her interest.

As Peggy sat thinking about all this, her chin resting in her hands, her eyes drifted over her colleagues in the open-plan office where she worked. She thought how surprising it was that so many people seemed to lie about their past, about

172

their qualifications. It would never have occurred to her to do that. In the Service, of course, you wouldn't get away with it for five minutes: the vetting process would soon find you out.

She looked at Denise from the library who was standing talking to an agent runner who'd just walked into the room. There was no chance at all that Denise didn't have the degree in library science or whatever professional qualification she claimed to have, or that the agent runner, who was now rather obviously flirting with her, had an undeclared wife somewhere.

On the other hand, there were spies working within the intelligence services. People who led a double life for years without being discovered. The most famous British ones, the Cambridge spies, were recruited before there was any kind of vetting. They just recruited each other. But there had been others much more recently, in Britain as well as in America.

She looked down again at the CV on her desk. She'd better talk to Liz about Mr Berger.

* * *

Liz was on the phone but she waved Peggy into her office and, while she waited, she stood by the window, looking down. The sun was out, and the Thames looked blue and sparkling and much cleaner than it really was—though she'd read that fish were now coming up the river as far as Westminster. Perhaps MPs, she thought, smiling to herself, would soon be fishing from the terrace of the House of Commons.

Liz put the phone down. 'What's amusing you?'

she asked. 'Don't say there's some good news for a change.'

'I wondered what you'd make of this.' Peggy put the sheet of paper on the desk and sat down opposite her.

'Mitchell Berger,' Liz said aloud in surprise. 'Don't tell me he didn't go to college either?'

'No, everything checks out so far. He was in the military, he did some contract work for the State Department, and he's worked for a bunch of NGOs. He was even a journalist—I found a couple of articles by him in the *New York Times Sunday Magazine*.'

'So what's the problem?'

'It's where he was—and when. I've highlighted the dates and places on his CV.'

Liz looked carefully at the document. 'El Salvador and Nicaragua in the seventies; Lebanon . . . that was when the Marines got blown up there, wasn't it? Haiti. What was going on there then?

'A coup.'

Liz nodded. 'Then the Dominican Republic. That must have been a few months before Reagan sent troops in. Then Kosovo in the nineties, and Afghanistan after nine-eleven. And now Athens?' She looked up at Peggy with a hint of a smile. 'Bit of a soft option after all that. He must have got tired of hot spots. But I see what you mean.'

'It's as if he's always wanted to be where the action is. A cynic might say he had a death wish.'

'Or else that he was paid to go there.' Liz raised her eyes from the CV and looked at Peggy. 'I know what you're thinking. This is either the résumé of a retired CIA officer or someone who's gone to

174

almost inconceivable lengths to pretend he's one. I know which option my money's on.'

'Do you think Blakey knows?'

'He didn't say anything to me, but you'd think he'd have spotted it when he appointed the chap. Blakey is ex-Six, after all.'

'What I was wondering is whether he appointed him *because* of it. Does that mean there's something going on in UCSO that we don't know about? And do you think Geoffrey Fane knows?'

Liz sighed deeply. 'He didn't mention it. Which, with Fane, doesn't mean he doesn't know.'

'Do you want me to do anything?'

Liz put her head in her hands. 'No. I'll have to go and talk to Geoffrey. And I was hoping not to have to see him for a while . . . fat chance of that now!'

30

It was eleven o'clock and Technical Ted and his colleague, Sammy de Silva, were strolling down the street where Boatman's uncle had his hardware shop. Ted, the Service's electronic wizard, had abandoned his favourite working clothes (biker boots and leather jacket), had removed his gold earring, and had tied back his long black dyed hair in a pony tail. He was dressed now, as was Sammy, in unremarkable shirt and jeans. Carrying their leather bags in their hands, they might have been tradesmen of any kind.

They stopped outside a café and seemed to be discussing whether they should go in. It was a café run by a Muslim family, which during the day was frequented by all and sundry from the flats, shops and offices along the street. In the evening, though, when the offices were closed, rather like Tahira's shop its customers were mainly Asian youths.

Ted and Sammy went in and sat down at a table by the window, putting their bags on the floor beside them. They ordered coffee, which they drank slowly. By the time they paid the bill and left the café, any conversation that took place at that particular table could have been heard in the Odeon cinema some distance away, which now served as MI5's Birmingham office. But until it got to 6 p.m. no one was listening.

*　　　*　　　*

The familiar voice shattered the silence like an explosion. In the back of the van, freshly resprayed and with new number plates, Dave Armstrong almost jumped out of his plastic chair.

'So how are you, brother?' Boatman's words boomed over the speaker in the van. Dave watched Sammy turn down the volume on the amplifier control. Next to Dave, perched on the edge of another plastic chair, sat Kanaan Shah, looking excited.

'I'm well,' said another voice. This must be Malik, Boatman's friend from the mosque. Boatman had arranged to meet him at the café after work. Under direction from Shah, Boatman had arrived at the café early, when it was still quiet, and had sat down at the table in the window. He probably thought it had been chosen because it was visible from the street. He didn't know that their conversation was being overheard.

The van was parked in a cul-de-sac less than five hundred yards from the café. In addition, one pair of A4 officers sat in a parked car a short distance from the café; another pair, an Asian couple, were in the café itself, sitting at a table near Boatman and Malik. Dave had an uneasy feeling about Malik, particularly since he'd heard that it was he and a pal who'd attacked Liz. He didn't think it was likely that there would be any trouble that evening, but he had laid plans to create a diversion, just in case.

'And how is my married friend?'

It took Dave a moment to realise that Malik was referring to Boatman himself.

Boatman said, 'It's going very well.' He hesitated. 'She is being very devout.'

'Ha,' said Malik with a throaty laugh. His voice was deep, with a Birmingham accent. 'That's not how a new wife's meant to behave—with her mind always on Allah and never on you. She's a very pretty girl, Salim. I hope you are making the most of it.'

Boatman didn't respond. Knowing him, Dave thought he was probably uncomfortable with the sexual overtones of Malik's banter. But Malik didn't seem to notice as he shifted the conversation on to football. He was a keen Aston Villa fan and spent several minutes discussing their manager and whether he would survive another season, and bemoaning the unwillingness of the owner to invest on the same scale as the moguls of the Premier League. There was an Asian boy in the youth team, but Malik didn't rate his chances of graduating to the first eleven. 'Too slow,' he said dismissively.

'You'll miss the football, won't you?' said Boatman.

'Yeah,' said Malik casually, and Dave could visualise his shrug.

Then Boatman asked, 'Are you ready for your trip?'

Beside him, Dave saw Kanaan nod intently, happy the conversation was getting down to business. Too soon, thought Dave, worried that the sudden shift of subject was too clumsy. Boatman had no subtlety and that put him at risk.

A waiter must have arrived at the table, for Malik said, 'Orange squash,' and Boatman asked for apple juice. There was a pause, then Boatman asked, 'How soon will it be then?'

Dave waited tensely for the reply; a date would help Pakistani liaison keep tabs on the group from the mosque when it arrived. But Malik only said vaguely, 'It won't be long now.'

Next to Dave, Kanaan sighed with disappointment. Then Boatman pressed on. 'Will you go before the football starts?'

Dave gritted his teeth.

'I'll go when they tell me to.' Malik's voice had lost some of its nonchalance. Leave it now, thought Dave, frustrated that he couldn't warn Boatman off.

'Of course, but do you know where you're going?'

Silence, an ominous sign. Finally Malik said, 'Salim, you know where I am going, so why do you ask?'

Fortunately Boatman didn't hesitate. 'I suppose it's because I'm jealous that you're going now, and I'm not.'

'You will have your own chance in time. Remember—this is not about either of us, OK? We are nothing. This is just our temporary life, after all. If you were never to see me again in this world, it wouldn't matter. Never forget that. Nothing else matters—not your friends, not your family. Not even your new bride.'

'You said you were briefed in London?'

'I was. It was very strange. To have a Westerner teaching you how to conduct *jihad*—it's like having a Jew telling you how to attack Israel.'

'Was the Westerner a Muslim?'

'Of course. Our faith is spreading around the world, you know. For you and me it is natural to think all white people are Infidels, but more and more of them are seeing the true path to Allah. They have the advantage of access to places and people you and I could not approach without people becoming suspicious.'

'That won't help you in Pakistan,' said Boatman.

Go easy, thought Dave.

But Malik replied conversationally, 'No, it won't. But from what we have been told, we won't be in Pakistan that long.'

'Really? Will you be back here for the New Year?'

'Who said I will be back?' There was a long pause before Malik continued, 'Our enemies are everywhere. They offer targets everywhere. Just look at what is going on.'

'Where?'

Malik sighed impatiently. 'Must I spell everything out for you, my friend? The brothers have dispersed across the world. The Middle East, North Africa—these are areas where we

179

can regroup while the Americans and the British remain fixated on Afghanistan. Eventually we will be acting at will in places where the Infidels still think they're safe.'

'You'd think they would have learned that when the Twin Towers came down.'

'They've learned nothing. The Towers will prove to be just the tip of the iceberg.'

'So would you be sent to America?'

Malik laughed. 'Not likely! I would stick out there like a sore thumb. There are plenty of more suitable volunteers—most of them white.'

'Then where will you go to after Pakistan?'

Dave groaned. Boatman was starting to sound like an interrogator. And sure enough, Malik seemed to sense this too, for he said sharply, 'Why are you asking me so many questions, Salim? You know it is forbidden to discuss orders from our leaders.'

'I'm sorry; it's just that we are friends, and I am concerned about you.'

There was the sound of a glass being put down sharply on a table top. 'I'd like to think that's why you are grilling me. I would hate to think there could be any other explanation. Anyway, I have to go.'

'Will I see you before you depart? It would mean a lot to me.'

Malik said icily, 'The cause is what matters, Salim. I have said that already. May we meet when Allah intends. Goodbye.'

The noise of a chair scraping back over the floor came through the amplifier, then there was silence. The technician looked at Dave, who nodded, and the man reached over and switched off the speaker.

A voice from the A4 car in the street reported Malik leaving the café and turning left. Should they follow?

'No,' said Dave. 'Let him go.' He didn't want anything else to happen that might spook Malik.

'Stand down, all teams,' came the instruction from Larry Lincoln in the control room.

Kanaan turned to Dave, beaming. 'Our man did very well.'

'Do you think so?'

Kanaan looked puzzled. 'Don't you? He's confirmed what we suspected—that they're being trained in Pakistan, but sent elsewhere. That's important.'

'Yes, but it could be Timbuktu for all we know.' Dave saw the crestfallen look on Kanaan's face and tried to reassure him. 'You're right, though—we know now he won't be coming back. That's a start anyway.'

'If Boatman can meet up with Malik again before he goes, perhaps he can find out more.'

'No,' said Dave quickly. 'Not a good idea. Please don't encourage him.' And though Kanaan looked puzzled, Dave didn't explain. He was thinking solely of Boatman now, wondering if he'd blown his cover. Malik's hasty departure had alarmed Dave. It was clear to him that Malik was a good deal cleverer than their agent.

31

Geoffrey Fane stalked into his office on the fifth floor of Vauxhall Cross. The room was flooded with light, shining in through the two large windows overlooking the Thames. He walked across and stared out at the little tourist boat just turning to go back towards Westminster, having completed its tour up river. He knew the boat's crew would be drawing the passengers' attention to the building, reminding them how it had featured in a James Bond film and giving them some garbled account of what went on inside. He himself wasn't at all convinced that they should ever have moved into such an exotic-looking place. Its outlandish appearance just invited people to gawp, and made it more of a target too. Admittedly the previous office block, Century House, where he'd worked when he first joined, was a dreadful hole, with masonry falling off the front and an interior like a squalid tenement. No one would ever have wanted to take tourists to see that or put it in a film. Good thing too.

Fane was feeling thoroughly out of sorts. He'd just been to a meeting in 'C"s office upstairs, to discuss the launch of the forthcoming *History of MI6*. Geoffrey didn't agree with that scheme at all—what was the point of it? he'd asked. There were other ways they could have celebrated the centenary. A Secret Intelligence Service should be secret. But he'd been unable to prevent it, especially when Five had announced that they were doing one, and the defeat had annoyed him greatly.

At least he'd managed to ensure the book stopped at 1949. Over at Five they'd gone almost up to the present day and then found themselves criticised because the last chapters were too thin. What else did people expect?

Perhaps it was time to retire, he thought, before he started to get the reputation of being old-fashioned and dyed in the wool. But retire to what? One of his troubles was that there was no woman in his life. Since Adele had gone off with her Frenchman, various short affairs had come to nothing. The women had all bored him; intellectually negligible, with nothing at all interesting to say. He still lived by himself in the flat in Fulham he'd bought after the divorce, since Adele had got away with—as he saw it—their house in Kensington. Not that she needed it (her new husband was as rich as Croesus), yet now she was pressing Geoffrey to sell the small country house that had been in his family for generations. It wasn't that he went there very often now, and there was no prospect of grandchildren to enjoy it with. But it was his, damn it, not Adele's.

His thoughts were interrupted by the buzzing of the phone on his desk. He picked it up. 'Yes, Daisy?' he said. A new girl, rather sweet if a little slow. Still, he'd get her up to speed soon enough. He prided himself on having a deft hand with his PAs, though it was annoying that they never seemed to stay with him very long.

'Liz Carlyle rang, Geoffrey, while you were upstairs.'

'Oh?' Fane said, a little tetchily, cross that Daisy hadn't told him straight away.

'Yes. She wondered if she could come across.

183

Preferably today, she said.'

'Hmm,' said Fane. He would have liked to tell Daisy to ask Elizabeth Carlyle to come over right away, but that wouldn't do. Though he would like to see her, he couldn't conquer a need to demonstrate what a *very* busy man he was; so busy that he might, just might, be able to squeeze her in between more pressing appointments. He said, 'Tell her I can probably fit her in at the end of the day. Let's say half-past five.' Then another thought came into his head. Perhaps he could persuade her to stay for a drink after their meeting.

Because the truth was that Elizabeth Carlyle was the one woman he'd met since Adele went who really aroused his interest. He found her attractive, both physically and intellectually. Her slim figure, brown hair and calm but watchful grey-green eyes fascinated him. She was a woman of real intelligence and he wanted to know what she was thinking about—other than the problem of the moment, which was all they ever found themselves discussing.

But now she'd got herself involved with that DGSE chap, Seurat. What was it with the French? First Adele and now Elizabeth. Anyway, he thought spitefully, he'd embarrassed them both that afternoon in the Athenaeum, telling neither of them that he was inviting the other. He toyed with the top of his pen as he thought of that awkward meeting, and of how Elizabeth's expression had stayed rigidly business-like while Martin Seurat blithely chatted on, all Gallic charm, assuming Fane did not know they were seeing each other. But Geoffrey Fane was always in the know. He prided himself on that.

By five-thirty the sun was in the west and glancing off the windows. Fane heard Reception ring Daisy to say that Miss Carlyle was in the waiting room. He got up from his desk and pulled a Venetian blind partway down.

'Liz is here,' said Daisy a few minutes later, poking her head round the door.

'Come in, Elizabeth,' he called out, frowning slightly to himself at Daisy's informality. Liz walked in, looking cool in black trousers and a satin blouse. Was she getting slimmer? he wondered, admiring her figure.

'Can we offer you some tea? Or something stronger perhaps, as the sun is almost over the yardarm?'

'No, thanks,' she said. Turning to Daisy, she added, 'I'd just like a glass of water, please.'

With a flicker of a smile and a nod he dismissed Daisy, and watched her blonde curls bouncing as she retreated from the room.

'Sit down, Eliz . . . Liz. What brings you over here on this lovely evening?'

'Sorry it's such short notice, Geoffrey, but it's rather important.'

'Ah, well, spill the beans,' he said, showing by his smile that he was not taking her too seriously.

Liz remained standing and looked straight at him without a trace of a smile. She said, 'We've come across something that makes us think Langley has an agent working in the UCSO Athens office.'

Fane was so surprised he said nothing. His

185

thoughts were racing: if this were true why hadn't Blakey told him? Or did Blakey himself not know? And how had Elizabeth found this out?

His voice remained unruffled. 'Sit down, my dear Elizabeth, and tell me what makes you think that.'

'It's perfectly obvious,' she said sharply, not sitting down. By now Fane was behind his desk.

'What is? Do tell.'

Liz fished in her bag and plonked Mitchell Berger's CV down on the desk. She stood back and waited while he scanned it.

'I knew nothing of this,' he said when he'd finished reading. 'All I know about the man is that Blakey vouched for him. In unequivocal terms.'

'Blakey must have known he was CIA.'

'I'm not sure he did . . . What's obvious to expert eyes is sometimes muzzy to the rest of us.'

'Don't patronise me, Geoffrey. Blakey's eyes *are* expert.'

'*Were* would be a better word. He's been out of the Service for ages now.'

'Five years,' she said through tight lips.

Fane shrugged. 'That's two decades in intelligence terms, as we both know. And between you and me, though David was a perfectly competent officer, he was not perhaps the sharpest knife in the box.'

'That's not how you described him before.'

'Loyalty is our business's first line of defence. You don't need me to tell you that.' Fane's lips curled in a slight smile.

'I don't buy it,' she said with an angry shake of her head.

'I'm not selling anything, Elizabeth,' he said

186

coldly. Who the hell did she think she was, acting as if he were on trial?

Nevertheless, he was put out when she shook her head again, unpacified. 'Blakey must have known . . . and you must have known as well. What I can't understand is why you didn't tell me.' She looked at him with open exasperation. 'You keep doing this, Geoffrey—you keep holding back information. I don't see how we can work together if you won't be straight with me.'

He thought how magnificent she looked when she was angry. Normally he wouldn't have been at all bothered to find that she suspected him of not telling her everything. Normally, he had to admit, she would have been right. But she was accusing him of holding back on her when for once he actually wasn't. He hadn't had the faintest inkling that Berger was a CIA man.

Why should he have thought it? Blakey had assured him that Berger was OK—and if Blakey turned out to have been economical with the truth, Fane would have his guts for garters. If it were true, it meant the Agency knew that the woman who'd been murdered had been put in by his Athens Station. That was embarrassing to say the least. Particularly as he suspected that Bruno Mackay had not conducted that operation very cleverly. Damn!

'Elizabeth, please hear me out. I give you my word that I hadn't the faintest idea until three minutes ago that this man Berger was anything but what I was told—a chap with a lot of international experience who was doing a fine job running a charity office in Greece, but whose ships had started disappearing.'

187

Liz did not reply, and Fane waited as the silence between them expressed her doubt as loudly as words would have done. He was frustrated by her refusal to believe him, but couldn't bring himself to reiterate his assurance. It was too undignified. Instead he said, 'Look, I see I can't persuade you now. But let me talk to the Agency. I'll get Bokus over from the embassy. You know him?'

She nodded, still looking sceptical.

'He's not going to deny it if this chap is one of theirs. Langley never actually lies to us overtly— just by omission. A point-blank question will get us the answer we need, one way or the other. Will that do?'

Liz pondered this as Fane watched her, wondering when she might decide to relax with him, when she might realise he wanted to help her if only she would let him. He found it galling to have his offers so consistently refused, especially by someone he would happily admit to admiring.

At last she said, 'All right. See what your friend Bokus has to say. But do it soon, please.'

Fane sighed as Liz made to leave. 'I haven't seen Andy Bokus for a while. I was hoping to keep it that way.'

An enigmatic smile appeared on Liz's face. 'That's funny. I was saying something just like that to Peggy Kinsolving earlier today.'

32

As it turned out, Fane decided to call on Andy Bokus at his office in the American Embassy, rather than summoning him to Vauxhall Cross as protocol would dictate. He thought he might get more out of Bokus on his own ground.

It was something of a sacrifice, though, for Fane hated the sight of Grosvenor Square, littered as it now was with concrete blocks, huge flower pots and metal barriers. He was in a bad temper when he got out of his taxi on the opposite side of the square into a steady drizzle. 'Can't get no nearer, guv,' the taxi driver had just announced.

Fane paid him off, unfurled his umbrella and strode round the barriers to the police post outside the embassy. He waved his Foreign Office pass and glowered as he waited for clearance to come through from inside. Thank goodness the Americans were moving south of the river, to a brand-new compound where they could be isolated and have no neighbours to annoy. The Mayfair residents would be delighted to see them go.

He thought about Bokus—a man with whom he had nothing at all in common. Bokus presented himself as the typical corn-fed Midwesterner; a man whose idea of a foreign country was New York City. Once when Fane had taken him for lunch at the Travellers, Bokus had asked for a can of Budweiser—Fane still smiled to himself at the memory of the waiter's expression. But Fane had come to suspect that this unsophisticated, not to say boorish, exterior was carefully cultivated.

Bokus disliked and distrusted the Brits, so he had adopted a persona designed to discomfit them. But Fane knew what he was up to; Bokus was no fool. In fact, Fane was certain that beneath that crude exterior lay a razor-sharp mind. Which made him simultaneously more interesting and more difficult to deal with.

'What's this all about, Geoffrey?' Bokus asked bluntly.

'We've got a rather interesting situation on our hands,' Fane replied languidly, shooting his cuffs.

'Well, take a seat and tell me about it.'

Fane sat down. Crossing one long leg casually over the other, he proceeded to outline the problems UCSO had been having with their shipments. As he talked, he decided that there would be no harm in mentioning the young British-Pakistani, Amir Khan, who had been picked up by the French.

Bokus nodded. 'Yeah, we heard from the French about that kid,' he said indifferently.

Fane raised his eyebrows but said nothing. He wondered for a moment why Bokus hadn't been more interested in Amir Khan. Why hadn't he enquired what the British knew about the lad, if he'd heard about him from the French? Were the Americans doing something with the French that Fane didn't know about? Was Elizabeth Carlyle right in thinking that the CIA had something going on in UCSO? But then he decided that Bokus' lack of interest was both genuine and utterly predictable—if something directly affected American interests you always had his full attention. If a US angle were less obvious, he'd play it cool.

190

Fane continued: 'We thought it best to take a look at all the UCSO employees, since one of them would be the most likely source of any tip-off to the pirates about shipments coming past the Horn. It seemed a bit hard to believe at first,' he added, 'but on the other hand, it seemed too much of a coincidence that UCSO was so repeatedly the victim of these attacks.' There were other reasons to think there was a traitor inside UCSO—including, of course, the wretched girl Maria's murder—but Fane saw no need to lay these on the table. Instead he took out a typed piece of paper and, leaning over, put it on the desktop under Bokus' eyes.

'What's this?' the American demanded.

'It's the CV of the head of the UCSO office in Athens. Or do you chaps say "résumé"? He's an American, as you see, and jolly interesting, I think you'll agree.'

Bokus bent his head over the desk and his bald pate shone in the light. After thirty seconds' silent inspection of the paper, his head lifted and Fane found Bokus' brown eyes fixed on him. The American said neutrally, 'What do you want me to say, Geoffrey?'

Fane decided to ignore this. 'The thing is, Andy, this chap is no doubt perfectly sound. Blakey, his boss in London, swears by him.'

Bokus interjected, 'Why does that name ring a bell?'

'Possibly for the same reason Berger's name rings bells for me.' Fane shrugged, unwilling to be deflected, and stared back at Bokus.

'Yeah, yeah,' Bokus said. 'I'll show you mine if you show me yours—is that it?' He laughed unexpectedly, a full-throated guffaw that Fane found intensely annoying. He liked it when Bokus stayed close to stereotype—the serious heavy-set ex-football player who thought the Limeys were all too arch and highfalutin' for words.

'You go first,' said Fane dryly.

Bokus thought about this for a moment then got up from his chair, which creaked when relieved of his weight. He went over to the wall and stood staring at a framed photograph of an American football team. Though Fane swung round in his chair, his only view was of Bokus' back.

'Mitchell Berger joined a couple of years before I did.' Bokus' voice sounded curiously disembodied, like the narrator's in a film. 'He was an operative in the field . . . kind of a famous one even when I started out. But he never had any interest in climbing the ladder.' Bokus turned back towards the room and lifted his right hand, in a gesture designed to encompass his surroundings, his office, his status, his rise through the ranks . . . everything apparently that Mitchell Berger had not had time for.

Bokus looked straight at Fane. 'I never met the guy. Heard he'd left the Agency a few years ago. Who knows?' He shrugged. 'Sometimes a fella wants a quiet life, and the way I heard it, Berger finally realised that one day his luck could run out. That's not surprising—most sane people wouldn't have taken half the postings he'd asked for. So I wouldn't think there was any other agenda going on—he just took the buy-out and opted for a safer berth. Certainly I don't know of any secret Langley agenda; like I said, the guy retired.'

This was as far as Bokus would go, Fane sensed.

But it was enough—Berger was ex-Agency, all right, but not working on Langley's orders. Fane believed Bokus about that; he had responded too quickly to have made up the story.

'Your turn,' said Bokus, without amusement. He clearly didn't like having to offer up information.

'In a minute,' said Fane. 'First, I'd like to ask you to find out if Mr Berger is active again.'

'I just told you, he retired.'

'You know as well as I do, one's always on call. We may not be priests, Andy, but we work under the same terms and conditions. I'd like to know if Berger's been reactivated.'

Bokus thought about this for a moment, then said, 'OK, I'll check it out. Now tell me why you want to know.'

And so Fane recounted the entire chain of events, from the first hijack to the phone call from Blakey and finally, reluctantly, Maria's Galanos' murder—there was no point in omitting it since it would be one of the first things Bokus would hear about.

When he'd finished the Agency man asked, 'What do you think's going on?'

'Hard to tell. I would think, as I said, that someone inside UCSO is tipping off the hijackers. Why, I don't know—it seems a pretty roundabout way to make money when other pickings off the Horn are so rich.'

'What are you going to do about it?' Bokus' voice had lost its detachment, and Fane sensed the American had something specific in mind. That was the last thing Fane wanted, so he said quickly, 'We've got some leads in Athens we're following up and Five are on to the UK end, trying to find out how Amir Khan got out there.'

'Yes, but what about Somalia? Don't you want to know what's happening there?'

'Presumably your asking means you do,' said Fane.

His subtlety was lost on the CIA Head of Station. 'Damn' tootin' I do,' he said vigorously. 'Yemen and Somalia are top of our list for Al Qaeda movements right now.'

'More than Afghanistan or Iraq?'

'I didn't say that. But in those places we know the bastards are there, and we can take the fight to them. We don't want them taking root all over the place or it defeats the purpose of our military campaigns.'

Precisely, thought Fane, who had never been gung-ho about either the Iraq or Afghan adventures. To him, Al Qaeda was a global movement that used criminal means; it was best tackled through intelligence and, when necessary, specifically applied force, not with the blunderbuss of NATO's military might—unless the US and its allies were going to be happy to fight a 'war against terror' on fifty fronts. But Bokus obviously didn't agree, so Fane merely nodded.

The American added enthusiastically, 'If we can find the Somalian end we could go in big-time.'

Fane had visions of F16s and Huey helicopters swarming over the Somalian coast, firing indiscriminately at targets that would turn out to be non-existent or entirely innocent. He suppressed a shudder, and the temptation to say 'Down, boy'. He extemporised quickly, 'That's exactly what we had in mind. We're planning to place our people on the next UCSO ship leaving Athens. We've

194

set it up so it looks like a particularly attractive shipment; if things run to form, they'll try to hijack it.'

'When does it sail?'

'Two weeks' time,' said Fane, thinking by then he could arrange to put someone on board. Anything to keep the Yanks from barging in; if Bokus had his way they'd never find out the truth. It would be lost in American overkill.

'All right, but we want in on this. You haven't got the firepower there to handle it yourself.'

Firepower was the last thing Fane was thinking about at this stage. But he replied, 'When the time comes, Andy, you will be kept fully informed. I'm sure there'll be a role for Langley in all of this. But let's see it play out first. No point scaring them off by showing our hand too early.'

And he stared at Bokus until the other man nodded his agreement. Fane did not find his response reassuring, but it would have to do for the moment.

33

The bar of the Venus de Milo was half-empty. A few couples sat at tables munching olives, pickled octopus and *taramasalata* with thin slices of pitta bread, to accompany their drinks. At the bar just one stool was occupied, and that by the broad rear of Hal Stimkin. Berger had been woken that morning by Stimkin summoning him to an urgent lunchtime meeting. Once again Berger had woven a circuitous path by foot from his office to the hotel, through half-deserted midday Athens, stopping periodically to peer into shop windows to check behind him for surveillance.

'Join me?' asked Stimkin, nodding at his glass of beer as the barman came up.

Berger shook his head. In this heat even a little alcohol made him drowsy for the rest of the day. 'A tall glass of lime and soda, please. Lots of ice.'

'If you're hungry the food's good here,' said Stimkin. 'My shout.'

You mean the Agency's shout, thought Berger, as he shook his head again.

'You're either a cheap date, pal, or a man in a hurry.'

'I've got a lot on. What did you want to see me about?'

Stimkin bided his time, taking a long pull on his beer. 'Well, it seems the situation at your office may be of interest to Langley after all.'

'Oh,yeah? Why the change of heart?'

'Hard to say. I get the feeling someone's been talking to them.'

'Like who?'

'Somebody on the Brits' side of things.'

'MI6?'

'It's gotta be, don't you think? They were already involved, and maybe after this girl got murdered they figured they should let us know what the score is.'

'What *is* the score then?' asked Berger. He couldn't see why Six would approach CIA Headquarters at Langley about a problem at the UCSO office in Athens. There didn't seem to be anything in particular about the hijacking of the UCSO ships or even the murder of Maria to make them go running to Langley. It wasn't that he'd expect them to hide stuff from the Americans—in these post-9/11 days there was a constant trans-Atlantic flow of intelligence. On the other hand, he couldn't imagine Six volunteering information that had nothing to do with the CIA. UCSO wasn't American-based—it didn't even have an office there.

'I was hoping you'd tell me. Any news about the girl?'

'The Greek police have interviewed me three times, and they're still all over the office and Maria's flat, but they're not giving anything away.' Stimkin raised an eyebrow, but Berger shook his head. 'It's probably because they don't have anything to give away. They seem mystified. Did Langley learn anything from the Brits—anything new?'

'I think the short answer's no. I was just told to make contact with you again—and from now on to do it regularly. They want to know what develops.'

Berger nodded, but he was still puzzled. 'What I can't understand is why Six went to talk to Langley.'

'They wanted something—it was standard *quid pro quo.*'

'What did they want?'

'Confirmation that there was an Agency operative in UCSO—ex-operative actually.'

'*Which* operative?' The barman looked over, and Berger realised he'd raised his voice.

Stimkin lifted his glass and turned to Berger with a smile as phoney as a $3 bill. 'Here's looking at *you*, kid.'

*   *   *

Berger's shirt was soaked with sweat by the time he got back to the UCSO office, but he felt as if he'd been hung out to dry. Now he was supposed to keep Stimkin and the Agency 'posted', when they still hadn't provided the protection he was looking for after Maria Galanos' murder. And if MI6 knew he was ex-Agency, who else did? There was no reason to suppose the Brits would have leaked anything, but he hated free-floating information; you never knew where it would end up. He'd survived a long career under cover in various hell holes and war zones, but he'd always been extremely careful who he trusted with information. The thought that stuff about him was out there, and he had no control of it, made him very uneasy. If it ended up in the wrong hands his life could be in danger.

All right, Berger told himself, so I haven't got the help I wanted. That's no reason to sit here like a patsy, waiting to become the next victim. He would have to take action himself. He needed to find Maria's killer—in his mind there was no doubt the murderer was the same person who'd been leaking information to the pirates. He didn't believe there was a larger conspiracy at work—the pirates in Somalia only needed a single person to tell them which ships to target; there was no reason to involve anyone else; that would just increase the risk of exposure. No, he was sure he was looking for one individual.

He told his secretary to hold all calls then took some blank pieces of paper and went to work.

Two hours later he looked down in frustration at several pages of notes. The task had seemed straightforward enough—he'd begun with the people in the office who had greatest ease of access to the cargo manifests. First was his own secretary, Elena, whom he relied on and trusted completely. She knew everything that went on in the office and could see any papers she chose. But he felt sure she was completely loyal, and there was also the simple fact—he felt guilty even thinking it—that she was very stupid.

Which still might have made her someone's dupe, except that everything about her history suggested she would never have been exposed to anyone with links to a band of North African crooks. She was from a remote part of the upper Peloponnese, and had grown up in near-poverty on a goat farm. When she'd left school, Elena had scraped together enough money to enrol in a correspondence secretarial course and had then taken a bus to Athens to find a job. She lived a simple and pious life, fuelled by her devotion to the Greek Orthodox Church and her duty to her ageing parents, to whom she sent a quarter of her monthly pay check without fail. Berger just couldn't see it.

Other candidates with access to the manifests included Katherine Ball. She was so English that again he found it difficult to imagine her involvement in an African-based conspiracy to rob UCSO, but unlike Elena she was very clever, and seemingly nerveless. They might have had an awkward relationship—she worked for Blakey in London, and when she visited Athens was clearly his emissary—but she never challenged Berger's authority. He liked her; she was quick-witted and amusing, and in any case she had been back in

London when Maria was murdered.

Of the likely candidates, this left Alex Limonides, since as the office accountant it was he who—until the arrival of Maria Galanos—had been responsible for drawing up each shipment's manifest. But the fact that he would be the obvious suspect seemed to make it less likely that he was involved. And he was the greyest of grey men— so utterly correct in his behaviour that it was impossible to imagine him leading a secret life. There was too the air of ineffable sadness about him since the death of his wife, to whom he'd been devoted. All in all, in Berger's assessment, it didn't add up to the remotest likelihood that Limonides was a threat.

There were others on the staff to consider, though none with an easy way to get at the manifests or even to know when shipments were scheduled. Only one of these stood out, the Frenchwoman, Claude Rameau, and Berger had to admit to himself that she figured in his calculations chiefly because he disliked her so much.

She was Parisian, Sorbonne-educated, attractive despite her unfeminine appearance—she stuffed her blonde hair under a beret, and usually wore baggy trousers and men's shirts, though she had been known to dress smartly when meeting potential donors. Claude held strong views— about the perfidy of George W. Bush, the endemic corruption in most aid agencies, the uselessness of the UN, and even about the operations of UCSO itself—and she was prepared to air them to everyone, from the newest recruit to the most august trustee on the charity's board.

Rameau had made it a condition of her

accepting employment with them that she should report only to UCSO's overall head, David Blakey. Berger had wanted to resist this as it made her an anomaly in the Athens office, which was her base, but Blakey was so keen to get her on the staff he had accepted her proviso. This made for a very difficult working relationship with Berger and she had become something of a thorn in his side. *Je m'en fiche*, her rude way of saying she didn't give a fig, characterised Claude's dealings both with him and with the logistical people— Limonides, who had the unenviable task of vetting her expenses, and Elena, whose job it was to make sure that air tickets, appropriate currencies and complex itineraries were all in order for her non-stop travelling. If perhaps too much to expect gratitude from Claude Rameau for these labours on her behalf, it would still have been good to have received something other than her manifest disdain.

He sensed that Rameau's political views were extremely left-wing, or more accurately anarchic, and that conventional views of what constituted a criminal act would not apply in her case. Berger wouldn't put any form of extreme behaviour past her, except perhaps murder. He tried to ignore his strong personal dislike of the woman but had learned to trust his instincts after so many years when they had proved to be life-savers, so he put Rameau at the top of his suspect list. But he did it rather half-heartedly. What after all would induce her to side with people stealing aid intended to improve the lot of the Third World?

Looking with dissatisfaction at his list, Berger decided he needed a break. Elena was out that afternoon at the dentist, so he went to make himself a coffee in the small cubicle kitchen along the corridor. As he waited for the kettle to boil, he went to the fridge to get the milk out. Through the thin stud wall he could hear the two Greek girls next-door, chatting away and laughing together. Suddenly their voices lowered. Berger closed the fridge door silently, the better to listen. His Greek wasn't entirely fluent, but he could follow their conversation easily enough.

'They were leaving the building when my friend saw them,' Anastasia was saying in lowered tones. 'It wasn't his wife he was with.'

Falana giggled briefly, then said soberly, 'It might be nothing. He does business with many clients, I'm sure. This could have been one of them.'

'Ah,' said Anastasia teasingly. 'It's admirable that you are so trusting. But there's a small problem with your idea.'

'What's that?' Falana squeaked.

'They were leaving a hotel. And not the kind with a restaurant or bar. More the type where you rent a room by the hour.'

They were both giggling now, and Berger suddenly reached out and quietly pulled the kettle's plug from the wall—he didn't want its boiling to be audible next- door.

Falana said, 'But how did your friend know it wasn't his wife? They might want privacy—who knows? Maybe his parents live with them.'

Anastasia laughed alone now, scathingly. 'Honestly, Falana, since when were you so naïve? Though I'm sure Mo would be delighted to hear you defend him this way.'

Berger was suddenly furious with himself. He hadn't even included Mo Miandad, the shipping agent, on his list—yet the man was in the office two, sometimes three, times a week.

'No,' said Falana stubbornly, 'it could well be his wife. It's perfectly likely.'

Now Anastasia's laughter was openly scornful. 'Don't be so stupid! Mo's wife is Pakistani, right?'

'So?' said Falana wearily.

'*So . . .*' said Anastasia mockingly '. . . the woman my friend saw him with was European. *She had blonde hair.*'

And Berger plugged the kettle back into the wall, happy now for the girls in the adjoining room to know that he was there.

But he was astonished by what he'd just heard. Years of being paid to know what was going on had prepared him for surprises—people were erratic, unpredictable, and sometimes fantastically secretive, which meant that however close you kept your ear to the ground, however canny a student of human nature you became, there was always room for the discovery that rocked you on your heels.

She had blonde hair. Well, that narrowed things down—zeroed them in, actually. Berger would have been prepared to believe a lot of things about the unpleasant Claude Rameau, but clandestine trysts with Mo Miandad in a flea bag hotel would not have been one of them.

34

To: Liz Carlyle
From: Peggy Kinsolving
Re: The *Aristides*
Ref: TH/CTE-cna342

The *Aristides* is a container ship leased by UCSO from Xenides Shipping. UCSO has an Athens office because Greece remains an important hub of commercial shipping, and it allows easy shipment of aid to either the continent of Africa, or via the Indian Ocean, Asia and the Far East. Though most ships, including the *Aristides*, fly flags of convenience for tax purposes (Liberia and Panama remain most popular), the Greek-owned maritime fleet is the largest in the word, accounting for 16% of global cargo tonnage.

The *Aristides* is a relatively small container ship, with a capacity of 2,500 TFO—TFO stands for Twenty Foot Equivalent Unit, which is the length of each container. A big cargo ship is anything over 7,000 TFOs and the largest can top 15,000. The advantage of the *Aristides*'s comparative smallness is that it does not have to use only those ports with crane facilities—it has its own small crane on board. This allows the vessel flexibility in its choice of harbours, though it most commonly unloads in Mombasa, Kenya, which remains the major distribution point for its African shipments—and Africa in turn is the largest recipient of UCSO aid.

Despite their size, container ships have small crews—as few as 15 or 20 on board. The *Aristides* sails with a larger contingent of about 30, because of the team required to maintain and operate the crane. All passengers and crew live in the accommodation block at the stern of the ship, near the engine room.

On the voyage when the most recent hijack attempt was made, the *Aristides* was sailing with 31 crew members, of whom 25 were seamen. These sailors were recruited by Xenides Shipping, and were a mixture of nationalities. The captain (Erich Steffer, to whom I spoke on the phone) was Belgian, as was his second in command; two other officers were Danes (brothers), one was Italian, and one Greek. The crewmen were from Asia and the Far East: 10 South Koreans, 2 Indonesians, 5 Filipinos, 2 Vietnamese, and 6 Pakistanis.

It is the last category who are interesting. Crew members have to show proof of identity in the form of passports, and they require temporary working papers from the Greek government. They are usually hired by Xenides through a local Athens employment agency which has strong ties to sources of labour— the Philippines, Indonesia, etc. In the past year, however, Xenides has used a new employment agency which is Pakistani-owned, so unsurprisingly more crewmen have started to come from Pakistan.

On this occasion, after the unsuccessful hijacking and a delay of half a day, the *Aristides* continued on down the east coast of Africa to Kenya, where it offloaded its cargo in Mombasa. Its crew were then granted shore leave of two days, but 6 of them did not return when the ship was due to sail. Occasionally crewmen jump ship during a voyage, usually when the ship stops at a port offering temptations—Marseilles and Beirut most famously. Mombasa is not known for its onshore attractions. But despite the Captain's delaying departure by 12 hours, none of the missing men reboarded, and Captain Steffer finally sailed without them.

The missing 6 were the Pakistani contingent. Steffer told me he had already formed suspicions about them because they spoke to each other in English rather than in Urdu. Greek liaison has sent copies of their employment papers and photocopies of their passports. There are many obvious irregularities: one passport gave the date of birth for a very young-looking man as 1960.

It is unlikely that any of the 6 Pakistani crewmen were who they claimed to be. It is highly probable that assumed identities backed up by forged or stolen documents were used to establish the credentials that allowed them to be employed on board the *Aristides*.

The questions that remain are who these people really were/are, why they enlisted on the *Aristides*, why they disappeared and where they are now.

PK

35

Peggy was sitting at her desk, just beginning to think about what she and Tim would have for supper. Around her, a few colleagues were packing up for the day. The phone on her desk rang; she picked up the receiver. As she listened, the blood drained from her face. She ended the call, picked up a sheaf of papers from the desk and walked quickly out of the office.

Liz was putting papers in her security cupboard for the night when Peggy appeared in the doorway. Liz knew immediately from her expression that neither of them would be going home soon. She sat down heavily at the desk and waved Peggy to a chair.

'What's up?'

'It's from the internet café at the mosque. You know we've managed to work out from Boatman's identifications that it's being used by several of Bakri's followers? They're in touch with all sorts of radical Islamic groups, in London and Pakistan. Up to now it's been general extremist chatter. But I've just heard that they're talking about "silencing" someone.'

'Oh, God. Who do they want to silence?' said Liz, putting her head in her hands.

'No names. But it's someone at the New

Springfield Mosque. That's got to be Boatman.'

'Yes, you're right. He's blown. At least, we've got to assume he is. We're going to have to pull him out right away. Where's Kanaan?'

'He's on holiday . . . back in the morning. He was going to see Boatman tomorrow evening.'

'We can't wait. I'll get hold of Dave Armstrong—we need to move on this right away. You'd better brief Lamb Lincoln—tell him it's urgent, top priority. We'll need total A4 coverage. If there's any problem, let me know and I'll ring DG.'

36

Salim had tried to see Malik again, but the other man had proved elusive. He had not been at prayers at the New Springfield Mosque and he hadn't attended the latest session of the imam's study group.

As Salim had left Friday prayers, he'd spotted Malik in front of the mosque, talking to a Yemeni man who had arrived only the month before. Salim had decided to wait on the front steps until Malik was free. But there had been a distraction—some white boys had passed by and shouted obscenities at the robed worshippers, and by the time they'd been driven off by a group of angry Muslims, Malik had disappeared.

Today, Salim left work slightly late, delayed by a lingering customer in his uncle's hardware shop—an Asian man, young and bearded, who'd walked slowly up and down all the aisles. When

Salim had asked if he wanted help, the man had brusquely said no. Then, a minute later, he'd left empty-handed.

Out on the High Street, seeing the bus approach, Salim ran to the stop. The effort made him pant and he realised how tired he was; he worked long hours for his uncle—6.30 to 7 on weekdays; 8 to 6 on Saturdays; only on Sundays did they close a little early. As a single man he hadn't minded; now he was married he found himself watching the clock, eager to get home to Jamila, his bride.

He smiled to himself at the thought of her. Four months ago he had not even seen her face; now its beauty lingered with him like a perfume. She was a good wife as well as a beautiful one; she had learned quickly how to run the household, even though she had only been in England for a few months. She was very bright—not much formal education, but full of a curiosity that Salim found exhilarating. The likes of Abdi Bakri would not approve, but Salim thought she should go to college.

Malik had been right about Jamila's beauty, but he was wrong about many other things—so badly wrong that Salim had no compunction about spying on him, and on the others at the mosque who thought the same way. To Salim, violence was not only futile, it was also wrong—and utterly alien to the true spirit of Islam. He'd been taught this as a little boy, by his parents and by his grandmother, whose brother had been one of Pakistan's most distinguished clerics, revered for his interpretations of the Koran. So how dare these others claim that Allah condoned what they wanted to do? Islam, in Salim's view, would only conquer the world through its beauty and its truth, not through force.

The bus was crowded and he went upstairs, where he managed to find an empty seat halfway down the bus. He sat next to an older white woman with a nose the colour of beetroot; when he smiled at her she shuddered and looked out of the window. Ignoring her, Salim was soon lost in his own thoughts.

He had been trying to see Malik for days because he wanted to find out more—about the strange Westerner in London and about where Malik would be going after Pakistan. And he wanted to find out about the young man in the photograph he'd been shown—the man called Amir Khan. He could tell that K had been particularly interested in him. The face had certainly been familiar, though Salim hadn't known he was called Amir Khan. But he did know the young man wasn't around any more; he was one of those who had just disappeared from the mosque. If he could find out where he'd gone, K and the lady he'd brought up from London with him, his boss, would be pleased.

But Salim hadn't been able to talk to Malik, so he'd decided to approach the one person who would surely know the answer to his questions— Abdi Bakri himself. When the meeting of the study group had broken up the previous day, and before prayers started in the large assembly room of the mosque, Salim had lingered in the small classroom with its cracked plastic chairs and cheap Formica-topped table, until only he and the imam were left in the room.

Bakri was tall and very dark, towering in his long white robes; his big sepia-coloured eyes were staring out from behind simple gold-rimmed spectacles. Salim had heard he was Sudanese, but he had never spoken to the imam alone before, and felt nervous in the presence of this daunting figure. He hoped the cleric would put his nervousness down to his being alone with him, rather than to anything else.

'Yes?' Abdi Bakri's voice was mild.

'Forgive me, but I was wondering if you had ever had a student called Amir Khan,' Salim replied, stuttering slightly.

Abdi Bakri's eyes studied him carefully. Then he said, 'The name is not unfamiliar.'

Salim nodded and tried to smile. 'I was hoping to make contact with him. It turns out he is a cousin of mine.'

Abdi Bakri did not return the smile. 'We are all brothers here, as I have taught you.'

'Of course,' said Salim hastily. 'But I thought . . . it would be polite to say hello.'

The imam shook his head. 'I do not know where he is now. He left the city some time ago.' He paused then said pointedly, 'I would suggest you make no further enquiries.'

Salim felt the strange sepia eyes scrutinising him, and sweat beaded his upper lip. He thanked the imam and left the mosque in a hurry, not waiting for prayers. He was sure now that the imam knew where Amir Khan had gone; sure also that he was not going to pass the information on. But at least Salim could tell K when they met the following evening that, yes, Khan had definitely been a student at the mosque.

His thoughts drifted then to K and the woman he'd brought with him last time they'd met, his boss. Salim had been surprised by the level of security they'd insisted on for meetings and had wondered if it was all done to impress him. But the more he got into his work for K, the more he saw the point of it. For the first time he was beginning to feel anxious, scared even. It wasn't just because of Abdi Bakri's frostiness and the way his pale brown eyes seemed to bore into Salim, looking for his secrets. In the study group the others had never been particularly friendly or welcoming, but the previous day they hadn't spoken to him at all, just turned their backs on him with barely concealed hostility. Yes, he felt scared, and suddenly he thought of Jamila; he didn't want to put her into any danger. He decided he must tell K about all this and look for reassurance. He sat up slightly taller in his seat. He didn't want to stop his work for K and his lady boss. It was worth the danger if it kept innocent people from being killed.

Salim's stop was approaching, and he got up from his seat and edged towards the stairs. The whole bus was packed. People were even standing on the upper deck and on the stairs themselves. He worked his way slowly down, muttering repeated apologies as he trod on toes and elbowed other passengers. At last he reached the steel-ridged platform at the bottom where he found himself wedged between a fat black woman with shopping bags to either side of her, and a businessman in a suit and tie, who was holding a briefcase in one hand while his other gripped the pole on the platform. Salim slid his hand on to the pole awkwardly, just above the man's, and steadied himself as the bus bumped along.

Then they slowed down, and he turned to the

back edge of the platform, ready to get off. But there was still a hundred yards to go, and the bus suddenly accelerated, lurching forward so that Salim had to struggle to keep his balance. He was being pressed from behind by the small crowd of people standing around him on the platform. He gripped the pole more tightly, but the pressure didn't ease, and when he tried to turn, he found his shoulders were wedged tightly against the fat woman and the businessman. Swivelling his head, he caught a glimpse of a man behind him: an Asian, bearded, young as Salim himself, and familiar. Was he from the mosque? Or was he the man Salim had just seen in his uncle's shop? He tried to get a better look, but the pressure on his back was growing more intense and he simply couldn't move.

He turned to the fat woman to ask her to move over, but stopped when a sharp shove in the small of his back made him arch backwards. Then he felt an excruciating stinging sensation in the hand that was gripping the pole. Automatically he let go, and at the same moment felt one of his feet slide on the steel platform. To his astonishment, he realised that he was being swept off the back of the bus.

He hit the street half-standing, landing on one foot as if he had jumped off the bus. But his leg crumpled underneath him and he fell heavily to one side, his elbow cracking against the kerb. And then his head hit the hard asphalt surface of the road.

A dim recollection of an egg being cracked ran through his mind as pain seared through both temples. The breath was knocked out of him as he rolled over the street. He was dimly aware of lights coming towards him. It's a van, he thought vaguely, and managed to lift up one arm, half in protest, half in self-defence, just before he blacked out.

37

It was 5 in the morning when the phone rang but Liz wasn't asleep. She'd done no more than doze all night. She'd got back to her flat at midnight feeling intensely frustrated. Dave Armstrong hadn't been able to raise Boatman on his mobile; he'd finally rung the landline at his house and got his wife, who turned out not to have heard from her husband either and was worried sick. As was Liz.

Now it was Dave again, and Liz heard the urgency in his voice. 'Liz, it's me. I've located Boatman. He's had an accident.'

'How bad?'

'Bad, but not terminal. The hospital thought he'd fractured his skull but the X-ray's come back negative. He's got a broken arm and jaw and another hairline fracture, but he's conscious again, and the doctor says he'll recover fully in time.'

'What happened?'

'He fell off the back of a bus. Literally.'

'Fell?'

'The hospital's choice of words. There were plenty of witnesses—the bus was packed. Apparently, he'd come down the stairs at the back and was standing on the platform, waiting for his stop. Somehow he lost his footing—he was lucky not to get run over.'

'When was this?'

'Yesterday evening on his way home from work. He's been in hospital ever since. Luckily there was a policeman nearby in the street when it happened, and he must have had some doubts about how Boatman came to fall off the bus. He made some inquiries, word got back to DI Fontana, and he rang me. That was an hour ago.'

'Is Boatman safe there?'

'Fontana's had him moved to a private room on the pretext that he needs quiet, and he's put a Special Branch officer in plain clothes, who's pretending to be a relative, inside with him. I don't think we've any worries on that score. It's when he gets out that I'll be concerned.'

'Me too.' Liz was fully awake now. 'Listen, I'm going to drive up. I'll come straight to the hospital. Can you meet me there in two hours or so?'

'That's where I am now. I'll wait here unless something else crops up.'

'What about his wife? We can't leave her out there. She may not be safe.'

'Fontana's gone to pick her up. He's told her to pack a few things in a suitcase but he's leaving the detailed explanations to us. He's told her not to tell anyone else what's happened for the time being.'

'Good. Let's hope that holds the situation for now. Any media interest?'

'Not so far. The hospital press office has been told to play it low-key—just a straightforward accident.'

'OK, Dave. Thanks. I'll talk to Mrs Boatman when I get there but it looks like a full-scale exfiltration job. I'll get Peggy to alert the team to expect a hospital case and a shell-shocked wife.

That'll give them something to think about!'

*   *   *

The ward was in a small two-storey wing, tucked away behind the enormous main block of the hospital. From reception Liz could see Dave standing by the nurse's station, and he came down the corridor to greet her, saying, 'I'm glad you're here.'

'What's happening?'

'Well, Boatman's parents have been and gone. They've just been told that he had an accident. They thought I was a plain-clothes policeman waiting to take a statement, in case the van driver who almost ran him over was going to be charged with dangerous driving. His wife's with him now; Fontana brought her here. She's very upset, but seems a sensible sort of girl and she's not panicking. Fontana told her there was a security issue, to explain why we're looking after her husband, and that someone was coming up from London to explain things further. That's you.'

'OK. I'll talk to her in a moment. What else?'

'His brother wanted to see him.'

There was something odd in Dave's tone. Liz stared at him. 'So?'

'The problem with that is he doesn't have a brother.'

'Christ. Who was he?'

'Don't know. One of the nurses thought the guy was acting oddly. When she asked him a few questions, he got spooked. By the time she called me he'd run off. Sorry, Liz.'

She waved Dave's apology aside. 'It just means

216

we're going to have to move a little sooner than I thought. I'd better see his wife now. Can you round up whoever's in charge of the ward while I do? I'll see them after her.'

*   *   *

What a stunning woman, thought Liz, as Boatman's wife joined her in the ward's small interview room. Jamila was tall, with fine regular features and big eyes, sad and tear-stained at present. Her raven hair was long and straight, held back by a large comb. Liz was surprised to see she was wearing white jeans and a silk shirt, which came down over her hips. She wasn't at all the demure, traditional spouse Liz had been expecting.

Liz introduced herself as Jane Forrester from the Security Service and they sat down side by side on a hard sofa.

'The doctors say your husband will be fine. They expect him to make a complete recovery.'

Jamila nodded and Liz said tentatively, 'I need to talk to you about what happens next.'

The younger woman's eyes widened involuntarily as Liz continued, 'The policeman who brought you here explained there was a security issue, didn't he?'

Jamila nodded, almost mechanically, and it was clear that she was in shock still, hardly able to take in the revelations of the last few hours. 'He said Salim had been helping the ... authorities.' She looked uncertainly at Liz, then her face creased into the hint of a smile. 'Is that you?'

'Yes, it is,' Liz said simply. 'Your husband has been helping us to find out what some very dangerous people may be doing.'

'He didn't fall off that bus, did he?'

'I can't say for sure, but I don't think so. We think there are people who want to harm him. It's possible that they caused his accident tonight.'

'Can you protect him now?' There was the first note of fear in Jamila's voice.

'Yes.' Liz was emphatic. 'But only if we get him out of here. If he stays in Birmingham, there's every chance these people will try again.'

'You mean, he has to go away? But what about me? Can I go with him?'

'Yes. Of course you can.' They could also stay put, for the couple might simply refuse to relocate, but that would be a fatal decision in Liz's view. It was much better for Jamila to think there was no choice.

'When do we have to go?'

'Straight away.'

'You mean, now?' she asked in disbelief.

'Yes. You've brought a bag?'

'The man said to bring the things that mattered most—my jewellery, family photographs, that sort of thing. But I haven't brought much else,' she added plaintively.

'We can buy any clothes you need.' It was best to be matter-of-fact, to deal with the small things and avoid discussing the sheer enormity of what was going to happen to this woman. That would all come later; one of Liz's colleagues was trained to deal with the inevitable emotional crisis that would follow when Jamila realised that her life was about to undergo a complete cataclysm. She would never see her home again; from now on she would have a different place to live, in a different city, and she would even have a different name. But Liz's first priority was to get her out of danger. Discussing anything else would only upset Jamila and make things even more difficult for them both.

'Where are you taking us to?' asked the young woman. Inwardly Liz sighed with relief that at least she'd accepted that she had to leave.

'We need to get you far away right now. There's a place in London we'll take you to, and a private hospital where your husband will stay until he's discharged. Our priority is to make sure you're both safe. And that's not possible for you in Birmingham.'

Jamila nodded, but Liz could see she still hadn't taken it all in. Suddenly she put her face in her hands, and her shoulders shuddered. Liz said gently, 'I know it's hard. Believe me, we wouldn't be doing this if it weren't necessary.'

Jamila took her hands from her eyes and slowly lifted her face. Behind her tears she looked bewildered. Liz put one hand on her shoulder as Jamila wiped the tears from her cheeks and said, 'I am sorry, but you have to understand ... five months ago I was in Pakistan, preparing for my wedding. To a man I had never met, about to go and live in a country I had never even visited. But I agreed to do it because ... because I had no choice. All through my childhood I did well at school, and I was determined to continue my education. But my parents would not allow me to go to university. I wanted to read law,' she added, half-proudly, half-hesitantly, as if Liz would not believe her. 'But it was out of the question if I stayed in Pakistan. So I let my parents arrange my marriage, and it turned out they chose well. Salim is a good man, a thoughtful man. I even had hopes of restarting my education.'

'That is still possible, Jamila.'

The other woman's eyes widened, and for the first time Liz saw hope in her them. 'Really?'

'Absolutely. But first I need to get you both out of here.'

*   *   *

Forty-five minutes later long strips of the yellow plastic tape used to secure crime scenes were being strung across the entrance to Ward 6, where in room 37B Salim lay half-conscious, his wife in a chair beside his hospital bed, and a 'friend' (the armed Special Branch officer) seated close to the door. Once the OK had been given by the hospital administrator, things had moved fast.

But that 'OK' had not been immediately forthcoming; the administrator, a fierce-looking woman called Albright, seemed to have a pre-existing low opinion of the police that she extended towards the Security Service also. Liz had listened patiently as the woman explained all the difficulties inherent in doing what they asked. Then, suddenly running out of patience, Liz snapped that if the hospital administrator didn't co-operate immediately, she would find herself being telephoned by the Home Secretary personally; furthermore, if anything happened to the patient in room 37b, it would be the sole responsibility of Ms Albright. After that, the OK had been forthcoming pretty sharply.

Liz overheard a nurse talking to a prospective visitor on the other side of the tape. 'I'm sorry but the ward's closed temporarily. One of the cleaners has spilled some chemicals, and we need to clean them up thoroughly before we can let anyone in.'

'How long do I have to wait, then?' asked a woman's petulant voice, uninterested in the reason for the delay.

'Won't be long now,' said the nurse briskly. 'No more than half an hour.'

*   *   *

And twenty minutes later Liz watched as a trolley was wheeled out through the rear door of the hospital by two orderlies, with a vigilant Fontana and his Special Branch colleague walking alongside. The ambulance was waiting, with Jamila and Dave Armstrong inside. As Boatman was gently stretchered into the rear of it, Jamila climbed out and ran across to where Liz was standing watching. Her eyes were wide and anxious. She reached out and touched Liz's arm, as though needing the reassurance of something solid in her rapidly shifting world.

'Will I see you again?'

Liz hesitated. Ordinarily, the answer would be no. Jamila and Salim would have a designated team to look after them and help them in their choice of new identities and location. Then a handler would be assigned to them, someone whose full-time responsibility it was to look after people like the pair of them. Liz would not normally be part of this equation.

But as she looked into Jamila's doleful eyes, she realised this young woman was desperately in need of continuity—any kind of continuity. Her

221

life had already been subject to so much upheaval: marriage to a man she barely knew, and a new life in a strange, foreign country, all in the space of not much more than six months; then to have that life stripped from her again, by people she didn't know, with her husband too badly injured to help and advise her . . . It was too much to expect most people to cope with, but Liz sensed an underlying resilience in Jamila and wanted to help her.

'Of course you will,' she said.

38

Martin Seurat finished his solitary supper and carried his coffee through into the comfortable sitting room. He stood by the window, looking out at the plane trees in the square across the street. It was high summer now and in Paris the days were breathlessly hot—hot enough to brown the foliage unseasonably—but now, as evening came on, a cooling breeze had sprung up, gently rustling the dry leaves. He stood watching the diners at the outside tables of Madame Roget's small restaurant and realised with a sudden feeling of surprise that the melancholy that had been his companion in recent years had lifted. He felt light-hearted and hopeful, thinking happily of the weekend he was about to spend with Liz Carlyle.

How his life had changed since they had first met! He'd had no inkling then that the attractive woman who had walked into his office that day barely a year ago, to question him about his former colleague, would have such an impact on it. When he thought of his ex-wife now, it was still with regret for the failure of their marriage, but without any of the lacerating sense of loss and betrayal that had afflicted him for so long. Now, not only could he imagine life without her, he could imagine life with someone else. The more he saw Liz, the more he wanted to be with her.

He remembered their last time together, the weekend when she had taken him to meet her mother at her childhood home in the country. As they'd driven down to Dorset on the Saturday morning, Liz had told him something of her family background. Her father had been the land agent for the Bowerbridge estate, and with his job had come a tied house, the gatehouse of the estate. He had died while Liz was still at school and she and her mother had been allowed to stay on in the house.

Then the estate had been sold and turned into a nursery garden, which her mother managed for the new owners; she had also been able to purchase the freehold of the house. Her mother had hoped for years that Liz would give up what she always called her 'dangerous job' in London, and nagged her constantly to come back home and settle down in the country with some 'nice safe young man'. But a few years ago Susan Carlyle had herself met a nice man, an ex-army officer who now ran a charity: Edward Treglown. Now that she was herself contented and happy, she seemed to have accepted that a safe life in the country was the last thing her daughter wanted.

Martin had been surprised to find himself as nervous as a teenager meeting his girlfriend's parents for the first time. He hadn't known what to expect and his heart had sunk a little as he'd thought of what might lie ahead. He sensed it would certainly be deeply English. The chairs would be covered in chintz; the garden would be ordered, full of flowers and rose bushes—there would be a lot of rose bushes, all neatly pruned. Liz's mother would be a tidy woman with tidy views, reserved and with a lurking suspicion of foreigners, particularly any foreign man attached to her daughter. They would have separate bedrooms, and the food would be heavy and stodgy.

Of course, he'd been quite wrong. Susan Carlyle was immediately welcoming, beaming at Martin and greeting him with a kiss on both cheeks. She was shorter than Liz, with a round pleasant face but without her daughter's striking eyes. There had been none of Liz's reserve about her; indeed there was an endearing warmth and openness instead. They'd found her in the kitchen of the small Georgian gatehouse, setting out a lunch not even a Frenchman could fault—homemade pâté, a tomato and basil salad, both French and English cheese, and freshly baked bread.

Susan's friend Edward had been a surprise too. Liz had explained that, like Martin, he'd been in the military, as a Gurkha officer. So Martin had expected a hearty, opinionated character, with firm views delivered in staccato bursts.

Instead, a tall, slightly rumpled-looking man had appeared, ducking down to avoid hitting his head on the lintel of the kitchen doorway. He was wearing a darned sweater and corduroys, and though his bearing was military, there was nothing remotely staccato about him. If anything he seemed a little shy. Having poured out two stiff

224

gin and tonics, he led Martin out into the garden, leaving Liz and her mother to catch up with the gossip. There, in the garden, through a wicket gate, Martin saw row after row of the dreaded rose bushes, all neatly pruned and bristling with flowers. He pointed at them politely. '*Formidable,*' he said.

'Do you think so?' said Edward. 'Can't say I'm keen on roses myself—and Susan can't stand them. Thankfully, they belong to the nursery garden.'

Martin laughed in relief and the ice was broken; by the time they'd gone in for lunch a bond had developed between them, two ex-soldiers who had seen their share of terrible things. But Edward's stories about his army days were light-hearted—a cache of plum brandy en route to the Falklands that gave his whole regiment a hangover for two days; a travelling circus, composed predominantly of dwarves, that had appeared out of nowhere during a patrol on the Northern Ireland border.

That evening they went to a village near Bowerbridge for a concert of chamber music, held in a primary school assembly hall. They'd sat on metal folding chairs and listened politely as Schubert's Trout Quintet was played with excruciating slowness. At the interval, as they stood up, Edward said firmly, 'I think we've earned a reward for that,' and led them adroitly past the tables offering apple juice, then across the street for more robust refreshment in the pub.

Later, back at Bowerbridge, they'd all sat up talking until after midnight. At one point Edward described two weeks he'd spent on manoeuvres in the Arctic, where he and his men were stalked by a polar bear. 'But, you know, we were never very cold there—thermal blankets work wonders. In fact, the coldest I have ever been was a winter in Kosovo . . .'

'I was in Kosovo', said Martin. And they discovered they had actually overlapped in their visits to that strife-torn country, had even known a few of the same UN monitors based there at the time. Then it turned out that Edward and Susan had recently taken a holiday in the Quercy, not far from Cahors, where until their divorce Martin and his ex-wife had owned a small cottage on the river. By the time they'd all retired to bed, he'd felt as if he were among old friends. He could see Liz was pleased by how easily they had all got on, and how much they'd laughed.

That was what he remembered most about the weekend—the laughter, and then the walk he and Liz had taken along the banks of the River Nadder on Sunday afternoon. She'd shown him her favourite spots, and where she used to sit as a girl to watch her father fish. Neither of them said much, but Martin sensed that Liz was letting him in to her past—and to her most private memories.

For the whole weekend they'd left their professional lives behind them—though there had been one moment when work fleetingly made its presence felt. On Sunday morning they had sat out on the small terrace, and while Liz and her mother read the papers, Edward had talked to Martin about his work for a charity which provided operations to improve the sight of blind people in the Third World. When he mentioned the staff in Mombasa, Liz looked up sharply from the *Sunday Times Magazine*. 'Did you ever have anything to do with a charity called UCSO?' she asked.

Edward shook his head. 'Not professionally.

226

I used to know its Director. Chap called Blakey. His wife was friends with mine, years ago—he was posted in Germany when we were there.'

'You've not kept in touch?'

'I have with his wife, but they're not together any more. Bit of a bad show.'

Susan Carlyle interjected, 'What Edward means is that David Blakey behaved appallingly.'

'Now, now, Susan. Always two sides to that kind of story. Anyway, sun's past the yardarm, at least in France. Who'd like a glass of wine?'

But that had been the sole remotely work-related moment of the weekend, and it was only as Liz and he drove back to London that Martin Seurat had felt his thoughts return to the job. He could sense that happening with Liz too, as they sat stuck in the traffic returning on the M4. Her face assumed a pensive, abstracted air, and he felt a momentary flash of sadness that she had drifted out of the weekend's mood of relaxed intimacy.

Standing now in front of his window, as night came down in a dark blanket over Paris, he remembered how his ex-wife had complained about the same thing. She'd say, 'You're always drifting away from me. Always thinking of something else.' That's how Liz had seemed as they'd returned to London and their respective problems. But Martin couldn't resent her for it; he understood it only too well.

39

The following morning he went straight to the Santé prison. He was focused solely on the interrogation to come and didn't allow any of last night's thoughts and recollections to distract him. A colleague had already questioned Amir Khan but had got nothing out of him. Liz had been slightly more successful on her visit, but hadn't managed to break through to the real story. Martin had listened carefully to her account of the interview, and of Amir's reactions to her line of questioning. He was determined to get something new out of this prisoner and not allow him to spin long and certainly misleading stories about his travels. He had some ideas of how he might do it. He had the advantage that Amir had been incarcerated in a foreign prison for a good many weeks and must by now be feeling both homesick and disorientated.

The traffic in the Boulevard Arago was light on this warm weekday morning and there were few pedestrians—tourists were not much in evidence in the 14th *arrondissement*. Martin turned on to the Rue Messier and showed his ID at the little window in the high, forbidding exterior wall of the prison. Once inside, he was met by a warder, who led him past the exercise yard, into the high-security wing and downstairs to the interview room.

Martin's questions about the condition of the prisoner met with a shrug from the warder. 'He speaks very little. As requested, we have segregated him from the other Muslim prisoners. He can't converse with the French cons when he exercises, since he hasn't any French. He hasn't asked for reading material. He mostly just sits and stares at the wall—or prays.'

'And his health?'

The warder responded, 'This is not a spa, M'sieur.'

Once within the high white walls of the interview room, Martin remained standing until Amir Khan was brought in. He watched as, closely escorted by a warder, the young prisoner shuffled to a chair on one side of the table and sat down heavily, resting his manacled hands on the metal table top. Martin thought he looked older than the scrawny youth he had seen in the photograph. He seemed to have put on several pounds, presumably from lack of exercise and the stodgy prison food, and had let his beard grow, which made his face seem fuller.

As the Frenchman sat down opposite him, Amir Khan slumped forward in his chair and stared down at the table, avoiding his gaze. He looked relaxed but his hands and legs were shaking, gently vibrating the light chain that connected them, setting up a faint metallic tinkling.

'Well, Amir,' Martin began, 'I have good news.' Khan lifted his eyes momentarily to look at him and then dropped them again.

'Do you want to hear it?'

Khan responded with a slight nod.

'It should be possible to arrange your transfer to the United Kingdom. This could happen in a matter of weeks, possibly even sooner, depending on our conversation today. I assume this is acceptable to you—you can of course fight the extradition if you like. A court will appoint a lawyer to act on your behalf if you do. Would you like that?'

There was no response.

'You understand that if you are extradited you may be tried in a British court, and if found guilty, sent to prison there. On the other hand, there may not be enough evidence to convict you, and then you would be released. Where would you go then? Back to your family in Birmingham? If that happened, I would expect the British security authorities to be keeping a very sharp eye on you and your contacts there—and on your family, of course. Perhaps that would not make you very popular in your part of Birmingham. What do you think?'

Still the prisoner did not look up or speak. The only sounds in the room came from the tinkling of his chains and the armed guard's shuffling feet.

'You have been away from Birmingham a long time,' continued Martin. 'Firstly with your trip to Pakistan to visit your relatives and then with all the other exciting journeys that you described in such detail to my British colleague when she visited you. You must miss your family. I understand they have not been to see you. Perhaps they don't approve of your activities.'

Khan moved uneasily in his chair, then slumped forward again and said nothing.

'I don't suppose you care whether your parents approve or not. Who doesn't want to rebel against their parents at your age? And I understand from the British that your father is fiercely traditional, so it wouldn't be surprising if he disapproved of you. But what about Tahira, your sister? What does she think, do you imagine?'

At the mention of his sister's name, Khan looked up and stared at Martin, his eyelids flickering with surprise. Martin pressed on. 'I would have thought you would be worried about her. Though of course she is a woman, and I suppose that means she doesn't matter to you.'

He paused and watched an expression of resentment spreading over Khan's face.

'I've noticed that your group of friends was all male. It's almost as if you don't like women very much . . .' He let the implication hang in the air for a moment, then added with the trace of a sneer, 'Though I gather your sister's nothing special.'

Khan suddenly sat up straight in his chair, exclaiming in protest, 'You know nothing about my sister, or me, or my friends!'

'That's where you're wrong, Amir. I know a great deal about you and your family and your sister and your friends. And as I say, you and your mates don't seem to like women very much.'

'That's not true,' Khan suddenly shouted. 'Ask Malik. He thinks my sister's—'

Then, realising he had lost control, he shut his mouth like a trap.

'What's that? He fancies your sister, does he?'

Khan's face was full of fury, and he tried to stand up. The guard moved quickly towards him but the prisoner was forced back into his chair, yanked by the chain; the prison officer went back to his post beside the door. The silence in the room was broken only by Amir Khan's sniffing as he wept quietly.

Martin let the silence hang for a time and then he said, 'Look, Amir, I think your sister needs you. I think she may be in some danger from these people you call your friends. From what I've heard, they may not be quite such good friends as you think. But there's not much you can do to help her, sitting here in this prison. Why don't you try being a bit more frank? You may be able to do her a lot of good if you talk a bit more truthfully about what happened to you. If you don't, you could be here for a long time—doing no one any good.

'There are lots of ways in which I can help you and your sister—but that means you've got to stop telling lies, and we all know you have been. I know, the British know, and you know. Just think about it—and if you want to talk to me again, tell the warders and I'll come straight away.'

And with that, he stood up and nodded to the guard, who opened the heavy metal door. A warder, standing outside in the passage, came in and led Amir Khan shuffling away.

Martin left the Santé feeling reasonably satisfied. He had certainly shaken up young Amir Khan and was hopeful of hearing from him before too long. He had got one name out of him at least—Malik. He would send his report over to Thames House that afternoon and hope that the name would mean something to Liz and her colleagues.

40

Dave Armstrong poked his head round Liz's office door minutes after she had read the message from Martin. 'Just the man I want to see,' she said. 'I've heard from the French. They've been to see Amir Khan again.'

'Any luck?'

'No breakthrough yet, though there may be a chink of hope. But there was something that's got me thinking. He was needled into saying that one of his group in the mosque has a bit of a thing for his sister, Tahira.'

'Not very pious, that.'

'Hmm. She's a beautiful girl. And it's somehow comforting to know that even an extremist has human feelings.'

'Do you know which one it is?'

'Yes. It's Malik, that guy who attacked me.'

Dave took this in for a moment. 'Is that all they got out of Khan?'

'Yes, for the moment. But it could help us a lot. Depending on Tahira, of course.'

He nodded. 'Yes. I know what you mean.' He thought for a minute. 'A4 have a good sense of her routine now, so I'm sure I could set up another meeting with her pretty easily.'

'Okay,' Liz said without enthusiasm.

'What's the matter?' he asked. 'You said she'd offered to help—and that was before this landed in our lap. If Malik is going to Pakistan, maybe she can chat him up and find out when . . . maybe find out more about this mysterious Westerner in London. This is just the kind of break we need.'

'I suppose it is.' But Liz's voice still lacked enthusiasm. 'It's just that asking Tahira to sidle up to Malik is like asking Daniel to enter the lions' den.'

'That turned out Okay.'

Liz smiled. 'You know what I mean.'

'Of course I do. But we've got to take the risk.'

'Even if it means putting Tahira in harm's way? Look what happened to Boatman.'

'Yes, I know. But from what I've seen of Tahira, I think she's a whole lot brighter than Boatman.' Dave was emphatic. 'There will be many more people in danger than Tahira if we don't do this.'

'Yes. But we're asking a lot of someone who's got no experience in our line of things. It's not as if Tahira's an extremist we've managed to turn. She's just a nice Muslim girl who works in her father's shop, for goodness' sake.'

Dave sat down on the other side of Liz's desk. She looked at him and sighed. She said, 'I know what you're going to say. But it used to be a lot easier: there were people on one side trying to blow things up, and there was us on the other side, trying to prevent them. We didn't use anyone to help us who wasn't part of the fight—and who didn't really understand the danger of helping us. In fact, we made jolly certain that they did understand.

'It's not that simple any more. We have to get help from anyone who offers it—we haven't the luxury of saying, "Leave it to us, you're not a professional so you can't get involved."'

'But Tahira volunteered to help; wants to help. I'm sorry, Liz, you have no choice. You can't say no.'

'I know,' she said. And later Dave's words stayed with her, only partly allaying the anxiety she felt about asking Tahira to put herself in harm's way.

*   *   *

234

Two days later Liz was sitting in the A4 transit van in the car park of a small industrial estate on the outskirts of Birmingham. She had driven up from London through very heavy rain and her eyes felt strained from peering through the spray thrown up by the lorries she'd overtaken on the motorway. Eventually the rain had given way to a sullen drizzle. She'd parked her car two miles away at another small group of factory outlets, and had managed to step in an enormous puddle as she'd run through the downpour to the waiting transfer vehicle that had driven her here. Now she sat with her shoes off, her sodden feet under a folding table. In another corner of the van an A4 officer called Felix sat crouched on a stool, reading the *Daily Mail*.

So far so good—Dave had left another note for Tahira in her father's shop the night before, just at closing time. They knew that this was the day each week when she came here, driven by her cousin Nazir, to buy bulk quantities of supplies from Costco for her father's shop. While she walked the aisles putting her order together, Nazir—not the sharpest knife in the drawer apparently—would cross to the other side of the overpass and visit an amusement arcade, playing pinball for an hour. They were relying on Tahira to have thought up some excuse to delay him there this morning for an extra half hour, while she met Liz in the van.

Liz leaned down and felt her toes; they were still cold, but just dry enough for her to slip her shoes back on. There was a tap on the van's back door and Felix sprang up and opened it. Liz caught a glimpse of Dave Armstrong, then another figure emerged from behind him and with his help climbed up into the van. Felix hopped out and closed the door behind him. He and Dave would watch outside from a waiting car; there were two other A4 cars parked at the front perimeter of the industrial estate, occupants ready to spring into action if needed.

'Sit down, Tahira,' said Liz, pointing to the chair on the other side of the table. 'I hope you didn't get soaked out there.'

'No, it's almost stopped raining.'

'Good. We haven't got much time, so let me tell you why I wanted to see you.' She explained that her French colleagues had talked to Amir in prison and that he was well. It was possible he might be returned to Britain, where he would be remanded in prison while it was decided if he should face charges.

At this, Tahira's face lit up. 'My father wouldn't let me go to France to see Amir,' she said. 'But if he comes back home, I want to visit him. Will I be allowed?'

'Yes, but possibly not for a while. Remember, he's been involved in an attempt to hijack a ship. That's a very serious thing.'

'I know,' Tahira said, and her face grew sombre. 'But it's not just the ship you're worried about, is it?'

'No, as I told you, we're concerned because we think he was sent to Somalia to take part in terrorist activities, after being trained in Pakistan. But what worries us most is that we're pretty sure he was recruited here.'

'At the mosque,' said Tahira bitterly.

'It seems so. And if he was recruited at the mosque, then others might have been recruited there too.'

Tahira said, 'I promised to try and find out more about Abdi Bakri. But I'm afraid I haven't been very successful.'

'Don't worry.'

'I will keep trying.'

'No, please don't.' Liz saw the puzzled look on Tahira's face. She took a deep breath. 'Actually, there's something else I'd rather you did instead.'

41

It was another gloomy day, precociously autumnal in its dankness. In Thames House Liz was writing a report of her meeting with Tahira when she became aware that someone was standing in the doorway of her office. She looked up—and groaned a secret groan. It was Geoffrey Fane. She hoped that at least he would have something interesting to tell her.

He did, though as usual he took his time getting to the point. 'I like this new office of yours,' he began inconsequentially, pointing out of the window. 'I find a river view lifts the spirits on a gloomy day like this. Even on a floor this low down in the building.'

Liz suppressed a sigh, thinking of Fane's eyrie high up in Vauxhall Cross. She said tartly, 'I'm suited for life at this level. I wouldn't want to develop ideas above my station.'

Fane allowed a smile to touch his lips. 'Touché, Elizabeth. But *à nos moutons*. I've been considering this hijacking business of yours. Bruno in Athens has been speaking to our friend Berger and there's another UCSO shipment planned for two weeks' time. Same vessel—the *Aristides*—and to Kenya again. The same route as before, right by the Horn of Africa.'

'I hope they stay a little further from shore this time.'

'That seems to make no difference nowadays. The pirates are becoming bolder all the time. They seem perfectly willing to go miles from shore if they think there's a sitting duck out there. And the whole point about this shipment is that we want them to think it's a fat bird, ripe for the plucking. The ostensible manifest is mouth-watering and its value is in the millions. It's a fake, of course, but it's been drawn up with the utmost security, so no one in the office has any reason to believe it's anything but legit. They may know we suspect a leak—and if this girl Maria was murdered because someone knew we'd put her in there, then they'll know what we suspect—but I'm willing to bet they'll still go for this shipment.'

'You're probably right. So what's this thought of yours?' She'd learned long ago in dealing with Fane that it was always best to stick firmly to the point. Otherwise, he'd lead you round and round, in a bewilderingly indirect dance. And you'd find yourself tied up in knots and agreeing to things that you'd regret later.

For once Fane was equally direct. 'I want to put a man on board. Undercover, of course.'

Liz looked at him with a slight frown. Behind her cool grey gaze her mind was racing. What was Geoffrey Fane up to now? 'And what would he do, your man?'

238

'Find out if anyone on the ship is helping the hijackers.'

'That seems most unlikely. If you're right, they'd already know which ship to attack, and what it's carrying. They don't need anything further from someone on board the *Aristides*.'

'Unless the pirates have people there to help them take control when they try and board.'

Liz thought for a moment. What Fane said made sense—there might well be an advantage to the pirates in having accomplices already on board. Or allies anyway, she thought, thinking of the crewmen who had jumped ship in Mombasa after the last hijacking attempt. And suddenly it occurred to her that this might be the whole point: men on board could certainly assist the hijackers, but more importantly, once on shore, they could stay there and join the pirates or else the forces of Al Qaeda, who might well have recruited them in the first place.

She realised, as she sat gazing blankly at Geoffrey Fane, that she hadn't thought through the full implications of all that Peggy had discovered. She'd been distracted: by the attack on Boatman, and the urgent need to get him and his wife to safety; by the recruitment of Tahira to cultivate Malik. All of this had taken her attention off Peggy's research.

Now, as she thought about it again, everything seemed a lot clearer. Amir Khan had attended the New Springfield Mosque. He had gone from Birmingham to Pakistan; from there he had somehow got to Athens, how or why he was still refusing to tell them. Then he had turned up with a band of pirates in Somalia. The six crewmen who had disappeared in Mombasa had, Peggy had discovered, been recruited for the *Aristides* in Athens, via a Pakistani company. They had false Pakistani passports but had spoken to each other in English, so were probably not Pakistanis at all. Had they come from Birmingham too? Could it be that Amir Khan was just the tip of the iceberg? Were many more British recruits heading for Somalia? She needed to think more about this idea before she shared her whole investigation with Geoffrey Fane. She'd rather talk to Peggy first, and then to Martin to see what he made of it.

Her eyes focused on Fane again and she realised he was still talking about his proposal to put someone on board the ship. But, if she was right, it was hard to see how placing a solitary undercover agent on the *Aristides* could do anything to foil a plot of this complexity. It was far more likely to blow the investigation and precipitate a change of plan by the plotters. She started to repeat her objections to Fane's proposal.

He cut her off with a raised hand. 'Hear me out, if you would, Elizabeth. If we have someone on board, with direct communications of course, he'll be able to alert us immediately the attack takes place—if it does. We'll have naval forces all over the area who can move in quickly—there's not a chance the pirates will get away. Then we'll discover what this is all about and who the leaker in UCSO is.'

The plan still seemed to Liz just the sort of John Buchan-like adventure that had filled MI6's past history—and which, in her view, rarely achieved its objective. Her scepticism must have showed clearly on her face. Fane said earnestly, 'I can see you're

240

doubtful about this, but what's the risk?'

In the first place, somebody's life, thought Liz, looking at him and remembering what had happened to Maria, his last attempt at infiltrating an agent. The dead girl seemed to hold for him all the importance of a tax deduction—something to be written off.

Fane went on, 'Look, the simple truth is, if we don't take charge of this operation, the Americans will.'

'The Americans? What have they got to do with it?'

'Quite a lot by now.' He was looking slightly sheepish. 'You were right about the head of the Athens office—he's ex-Agency. Langley has suddenly started to take an interest in what they'd previously dismissed as a parochial Greek affair. It feeds into their growing concern about Somalia.'

'What's that got to do with putting someone on board the *Aristides*?'

'Simply this: if we don't do it, Langley will. And I'm sure that neither of us wants that to happen.'

She didn't answer at once. Fane was right to think that it would be disastrous for the CIA to come charging mob-handed into the case. Now was not the moment for a 'bombs away' approach.

But Fane's alternative, putting a Six officer on board, was equally unpalatable to Liz. The emphasis then would be less on discovering any links between the Birmingham mosque, Al Qaeda and Somalia, and more on adventures against pirates and ... well, ultimately, she thought cynically, furthering Fane's own glory. No, thanks, thought Liz.

She said, 'I agree we don't want the Americans

241

taking over. But I don't think it should be one of your people on board.'

'Why not?' demanded Fane, looking affronted.

'Because if anyone's going to do this, it should be one of us.' Before he could object, she continued, 'If there are people on board who are in collusion with the pirates, the likelihood is that they will be British masquerading as Pakistanis.' She told him what Peggy had found out about the six crew members who had disappeared during the *Aristides'* previous voyage. She went on, 'And we're obviously in the strongest position to spot them. We're already investigating the mosque in Birmingham that Amir Khan used to attend. We think that's where he was recruited to do whatever he was sent out to Somalia to do. It may be that all this links together. Anyway, it's in our bailiwick. So whoever we put on the *Aristides* should know the details of our investigation and be from this side of the river.'

She pointed out of the window. 'Low floor perhaps, but the view from here looks pretty clear to me.'

42

In the Athens office OF UCSO, the shock of Maria Galanos' death had begun to wear off, to be replaced by an atmosphere of oppressive gloom. The usual high spirits of the Greek girls were dimmed, and Mr Limonides had become even more withdrawn. Katherine Ball was due in from London the following day, and Mitchell Berger was hoping that her brisk professionalism would lighten the mood and return them to normality.

Claude Rameau had come back from ten days in Rwanda, and Berger had been trying to keep track of her—not an easy task since she clearly regarded the office as merely a convenient place to drop in to from time to time when it suited her. The more he thought about it, the less likely it seemed that Claude Rameau was the source of the leak about the UCSO shipments. An accomplice, possibly, but not the prime mover. For a start, she wasn't in the country enough, let alone in the office, to know in detail what was going on—or to keep an eye on the ships' manifests.

No, the obvious suspect was not someone in the office at all. Berger's suspicions were now focused on the shipping agent, Mo Miandad. Acting on these suspicions, he had followed Miandad the previous week when the man left the UCSO offices in the late afternoon after one of his regular visits to Mr Limonides. When Mo got on to a bus, Berger hailed a passing cab and, to the obvious delight of the taxi driver, told him to follow the bus. They'd stopped and started, keeping closely behind the bus as it made its way for two miles or so across the city, until Berger saw Miandad alight. The taxi driver had been disappointed when Berger leaped out and paid him off. He'd asked if he should follow on slowly behind, ready in case he was needed again, but Berger told him to go away.

They had ended up in a part of Athens that Berger did not know—a suburban enclave of flats and small houses, which from the look of the pedestrians on the street seemed to be occupied largely by older people, with a good smattering of ethnic minorities. He followed Miandad from a distance, and spotted him turning into a terrace of stuccoed houses where he opened a front door with a key. This must be where he lives, thought Berger. That seemed to be confirmed when, minutes later, an Asian woman and a teenage girl, both wearing headscarves, came out of the same front door.

There was nothing suspicious going on here, it seemed, and Berger turned away to return to the office. It was as he was walking back to the bus stop that he noticed a name on one of the streets that rang a bell with him. He'd seen it somewhere before, but couldn't recall where. It was only as he was sitting on the bus that he remembered— he'd seen the name in the police report on Maria's murder. It was the street where she had lived.

*   *   *

Now, a week later, Mo Miandad had come into the office for a morning session with Limonides. Berger hovered in the corridor, keen to see if the Pakistani would go and talk to the newly returned Claude Rameau. He didn't, but when the Frenchwoman left early for lunch, followed only a few minutes later by Miandad, Berger decided to follow the shipping agent again.

This time Miandad stayed on foot, walking quickly through the middle-class neighbourhood where the UCSO offices were situated, heading towards the harbour. Berger found him easy to track. Though he was comparatively short, he was wearing a hat—an old-fashioned fedora, which could be spotted from a good distance. Berger followed him through a commercial zone of rough bars and fast-food outlets, then into a better neighbourhood with modern office buildings and an American chain motel three storeys high.

Mo walked on, past the entrance to the hotel's reception area. And then suddenly he turned and went up an external flight of stairs which led to the walkways that ran around the second and third floors of the motel. He must be meeting someone in a room up there, thought Berger, with increasing excitement. Maybe it was Claude Rameau—she could have taken a cab and be waiting already inside the room.

Quickening his pace, Berger followed him up the same staircase, listening for his quarry's steps on the treads above him. *Tonk-tonk-tonk.* The metal stairs reverberated as the man climbed. Then suddenly the noise stopped; Berger stopped too. When the steps resumed he continued climbing, treading lightly, two steps at a time, until he reached the third floor where he paused just short of the top of the flight of stairs. Slowly he extended his head and peered cautiously along the walkway, first in one direction, then the other—where he saw, at the far end, almost a hundred feet away, the familiar figure of Mo Miandad. There was someone else there, in front of him—a blonde woman with her back to Berger, wearing what looked like a black raincoat. It could be Claude Rameau; Berger's pulse quickened. Mo Miandad looked back for a second and then they both disappeared around the corner. Had he spotted Berger?

He sprinted after them along the gallery, then slowed as he reached the corner, listening for footsteps. He saw another stairway leading down and could hear footsteps on the treads. He went to the top of the steps and peered down. Two floors below he spotted Mo and a fleeting glimpse of the blonde woman, just as she left his field of vision. Damn!

He ran down the staircase without any thought for the noise he was making—his only aim now was to catch up with them and confront them. When he reached the bottom of the stairs he hesitated. There was no one in sight. He turned along the passage which led past the long line of ground-floor rooms. A door halfway along was ajar, as if someone had just gone inside. Running towards it, he realised that he didn't know what he was going to say to explain why he was there—but it was they who needed to do the explaining.

As he came up to the open door he slowed down. Inside, the room was pitch black. He stepped through the doorway, reaching out for the light switch. He flicked it on and at the same moment felt a hand on his back. Before he could turn around, the hand pushed him—hard—and he stumbled forward, landing on the concrete floor with a painful crack to his knees. He winced and tried to get up to confront his assailant. But the door behind him closed with a sharp click. Trying to ignore the pain in both his legs, Berger reached for the door handle. It was locked.

He looked around and saw that he was trapped in a service cupboard, facing two brooms and a row of mops, bolt upright in their buckets. A trolley against one wall held piles of clean sheets and folded towels. On the wall, bottles of disinfectant and liquid cleaner crowded a shelf. This was obviously not where Mo conducted his assignations.

Going back to the door, Berger began to pound on it with his fist. When there was no response, he shouted, 'Help!' Then 'Help!' again. He felt very stupid. He had fallen for one of the oldest tricks in the book. I'm past it, Berger thought to himself. He remembered his old colleagues in the Agency. How they would love to hear about this.

43

Tahira did not usually wear the *hijab*, just a scarf loosely thrown over her hair when she went out. But today, before she went into the café, she carefully adjusted the scarf, pulling it forward to cover her hair entirely. She had swapped her heels for flat walking shoes, and her *shalwar kameez* covered everything else, including her ankles. It would be unusual for a lone woman to go into the café, but no one could say she was dressed improperly.

Several pairs of eyes watched as she went inside. A4 were stationed at various strategic points in the street outside and inside the café. They knew her quarry was inside; they had been watching him most of the day.

Tahira collected a small pot of mint tea from the woman behind the counter and walked with her tray towards a table by the window. Only as she crossed the room did she look up, and it was then she saw Malik in the corner, staring at her.

'It's Tahira, isn't it?' he called out. She smiled at him shyly.

247

'I'm Malik, a friend of your brother's. Are you meeting someone?' He stood up, looking around the café. Only two other tables were occupied, by groups of much older men who were not paying them any attention.

'I was supposed to meet my cousin here. But he's just rung me to say he can't make it.' She gave a small shrug. 'I thought I would have some tea anyway.'

'Come and sit with me,' said Malik, and giving her no chance to protest, he took the tray from her hands and led her to his table.

Sitting down, they looked at each, and Tahira adopted an expression of modest embarrassment.

'Do you not remember me, Tahira?' asked Malik.

In fact she did recognise him, but only just. She knew vaguely that she'd seen him in her brother's company. They had certainly never been introduced; none of Amir's friends from the New Springfield Mosque had, for her father had forbidden them to enter the family house.

'Of course I remember you, Malik. Amir often spoke of you.'

'Not badly I hope,' he said, though he didn't sound worried.

'Of course not.'

'Have you heard anything from Amir?' he asked.

'Not lately,' she said. She knew her parents were too ashamed to have confided in anyone about their son's whereabouts, not even extended family. And the woman from MI5 had been confident that word would not have got out about Amir's capture and imprisonment in Paris.

'Is he still in Pakistan?' Malik asked, though

248

Tahira sensed he knew the answer to his question.

'We don't know where he is. Our family out there said he went travelling. That's the last we heard.' She faltered. 'I just hope he's all right. We are very worried about him.'

Malik shot a comforting hand across the table, though he stopped short of touching her. 'Don't worry, Tahira. He's fine, I'm sure of it. Your brother knows how to look after himself.'

'You think so?' she asked, trying to sound hopeful and pathetic.

'Yes, I'm sure. It's not as if he's in enemy territory out there. Now in America, who knows what could have happened to him. They lock you up over there, you know, just for practising Islam. Half the inmates in Guantanamo didn't even know how to spell Al Qaeda, much less belong to it. Their only crime was being Muslim.'

'Really?'

'Absolutely. The Jewish lobby sees to that. Look at the media there—the television stations, the newspapers. All owned by Jews. And they control the views people have all over the West. When was the last time you saw anything favourable about Islam on TV or in the Western newspapers, tell me that? They'll praise Dubai all right, run features about its new hotels, and the way it lures white English people to spend their money on gambling and drinking and all sorts of decadence. But nothing about the real faith that is Islam.'

Tahira nodded submissively, knowing that he didn't want anything but agreement from her. Malik went on, 'You can be sure that Amir wasn't going there. He is a messenger of true Islam, your brother, and he would only visit those places where

249

Allah is respected. I am sure of that.' He waved one hand dismissively, and Tahira sensed he didn't really want to talk about her brother. What he really wanted to talk about was himself.

'You know, I have always been interested in you.'

She stiffened slightly—it was important for her to seem demure. Malik quickly added, 'Not improperly, Tahira. I mean, your brother always spoke of you in such a way that I thought you must be a very good person.'

'We are very close,' she said. 'But,' she paused, 'we are so worried about him. Do you think the imam at the mosque might know where he has gone? I thought perhaps I could ask him. Would that be a good thing to do?'

'Abdi Bakri?' Malik stared at her, his eyes suddenly suspicious. 'I don't think that would be a good idea at all.'

'Why not? Amir always spoke respectfully of him.'

'I am sure the imam thought he was a good and loyal student.' Malik paused for a moment. 'Someone else has been asking the imam about Amir. Someone who said he was his cousin.'

'Really?' She was as genuinely surprised as she sounded. 'Who was that?'

'A bloke called Salim. I know him pretty well but he never said before that he was related to your family. Is he?' Malik sounded casual, but his eyes were hard now and searching.

'It's possible. Even my father sometimes has trouble keeping up with all the relatives we have over here. Especially on my mother's side.'

'But you don't know Salim yourself?'

'No,' she said.

He seemed satisfied by this. 'I thought not, somehow. Anyway, it's better not to ask the imam yourself. Let me make some enquiries.'

When she nodded her agreement to this, his face lightened momentarily then grew serious again, though this time there was nothing hard about his eyes. 'Tahira, I am going away soon.' When her eyes widened he looked pleased. 'To Pakistan. It is something of a . . . mission, you could say.'

'It sounds serious.'

'It is, and possibly quite dangerous. I must ask you to tell no one I spoke of it.'

'Of course not, Malik. When will you go?'

'Quite soon, and it may be some time before I come back.' He hesitated, and Tahira wondered if he expected to come back at all.

'I will miss you,' she volunteered, then realised how absurd this might sound—this was the first time they'd met. She blushed. 'I mean, it is very nice speaking with you. I have so often heard Amir talk about you that I feel as if we have known each other for a long time.'

'I know exactly what you mean,' he said approvingly. 'Perhaps before I go, we could meet again? I have enjoyed this talk.'

'I would like that very much,' Tahira replied with a smile. It was after all just what she'd been aiming for.

44

Geoffrey Fane had reluctantly conceded that it should be one of Liz's colleagues, rather than one of his, who would join the crew of the *Aristides* on its next voyage from Athens to Kenya. But it seemed that he was still trying to run the operation. Liz had been astonished to receive an invitation to what he was describing as a 'co-ordination meeting' at Vauxhall Cross. She suspected that he had not been completely frank with her about the extent to which he had already involved the Americans, and that he was now trying to 'uninvolve' them and hoping she could help.

Not much chance of that, she thought, once Langley had got a sniff of it. She wondered who else he had invited to the meeting. The room would probably be full of people, all vying for position: Bokus and colleagues from the American Embassy, a team from MI6, probably the Navy, the SAS, the Cabinet Office, the Foreign Office ... and heaven knows who else. It was all far too premature, and would be sure to result in a muddle.

She decided to go to the meeting alone and let them all talk. Her aim was to avoid anything happening that might mess up the operation in Birmingham which, now she had Tahira in play, she felt might at last be getting somewhere. All this had put her in a thoroughly bad temper, and she was crossly putting her papers away in her security cupboard, ready to go across the river, when Peggy came in with the latest update on the monitoring of emails from the mosque.

'I can't stop now,' Liz said, 'or I'll be late for the Fane jamboree.'

'I think you'd better read it before you go over there,' said Peggy. So Liz sat down and read:

URGENT
Re: New Springfield Mosque Communications

We have had some success in analysing the internet communications from the New Springfield Mosque. A variety of machines are in use, mainly laptops which appear to be used by different individuals and are probably brought into the premises and used in some sort of library or study room. A4 surveillance linked with emanations has enabled us to identify several individual users.

There is one particular machine that remains in place. It has an Arabic keyboard. We believe, again from A4 observation, that this machine is used only by Imam Abdi Bakri, and is probably situated in his office.

Bakri sends messages to a variety of radical Islamic groups throughout the Middle East and North Africa. In addition, he is a contributor to message boards based in Europe but consulted by Arabic-speaking users. Many of Bakri's contributions could be considered inflammatory or even illegal under existing UK incitement laws, but none so far has suggested involvement in or planning of actual terrorist missions.

The exception is a series of messages, increasing in number in the last five days, which are clearly designed to be unbreakable by monitoring. These messages go to a parallax repository, which functions as a depot to which outside visitors travel; in that sense it is not unlike a bulletin board in a chat room. The key difference is that access is restricted, and the identity of visitors is technically almost impossible to back-trace as they arrive through a series of relays, each of which can involve half a dozen different ISPs as well as literally dozens of different national boundaries. At present we cannot identify individual visitors to the depot.

Attempts at decryption are complicated by the twin facts that a) the encryption is double-ended and intrinsically hard to crack; and b) it is changed algorithmically every hour—which means we have effectively to decipher an algorithmic adjustment within another algorithm every sixty minutes to keep up to speed with the contents of the transmitted messages.

Nonetheless some deciphering has taken place. Particles and conjunctions—'the', 'and', 'or', etc.—have been relatively easy to decipher and freeze, and increasingly we have isolated recurring proper nouns as well as base verbs and nouns. For example . . .

There followed a series of transcribed bits and pieces—mainly phrases, few of which made any sense to Liz. But her eye was caught by one phrase that stood out, even with all the synonyms provided by the technical team:

Passengers [[travellers, voyagers]] due in ten days city [[town, village]] will require// need//want immediate transfer [[relay, travel, shipment]] out.

It would have been meaningless without everything else she already knew, but as it was she thought she could fill in the blanks. People were travelling to what was most likely a city—that could be Islamabad or Athens since both were cities. Or somewhere else perhaps. But if, as was most likely, these communications were connected to the goings on at the mosque she already knew about, then Athens seemed most likely. Interestingly, it appeared the travellers were then being moved on right away. Where to? Could it be Somalia? She would have put money on it; in any case, it was happening soon.

*   *   *

Liz was only five minutes late for the meeting at Vauxhall Cross. Fane had chosen the grandest of the conference rooms for the get-together, with a river view and a gorgeous Georgian burred oak table that could have seated twenty-five people. It seemed a bit unnecessary, since to her relief the only others present, apart from Fane, were Andy Bokus from the US Embassy and Martin Seurat, whom she was very surprised to see—he hadn't told her he was coming over. He had broken with protocol, moreover, in coming without anyone to accompany him from the French Embassy in London. When Liz gave him a quizzical look, he smiled apologetically. He must have been called in by Fane at the last minute.

Fane gave Liz a frosty nod as she entered and made her excuses to the other two men, who were standing by the window while they waited. Martin smiled warmly at her, and Bokus solemnly shook hands. She knew him of old and was well aware that the big man in the olive-green gabardine suit was deceptively sharp. She was not taken in by the Midwestern twang and the hearty vocabulary; she'd learned not to underestimate Mr Bokus or the other CIA agents stationed in London.

They all sat down at the table, Fane taking the chair at the end. 'Now that we're all here, shall we get started? Thank you for coming over, Andy and Monsieur Seurat. I decided to keep this meeting small since we're in the very early stages of considering what action might be appropriate. I think we are all familiar with the background. The *Aristides* is leaving Athens in four days' time, with a cargo of aid from UCSO for Africa. As you know, we suspect a leak from that charity to a pirate group in Somalia. We have artificially inflated the apparent value of the cargo on board, in an attempt to flush out the link to the pirates and to discover whether anything else is going on. We expect a hijacking attempt to take place off the coast of Somalia—south-east of the Horn, and not in the Gulf of Aden. The pirates in question are based south of Mogadishu and, because of the information we already have from the earlier hijacking attempt that was thwarted by the French Navy, we believe the gang in question to be Arabs not Somalis.

'In discussion recently,' continued Fane, leaning forward, 'my colleague Eliz . . . er, Liz Carlyle and I decided to put one of our colleagues on board the ship.'

'Yes,' said Liz, quickly interjecting, 'It will be Dave Armstrong, one of our best intelligence officers.' She wanted to make quite clear that this was primarily an MI5 operation.

Bokus, who had been chewing gum placidly, now said sharply, 'And just what's this Double-O Seven supposed to do? Take out the pirates single-handed, then find Osama Bin Laden for an encore?'

Liz took this calmly. 'We have slightly more modest aims for him. One—identify any collaborators with the pirates who are on board; it's possible someone on the ship is helping these guys. Two—alert the patrols we'll have in the area so they can intercept the pirates and arrest any collaborators.'

Bokus said, 'I say we supply the firepower. We've got a carrier in the vicinity, and two frigates alongside as escorts. Plus, if it gets really heavy, we can have air support along in minutes.'

Liz could see Fane wince. Air support was the last thing either of them envisaged. If it were called in, there was no question that the pirates would be blown out of the water. But there was also a strong likelihood that the *Aristides* and Dave Armstrong and any British Pakistanis who might be on board would be bombed to smithereens as well.

Fane said, 'I don't think firepower is going to be an issue. Something a little more subtle is required.'

Bokus bristled. 'Are you saying we can't do subtle?'

'Not at all, Andy,' Fane said soothingly. 'But

257

I think we're best placed to handle the policing aspect of this.'

The atmosphere between them, never easy, had turned tense. Liz watched as the argument progressed, Bokus emphasising the sheer might of American forces, Fane the need for stealth and surprise, which would be helped by having an agent on board. When Bokus returned to the possibility of air strikes—'That way we can keep their colleagues on shore from coming out to help. Do we know where they're based anyway?'—Liz reached for her briefcase. She took out a stack of photographs and passed them around. 'These are satellite pictures of the camp.'

'Pretty big site,' said Bokus as he looked at them.

'The compound in the middle belongs to the pirates. We think the tents at the bottom are their Middle Eastern visitors.'

'Al Qaeda,' Fane declared.

'Or Al Shebab,' said Bokus.

'Same thing to all intents and purposes,' snapped Fane.

Martin, who had been quietly watching this Battle of the Titans, winked at Liz.

Then Bokus said, 'An F-16 could keep these guys pinned down easy.'

'There are almost certainly hostages in the camp,' Liz said firmly. 'Attractive as an air strike may sound, think of the repercussions if you kill the captain of an oil tanker being held to ransom.'

'Shit happens,' Bokus said with a shrug, and turned to resume his argument with Fane. We're getting nowhere, thought Liz, her mind busily reviewing options to resolve the stalemate.

Then Martin Seurat broke in, so quietly at first

that it took Fane and Bokus, in mid-argument, a minute to realise he was speaking. 'Gentlemen, it seems to me each of your positions is reasonable. But also completely incompatible. I have an alternative to propose.'

Bokus and Fane stopped talking and both turned to look suspiciously at him as he continued. 'You will remember that the last time pirates attempted to seize the *Aristides*, they were foiled by the French Navy. It so happens that the corvette responsible is currently patrolling the same waters. I would propose that this be the vessel that should intervene if there is a new attempt—we are talking days from now, and the ship is already in place.'

'So you're saying the French should run the show?' said Bokus irritably.

'Not at all. I am merely pointing out that we have the advantage of knowing the *Aristides*, and that we are already in position.' Before Bokus could protest, he went on, 'I suggest the British be responsible in the event—unlikely, we hope—that it's necessary to put a force down on land. I am sure our own commandos could do the job, but I am happy to defer to the expertise of your special forces, Geoffrey and Liz.'

That should satisfy Fane, thought Liz, as she quietly assessed Martin's diplomacy, but it still left Bokus to be appeased. Martin now turned to the American. 'Monsieur, I accept your argument that airpower might be useful. But in this situation, where it will be very difficult to distinguish between the innocent and the enemy, I think helicopters would be the most advantageous. If you can have a ship within ten miles or so of the coast, they could put in reinforcements as needed to either the *Aristides* or the pirates' camp. They would have adequate firepower if there is resistance, but also have the ability to be—how should I say?—*discriminating* in who they attack. And, most important, they could transport people out if needed—casualties, freed hostages or prisoners.'

It was a good argument, Liz thought, and to his credit Bokus seemed to see that. Moreover, if Bokus couldn't win the argument with Fane, Seurat's solution also meant he wouldn't entirely lose. He conceded, 'It makes sense.'

'Yes, it does,' said Liz.

Fane didn't say anything. He looked unhappy, though Liz sensed this was not because he had any objection to the plan itself, but because the compromise came from Seurat. Eventually Fane gave a grudging nod. Then, reasserting his position as chairman of the meeting, he said, 'Well, if that's agreed then we'd better decide how to co-ordinate all the planning.'

Well done, Martin, thought Liz, as they exchanged glances.

45

When Peggy Kinsolving had done her research on the background of the various employees in UCSO's two offices, she hadn't bothered with UCSO's Chief Executive, David Blakey. She knew he was an ex-MI6 officer and had left it at that. After all, no one could say that MI6 was casual about its recruitment and he certainly wouldn't have been employed there if there had been any doubt about his background.

But Peggy hated loose ends and the loose ends in Blakey's case were the five years since he'd left MI6. So really just to satisfy herself, she decided to put him under her investigative microscope.

Her friend Millie the Moaner was now working in the Personnel Department of MI6—or Human Resources as even MI6 called it now—and she got permission for Peggy to see Blakey's file. It recorded his recruitment, after he'd been talent-spotted while working on a postgraduate Politics thesis; his various postings; his marriage to Dorothy, who had been his secretary in Copenhagen, and their separation and divorce. It was clear from the confidential reports by his various Heads of Station that his performance had been acceptable if never outstanding. But there was something about Blakey that was frequently mentioned; his relationships with women, both before and after his marriage. He had been warned repeatedly that his behaviour was not compatible with his secret work, and eventually his blatant relationship with a woman from the German Foreign Office, whom he met when he was posted to Berlin, had caused the break-up of his marriage, and ultimately his departure from the Service.

Peggy thought she now had a pretty clear idea of the sort of man David Blakey was, but she did not immediately see how that could be relevant to the goings on in the UCSO office in Athens. In any case, he might have changed; it was more than five years since the last page in his file had been added—the reference the Service had written in support of his application for the post he now held in UCSO. But Peggy was like a bloodhound once

261

she was on the trail, and she decided to take a closer look at Mr Blakey.

David Blakey lived in a flat north of Baker Street. It was an area that had once been a mixture of working-class housing and quiet middle-class mansion blocks, a neighbourhood that had never been chic—until the last ten years, when prices for even a studio apartment topped £400,000 and many property owners found themselves, on paper at least, millionaires. When a newsagent's closed, or the local ironmonger's, it was replaced these days by an estate agent or a smart flower shop. Like all Londoners, Peggy looked at the affluent area and wished she had bought something there when she first came to London six or seven years before; though, like most Londoners her age, she hadn't had the money then to buy property of any sort.

She stopped at the corner nearest to Blakey's flat, and took a clipboard out of her briefcase; fastened to it were a few official-looking forms she'd had run up by Printing. She pushed her glasses higher on her nose, buttoned up her jacket, and walked purposefully up to the door of the mansion block. She rang the bell of 2C, which her researches had told her was on the same landing as Blakey's flat, 3C. After a moment a woman's voice said, 'Yes?'

'Mrs Goodhart? I'm from the Electoral Register,' Peggy said, holding up to the entry camera a quite realistic-looking identity card, also run up by Printing. 'I'm confirming current occupancy in this block. May I have a word, please?'

'All right,' the woman said resignedly, and buzzed her in.

Inside, the entrance hall was deserted. Peggy ignored the brass cage lift and took the stairs, arriving on the second-floor landing only slightly out of breath. The door of 2C was on its chain, open just a crack, but the sight of Peggy apparently reassured Mrs Goodhart and she took off the chain and opened the door.

To Peggy's eyes, Mrs Goodhart looked as if she had dressed for a wedding—smart silk suit, golden hair swept tightly back into a knot at the nape of her neck. 'Will this take long? I'm going out for lunch and I need to leave in five minutes.'

'No. I just have a few questions,' said Peggy, flashing her a charming smile. 'Only one side, you see,' she added, holding up her clipboard.

The woman laughed. 'Come in then. It's a bit bleak standing out here on the landing.'

Peggy followed her into a sitting room that seemed to be crammed with furniture. Georgian side tables covered with china ornaments jostled with silk damask-covered chairs and sofas. Peggy found herself staring at a large portrait of a cavalry officer on a horse, which dominated the far wall. 'My great-grandfather,' the woman said simply, and motioned her to sit down.

Perched on one of the pristine chairs, Peggy held her clipboard upright on her knee. 'If I could just check some details, Mrs Goodhart,' she began.

Peggy asked a series of questions in her version of the bland tones of officialdom: what was her name, her address (with a laugh), was she over seventy, the names and details of any other occupants of the flat—'I have lived alone here since the death of my husband,' Mrs Goodhart answered stiffly.

When she got to the end of her questions, Peggy slid her pencil through the metal rung of her clipboard and stood up. 'Thank you very much,' she said, and started towards the door. Then stopped, as if she'd thought of something else.

'Yes?' asked Mrs Goodhart.

'Sorry, I was just wondering . . . I've been trying to check the present occupants of Flat 3C.' She waved vaguely across the landing. 'But no one ever seems to be in.'

'Ah, that's David Blakey. He works during the day but he's usually at home in the evening.'

'Oh, yes, that's the name I've got—and Mrs Blakey?'

Mrs Goodhart gave her a knowing look. 'There isn't a Mrs Blakey. But there is a lady there who— well, as you might say, keeps him company.' She looked down, suitably abashed by her own candour.

Peggy let her eyes widen to display mild surprise. 'Is this lady . . . uh . . . resident with Mr Blakey?'

'I think they say "cohabitant" nowadays, my dear. I don't think she's moved in. It's strictly a nocturnal arrangement, if you see what I mean.' Mrs Goodhart emitted a small snort, as if to say, *Men!* 'She *is* attractive. Not young, you know, forty if she's a day and I don't think the blonde hair is completely unaided by the bottle. But Mr Blakey is utterly smitten, according to Howson.'

'Howson?' asked Peggy politely, looking at her list. 'Does she live here too?'

'Oh, no. She's my daily and she does for David Blakey too. A nice woman, if a little prone to gossip,' said Mrs Goodhart with a small sniff. Then, perhaps realising the hypocrisy of this, added briskly, 'Is that all, because I must be going now?'

264

'Oh, I'm so sorry. I hope I haven't made you late.' But Peggy wasn't sorry at all. She'd learned rather more than she'd expected.

46

No one had briefed Dave Armstrong on how boring life was on board a container ship. In fact, no one had briefed him on much about this operation, which saw him posing as medical assistant to the ship's doctor on board the *Aristides*. A ship of this size would not normally have carried a medical assistant, but none of the officers had queried his presence. The Captain was fully in the picture and the ship's doctor, an old Scotsman called Macintyre, had been told only that he must treat Dave, alias Tony Symes, as he would a genuine medical assistant. Dr Macintyre had been around far too long to be surprised by anything and was finding Tony Symes' presence quite agreeable, as it allowed him to spend more time playing bridge with the other officers.

Dave had been whisked out to Athens by the RAF at a week's notice, with just enough time for him to brush up on the First Aid course he'd taken years before. Having been closely involved with the Birmingham end of things, the extraction of Boatman and the recruitment of Tahira, he knew the operation's background, but was far from certain what he was expected to achieve by being on board the ship. 'Get to know the crew,' Liz had said, 'particularly the Pakistanis. Find out if any of them are British and learn as much as you can about where they're going and why.'

Well, that was easier said than done. The four Pakistani crewmen had formed a tight group and spoke hardly at all to the other seamen, let alone the officers. But what concerned Dave most of all was what he was supposed to do if, as everyone seemed to be expecting, the ship was hijacked. He just hoped that Geoffrey Fane had thoroughly sorted out the back-up with the Americans and the French, and that he wasn't going to find himself the target of 'friendly fire'.

He had not been much reassured when he'd stopped briefly in Athens and had dinner with Bruno Mackay at a small restaurant near the embassy. Though he'd never met him before, he had heard about Mackay from Liz and was not expecting to discover a soulmate. Mackay turned out to be just as Liz had described him—the perfect suntan, the elegantly cut hair, the smart suit and the shirt cuffs with gold cufflinks on display. Mackay did a competent job, briefing Dave on the Athens end of the operation. Dave was not surprised that he made only passing reference to the murder of his agent Maria Galanos; in spite of his self-confident front, Bruno Mackay must be very embarrassed by that. They went on to discuss the leasing, loading and despatching of the UCSO aid ships by the shipping company. Mackay had obtained a copy of the crew list, which revealed a mixed bag of Filipinos, a Cypriot, Koreans and four Pakistanis. 'These are your targets,' said Bruno, unnecessarily, pointing to the Pakistani names.

'Does anyone at UCSO know I'll be on board?'

'Absolutely not. Even their head man in London hasn't any idea we're putting someone on the

Aristides. And we didn't want this chap Berger to know either, since it looks like the leaks have been coming out of his office.'

For communications, Technical Ted had handed over a laptop containing gizmos which he'd assured Dave would be completely invisible to anyone looking at his machine except the most sophisticated technician. They would enable encrypted messages to be sent directly to and from Thames House. Bruno's office in the Athens Embassy was to act as fallback communications in case the system failed.

All that sorted out, Bruno ordered another bottle of wine and said, to Dave's surprise, 'You've worked a lot with Liz Carlyle—tell me about her.' And for the rest of the dinner Dave had ducked his probing questions about Liz as best he could, saying nothing revealing, and unsuccessfully trying to change the subject. By the end of the evening, he was left with the distinct impression that Bruno's interest in Liz was not on his own account; he was trying to find out whether she was involved with his boss, Geoffrey Fane.

*   *   *

The ship had already reached the Red Sea and Dave had as yet made very little headway in getting to know the Pakistani crewmen. In the Mediterranean, two small storms had blown up and the *Aristides,* with no stabilisers, had been tossed about like a yo-yo. All the Pakistani crew members had been seasick for almost two days and Dave himself had had to retire to bed at one point. Even when they were well, the four men did not mingle with the other crew, and at meals occupied a table of their own. When he'd encountered them on deck and had tried to make conversation—about cricket, or the floods in Pakistan that had been on the news—they had just nodded and moved away.

But then one of them, a crewman called Fazal, had gashed his hand lashing down some containers on the deck. Dave had noticed Fazal at the beginning of the voyage, and had thought that he looked much younger and more vulnerable than the other Pakistanis. And, interestingly, when he had first come into the surgery to have his hand treated after the accident, he had answered Dr Macintyre's questions about it in fluent English, with a definite trace of a Birmingham accent.

Now Fazal was due to come in and have his dressing changed, and Dave was hoping that he could use the opportunity to get him talking. When he suggested that Dr Macintyre might like to go and play cards, leaving Dave in sole charge for the hour the surgery was open, the Scotsman had understood at once, and made himself scarce.

Fazal turned up on time and sat down while Dave changed his dressing. 'Tell me how it feels now,' said Dave, assuming a medical manner. 'Has it stopped hurting?'

'Yeah, it's all right.'

'I hope you're not putting any pressure on it.'

'No. I'm on light duties.'

'You don't sound like a Pakistani.' Dave looked up from his bandaging and smiled. 'That sounds like a Brummie accent to me. My mum came from Birmingham; grew up near Springfield Park.'

Fazal's eyes widened. 'That's where I come from.'

'Really?' said Dave. 'It was all Irish back then.'

'Not any more,' said Fazal, with a hint of a grin.

'What brings you here then? We're a long way from home.'

Fazal hesitated, then said, 'I wanted to see the world. My mum had family in Pakistan; one of them put me on to this.'

Dave pointed through the porthole, where the sandy shoreline of Saudi was still visible. 'Didn't you want to go there? To Saudi, I mean. Mecca and all that.'

Fazal thought about this. 'Some day,' he said at last. 'But they're not true followers of the faith. The ruling family's corrupt.'

Dave shrugged. 'Can't be worse than Africa. Wait till you see Mombasa. We'll have to bribe the harbour master before we can put the gangplank down.' He finished off the dressing and laughed. 'Not many followers of the true faith there, I think.'

Fazal shook his head. 'You're wrong.'

Dave raised his eyebrows. 'Really?' He was about to ask Fazal if he would be meeting any of these 'true believers' when he saw the boy's face freeze. Someone was standing in the doorway of the consulting room and when Dave looked round he saw it was another of the Pakistani group—an older man called Perjev, who seemed to be in charge of the others. He barked something in Urdu and Fazal looked briefly at Dave, then got up and quickly left.

It was disappointing, but at least he'd made contact with the boy and confirmed not only that he was from Birmingham, but also that he came from the Sparkhill area. At last he had something to report. And Fazal seemed vulnerable—that

269

could be useful if things got heavy.

At the end of the hour, Dave locked up the surgery and went back to his cabin. He checked the slightly primitive security measures he set every time he left his room: a single strand of hair balanced across the handle of the top drawer in his desk; and the items in his shaving kit, seemingly a random jumble of toothpaste, razors and shaving cream, which were in fact carefully arranged.

The hair was missing, and he found it only when he got down on his hands and knees and inspected the linoleum floor. It didn't necessarily mean anything—the draft when he opened the door could easily have blown it off. The contents of the drawer seemed fine; his laptop was where he'd left it, apparently untouched. He went across to the washbasin to look at his shaving bag. Everything was there, he saw to his relief, but then he realised something was wrong. The tube of toothpaste was the wrong way round.

Someone had been in his room.

47

They were putting up a stage at the bottom end of Springfield Park. From the bench where Tahira sat, she could see scaffolding and two workmen fitting stairs at one end of the platform. Beside a van, parked on the grass, an electrician was sorting out a spaghetti-like tangle of wires.

Tahira was waiting for Malik. He'd rung her on her mobile the day after their first conversation in the café, and she had agreed to meet him here.

Other ears were listening when he rang—Liz's colleagues were tracing all calls going to and from Malik's mobile phone.

He had suggested they meet in the park, specifying this particular bench on the hill, where large chestnut trees offered shade and privacy. Tahira sensed he was torn between a wish to see her, and an unwillingness to be seen talking to an unmarried young woman who was known more for her forthright character than for her Islamic piety.

Turning round, she spotted him coming through a rear entrance to the park. He was wearing jeans and a dark T-shirt, and carried a mobile phone in his hand. As he sat down beside her on the bench he looked round anxiously, though there was no one within a hundred yards of them.

'Hello, Malik, it is nice to see you again.'

'Likewise. You look lovely today.'

'Do you see what's going on down there?' asked Tahira brightly, pointing to the stage at the bottom of the hill. 'There's going to be a pop concert here on Saturday.'

'I know.' Malik sounded unimpressed.

'I've got tickets. My cousin and I are going.'

'What do you want to do that for?'

'It's the Chick Peas. I love their music.' Which was true. The all-girl Asian group had recently become famous with their single 'Biryani for Two'. Their lead singer, Banditti Kahab, had been on *Celebrity Big Brother,* wearing lots of make-up and an ever-skimpier succession of miniskirts. Tahira knew the girls were vulgar, but their songs were catchy, and in any case she admired them for their gutsiness. She liked the way they defied the conventions they'd grown up with and still

271

managed to remain as much Asian as English.

Malik groaned. 'Oh, Tahira, you've got so much to learn. The way you talk, you sound as though you've been brainwashed.'

'Brainwashed. Who by?'

'The so-called culture of the West, what else? Can't you see? The girls in that band stand for the very worst things in this country—sexy clothes, flashy jewellery, lots of make-up. Flaunting their bodies. All the things they have been seduced into thinking are glamorous. And what has seduced them? The TV and the tabloids and adverts—especially the ads. You see them everywhere. For short skirts and bare skin and all the things our own religion condemns.'

'They're just a girl band, Malik.'

'That makes it even worse—their only aim is to be famous. They've sold out in the worst possible way.'

He sounded angry now, and Tahira didn't argue. Liz had told her to play him along, whatever she really felt about the things he said. He went on, 'When will we ever learn? The way ahead is not through aping the West. We should be getting the West to accept our standards, not the other way around.'

'But is that possible?' asked Tahira hesitantly.

'It may take time,' Malik conceded. 'But it will happen some day. You watch. I have seen for myself Westerners who have embraced Islam.'

'Really?'

'Yes.' He gave a patronising laugh. 'One of them was even a woman. A blue-eyed devil,' he added, laughing at the cliché.

'Where did you meet her?' she asked.

272

Malik hesitated. 'It had to do with the mission I told you about. I hope you have kept that secret.'

'Of course.' She paused then ventured, 'I'm sorry you're going away.' She hoped the words didn't sound as ridiculous to him as they did to her, but she was gambling on his ego being big enough for him to accept them without question.

To her surprise, he said, 'I'm not going to Pakistan after all.'

'You're not?'

'No. Plans have changed.'

'But what about the others?'

'They've already gone.'

'Gone without you?' She was surprised but didn't dare ask why he had stayed behind. So she just said, 'Well, that's nice for me.'

But Malik looked uncomfortable. She wondered why—if he was keen on her, he ought to be glad he wasn't going away. She looked at him. 'What's the matter, Malik? Are you upset that you aren't going?'

He shrugged and said nothing, but Tahira knew there was something wrong.

'Perhaps you are more interested in this blonde blue-eyed devil than in me,' she teased.

'I didn't say she was blonde,' Malik snapped. He looked around, suddenly tense again. 'I've got to be going.'

'All right,' she said, as if her feelings were hurt. 'Do you want to meet again, Malik?'

He hesitated, and she could see his conflict reflected in his face. He was obviously attracted to her, but there was another side to him—the side that had him looking around tensely, the side that had no place for her or any woman.

273

Eventually Malik smiled at her. 'Of course we'll meet again. It is the one good thing about my change of plans.' He reached out and put a hand on her arm. 'Let's see each other on Saturday, before you go to the concert. We could meet at the café.' He wasn't looking at her as he spoke; his mind was on something else, and she had no idea what that was.

48

They came under cover of darkness and mist just before sunrise. Captain Guthrie had sent for Dave Armstrong, and when he arrived in the pilot's house on the top deck of the accommodation block, the Captain pointed silently at the newly installed radar screen. It showed four tiny blips making straight for the *Aristides*.

Like the crew and the officers, Dave was unarmed. No weapons were allowed on board: the owners of ships sailing through the pirate-infested waters off the Horn had long ago decided that resisting the pirates would only lead to violence. It had turned out to be the right decision—not one hostage had been killed during the spate of hijackings in recent years. But just at that moment, Dave would have liked to have a weapon in his hands to defend himself.

He watched as the blips drew closer to the centre of the screen, then began to fade. He looked questioningly at Guthrie, who said, 'The radar starts to dissolve at five hundred yards. That means they're very close. Look.' He pointed to the monitor where a larger blip had appeared in its upper corner. 'That must be the French corvette. Our chaps should be in view any moment now.'

CCTV cameras had been positioned at the stern and bow of the *Aristides*, tilted down to show the waterline. Daybreak had come, but the fog had not yet lifted. Dave stared at an overhead monitor as a skiff came murkily into view at the stern. He could just make out three men in it, one of whom was manhandling the lower section of a ladder, holding it upright until its upper rungs were perched against the side of the *Aristides*. The man began pushing the bottom rungs of the second section, which slid upwards towards the rail of the stern deck.

Dave felt a tap on his shoulder and Guthrie pointed to the other monitor, which showed a skiff nestling up to the bow of the ship. There were also three men in this boat, and one of them, bare-chested and of Arab appearance, was standing up, holding a harpoon gun. He took careful aim then fired. A steel grappling hook shot up into the air, trailing an unravelling length of rope. Dave couldn't see where the hook had landed but the line tautened sharply, almost pulling the harpoonist out of the skiff. One of his associates quickly cut the rope free of the harpoon gun, then lashed it around the low gunwale. Now the Arab who had fired the harpoon gun swung himself up on the rope and began climbing, hand over hand, towards the bow of the *Aristides*, which loomed above him. It would have been easy to go along the deck to the bow and cut the rope, thought Dave, but both men still in the skiff held AK-47s, trained upwards to cover the climbing man.

'Time to go,' said Guthrie; the other monitor was showing one of the pirates halfway up the ladder at the stern. Guthrie reached down and flicked a switch. The noise of a klaxon horn filled the air, and within seconds crew members were running along the deck towards the accommodation block.

Dave followed the Captain to the companionway, where they quickly descended two flights of steel stairs down to the ship's staff room, which was level with the main cargo-laden deck of the tanker. The crew members, about twenty of them, were gathering there, looking uneasy. They formed a rough semi-circle as Guthrie stepped forward to address them. Dave noticed the Pakistanis weren't there.

Guthrie clapped his hands together and the room went silent. He was not a big man but he looked tough, with square shoulders and an air of grizzled authority. Just what you needed in a crisis, thought Dave. Guthrie said, 'Listen, men. Pirates will soon be on board this vessel. We expect them to head down here without much delay. You may have noticed that some of your fellow crewmen are missing ... we think they may be helping the pirates.' The men started to talk among themselves, and Guthrie held up his hand for silence. 'Here's what we're going to do. We've locked the steel doors over there, though eventually the pirates will be able to open them and get in. But by then we'll all be safely on the lower deck.'

There was more murmuring and one of the crew raised a hand—the Cypriot, who spoke very good English. 'If they have control of the ship, they can just wait for us to come out.'

Guthrie shook his head. 'Help's on the way. With any luck we won't be down below for long. Now get going!'

The men moved towards the rear door of the room, which led to the interior companionway that ran up and down the accommodation block. Dave lingered, waiting for Guthrie, who was checking the bolts on the door that led to the deck. Finished, he said, 'That should hold them off for a while. And once we close the steel door to Level Two we'll be safe until the cavalry rides to the rescue.'

The two of them started for the companionway, where they could hear the crew clanking their way down. Suddenly a figure appeared in the rear doorway. It was Fazal, who must have been waiting in the stairwell. He held a 9 mm handgun in his hand—the same one Dave had recently bandaged.

'Drop the weapon!' Guthrie barked. 'That's an order, sailor.'

Fazal shook his head, and tightened his grip on the handgun as he stepped into the room. He looked so nervous that Dave was scared he'd fire the gun by mistake. 'Fazal, listen to me,' he said, taking a small step forward. 'If you hand over the gun, I promise nothing bad will happen to you. But if you hold us here with that, I can't make any guarantees.'

From outside the accommodation block they heard the sound of a loud hailer, though the words were unintelligible. That's the cavalry, thought Dave, and just in time. He pointed towards the bolted door leading to the main deck. 'There's a French patrol boat full of commandos out there. They're heavily armed, and they won't hesitate to shoot you if they see the gun. Make the smart move, Fazal, and give me the pistol.'

The boy hesitated, and for a brief moment Dave thought he was about to relent. But suddenly, from behind him, Perjev came rushing through the doorway, holding an AK-47. Seeing Fazal, he shouted at him in Urdu, and the boy swung his pistol up to cover Dave. As he did so, Perjev went over to the door leading to the deck and undid the bolts. Using both hands, he swung the steel handle to vertical and heaved the heavy door open.

A man stepped in from the deck, a tall Arab with hard eyes. He looked agitated. Waving his gun, he motioned Dave and Captain Guthrie out of the open door. 'Go!' he shouted, following closely behind as they stepped through on to the deck. Perjev came too then stopped and gestured back inside. 'Our two mates are down below. We'll get them.'

The Arab hesitated then said sharply, 'Quick! The French are here.'

Turning to Dave and Guthrie, he pointed down the long central corridor on the deck with twenty-foot containers lined up on either side. It stretched to the bow of the ship almost two hundred feet away. 'Move—to the bow—fast,' the Arab said, waving his gun.

Guthrie hesitated, and the Arab pointed the AK-47 straight at him. 'Go or I'll kill you both.' His English was excellent and only lightly accented; Dave guessed he had lived in the States.

They ran then, ran as fast as they could, with the Arab right behind them. Dave couldn't understand what this man was up to. The French must already be on board at the stern. What on earth was he hoping for?

As they reached the bow, the figure of another man appeared out of the mist, standing by the rail. He also held an AK-47, upright in his hands like a barrier, forcing Dave and the Captain to stop. Beyond him Dave could see the sea, still shrouded by a low mist. He could just make out a skiff far below, nestled near the port side of the bow of the *Aristides*. In it sat a single armed pirate; it was secured by the long rope that Dave had seen fired from the harpoon gun just minutes before. The tall Arab came up behind them, and the guard with the AK-47 asked him, 'Where are the others?'

'They're coming,' he said curtly. But just then a crackle of automatic weapons fire came from the stern of the ship. The French had boarded, thought Dave.

The tall Arab cursed. 'We must go.' He turned to Dave. 'Down!' he ordered, gesturing at the rope.

'What?' asked Dave incredulously.

'Down the rope.' He waved his gun menacingly. 'Hurry.'

Dave hated heights; he couldn't climb down all that way on that little rope; he'd fall off into the sea. He gulped as he moved to the rail and looked down. He turned back, but the pirate was threatening him with the gun. There was no choice. Gritting his teeth, he threw one leg over the rail, then the other, and slowly crouched down, grabbing on to the rope just below its thickly knotted end. He closed his eyes and began to lower himself down along the rope as Guthrie watched from above, waiting his turn.

Dave descended slowly, trying to keep control of his speed, his hands burning on the coarse thick

279

hemp. What the tall Arab had done was clever. The French would have sent a boarding party in dinghies to the stern of the *Aristides*, knowing that the crew had locked themselves in the lower floors of the accommodation block. The corvette would be anchored a hundred yards away, and in this mist the French would never see the skiff at the other end of the ship. They'd free the crew, capture some of the Arab hijackers and, crucially, the four Pakistanis, but they wouldn't have the slightest inkling that others were getting away. By the time the rest of the crew told them that the Captain and Dave were missing, it would be too late.

*   *   *

And two hours later, as a French sailor was showing his commanding officer a rope hanging from the bow rail of the *Aristides*, Dave Armstrong and Captain Guthrie were being led across a beach at gunpoint ten miles south of Mogadishu.

49

Liz was fast asleep in her flat when the phone rang at 5 a.m. 'Cabinet Office duty officer here,' said a voice, in reply to her drowsy greeting. The caller told Liz that pirates had stormed the *Aristides*. 'A French corvette, part of the International Protection Force, intervened,' the voice went on, 'and the ship and most of its crew are safe. Unfortunately some of the pirates escaped, taking with them Captain Guthrie and your colleague

280

Dave Armstrong.' COBRA was being opened, she was told, and she was required to attend as soon as possible.

When Liz arrived in the Cabinet Office Briefing Room, known as COBRA, deep underneath the Cabinet Office in Whitehall, things were buzzing. Peggy was there with some others from Thames House, sitting at computer screens, alongside colleagues from MI6 and GCHQ. The SAS's area was manned up; Bokus was already in evidence, with a small team from Grosvenor Square with their own communications, and, in a corner, sat a team from the French Embassy.

Geoffrey Fane came into the room just behind her, looking as smart as ever in a three-piece suit and silk tie and handkerchief, as though he had never been to bed. 'Good morning, Elizabeth,' he said cheerfully. 'Bit of a pickle your chap's got himself into.'

Liz started to say something cutting, along the lines of 'Whose idea was it to put him on board?', but thought better of it. With Dave in serious danger, this was no time to be sparring with Geoffrey Fane, so she merely replied, 'Good morning, Geoffrey. You're looking very dapper.'

Considering how many people were present, there was surprisingly little noise in the room, just quiet voices and the hum of computers and TV monitors with their volume turned low. Information was streaming in and being collated and assessed by a Cabinet Office team at the back of the room, in preparation for a meeting to be chaired by the Foreign Secretary.

At 9 a.m. he swept in, followed by a team of officials. Those who had been working at computers left their desks and came to sit in the rows of chairs facing the platform on which the Minister and his senior advisors sat, and the briefing began. The Naval Attaché from the French Embassy gave the latest information from the corvette about exactly what had happened on board and who they had in custody; Geoffrey Fane spoke about the background to the UCSO shipments and what was known about the group who had taken the hostages (not much); Liz gave a brief account of the investigation in Birmingham and their suspicions about the Pakistani crew members who had been arrested on board; a Defence intelligence officer produced satellite imagery of the coast of Somalia, pinpointing the best assessment about where the hostages were being held and a woman from the Meteorological Office described the weather conditions there.

The Foreign Secretary refrained from asking why the MI5 officer had been on the ship—no doubt that question would be picked over to death later on. The present meeting was about rescuing him and the Captain. He listened closely to debate about the viability and logistics of a rescue operation and negotiated his way courteously through a proposal from Andy Bokus that they should go in heavy with maximum firepower, eventually coming down on the side of the Colonel from the SAS who outlined his plan for a small, quick in-and-out operation. He listened sympathetically to Liz when she argued that the rescue attempt should be mounted without delay. The pirates, she said, must have taken Dave Armstrong because they suspected that he had some special role. That being the case, his life was in hourly danger.

The SAS Colonel was invited to speak about timing, and after consulting his team, he confirmed that they could be ready to go at 05.00 Mogadishu time the following morning, 03.00 hours London time, when the light conditions would favour the attackers. Provided of course that it could be established without doubt where the hostages were being held. The Minister called for comments or objections. Bokus remained silent and it was agreed that the SAS should go in at 05.00 local time the following day.

The Minister withdrew with his supporting team of civil servants, asking to be kept up to date with developments, and the room returned to its working mode, while in the SAS corner the decision was relayed to operational control in Hereford.

Liz left Peggy in charge of the Thames House team and went back to the office to brief the directors' meeting. Peggy would keep her in touch as events developed.

50

Many years before, Taban had been told a fable about twin brothers who had been raised by a violent father. Instead of uniting against this tyrant, the brothers had fallen out between themselves and become bitter enemies. They argued endlessly and often fought—and one day they fought so fiercely that one of them died from his brother's blows.

At first the surviving brother was happy to be rid

of his detested sibling. But over time he became uncertain and afraid, and started telling everyone that the ghost of his dead brother had come back to haunt him. Asked what this ghost looked like, the surviving brother cried, *It's a shadow and it looks like fear.*

That was exactly how Taban would have described the shadow cast over his own life by the Middle Eastern men at the camp. He tried to avoid them, but his duties at the compound meant that inevitably he came across these Arab strangers almost every day, and when he did they were hostile and aggressive. The Tall One in particular seemed to enjoy frightening the boy, and had taken to pointing his gun at him every time he saw him. The first time he'd done it, Taban had flinched in fear, and the other men in the gang had laughed. Now he'd steeled himself not to react when the gun was aimed at him, but he sensed that it was just a matter of time before the Tall One actually pulled the trigger. Taban had told Khalid about this terrifying game, but the leader of the Somali pirates had just shrugged and said that there was nothing he could do about it. It was clear that if Khalid was ever going to stand up to the Tall One, it wasn't going to be on Taban's behalf.

Very early this morning, for the first time in weeks, six of the Arab men had gone out to sea, 'borrowing' skiffs from Khalid and the other Somalis. But Taban's relief at their departure was short-lived; they returned before midday, though only three of them came back. They were in a hurry, too, running from the beach into the camp, pushing two Westerners towards the pen at gunpoint. The younger of the two had a massive

284

bruise on one cheek, and when he was slow entering the pen the tall Arab pushed him so hard from behind that he hit his head on one of the timber frames.

Hostages, thought Taban. But this didn't look like the usual situation. Why were there only two men and not a whole crew? And where were the other Arabs and the ship? And why did the Middle Eastern men seem so jumpy and nervous? Normally when hostages were taken there was celebration and feasting while the pirates waited happily for the first phone calls to come through, signalling the beginning of negotiations for the release of the ship and the hostages. But the Middle Eastern men were on edge, talking together loudly and looking out to sea and up at the sky. None of them had put down their weapons, and the Tall One had ordered several of the ones who had stayed behind to guard the perimeter of the camp. He himself was standing in the centre of the compound, holding an AK-47 and constantly looking around.

The noise made by the men must have wakened Khalid, who usually slept until early afternoon, after staying up late watching Western movies on the big screen in his house. He came out and asked the Tall One what was going on. Taban could only hear snatches of what the Tall One said, but it was clear that the hijacking attempt had gone wrong—the Arabs had brought back hostages without a ship. Khalid was visibly alarmed and, for the first time, he seemed to be standing up to the Tall One. Taban edged closer so he could listen.

'What is the point of holding these two men if you don't have their ship?' Khalid demanded.

The Tall One glared at him furiously. 'Listen, you snivelling piece of dog! Three of my comrades have been captured by foreigners along with four new fighters from Pakistan who were supposed to join us here. They may be dead for all I know. So I have no time for your moaning.' He pointed to the pen. 'I have to deal with this scum here—the Pakistani leader told me on board that the younger one is a British spy. And the other man is Captain of the vessel. He will be valuable to its owners.'

'Bah!' said Khalid derisorily. 'He is nothing to the owners. It's the ships and the cargoes they want.'

'This British spy is a different story.'

'He certainly is, and it is a dangerous one. Can't you see? They will come after him.'

The Tall One said, 'Let them come. They will find more than they bargained for.'

'Are you mad?' Khalid's voice was rising. Taban knew that the last thing he would want was a confrontation in his own camp. 'They will kill us all.'

'Not before we kill many of them,' said the Tall One. He spoke with an eerie calm. 'I can think of no finer way to die. No real warrior is frightened of death.'

Khalid ignored this. 'I can't have them coming here. It would destroy our entire operation.'

'Operation? You mean making money. That should not be the priority for any true Muslim.'

But Khalid wouldn't yield. 'I cannot have them coming here,' he repeated. 'You will have to go. And take the hostages with you.' Taban could tell that Khalid was scared of the Tall One, but he could see that he was even more scared of an

286

attack by Western forces.

'Say that again,' said the Tall One coldly.

'You will have to go,' repeated Khalid. The Tall One's eyes widened at Khalid's unprecedented boldness. He stood back for a moment, scratching his chin thoughtfully. Then the Tall One's face hardened, his jaw clenched and his eyes narrowed. He suddenly swung up the AK-47 he was holding and fired a burst straight at Khalid.

Khalid fell backwards on to the ground, blood pouring from what was left of his head. Taban stared, too stunned to move. He didn't dare look at the Tall One but waited, expecting to be next and wondering what it would feel like to die.

Suddenly a man shouted from nearby. The Tall One looked round, distracted by the sound, and Taban dared to turn his head too. The younger hostage had his face pressed up against the wire of the pen. 'Water! My friend needs water!'

The Tall One strode over to the pen and unlocked the door, all the while pointing his rifle. He trained the gun on the younger man; the older hostage was lying down in the rear of the pen, and looked ill.

'On your knees,' ordered the Tall One.

The younger one obeyed, slowly getting down on all fours. The Tall One stepped forward, swinging his rifle slowly round until its barrel end touched the forehead of the hostage. 'I am told you are an agent of the West.'

The man said nothing, and the Tall One moved the barrel away, then suddenly swung it back fast across the man's face. He winced in agony, and Taban saw blood flowing in a swelling line from the bridge of the hostage's nose.

'Do your people know where this camp is?' the Tall One demanded. This time he didn't swing the gun away, but pushed it straight against the man's forehead. The man closed his eyes, and Taban knew he thought he was about to die.

Taban had to do something; any moment now, the Tall One would pull the trigger. So he shouted, a loud inarticulate cry designed purely to attract attention. Momentarily the Tall One looked behind him, startled, then snapped, 'Shut up,' at Taban and turned back to the hostage.

'They're coming!' Taban shouted again.

'What?' This time when he turned the Tall One kept his gaze on the boy.

'Over there!' Taban was pointing frantically towards the nearby dunes. 'They're landing—the enemy!'

And without thinking how the boy could know this, standing just twenty feet away from him, the Tall One came out of the cage quickly, stopping only to close the padlock. Then he ran across the compound towards the dunes.

Taban breathed out; his heart was beating like a drum. He walked over to the pen, where the younger man was now sitting on the floor, all colour drained out of his battered face. The hostage said, to Taban's surprise, 'A man was here once called Richard Luckhurst. Do you remember?'

Of course he did. Captain Richard had been his friend. He nodded vigorously. The hostage added, 'You are Taban, right?'

Taban nodded again and smiled. 'I help you,' he said eagerly.

'No. You need to get out of here . . . fast.' When

288

the boy looked puzzled, the man made gestures as if shooting a gun.

'Go,' he said. 'Quick. Vamoose. He was going to shoot you. If you stay here any longer, he will do it.'

'But I—'

The Western man interrupted, shaking his head. 'You must go. Run and get help. Or they will kill you.' And he drew his finger across this throat. 'Now!' he said urgently.

Taban hesitated no longer. He struck out at once, not towards the dunes, where men were already positioned with guns, but north, over a section of low wall. Once out of sight of the compound, he started to run. He ran straight on without looking back, then he turned towards the coast. He was heading for the sanctuary of his past—the village, less than two miles away, where he had grown up with his father and brother; the village from which he had gone out to sea each day to fish; the village where he had seen his father murdered. He wondered who would still be there; the last he had heard, some other pirates were using the dilapidated huts as shelter, in between their hijacking runs.

He ran as quickly as he could. He was young and fit, but the soft sand slowed him down. At last, as he climbed up to the top of the dunes, he could see the huts and the splintered wooden landing stage beside his former home. It was beginning to get dark now and he ran faster, fuelled by the adrenalin of fear, sprinting down the last few yards of sulphur-coloured sand to the hamlet nestled on the shore. As he reached the straw-roofed huts he could see that none was inhabited—they had been stripped bare by raiders, who had taken everything from chairs to cooking pots. There was nowhere to hide: not a bed to crouch under, no cupboard to conceal him, just sand floors and bare board walls and open squares for windows. Soon it would be pitch black, so propping himself up against the back wall of one of the huts, he sat down to wait till dawn.

*   *   *

Taban opened his eyes suddenly to grey daylight and the low throbbing of an engine. Peering round the wall of the hut, he could just make out, far in the distance, near the compound, a jeep moving along the beach in his direction. Men had been sent to bring him back. No, not to bring him back; they would have been sent to kill him.

The noise of the jeep was growing louder; he could hear the harsh cough of its carburettor, but didn't dare wait to watch his pursuers draw closer. He looked desperately about for some way to escape. Then he spotted a single skiff moored at the end of the landing stage. But was it still seaworthy or had it been holed? He ran out along the splintered boards to where the little boat floated at the far end, tethered by a fraying piece of rope. It had no engine, and its mast was badly split—too broken to support a sail.

Taban jumped in regardless; to stay on land would mean certain death. The bottom of the boat was fairly dry, and tucked under one gunwale was a pair of oars. He undid the rope, pushed off as hard as he could from the wooden platform and quickly slotted the oars into the rowlocks. He heard the jeep roar into the hamlet and heard its engine cut out. They were here.

Struggling at first with the long oars, he gradually found a rhythm. The tide was going out, which helped, and he made rapid progress, pulling away from shore—when he allowed himself a glance back he was almost a hundred yards out. The men couldn't have looked out to sea at first— they must have started by searching the huts— but now one of them appeared at the far end of the landing stage, shouting and gesturing to his comrades.

Soon there were three men running along the wooden planking, all armed, and as the first got to the end, he started firing. A bullet sang by Taban with the buzzing whine of an angry bee. He tried to row faster but almost lost an oar, so he forced himself to row calmly, rhythmically. The bullets were hitting the water well short of him now and the firing paused; then it resumed and they must have been using a different weapon, for he heard a sharp crack and realised that a bullet had found the side of the boat.

Another bullet struck, low down, near the keel. Water began to trickle in at first, then flow freely, like a tap gradually opening—soon it lay an inch deep in the bottom of the boat and it was rising fast. Taban was well out to sea now, at least two hundred yards from the beach. The firing was intensifying, though it seemed to be getting less accurate. But his progress was slowing as the boat grew heavier, with more and more water accumulating in the bottom. He was afraid that if the boat stopped moving he would be an easy target. The water was over his ankles now and he knew the boat would not stay afloat much longer.

What should he do when it sank, as it soon would? Should he try to cling on and hope the timbers would be buoyant enough to support his weight? Or should he abandon it and try to swim back to shore further along the coast and hope to avoid the Arabs there? He was not a strong swimmer, and the thought frightened him.

Then he heard the noise of an outboard engine, and turning around he saw a bright yellow inflatable, a quarter of a mile further out, coming straight towards him. His heart sank—he hadn't realised that the pirates had their own boats; he'd thought they relied entirely on Khalid's skiffs to go out to sea.

He could see, in the bow of the approaching boat, a crouching figure, holding a weapon. As the boat drew closer the man in the bow began firing, and Taban saw bullets soaring above his head, making long trails against the sky.

He ducked instinctively, but the bullets were not for him, they were aimed at the men on the shore. Taban lifted his head cautiously—the dinghy was no more than a couple of hundred yards away from him now and he could make out the face of the man holding the weapon. He was a Westerner. And as the bow of the boat bumped up and down over the little waves, Taban could see painted along its side a familiar flag. The same flag that his friend the Captain had worn on his jacket. These men were British, and when Taban looked back at the shore, he saw that the Arabs had fled.

51

Dave did not sleep. His head was throbbing after the blows from the Arab's gun and his boot. The wind blew remorselessly, carrying sand up from the beach and filling his mouth and the cut on his face with grit. His nose was still bleeding on and off and he was trying to stop the blood by stanching it with what was left of his shirt. Guthrie had been suffering from the heat during the day, sweating profusely and complaining of dizziness. Now he seemed to be asleep but was shivering continuously.

The Somali pirates had fled the compound the previous evening after Khalid had been shot dead, and now only the Arabs remained. Dave reckoned at least three must have been captured on the *Aristides*, along with the four British Pakistanis meant to join them. But the ones who remained were well-armed, seemed well-trained and very determined.

Dave hoped Taban had got away safely. Ten minutes after the boy had left, having distracted the tall Arab by claiming troops were on the beach, the leader had returned, furious at the false alarm. Coming over to the pen he had motioned Guthrie to stay where he was, then forced Dave out at gunpoint. As he emerged, the Arab had hit him with his free arm, knocking him down. The punch had been followed by a kick to the back of Dave's head, which had left him stunned.

He had not tried to get up again, and was lying there, curled into a ball, waiting for the Arab to hit him again, when someone shouted from the edge of the camp. Dave heard the name 'Taban' and realised the boy's escape had been discovered. The tall Arab kicked Dave one more time, then dragged him back into the pen, before turning to give his men orders. He seemed to be telling them that the boy could not get far and they should wait till morning to go after him.

What a cock-up. Dave wanted to blame the French for the mess that had brought him here, but he knew the operation had been a joint Anglo-French one. The combination of mist and darkness and the surprise boarding of the *Aristides* via the bow as well as the stern had caused the disaster, allowing the leader of the hijackers to get away and take Dave and the Captain with him as hostages. The only consolation, he thought, was that none of the Pakistanis had escaped.

What was going to happen to him and Guthrie? He had assumed they would be held to ransom, and had pictured Geoffrey Fane receiving the demand then trying to buy time to mount a rescue operation. The Government would never agree to pay a ransom. He had hoped that Liz would be involved in any response. She knew the background to all of this and would have a pretty clear idea of the sort of people they were dealing with.

But now ransom seemed the least of the Arab leader's priorities. If this were a group of Al Qaeda or one of its affiliates, they would be looking for something other than money in return for their hostages—if they were interested in negotiating at all. Dave's main fear now, which he wasn't going to share with Guthrie, was that since their leader seemed to know that Dave was a British

294

intelligence officer, he would be keen to extract whatever useful information from him he could, doubtless using very unpleasant methods. How far would he go? From the egg-sized bump on his head, the bruise on his cheek, and the cut on his nose that kept dripping blood, Dave guessed that when the man really got to work he would show no mercy. He would enjoy inflicting pain on the West's spy. And after that—well, he had shot the Somali without compunction so wouldn't hesitate to kill a British agent, though Dave feared his death would not be so quick or easy.

He assumed an assault on the camp was being considered, and the helicopter he'd heard half an hour before flying overhead was probably pinpointing their location. Daylight was slowly breaking, the ideal time for such an assault. But would it be in time? And even if it were, it posed its own dangers—the men here in the compound wouldn't stand a chance in a fire fight with the SAS, but that would be small solace if their first act, in the event of an assault, were to open fire on the pen holding him and Captain Guthrie.

As Dave lay sleepless, brooding about this, a jeep started up and drove away along the beach. There was silence after that and then the sound of desultory gunfire from a short distance away. Then, suddenly a fusillade much nearer, from the dunes towards the sea. Within seconds the men in the compound were running to the beach, holding their guns at the ready. A muffled explosion sent a cascade of sand blowing across the open compound into the pen. As it settled, Dave saw an object the size of an apple, just visible in the early light, land on the soft sand, short of the compound's edge;

whoof it went, and again sand flew through the air. Grenades—thrown from the other side of the dunes, where soldiers must be crouched, having landed on the shore. They would be safe from outgoing fire as long as they stayed on the other side of the dunes, but there was no way they could take the camp without directly assaulting it.

The Arab leader was barking orders as more gunfire came from the beach. Suddenly the men in the compound started shooting—one of the assault force must have put his head over the top of the dunes. The firing was disciplined; these guys are well-trained, thought Dave as he watched the men around him taking up cover positions, behind the big tables in the middle of the compound where they ate their food, and behind empty oil barrels and chairs. They would not be easy to dislodge, heavily armed and well-positioned as they were.

But suddenly two of the Arabs fell to the ground, hit. Others followed. Their leader turned round and began firing back—towards Khalid's house at the rear of the compound—and now Dave understood.

The firing and the grenades from the beach had been a diversionary tactic, designed to lure the pirates towards the dunes. As had the appearance of some brave soldier on them, intent on drawing enemy fire. But the main rescue force was firing at the terrorists from behind. They must have landed from that helicopter in scrubland, a mile or so away from the camp, and made their way silently overland on foot.

Pinned down, the Arabs fought tenaciously, but the assault from behind had caught them by surprise—within minutes most of them lay dead

296

or wounded. Only the tall Arab, their leader, was still unharmed. Swivelling a round wooden table on to its side, he used its top as a shield, and from a kneeling position continued to fire towards Khalid's house.

On the far side of the open sandy square a British soldier appeared, climbing over the low compound wall. He was checking the dead nearest him, his attention focused on the Arabs lying on the ground, making sure none was still capable of firing. He was so intent on the task that he didn't see the leader, hidden by the table, who had turned towards him, ready to fire. Watching this with horror, Dave knew he had to act, but what could he do, locked in this pen? The next instant, as the tall Arab stood up to aim and fire, Dave shouted at the top of his voice, '*Incoming!*'

The soldier turned and jumped behind the low compound wall just as the Arab fired, and fired again, in vain. Then another soldier seemed to come out of nowhere, not ten feet from the pen. Standing directly in front of Dave, he shot the leader dead with a burst of automatic-weapon fire.

Turning to the pen, the soldier said nonchalantly, 'All right, mate?'

'We're OK.' Only then did Dave realise how frantically his heart was pounding.

'Good thing you called out or Tony over there would have had it. Cheers!'

For the second time in twenty-four hours, Dave had saved someone's life merely by raising his voice. Maybe I should audition for RADA, he thought. It's got to be safer than this.

297

52

Peggy had stayed in COBRA all day with a small group from Thames House, working closely with the intelligence analysts from the other departments as they put together as much information as they could find to help the SAS plan their rescue mission. From time to time Liz had rung in for an update, and at six o'clock in the evening she had joined the substantial group of people from various departments who'd assembled to hear the SAS's presentation to the Foreign Secretary of their operational plan for the rescue attempt the following morning.

In the pre-dawn darkness, Liz again climbed the few steps from Whitehall to the door of the Cabinet Office, to wait for news to come in of the progress of the operation. By the time she reached the windowless briefing room, reports had started to arrive of a fire fight at the camp; a little later she heard with relief that Dave Armstrong and Captain Guthrie had been successfully rescued. She was still there several hours later when medical reports came in that Guthrie was suffering from what appeared to be pneumonia and that Dave had been beaten badly but was not seriously injured.

Shortly afterwards, as she was watching a shaky hand-held video of the rescue on one of the screens, Peggy waved her over. A call had come in for her from Martin Seurat's office in Paris. Liz took the phone, expecting to hear Martin congratulating her on Dave's rescue, but it was one of his colleagues telling her that M. Seurat had gone over to the Santé prison with a colleague from the DCRI. Amir Khan had told his warders that he was prepared to talk.

Much later, after Liz was back at home, exhaustedly downing a glass of Sauvignon in celebration of Dave's rescue, Martin himself rang. 'I have heard that your colleague is free. Congratulations.'

'Thank you. It's a great relief,' Liz said. Enough had gone wrong in the operation for her to feel that they were very fortunate things had turned out as well as they had.

'It's not the only reason I am calling. I hope you got my message that I went to see our friend in the Santé with Cassale. He says he's willing to talk some more, but he's scared—he knows there are Al Qaeda prisoners in there who would not hesitate to kill him if they thought he was talking to us. He wants reassurances about his safety before he gives out any more information.'

'Can you or Cassale give those to him?'

'I could try, but there's a problem. He wants reassurances from you too. And in person—I'm afraid he was insistent on this point.'

So, this morning, Liz had dragged herself out of bed to catch an early Eurostar. It was clear when she arrived at the prison that something fairly dramatic had occurred to change the French attitude to Amir. She had been surprised to be told that the interview was not to take place in the high-security wing. She had instead been shown into a small, comfortably furnished office, where she settled into an armchair, with a cup of coffee to wait for Amir Khan.

The door opened and Amir walked in, followed

by Martin. The armed guard had gone, as had the chains that had bound Amir's arms and legs. Now he walked upright instead of shuffling, his head no longer bowed. Looking straight at Liz, he nodded and said 'Good morning' with a slight smile, then sat down on the chair that Martin indicated.

Martin said formally to Liz, 'I have had a long talk with Amir and he says that he wants to tell us his story. There are some reassurances he is asking for that only the British can give, so I thought it best that you come in person to hear what he has to say.'

Amir looked at her and nodded. 'I want to tell you what happened because I want you to stop it happening to anyone else. If I do this, then I want to see my sister so I can explain things to her. But you must guarantee she'll be safe if she comes to see me here.'

Liz said nothing while she thought about this. What Amir was asking for was perfectly reasonable from his point of view, but it was not something she could immediately agree to. It would take a lot of sorting out. Liz couldn't give him any reassurances about his own position, since it hadn't been decided yet what if any charges he should face, or in which country he would face them: France or England.

Tahira, moreover, was now effectively a recruited agent and vital to the investigation. If she were suddenly brought over here, she would have to be pulled out of the operation, which would mean they'd lose their one means of contact with Malik. And what's more, as Amir himself understood, just bringing her to the prison to talk to him might put her in serious danger. This would

300

need careful thinking about.

Amir was watching her closely; Liz could see from his face that if she said the wrong thing he was going to refuse to speak. She had to take a risk.

She said, 'Amir, I'm very glad that you have decided to help us. We also want to stop others getting involved in all this. I'm going to explain what I can do to meet your terms. First, about Tahira. I've met her and talked to her.' Amir looked surprised, but Liz went on, 'She is terribly worried about you. She wanted to come and see you but your father wouldn't let her.'

He nodded as if that were no surprise.

'I'm sure she would want you to know that she is helping us, and I'm equally sure that she would want you to help us too.' Amir frowned and Liz went on quickly, before he could speak. 'I can promise you that when this is over, we'll look after her. But I don't think it would be a good idea for her to come over to Paris to see you now. If she did, I could not guarantee to keep her safe, as we couldn't be sure her trip would remain secret—not right now, at any rate. But I will ask her to write to you and I'll either bring the letter myself or give it to my French colleagues to give to you.'

'What is she doing to help you? Are you putting her in danger?'

'She is only doing what she wants to do.' Liz's eyes were focused on Amir. 'No one is putting any pressure on her. She's helping us because she wants to help you. You are lucky to have such a sister.'

'I know.'

'Now about your position, Amir. As you know, it hasn't yet been decided whether you should be charged, or even whether you should remain in

France or return to the UK. I can't give you any guarantees. But if you talk to us truthfully, that will certainly be taken into consideration, both by us in the UK and,' she looked at Martin with raised eyebrows and he nodded, 'by the French.'

'But if I talk to you, they'll kill me if they can.'

'If you talk frankly to us, we and our French colleagues will have the responsibility of looking after you—and Tahira, of course. And if that meant you couldn't go back to Birmingham, then we would help you go somewhere else.'

Amir had been staring at Liz as she explained all this. Now he was hesitating, clearly trying to make up his mind what to do.

Martin said gently, 'My advice is that you should tell us your story.'

Amir nodded. 'I haven't got a choice really, have I?'

And he began to talk. He'd first gone to the New Springfield Mosque with Malik and had been fascinated by the preaching of Imam Bakri and his message of the duty of all true Muslims to wage war against the infidel. Amir described how he'd been asked to join an inner group of true believers which had met weekly for several months. Then they had all gone three times to a mosque in North London where they had met a woman—a white woman, who spoke beautiful Arabic and talked enthrallingly about *jihad*.

'She was a witch. A blonde witch,' he said. 'She enchanted us and took away our souls. She told us we had been chosen to be on the front line of the fight and we would be blessed. No one told us where we would go, but we thought it would be Afghanistan.'

The officials of the New Springfield Mosque had made all the travel arrangements and they were kept very secret. 'They told me to go to my uncle in Rawalpindi, where I would be contacted, so I did. One day three men came to see me there, and I went with them. They gave me Pakistani travel documents and arranged for me to go to Athens.'

He went on to describe how he had got to Mombasa by ship, then by road to Somalia where he joined a group of Arabs who ran a training camp in the desert. 'It was very difficult getting there overland—we arrived ten days later than expected.' It was then that the decision was taken to take new recruits in future directly from the ships off the Horn, rather have the human cargo unloaded a thousand kilometres away in Kenya and wait for it to make its way north to Somalia.

So the Arabs moved camp, to a compound that was already inhabited by Somali pirates, on the coast about ten miles south of Mogadishu.

Liz interjected, 'And the Arabs then tried to hijack the *Aristides*?'

'Yes. They saw how easy it was—the pirates had been doing it successfully for years, so the Arabs decided to do it themselves. That way they'd get their new recruits and also make money by ransoming the ships and stealing the cargoes.'

'Didn't the Somali pirates object?'

Amir shook his head. 'Their leader wasn't happy, but he was frightened of the Arabs. So was I, to tell you the truth; and the Arabs knew it. The leader was a tall, thin man with burning eyes—I think he was mad—who made me go with the others on a pirate raid because he claimed it would make me brave. I think he just wanted an eye kept on me.

'It was terrifying. They made me go up the ladder first and when the French Navy boat came up, they sailed off and I fell in the sea. And that's how I got captured. The others were captured, too, and they told me if I said anything they'd find out, and then they'd kill me. Are some of them are here in this prison?'

He looked at them both with frightened eyes. Martin shook his head. 'They're not here, and there is no way they could know anything about what's happened to you.'

I hope you're right, thought Liz, as she sat and listened to Amir's story unfold. And as she and Martin questioned him further about the details over the next two hours, she couldn't get out of her head her first visit to this prison, and the man with the book in the back pocket of his jeans whom she had felt sure was following her. Was he Al Qaeda too? Possibly, which meant Amir was right to worry about his safety and Tahira's if she ever came here.

53

'I have some news for you,' said David Blakey, leaning forward in his chair and putting his elbows on the desk. There was a self-satisfied air to the man which surprised Liz, since she had come to his office after getting back from Paris, expecting to be the one who did the talking. But she let him speak first, knowing that nothing he was going to say would alter the facts that had come to light.

He went on: 'Mitchell Berger in Athens has been

doing a little investigating of his own. He's grown suspicious of the man who arranges the leasing of our ships there. His name is Mo Miandad and it turns out he isn't entirely what he seems. Berger has discovered that he's been meeting a woman who works in the UCSO office. Her name's Claude Rameau—she's been with us a long time. Quite senior; she's a roving co-ordinator for our local aid supplies. Travels all the time, mainly in Africa.'

'Why is she based in Athens?'

'There's no real reason—I inherited her, she'd got a routine, and frankly, I didn't see any reason to change it.'

'Why does this mean that Miandad is the source of the leak?'

Blakey seemed a little taken aback. 'Well, we haven't got any hard evidence, if that's what you're driving at. But Rameau has always been a bit of an anarchist—she's very anti-American, for one thing. And of course it means Miandad has a secret life.'

'Cheating on his wife doesn't make him an Al Qaeda agent.' Liz sighed at Blakey's reasoning. None of this would stand up in court; none of it, in fact, was standing up with her.

'I think you're missing my point. It's not his choice of bedmate that's at issue here.' Blakey looked at her resentfully. 'I thought you'd be interested in this. Berger's convinced Miandad's up to no good. Remember, you don't know the people we're talking about.'

'That's true,' said Liz. 'But there are some other things I've discovered which you ought to hear.'

'About the Athens office?'

'Actually, no. A bit closer to home.'

Blakey looked uncomfortable for the first time.

Liz said, 'There's another woman we've had under surveillance. Not Rameau, though this one's also blonde. She attended a mosque in North London that we've been investigating for some time.'

'What's that got to do with the leak from UCSO?' asked Blakey.

Liz ignored him. 'Radical Islamists have taken this mosque over; we suspect they've been recruiting young British Muslims and sending them to Pakistan for training in their camps. This woman addressed some of the recruits, and a week later, bingo, off they went to learn how to wage *jihad*.'

Blakey was listening intently.

'Then the scene shifts to Athens. I don't think the woman seeing Mo Miandad is Claude Rameau.'

'You don't?' It was impossible to tell if Blakey's surprise was genuine.

'No. I think it's the same woman who was seen at the North London mosque. Which disqualifies Rameau.'

'So who is it then?' But Blakey's question seemed rhetorical. The expression on his face had changed from scepticism to curiosity to alarm—he was clearly starting to draw his own conclusions. And not enjoying them.

'I'm pretty sure you have as good an idea as I do.'

'What do you mean?' Blakey looked shaken.

'Katherine Ball.' Liz let the words hang between them.

'You think . . .' Blakey started to say, his voice rising, and then the possibility that she might be right seemed to stop him short.

'I *know* that she has visited a North London

mosque. I *know* that she's addressed recruits there. And I *know* that she's been your lover for some time.'

Blakey wanted to speak: his lips moved; a croaking sound came out of his mouth but there were no words. He was staring at Liz without really seeing her. Suddenly he dropped his head into his hands. Liz thought for a moment that he was going to burst into tears, but when he lifted his head again his eyes were dry, and he seemed to have pulled himself together. He said quietly, 'What a fool I've been.'

'How much does she know?'

'Katherine? What about?' Then, seeing Liz's cold gaze, he said, 'She knows the lot.'

'That won't do. You need to be more specific.'

Blakey threw his hands up in the air, almost in despair. 'She knew I asked Geoffrey for help, and she knew when you came to see me.'

So the MI6 and MI5 operations had been blown from the beginning. Liz sighed, and Blakey seemed to sense her disgust. He protested, 'I don't see what use that would be to Islamic militants in Birmingham.'

Liz shrugged. 'I wasn't thinking of Birmingham; I was thinking of Athens. Did she know about that?'

Blakey flushed. 'You mean, the girl?'

'I do. Let's give her a name,' Liz said icily. 'Maria Galanos.'

Blakey wouldn't look at her, which gave Liz her answer. At last he said, in a voice that was barely above a whisper, 'Oh, God.' He was rubbing his hands together now, as if trying to wash everything away. 'But Katherine couldn't have killed her,' he

307

said, almost hopefully. 'She wasn't in Greece when Maria was murdered. She was here.'

'Enter Mo Miandad,' said Liz.

Blakey's hands stopped moving, and he stared at them as if they had been stained again by her words. Then he spoke without looking at Liz, averting his face, as if it would somehow make the horror less. 'You have to believe me, I had no idea. She never gave the slightest indication of sympathising with Islam—I'd have bet you anything that she'd never set foot in a mosque in her life. Her husband was Middle Eastern, but from everything she ever said he was thoroughly Westernised—educated in the States, enlightened, liberal. And the information she got from me—well, I'll be honest, it was me telling her; I wasn't being pumped.'

Pillow talk, thought Liz bitterly, which had cost Maria Galanos her life. Blakey seemed to sense this, for he continued, 'I have no excuse, I understand that. I'm just trying to explain things. Even now that I know, I find it hard to believe. If she was trying to entrap me, she did a miraculous job of disguising it. I made all the running,' he said emphatically.

Yes, thought Liz. An attractive intelligent blonde woman who works in the same office didn't have to do a lot to catch the interest of a known womaniser whose wife had left him. The smallest signs would do—the chance arrival at the lift when her target was leaving for the day, perhaps turning down the first invitation for a drink but making it clear a second offer would receive a different reception; a few sympathetic words about his personal troubles, a suggestion that she knew 'how it was' since she was lonely too. She'd played him very cleverly, you had to give the woman that—even now Blakey was thinking he had seduced her, that he had made all the running.

Blakey was waiting anxiously for her to say more. 'When are you due to see Katherine next?' she asked.

'This evening. She's at a meeting away from the office today; a get-together of other similar charities—it happens twice a year. She said she'd come round to my flat at seven or so. I can give you the address.'

'We've got that already,' said Liz. It was somehow worse having Blakey trying to be helpful.

'I don't know how I'm going to face her,' he said plaintively.

'I don't think you'll find it's much of a problem.'

54

Normally Ivy Howson would have been at home by now. Thursdays were her late day working for Mr Blakey, but even then she was usually off by four, having done two loads of laundry, put them through the dryer (she'd told him twice now it was on its last legs), and ironed the sheets and pillow cases as well as the shirts she hadn't got round to on Tuesday.

But today she was still in the neighbourhood a good three hours later, though in fairness it was not because of Mr Blakey. Before she'd gone to work for him, she'd worked for an American family who'd lived around the corner, in a trim little house that the American woman had insisted on calling 'cute'. It was there that Mrs Howson had met Eloise the au pair, a nice New Zealand girl who'd looked up to Ivy like a second mum. And it was Eloise she'd gone to see today, still working as an au pair, in the same house funnily enough, though now it was for a Chinese couple called Tang or Tong or Ting—Mrs Howson didn't know.

Though Eloise was working so close by, Ivy hadn't seen her for yonks, so they'd had a lovely time over tea, catching up and chatting. Not that Eloise had that much to tell—the Tangs or whatever they were called were quiet people, with one young child, but they didn't speak that much English, according to Eloise, so it was a bit boring for her. Yet Ivy Howson had more than filled the conversational gap, what with the goings on in the Blakey household since she'd last seen Eloise. How they'd laughed as she'd described this new blonde woman that Mr Blakey didn't like to admit was his girlfriend. She wasn't a patch on Mrs Blakey, who, poor thing, was said to be living in Acton now, all on her own. 'It's tough on a woman if she gets hitched up to a bastard,' Mrs Howson had said. 'You watch yourself, Eloise,' she'd warned, more than once.

They'd had a lovely chat, though Ivy had got a bit of a shock when she looked at her watch and saw it was ten to seven. 'Lordie,' she exclaimed, thinking how cross Stanley would be, sitting waiting for his tea in the ground-floor flat in Streatham, where they'd lived for seventeen years. Lived ever since Maureen their daughter had moved out to shack up with the first of what even Mrs Howson, loyal mother though she was, would acknowledge had been a string of unsatisfactory partners. Stanley was retired now, and hadn't found a lot to fill his time, so he didn't like it that she still went out to do for Mr Blakey. He'd be furious when she got home a good three hours later than usual.

She put her coat on hurriedly, grabbed her bag and said a quick goodbye to Eloise, promising to come and see the girl again sometime soon. She was bustling down the street, retracing her steps past the mansion block where Mr Blakey lived, when she noticed the cars. They were parked within twenty yards of each other, three of them, all exactly the same, which was why she noticed them in the first place. They were black and as she walked past them she saw that inside each car two men were sitting. Mrs Howson stopped for a moment, simply because this seemed so odd. She found herself waiting, not quite sure what she was waiting for.

It didn't take long to find out. A taxi came along fast from Marylebone High Street, its orange 'for hire' light going on even before it had stopped. The driver braked sharply and came to a halt across the road from Mr Blakey's block. Mrs Howson tutted to herself disapprovingly as she recognised the woman who got out. It was that blonde woman Mr Blakey insisted on referring to as 'Mrs Ball', and whom Ivy Howson never addressed at all.

She watched as the woman paid the driver, then swung her expensive-looking bag over her shoulder and started to cross the road. She was smartly dressed in a belted raincoat that reached just below the knees, showing off her well-formed calves, encased today in shiny black tights. I'll bet they'll be at it before the clock strikes seven, thought Ivy, then chided herself for her crudeness. Still, there was something that invited it in the way this woman dressed, and walked—she was on the pavement now and heading for the mansion block's outer door.

It was then that the most amazing thing happened, something Mrs Howson would never forget. From out of nowhere all the blokes in the cars had suddenly appeared—there on the pavement. It was like magic, she later said to Stanley, who couldn't understand why she'd been so surprised by the sudden appearance of six fellows who just had to be coppers. You don't understand, she'd complained. It was like a conjuring trick. One minute they weren't there and the next they were, and I never noticed it happening.

One of the chaps had approached Mrs Ball just as she was about to enter the building, and she'd smiled—Ivy could still remember the flirtatious curve to the woman's lips. At the same time another bloke had moved in from the other side, taking her by the arm. It was then that alarm had replaced polite curiosity on the woman's face. By now the taxi had left and the street was deserted— thinking back, Ivy Howson realised that she'd been the only witness.

But witness to what? The men had taken the Ball woman to one of the black cars, and you could see she wasn't given any choice—she was going with them like it or not. But she hadn't screamed; she hadn't even looked around. She couldn't have been abducted because she didn't struggle. If she was being nicked, the odd thing was that she didn't seem to mind. What Ivy remembered most of all

was the way Mrs Ball had got into the back seat of
the car with a smile on her face.

55

Paddington Green police station was a grim place,
even grimmer than Liz had expected. A colleague
had once described to her his interrogation of a
suspect there and had said that it made Wormwood
Scrubs look like a five-star hotel. Now, as she was
escorted down two flights of stairs and along a
narrow corridor, flanked by cells, Liz understood
what he meant. Forbidding though the Santé prison
in Paris was, at least it had a history, both fictional
and real. Carlos the Jackal and Noriega rubbed
shoulders in its corridors with characters from the
novels of Alexandre Dumas and Georges Simenon.
Here, in Paddington Green, there was no gloss
of history, and the brutal concrete walls seemed
to match the squalid violence of the modern-day
terrorists whom it had been built to accommodate.
It was, thought Liz, a truly awful place.
   The police officer escorting her opened a steel
door and stood back to let her enter the room,
then followed her inside. A single light bulb
illuminated a bare table and chairs, cement floor
the colour of day-old porridge, and blank walls.
Liz was expecting to find that the prisoner she'd
come to see would introduce a note of elegance
to these stark surroundings. She remembered
the stylish even glamorous woman she had met
in David Blakey's office at the beginning of this
whole business, and how she had admired, not to

say envied, the understated linen dress the other woman had been wearing and her gold jewellery.

So she was startled by the appearance of the person sitting at the table. It was difficult to believe it was the same one. Katherine Ball was wearing a plain cotton caftan and long, wide trousers over flat pumps. At first sight Liz wondered if this was some sort of prison uniform, but Katherine Ball had not been charged and was entitled to wear her own clothes, so these must be her choice. Her face was bare of make-up and her hair, which Liz remembered as fashionably tinted blonde, was completely covered by an unflattering scarf. Only her bright blue eyes were unaltered and they seemed to burn as they stared at Liz.

'Mrs Ball,' said Liz, taking a seat across from her. 'We met in David Blakey's office some time ago. My name is Jane Forrester.'

Katherine Ball arched an eyebrow. 'I remember you well. You work with that man who was a colleague of David's when he was in MI6 . . . what's his name? Tall, dark and not entirely handsome. Fane—that was it. So you're a spook too.'

'I'm with the Home Office.'

'Oh, I see, we're talking in euphemisms. What you mean is that you're MI5, not MI6. Isn't that what you're trying to say, Miss . . . *Forrester.* Now, tell me, what are you here for?'

' I was wondering—'

'Don't wonder,' said Katherine Ball fiercely, her eyes suddenly ablaze. 'There's nothing to speculate about, nothing ambiguous in any of this. Believe me: if you want to know about me, I'll tell you. Frankly, I'm delighted you're here; nothing will please me more than to say what I have to say to a representative of Western Intelligence.'

'What is it you'd like to say?'

But Katherine did not need to be asked. Liz's presence seemed to have breached the dam behind which she had been concealing her true personality and feelings.

'You in Western Intelligence—you once had something worth defending and an enemy worth fighting. For all the shortcomings of life in the West, Communism was worse, much worse ... corrupt, oppressive of its people, twisted. Getting rid of them was a just cause.' She paused for breath and went on, 'But when the Wall fell, so did your *raison d'être*. You didn't have a role any more. Just what exactly were you fighting after that, and what were you defending? I mean, what does democracy consist of when a hedge fund trader makes three billion dollars trading off the back of some poor black people in Detroit who've taken out a mortgage?

'So you became stooges of the Americans. Dancing to their tune. Fighting a war on terrorism—"those who are not with us are against us". Anyone who thinks differently from them is a threat and has to be destroyed. And the rest of the world is supposed to admire this, and stick out their bowl for the thin gruel the likes of UCSO graciously bestow on them.'

'So you chose an alternative solution.' Liz kept her voice cool. There was no need to needle this woman to get her to talk.

'I'd have thought that was obvious. There is only one positive ideology in the world today, don't you think?'

Liz ignored the question and replied, 'I'm

315

curious to know how you found this cause. I know your husband was Middle Eastern, but my understanding is that he was Westernised.'

'You know nothing about my husband.'

'I'm told he was a businessman in Beirut.'

'He was. But the 9/11 pilots were living quietly in America while learning to fly planes. You should know about cover stories, Miss Forrester. It's your job—playing a role. But others can do it too. My husband played a role. He lived and breathed it and I've been doing it ever since he died.'

'But why? What was he trying to achieve?'

'He was half-Iranian, and always said he wished he'd been a hundred per cent Iranian. If he hadn't died so suddenly, we wouldn't be sitting here, Miss Forrester. I'd be in Beirut, helping him organise resistance to Zionist incursions. My husband made a lot of money and he used a good deal of it to underwrite Hamas.'

'I'm sorry your husband died. He had a heart attack, didn't he?'

'Is that what your research department told you?' She was growing angry now. 'Tell them to have another look. My husband was murdered—he dropped dead in a Damascus souk. A coronary, they tried to say, but he had the heart of a lion. Mossad killed him—who else?'

Maybe God did, thought Liz. Or Nature, depending on one's theological views. 'Is that when you took up his cause?'

Ball looked at her scornfully. 'I was already on his side. Who wouldn't be? Have you seen the camps in Gaza, Miss Forrester? Have you asked your Jewish friends why they're letting people die there? Why they continue to take other people's land? Have you ever discussed with your American bosses what their "policies" are doing to people all over the world, or why their impact is never reported in the *Jew York Times*?

'When he died I went to Iran to live with his family. I studied and converted to the true faith, Islam.' She stopped talking for a moment and closed her eyes. Then suddenly she opened them again. Glaring at Liz, she half-rose from her chair. 'I don't believe you have any faith at all. You disgust me, you know; you have the nerve to oppose us without having any beliefs of your own. Even our worst enemies, the Jews, believe in God.'

'Sit down,' Liz said sharply, and the woman slowly did. 'So you studied in an Islamic school. What else did they teach you beside the faith? Did they teach you to wage war on the West?'

'They taught me to teach.'

'I've heard about your teaching,' said Liz. 'In a mosque in London. I gather you were inspirational.'

For the first time Katherine Ball hesitated.

'Inspirational,' Liz repeated.

'Whoever told you that is flattering me.'

'Ah, flattery,' said Liz thoughtfully. Then, suddenly, 'Was it by flattery that you attracted David Blakey?'

Katherine Ball's face twisted in distaste. 'It's one thing playing a role; it's quite another pretending you're enjoying it. I found that side of things revolting.'

'Was that true of Mo Miandad as well?'

'What do you know about him?'

'You two slipped up. You were seen at a hotel in Athens. You were supposed to be flying in the

317

following day, but we checked with the airlines and you landed a day early. In time for a rendezvous with Mo.'

'Not that kind of rendezvous,' she snapped. 'What an ass your friend Berger made of himself. He hangs around, thinking he's a detective in a Raymond Chandler novel—then ends up locked in a broom cupboard. As for Mo, he may have been wild once upon a time, and he was happy for people to think he was still a corrupt philanderer—it was the perfect cover story. But he's a true Muslim,' she declared defiantly.

'And a murderer it seems. You have an alibi for the death of Maria Galanos—you'd gone back to London. He doesn't.'

'Try proving that. You'll need more than speculation for the Greek authorities. Speaking of slip-ups, placing that girl in the UCSO office was a very stupid thing to do. She stuck out like a sore thumb. Ingratiating herself with the two Greek girls, trying to find out about everybody—it was ridiculous.'

'Yes, I'm sure you're a far better actress than Maria.' Liz added coldly, 'And she paid the price, didn't she?'

Katherine said nothing, so Liz went on, 'Speaking of acting, your performances at the London mosque seem to have had quite an impact. Several British Asians have left this country to fight *jihad* because of you.'

'That wasn't acting, Miss Forrester. I only preach what I truly believe. But you have no proof that I persuaded anyone to go anywhere.'

'I wouldn't be too sure of that. And I don't think it was only persuasion. I think you were a key part of the organisation that recruited young men and sent them out to train and fight. We've managed to detain the four most recent travellers on their way to Somalia. They'll be extradited here, and in the fullness of time put on trial. I wouldn't rate their chances myself. And some of them may choose to tell the whole story.'

But Katherine Ball seemed unmoved by this news. In fact it seemed to calm her. Her voice became less excitable and her face looked almost serene. If she answered Liz at all, it was in monosyllables; her attention was elsewhere. Liz drew the interview to a close but she felt dissatisfied. She had an uneasy feeling that for all Katherine Ball had revealed, she was still hiding something important.

56

Geoffrey Fane had been delighted by the outcome of the operation off the Somalian coast. 'Despite your colleague's misadventure,' he had said smoothly, 'I think you'd have to agree it's a very satisfactory result. Between us, Elizabeth, we've captured some pirates—who I'm certain will turn out to be Al Qaeda or Al Shebab, not that I think there's much difference—and we've killed the rest of their gang. We've prevented the Birmingham recruits from reaching Somalia, where they would have been trained and hardened and probably sent back to kill us, and we've got your friend Dave out safely. Good job done, I'd say. We must have a drink on it. Perhaps you'll join me at the

Athenaeum one evening.'

Liz wasn't so sure. The Somalian end of the operation might have been shut down, and thanks to Peggy's research into Xenides' role, the Athens conduit for Al Qaeda recruits had been closed by the Greek authorities (though Mo Miandad was still at large). But Liz was worried about Birmingham. As she sat in her Thames House office, gazing out of the window at the Embankment, dry and dusty in the evening sun of a late August day, she reviewed the strands of the UK investigation.

Katherine Ball, the woman who had inspired young recruits and organised their journeys out to train for *jihad*, was safely held in Paddington Green police station. She would not be doing any more harm, but Liz still felt uneasy about her. She had ranted and poured out her hatred, yet at the end, even when she had learned that her mission had failed, had seemed calm, almost satisfied. Was it just a reaction to all that bile spilled or was there something else? And Abdi Bakri—he was still preaching at the New Springfield Mosque and no doubt still inflaming malleable young people with talk of their religious duty to wage war.

'Liz?' It was Peggy. Liz came out of her reverie and waved her into the chair opposite the desk. Peggy sat down, clutching a sheaf of paper. She looked flushed.

'I've got more info—two things actually. The Techs say Abdi Bakri has been emailing this parallax repository again. They've made some more progress with the encryption, and they say Bakri's talking about something on for this weekend. No real indication of where, though, or what.'

Liz thought for a moment. 'It can't be the hijack in Somalia. That's already happened.'

'No, they think it's closer to home. Somewhere in the UK.'

'I bet it's Birmingham. His acolytes all come from the New Springfield Mosque. Like the four we captured on the *Aristides*.'

'But we've had nothing before from Bakri to suggest any UK plans for action. He's more of a preacher, surely. He preaches *jihad* but leaves it to others to organise it.'

'I know,' said Liz, thinking of Katherine Ball.

'Where do we start?' asked Peggy despondently. 'This is when we could have used Boatman.'

Liz thought fleetingly of Salim and his wife, who were ensconced in a safe house well away from both Birmingham and London. Kanaan Shah was looking after them and doing a good job, she'd heard. She would visit them as she'd promised, but only when this new threat had been dealt with. She said to Peggy, 'I know what you mean, but we've still got one agent in place.'

'Who?'

'Tahira.'

'She's not close to Abdi Bakri and the mosque.'

'No, but she is close to Malik. And he's close to Abdi Bakri. And Malik keeps popping up in all this—he helped attack me near the mosque; he knew Boatman, and seemed to become suspicious of him; he may have had a hand in the "accident" on the bus. Plus he knew Amir Khan, apparently quite well.'

'And he's still in Birmingham.'

'Exactly. Remember, he boasted to Tahira that he was going on an important mission to Pakistan,

321

but then he didn't go. Why not? He gave her no explanation. He just said the plans had changed. What plans? And why was he kept behind when the others went? It doesn't make sense.'

'Unless . . .'

Liz was nodding. 'Unless he's got a mission here, in the UK.'

'Tahira is due to see him again tomorrow.'

'I know, and that worries me. He wouldn't hesitate to hurt her if he knew she was working for us.' Liz remembered the strength in his arm when he'd grabbed her.

'But maybe she'll be able to tell us something after their meeting.'

'Perhaps. But I don't think we can risk waiting till tomorrow.' She paused, making up her mind. 'I want Malik placed under surveillance as soon as possible—within the hour if they can do it. We need to know where he is every minute of this weekend—even if he isn't involved. Will you set it up with Lamb Lincoln in Birmingham and get them to patch real-time reports through to A4 Control here? I'm going to alert Fontana and tell him what we've learned. I'll see if he's got any idea of what might be happening. I don't want any crossed wires; I'll warn him we may need armed support if anything unravels. Then I'm going to ring DG. I'll meet you in A4 control in an hour or so, when we've done all that.'

Two hours later lights were burning on several floors of Thames House. Peggy was at her desk, receiving reports from the monitoring of various telephones that Malik was known to use; the Techs were on alert for any email traffic. In the A4 control room Liz was sitting on the battered leather sofa reserved for case officers, listening as Wally Woods, the Thames House controller for the evening, liased with Lamb Lincoln in Birmingham. Reports were coming in from A4 teams as they searched for Malik in all his known haunts, but so far there had been no sign of him. He had not been spotted in the crowd coming out of the mosque, a disguised call to his parents' house had elicited the information that he was out, he was not at the café, and A4 was running out of ideas of where to look as the evening drew on. Lamb was asking how long they should go on looking as he was beginning to fear they might be getting exposed.

Liz took a deep breath. 'OK,' she said. 'There's no point in going on with this tonight. Stand them down. We know he's meeting Tahira in the morning, so let's put the teams on to her first thing. She'll be at her parents' house. They can follow her to the meeting and then take on Malik as he leaves. We'll need real-time reports. I'm going up to Birmingham. Tell Lamb that I'll see him early on.'

Leaving further instructions that if the Techs or the monitors got anything of interest she was to be told right away, Liz went back to her flat for what by now would be a short night's sleep.

57

The alarm went off at 4.30 and Liz got up immediately. She had only been in bed for four hours and felt as though she'd been awake for every minute. She knew she hadn't, because she could remember dreams where Amir Khan, Malik and Tahira whirled together in a meaningless but alarming ballet in her subconscious.

By 5 she was on the North Circular Road, heading for the A40. This early on a Saturday morning, even the notorious Hanger Lane gyratory was clear, and once on the A40 she made steady progress past the old Hoover building and Northolt airfield towards the motorway. Over the M40, the sun slowly rose into a cloudless morning sky, and was soon filling the fields of Oxfordshire with golden light.

At 6 she pulled over at a lay-by and rang Peggy, who would have spent the night in one of the small bedrooms at the top of Thames House, ready for any new development. She would be awake by now and at her desk.

Peggy said, 'Nothing's happened. The monitors and the Techs say it's been quiet all night. A4 in Birmingham are checking out Malik's place, but there's been no movement so far. They're ready for Tahira when she leaves home. I spoke to DG on the phone last night. He's got a call booked to the Home Secretary at ten and I've told Private Office I'll bring them up to date just before then. A4 up there say they're looking forward to seeing you.'

Thank God for Peggy, thought Liz. She was a

real rock in troubled seas.

In the Birmingham suburbs, the first signs of life were appearing; some of the small mini-markets were open and cafés were serving breakfast to stall holders setting up a street market. It was 7.30 when Liz turned into the old Odeon cinema building and tapped in the code to open the tall iron gates that let her into the car park at the back.

Inside, the A4 Ops room was a low-ceilinged windowless space at the top of the renovated cinema. One wall was covered with screens, mostly dark at present, but when the operation got underway they'd be taking real-time feed from cameras in the area and from some of the A4 cars.

As she went into the gloomy room, Liz saw DI Fontana sitting on a large leather sofa. A4 must have a secret source of battered furniture, since these brown sofas, placed for case officers to sit on when an operation was in progress, always appeared as if by magic.

Lamb Lincoln at the control console waved to Liz as she walked into the room. Handing over to his deputy, a morose-looking man called Faraday, he walked across to brief her.

'Good morning,' he said cheerfully. 'All's quiet on the Western Front here; so far anyway. There's activity in the park, setting up the concert—it starts at twelve. Tahira's at home as far as we know, but still no sign of Malik. I don't suppose she's going into the shop before she meets him?'

Liz shook her head. 'From what she said, I don't think so.'

'Then she won't be leaving home for a bit. But anyway the teams are all ready, on her house and the café, so we're OK whatever she does. We'll be working with two police teams when Malik appears, in case there's any need for an arrest. '

Liz nodded her thanks to Lamb and looked at Fontana.

'This pop concert's taking a lot of police resources,' he said. 'They've put twenty-five crowd-control and drugs officers in the park and just outside it. In addition to the two surveillance teams out with your guys, we've got an armed team standing by and ready to go.'

'OK, thanks. There's not much more we can do till Tahira appears.' Liz walked across to the table at the end of the room where a jug of coffee was standing on a warmer beside a plate of Danish pastries. Yet another unhealthy breakfast, she thought to herself, as she selected a large cinnamon bun.

58

'You keep an eye on that little monkey Nazir,' warned Tahira's father. 'He daydreams, that boy. Anyone could steal us blind when he's behind the till.'

'Don't worry, Papa. I always watch him very carefully.'

Tahira closed the front door behind her, then walked quickly down the road. If her father was standing in the sitting-room window to watch her go, he'd see that she was heading for the shop. It wasn't until she knew she was out of his sight that she turned up a side street, cutting across the hill towards the café where she'd agreed to meet Malik.

She'd asked her cousin Chunna to stand in for her today, though she hadn't told her father that. Chunna would keep an eye on Nazir and was glad of the work—it would give her a bit of pin money to spend on herself. Her husband was a bully and mean with it; he only gave her the barest housekeeping. But he'd gone on a trip to Pakistan, so Chunna was off the hook for a few weeks, though her mother-in-law was a mean old cow too and kept a very close eye on her. Tahira had sworn Chunna to secrecy. If her father ever found out she'd gone to a pop concert, let alone taken a day off work at the shop for it, he'd be furious.

Tahira was nobody's fool, but she'd trusted the MI5 woman from London as soon as she'd met her. Not that she believed she was called Jane Forrester, but that didn't matter—Tahira wasn't surprised that she didn't use her real name in her line of work. But she'd seemed very straight and she'd spoken kindly about Amir, not blaming him as though he was some kind of criminal—though it did seem from what she'd said that he had got himself into something dreadful. Jane had seemed anxious about Tahira too, particularly when she'd told her she was meeting Malik again this morning. Jane had made her promise to ring as soon as he'd gone, and tell her what had happened.

Tahira didn't know Malik very well, but it was hard to believe that someone like him, who'd lived all his life just a few streets away and who'd been to the same school as her, would want to kill people, though Jane had said he did. In his way he was quite attractive, and when you talked to him he could be interesting and even funny sometimes—in a different world they might have

327

had a real friendship. But he had shown another side too, when he'd started lecturing her about the Islamic duty to fight the West and defend Islam. Why should defending Islam mean hurting people? She didn't get it. It was men like Malik who'd led her brother astray. She was sure it was him and the others at the New Springfield Mosque who'd arranged Amir's trip to Pakistan and put him in the hands of other extremists, so that he'd ended up in prison in Paris. She'd never forgive Malik for that, and that was why she'd agreed to tell the MI5 woman everything that he said.

Tahira was hurrying now; she didn't want to be late at the café and start the conversation on the wrong foot. There was something rigid about Malik that made her sure he'd be angry if she wasn't on time. In that way he reminded her of her father. Were all Pakistani men tyrants? She sometimes wondered. Englishmen seemed more relaxed, not that she could speak from personal experience— she'd never got to know any. Her father, her mother, and the whole culture she had grown up in had made sure of that. So far she had managed to avoid the arranged marriage her parents wanted for her. Her father had been prepared to wait, but only because she was useful to him, being so good at running the shop. But he wouldn't wait for ever, and it was certain that if she showed any interest in an Englishman she'd end up married to some dire cousin from Sadiquabad. Then she'd be like Chunna: bullied and tied to the house.

She crossed over the side street, noticing a couple of builders sitting eating sandwiches in a van. She wondered why anyone would work on a Saturday if they didn't have to. Maybe they worked

328

at something else during the week. Not that they were working now, just sitting eating and reading the paper.

'You're looking very lovely today, Tahira.' The voice came from behind her; she was still a hundred yards away from the café. Tahira was used to casual comments on the street—wolf whistles from men on building sites, muttered compliments from shy teenage boys when she passed them—but this sounded different. He knew her name.

She turned around and saw a short man who looked familiar, beaming at her. She looked more closely.

'Malik?' she asked cautiously.

'Don't say you've forgotten me already,' said the man with a laugh. It was Malik, she saw now, but he had shaved off his beard and he was wearing trousers and a jacket. He even had a pullover on. He's going to be hot, thought Tahira; the forecast was for a day of sunshine and it was already warming up.

Malik came closer and shook her hand, holding it for a moment. He seemed less formal than usual, much friendlier. 'Let's have some tea,' he said, taking her arm and leading her towards the café.

It was crowded with Muslim men in white shirts and skullcaps. Tahira was one of the few women there. Two men at a corner table got up to leave as they came in, so Malik and Tahira sat down there, Malik facing the door. He poured out the mint tea they had ordered, talking all the time—asking Tahira about her job in her father's shop, telling her about his little nephew's football team and his brother's hopeless efforts to set up a kebab stall. He was doing his best to be charming; she might have warmed to him if she hadn't kept in the forefront of her mind everything else she knew about him.

He stopped talking just long enough to drink his tea, then asked, 'Are you still going to the concert?'

'Of course. Though my cousin's cancelled on me.' She looked down at her watch. 'I'll have to go soon if I'm going to get a good place.'

She was finishing her tea when Malik said, 'You know, I have been thinking about this group you like. Perhaps I was a bit too down on them. After all, if we live here in the West, then we have to live *with* the West. There is no point pretending we are in Pakistan, is there?'

Tahira nodded, but she was puzzled. Why was Malik sounding so reasonable? Where was the firebrand of their last meeting? He went on, 'I can't say these Chick Peas are much to my taste—bit of a girls' band with all their fancy clothes and hair-dos and stuff. And they're Indian as well. But I have to admit,' and he gave a sheepish smile, 'that their songs are quite catchy. I heard one on the radio this morning and I've been humming it ever since. What's it called?'

' "Biryani for Two",' said Tahira. 'But you ought to get their CD. Some of their other songs are better.'

'Really? Well, perhaps I should hear them live. I'm not doing anything special today—I could come with you to the concert, especially since your cousin's let you down. If you don't mind, that is?'

'Of course not,' said Tahira, but her mind was racing. It didn't make sense—Malik had been completely contemptuous last time, when she'd said she was going to hear the all-girl band. Why

330

had he changed now? And why had he shaved off his beard? She didn't like to ask him, but it was a very odd thing to do for someone as religious as he professed to be. She didn't trust this new Malik— something was going on. She needed to tell Jane right away.

'Excuse me a minute,' she said, getting up to go to the lavatory.

Malik stood up too. 'I'll pay the bill,' he said, 'then we can walk to the park together.'

Tahira found the women's room at the back of the café, and locked the door firmly behind her. She turned on the tap in the washbasin to cover the sound of her voice, in case anyone was listening outside, then she hit the predial number for Jane.

There was no signal.

She went out to find Malik waiting for her by the door. 'Ready?' he said with a smile.

'You go on. I just need to phone my father. I'll catch you up,' she said, reaching into her bag for her phone.

'Your father's a bit of a tyrant, if you don't mind my saying so,' said Malik. He was holding her elbow now. 'Ring him later?'

'But I promised—' she said, and felt his fingers tighten their grip on her arm.

'You can ring him when we get to the park. Come on, let's go. Don't forget, I've got to buy a ticket.'

*　　　*　　　*

As Malik and Tahira left the café, tension was rising in the Ops room. There had been some initial confusion in the A4 teams as to whether

331

the man who'd joined Tahira was Malik or someone else, as he looked so different from normal. There'd been a discussion about why he was looking so Westernised; they'd come to the conclusion that he must suspect surveillance, so Lamb had warned the teams to hang back, as their target might be alert to them.

'Looks like he's going to escort her to the concert,' said Lamb to Liz as the reports came in that the two targets were still together and walking towards the park.

Liz didn't reply at first. A thought came to her and she asked Fontana, 'Is the concert sold out or are they selling tickets at the gate?'

'It wasn't sold out yesterday,' replied Fontana. 'The organisers asked permission to erect ticket booths and there was concern in the crowd-control unit that there might be trouble if a lot of people were scrambling for tickets. But they let them go ahead in the end. What are you . . .'

Liz broke in, 'I think that's where Malik's going. He's going to the concert.'

'What? A good Muslim boy like him? I wouldn't have thought he'd be seen dead at a pop concert. Especially when it's an Indian group.'

'Dead may be the right word. He's going *because* they're Indian, and Westernised, and vulgar and decadent—just like the rest of us, in Malik's view. And there will be thousands of people there listening to this girl band. I think the band's his target—but anyone else will be a bonus for Malik.'

'God, I think you're right.' And Fontana seized a radio from one of the spare console desks and started barking out a series of orders—mobilising the armed teams and passing the description of

Malik and Tahira to the police control room to send to the officer in charge on the ground.

'I'm going to the park,' he told Liz.

'I'm coming with you. I know Tahira, I can help look for her.' As they left the Ops room she said to Fontana, 'Tell the men on the ground that they have to get her away from Malik.' She was afraid that whatever the extremist was planning to do, he was intending to take Tahira with him.

59

'Are you OK, Malik?'

'I'm fine. Why shouldn't I be?'

'It's just the way you're walking—all stiff. You look as if you've hurt your back or something.' Malik usually strolled along, his arms hanging loosely by his sides, but today he was almost marching, his back very straight and his head up. He looks like a soldier on parade, Tahira thought.

'I went to the gym yesterday for the first time in ages. I think I overdid it a bit. But I'm fine. Who wouldn't be, walking with a beautiful girl to a decadent pop concert?' he added with a laugh.

Tahira was struck by how light-hearted he seemed. Maybe the Jane woman from London had got it wrong about him. She hoped so.

On the Stratford Road the traffic was gridlocked. Cars sat motionless in two long lines, completely blocked by the swarm of mainly Asian young people who, bunched up at the entrance to the park, were spilling over on to the road. They made a colourful crowd on the sunny morning, many of the girls in very short skirts that barely covered their pants, tottering along in high-heeled sandals; the men, fewer in number, were wearing bright shirts and jeans, some of them pushing buggies or carrying small children on their shoulders. Tahira thought Malik looked very out of place in his jacket and pullover, but if he'd never been to a pop concert before, perhaps he didn't know what people wore.

As they were carried along by the crush of people towards the entrance gates, she grabbed Malik's hand. It would be easy to get separated in this crowd. Closer to the gates, stewards in orange jackets were trying to divide the crowd into those who had tickets and those who needed to buy them. Two booths had been erected, one on each side of the gate, and tapes marked where the queues were supposed to form. But the lines were already longer than the tapes and there was a lot of confusion about where each queue ended and who was in front of whom.

As they stood waiting, Tahira watched the uniformed policemen who had joined the stewards at the gate. It struck her that they seemed more concerned with scanning the concert-goers than with helping the stewards sort out the chaotic crowd. There was a man in a parka with a camcorder. She thought he must be from local TV because he was filming them all as they approached the gates.

'Come on,' said Malik. 'I'm not waiting here any longer. The concert'll be starting soon.'

'How are you going to get in without a ticket?'

'I've been watching them and they're not checking very carefully.' He took her arm and pushed her towards the dense crowd going through the gates, walking closely behind her. He was right—there was such a crush that the ticket checkers had more or less given up. They were reduced to looking cursorily at tickets when people held them out, but they weren't able to stop anyone who didn't. A sudden surge from the crowd pushed Tahira through the bottleneck of the entrance, Malik hanging on tight to her arm. As they came into the park the pressure eased and the crowd spread out, like water pushed through a narrow channel suddenly finding room to flow.

Tahira took a deep breath and realised that Malik had let go of her. She looked around for him, panicking slightly when she couldn't see him. Then his now-familiar face materialised behind her, and she saw with amazement that he'd put on an orange baseball cap, which had a big blue *P* emblazoned on the front.

Tahira laughed at him. 'Where on earth did you get that from?'

He grinned. 'I went to Tesco earlier this week for my mum. They were selling them there and I thought I could use it today. Isn't this what you're meant to wear at a pop concert?'

She shook her head. 'You're a clown.' But as she said it something was occurring to her. If he'd bought the cap in Tesco earlier in the week, he must have meant to come to the concert all along. Why had he pretended to her that he'd only had the idea this morning?

She had no time to think this through, jostled into following the crowd of people moving in the direction of the stage, but Malik steered her towards the side where ropes strung loosely

335

between stakes marked the boundaries of the audience area. She pulled the other way. She wanted to get up to the front, near the stage, and join the girls there who were jumping up and down and clapping in time to the warm-up band. But Malik tugged her back and pointed to a huge screen showing the performers on-stage. She realised that she'd get a better view from here, and it would be more comfortable than being squashed in the crowd and probably seeing very little.

The warm-up band finished playing and the crowd clapped and shrieked as they went off the stage. Then a tall Asian man came on with a microphone in his hand. It was Amrit Sandhu, presenter of the local TV station's music channel. The crowd roared as he waved to them, then gradually the noise died down.

'*Namaste*, everyone,' he shouted.

'*Namaste*,' the crowd roared back.

'*Salaam*,' he shouted.

'*Salaam*,' they roared back.

And finally 'Hello,' and back from the crowd 'Hello.'

'Are you enjoying yourselves?'

'Yes,' the crowd shouted back.

'Well, now you're in for the treat of the afternoon. They're here, straight from their successful European tour, already booked for a US tour and waiting to perform, just for you. Put your hands together. It's . . . the Chick Peas!'

A huge answering roar came from the crowd.

Tahira was watching the big screen beside her as the group's band began to play a heavy bass line accompanied by loud insistent drums. Suddenly from the wings the lead singer, Banditti Kahab, marched on to the stage wearing a white leather miniskirt, stamping her tall, shiny, high-heeled boots in time to the beat. She had huge silver hoop earrings in her ears, silver bangles on her arms, and her hair was brushed out in a lustrous black mane.

The two other Chick Peas now came on to the stage, one in wide-bottomed silk trousers displaying a bare midriff, the other in skintight crops and what looked like a bra made of sequins.

They stood side by side at the front of the stage, waving and smiling at the audience. Then suddenly the band started to play the intro to their hit single and the girls began to sing. Banditti waved to the crowd to join in and the resulting noise was deafening.

Tahira sang too, and glanced over at Malik to see if he was joining in. But he wasn't singing; he was looking at her. She smiled but he didn't smile back. She felt uneasy again. What was the matter? As the song ended and the applause died down a bit, she said, 'That was great, wasn't it?'

He didn't reply. A guitar was being tuned before the next song and over Malik's shoulder, on the screen, Tahira could see Banditti moving around the stage, waiting till the band was ready. Malik said, 'Listen, I have to go now.'

'What do you mean, go?' She couldn't believe it.

He nodded. She said, 'So you *aren't* enjoying it.'

'No, no. It's not that,' he said. 'I just have to leave.'

'I don't know what you're talking about. Why have you got to leave?'

He gave a thin smile. 'It doesn't matter. Just trust me.'

'But where are you going? You'll never be able

to get out in this crush. When will I see you again?'

He looked at her and said, 'I can't predict that. But I am sure we will meet again. Maybe not in this world, but certainly in the next one.'

As he said these words, Tahira went cold from head to toe. She stared at him open-mouthed. There was a dreamy look on his face now, as if he was already somewhere else.

She didn't want to think about that. Instead she said, 'Why are you talking like this? Why can't you stay here with me? You wanted to come,' she added accusingly.

But he wasn't listening. Malik seemed to be drifting away from her, right before her eyes. She was helpless to call him back.

He said slowly, 'You are very special, Tahira. Please always remember that I said that. Goodbye.' And he reached out his hand and touched her lightly on the cheek, then turned and walked away. She watched, mystified, as he headed towards the gates.

Then Malik suddenly changed direction, angling sideways into the back of the crowd. She lost sight of him for a moment, then saw the orange baseball cap bobbing among the excited teenage girls. What was he doing?

And then she realised he was heading for the stage, and suddenly she knew. It had all been a sham. He hadn't changed his mind about the Chick Peas, or the West, or the evil he seemed to see in everything Tahira enjoyed. He had tricked her, pretending to have changed; he'd used her as cover to get into the concert. He was going to do something terrible.

60

'We've lost them.'

Lamb's voice came over the radio just as Fontana pulled up at the back entrance to the park. By coming this way, he'd managed to avoid the worst of the traffic. 'NO ACCESS TO CONCERT' read a makeshift notice stuck on the gate. A couple of stewards wearing armbands were directing hopefuls around to the other side of the park.

The radio crackled and Lamb's voice came through again: 'Both targets were together outside the entrance gates two minutes ago, but we lost them in the crowd.'

'Damn!' said Fontana, banging his hand on the steering wheel in frustration.

'Come on,' said Liz. 'Everyone's looking for them. Let's go and help.'

They left the car by the entrance. Fontana flashed his badge at the stewards and one of them opened the gate to let them in. The combined noise of the music and the audience was ear-splitting, even here behind the stage. Liz could see the vast crowd gathered in front of it, swaying to the music as the girls began to sing. A group of roadies stood smoking by the short flight of steps that led up to the rear of the stage. As a policeman walked towards them, waving his arm, they ground their cigarettes out in the grass.

Fontana was on his radio, talking to the crowd-control officer in charge of the concert, who was saying, 'Four armed officers in the front few rows, ready to intercept anyone trying to reach the stage. The others combing the crowd. All uniform have the description of the suspect and the girl.'

The officer went on, 'We've taken the decision to let the concert carry on. There's a serious risk the crowd will panic and stampede for the exit if we make any announcement or try to stop it now.'

Fontana shook his head. 'I'm sure he's right,' he said to Liz. 'But I'm glad it's his call and not mine.'

From where she now stood, by the side of the open-air stage, Liz had a clear view of the crowd. At the front it was overwhelmingly female, young Asian girls happily singing along with the group. Many of them were dancing to the music; a few sat on the shoulders of their friends, waving their hands from side to side in time to the rhythm. Finding anyone in this throng was like looking for a needle in a haystack. The only hope was that a single male figure would stick out in this predominantly female crowd. But the audience stretched almost to Stratford Road, and further back there were couples and families. If Tahira and Malik were still together and towards the back of the crowd, finding them would be well-nigh impossible. Liz did a rough calculation and reckoned there must be five thousand people in the park.

And then, incredibly, she saw Tahira. She was standing by herself to one side, just outside the ropes that cordoned off the audience enclosure, near a huge television screen. She was holding something in her hand, and looking to one side. There was no sign of Malik.

'I see the girl,' Liz shouted at Fontana over the din. 'Tell your men Malik will be on his own.'

She ran along the edge of the vast crowd,

outside the ropes. No one paid any attention to her; all eyes were glued to the stage as Banditti began to sing a new song. The noise was deafening, and when Liz shouted at Tahira as she drew closer, it was like shouting into the mouth of a gale. Liz could see the girl clearly now; she was holding her mobile, looking as if she were trying to make a call. When Liz reached her, out of breath and panting, Tahira still hadn't seen her. She tapped her on the shoulder and Tahira looked up in astonishment.

'I was just ringing you,' she said.

'Where's Malik?'

'He's gone.'

Fontana joined them as Liz asked urgently, 'Did he leave the park?' Tahira shook her head. 'He started to, but then he moved into the crowd.' She pointed at the semi-hysterical mass of girls.

Fontana shook his head. 'How are we going to find him in that?'

'You might spot him,' said Tahira. 'He's wearing a baseball cap now. He put it on when we got inside the gates. It's orange.'

Fontana began shouting into his radio while Liz scanned the audience. Her heart sank as she scanned a sea of pulsating bodies and countless flashes of orange—baseball caps, and Chick Peas T-shirts emblazoned on the back with the band's bright orange logo.

Then she felt a sharp nudge in her ribs. 'I can see him,' cried an agitated Tahira. 'He's taken his cap off. Look, he's that one there, pushing through the crowd.' She gestured towards the middle of the audience, about halfway between where they stood and the stage. Liz peered at the waving throng, then she suddenly spotted a bareheaded man, moving through the crowd, slowly working his way towards the stage. It was Malik.

'Look, can you see him?' Liz said to Fontana, lifting her arm to point to the figure forcing his way through the onlookers.

Fontana stared and stared, then suddenly said, 'Got him!' He spoke into his radio, and listened to the response crackling back. He shook his head in frustration. 'There's no one near him. We're going to lose him again.'

But Malik was clearly visible now. He was no longer heading for the stage, but was moving slowly towards the rope cordoning off their side of the crowd. Fontana was on the radio again, giving a running commentary. 'He's coming out of the crowd. Left-hand side facing the stage . . . halfway down . . .'

He turned to Liz. 'He must have found he couldn't get through all those people.'

They stood watching, the distant figure becoming clearer with every second that passed. Two armed policeman came running from the side of the stage just as Malik—distinguishable now in his suit jacket—pushed his way out of the heaving mob of girls and started to run along beside the rope towards the stage.

Then he saw the two policemen ahead of him and hesitated. One hand moved towards his jacket pocket, and for a moment Liz thought he was going to blow himself up right there. One of the policemen shouted at him—Liz could see his lips working furiously. His colleague was crouching, his weapon held in both hands, aimed and ready to fire.

But Malik must have changed his mind. His

hand came out of his pocket again and he turned round, now facing their little group of three, less than a hundred yards away. He started running towards them, moving awkwardly in his heavy jacket.

Liz heard Tahira shriek, and Fontana stepped in front to shield them. The two policemen sprinting after Malik were catching up fast. Both had their weapons out now, and both were shouting—though with the music so loud there was no chance Malik would hear them.

He was now only fifty yards away from Liz and Tahira, but the two Special Branch men were very close behind. They were trying to get into a position where they could fire away from the crowd and avoid hitting Liz and her two companions.

Malik was within thirty yards now and suddenly his hand moved quickly into his jacket again. Both policemen fired. The Glock pistols made a flat metallic noise, hardly audible over the beat of the Chick Peas' backing band.

As Tahira screamed Malik fell, flat on his face. He lay unmoving on the ground as blood seeped slowly out of his head.

61

Amazingly, virtually no one in the crowd had paid any attention to what was going on at the side of the park. The armed officers quickly put away their weapons, as uniformed police arrived to shield the body from view, and gently but firmly move the crowd away from the ropes, telling them that someone had had an accident. People were happy to comply since they were far more interested in the music being played on stage than in someone who'd been taken ill.

Whatever explosives there were beneath Malik's jacket, the man was not alive to detonate them. But within minutes the bomb squad arrived, coming in discreetly from the back of the ground while the police finished erecting a tent over the body and placing a cordon round the area. The concert was nearly over now, and people were beginning to drift away from the back of the crowd. Soon the rest of the audience would be on the move, shepherded out by the police; then the park would be closed while the forensic team moved in.

Liz walked with Tahira to the back entrance where they sat in Fontana's car watching as various police units came and went. Tahira had said nothing since Malik was shot. She was shaking and was obviously in deep shock. Suddenly she started to cry—big shuddering sobs. Liz put an arm round her. 'You were very brave,' she said, meaning every word.

Tahira was trying to speak through her sobs, 'He was heading straight for me. He wanted to kill me. He wanted to kill all of us.'

Liz had no doubt that Malik had decided to take them with him once he saw he couldn't get near the stage. Ten more seconds and he would have succeeded. But that wouldn't help Tahira. So she said gently, 'You know death didn't mean the same thing to him as it does to you and me.'

Tahira looked up, wiping her streaming eyes with the back of her hand. 'What do you mean?'

'For Malik this was only a temporary world,

a brief stop on the way to Paradise. That's why he wanted to kill himself. Death is welcomed by someone who thinks they're going to another, better life.'

'But we would all have died! And he said he cared about me. He told me I should always remember that. He said I was special . . .'

'I know. And he meant it. But he also believed you would meet again—in this other, better world of his.'

Tahira nodded. 'That's what he said—that I might not see him again here, but that he was certain we would meet in future.'

'Yes. I am sure that's what he thought,' said Liz, and Tahira seemed satisfied by this explanation.

But Liz wasn't. From where she sat in the car, she could see down the side of the stage to the park. It was a sad sight on that late-summer afternoon: the litter-strewn field, the stage being dismantled, and two white-coated orderlies lifting a stretcher into the back of an ambulance.

Her mind was full of questions. If Malik really had cared for Tahira, would he have wanted to murder her? It certainly looked as if he'd intended to. But did he actually believe he would see her again in Paradise? As far as Liz understood, the celestial rewards were reserved for martyrs—and though Malik might have considered himself a martyr, it was hard to see how his killing Tahira would have made her one as well.

No, he must just have seen her, like the Chick Peas and everyone else at the concert—men, women and children—as a sacrifice, to be killed in pursuit of his objective. And what was that objective anyway? Was it his personal desire to become a martyr, or did he really think of himself as a warrior in a justified war, defending his religion?

Yet he'd had more than half a chance to do what he'd set out to do. He could have exploded his suicide belt at any minute—he'd had plenty of time, even after he'd spotted the armed police coming towards him. The Chick Peas would have escaped—he hadn't got close enough to the stage—but he could have killed dozens of 'Infidels', mainly silly teenage girls, having fun at a harmless entertainment that he disliked.

So why hadn't he? Why didn't he pull the cord as soon as he thought he would be captured or shot? If he was the loyal *jihadi* that he seemed to have been, why hadn't he gone ahead and achieved his aim?

It didn't make sense. All these contradictions—to kill but not to kill; to kill a friend but not to kill strangers. There'd never be an answer now. Not with Malik lying dead on a stretcher.

There was only one thing left to do—look after the living. Liz put her arm round Tahira's shoulders again as Fontana arrived back at the car. This girl still had a life ahead of her.

62

'Liz around?'

Peggy looked up to find Kanaan Shah standing in front of her desk. 'No, she's away for a few days. Holiday.'

'Well deserved.'

346

'I'll say. How's it going with you?'

'Fine, thanks. I've just come from seeing Salim and Jamila. The Boatmans. They're adjusting pretty well, all things considered. Jamila would love to see Liz sometime.'

'Liz said she'd visit her as soon as she gets back.'

'Good. I've got something here for you both to read. The last sentence is mind-boggling.'

He handed a ragged piece of newsprint to Peggy. It was a cutting from a recent edition of the *Birmingham Asian News*:

Local cleric Abdi Bakri has strenuously denied police allegations that he masterminded a plot to detonate an explosive device at a pop concert. A 27-year-old man identified as Malik Sukari, a native-born resident of Birmingham, was shot dead by Special Branch officers during the concert, featuring the all-girl Indian group, the Chick Peas.

Labelled a suicide bomber by police, Sukari was found to have been wearing a belt containing enough explosive, in the words of one officer, 'to blow up half of Birmingham'.

Somalia-born Bakri, founder of the New Springfield Mosque, claimed he was the victim of a smear campaign designed to link him not only with Sukari but also with four British Pakistanis, all members of his Birmingham mosque, who were recently arrested during the attempted hijacking of an Athens-registered tanker off the Horn of Africa.

Speaking to the *Asian News*, Bakri said, 'I had no knowledge that these young men were going to Somalia and did not assist them in any way.

As for Sukari, he was acting entirely on his own, and I do not condone what he did—though when the Western powers are daily killing our Muslim brothers all over the world, actions like his must be expected.'

Bakri claimed to have been a victim of religious persecution as a young man in Somalia, and said he would resist any efforts by British authorities to deport him there.

Bakri also announced that he planned to ask for political asylum from the UK government.

*　　　*　　　*

In the UCSO Athens office, Anastasia was typing a letter for Claude Rameau when Falana walked across to her desk. It was Thursday afternoon, the usual time for the two girls to discuss which club to go to on Saturday night. But Anastasia could see something else was on Falana's mind—her dark eyes were wide with excitement.

'I've just seen Elena. She said a policeman's been to see Mr Berger,' she whispered.

Anastasia sighed. 'It'll just be about poor Maria Galanos again, I bet.' The police had visited the office so many times that their visits had become routine.

'Yes, but not in the way you think. They were asking about Mr Miandad.'

'Mo?' she asked, not being as deferential as Falana.

Her friend nodded. 'Yes. They wanted to know where he was. Mr Berger said we hadn't seen him here for weeks and they should ask the shipping agency, but the police said they already had. No one knows where he is.'

Anastasia scoffed. 'He's probably run off with yet another woman.' They had heard about Katherine Ball's arrest in London, and decided she must have been the blonde who had been spotted with Miandad in a sleazy hotel.

'No. That's not it,' said Falana. 'Apparently they want to talk to him about the murder of Maria Galanos.'

'They think Mo knows something about that?'

'They think he did it.'

'Mother of God! No wonder he's disappeared. I wonder where he's gone.'

'Pakistan,' said a voice, and the girls looked up to see Alex Limonides in the doorway. 'That's where he'll be. And they'll never find him there.'

*   *   *

'Coke and a slice of lemon,' said the CIA Station Head, London, Andy Bokus. 'Lots of ice.'

The Athenaeum Club wine waiter allowed the merest flicker of surprise to cross his face. But when Fane ordered a glass of Chablis, he smiled.

Bokus leaned forward and said, 'I hear one of your former colleagues has gotten the push.'

'Who might that be?' asked Fane mildly, though he knew full well who Bokus was talking about. David Blakey had resigned as Director of UCSO three days before. Word must have travelled fast if Bokus already knew about it.

'You know who I mean. What exactly did he do? Get caught with his pants down? I hear it's not the first time.'

'Something like that,' said Fane mildly.

'He got taken for a ride by that Ball woman. Some piece of work she is. I hope she gets all the payback that's coming to her.'

'Evidence, Andy. Evidence. We'll have to see what we can prove. Her partner in crime, that Pakistani shipping agent Miandad, has disappeared.'

'Yeah, I heard that. He'll be in the tribal region by now. The only thing that'll get him is a drone.'

Their drinks came, and Fane decided on a charm offensive. 'Cheers, Andy,' he said, raising his glass. 'Nice to see you in more peaceful surroundings. Last time we met, the fur was flying off the Horn.'

Bokus grunted and studied the menu. He had been furious that the British Special Forces had gone into Somalia without even informing the American warship that had been especially despatched to provide firepower.

Fane couldn't resist rubbing it in. 'Sorry you couldn't take part in the show, but I think you'd agree our chaps handled the whole thing rather successfully. We managed to pull MI5's irons out of the fire and get their chap out safely. Can't think what he was doing there in the first place. Anyway, it all worked out in the end. I hope it was useful for your lot to see how we do things.'

Bokus' face turned red.

'Well, we should order,' said Fane, taking up the little pad to write the order down. 'What will you have, Andy?'

'I'll have the lobster. A whole one,' Bokus said angrily, ignoring Fane's raised eyebrow. 'And I'll start with the caviar.'

God knows what they'd make of his expense

account this month, thought Fane, but he'd happily have paid for dinner himself just to see Bokus' reaction to being . . . what did the Americans say? Ribbed? Yes, that was it. *Ribbed*.

*   *   *

For a luxury cruise ship, the SS *Tiara* was small, but its amenities were second to none. An indoor pool, an outdoor pool, three restaurants (including a sumptuous seafood buffet), a bar that literally never closed, a casino and a live entertainment show each evening (admittedly pretty dire), and enough boutiques to keep the most shopaholic matron satisfied.

After Dave Armstrong had been freed from the pirate compound on the Somalian coast, he'd spent three days on board a French corvette sailing back to the Mediterranean, from where he'd been choppered to the French naval base in Toulon. There he'd been debriefed by a pleasant man from the French DGSE, Martin Seurat, whom he'd met the previous year when an operation had ended in France. Seurat had kept in touch with Liz Carlyle and, from what Dave had heard, they were now an item. Then an MI6 officer from Paris had turned up to question him; he'd assumed Dave would want to fly back to England straight away and had offered to arrange it.

But Dave knew exactly what he wanted, and it wasn't a flight back to England. He needed a break. He wanted to go somewhere comfortable but not over the top; somewhere where he could do nothing and be alone when he wanted to, but with people around if he felt like socialising. In short,

351

somewhere where he could completely relax.

So, instead of flying to London, he had joined the *Tiara*, which was sailing from Toulon, down the coast of Italy and up the Adriatic to Venice. The shipping agents for the *Tiara* were contacts of the DGSE, and after Martin Seurat had spoken to their CEO, it turned out that there was a vacant berth in first class and that Dave would be welcome on board as an honoured guest of the company.

Now as the ship cruised gently through the Ligurian Sea, he looked out from the deck at the coast of Italy in the evening sunshine and saw the island of Elba rising from the deep blue water. He found himself beginning to feel very fortunate to be alive.

He thought of his narrow escape from the pen in Somalia. It was the second time he'd been abducted within the space of a year. Was he getting careless? Had his capture each time been his own fault? It was hard to say. He still loved his work, but without the youthful passion he had brought to it during his early years in the Service. Now, there were times when he'd encounter a situation and feel an almost weary sensation of déjà vu, a feeling that he'd seen the same thing many times before. There were only so many variations to an intelligence operation, only so many different kinds of terrorist to pursue or agent to run. Maybe he was just getting stale. Maybe it was time to look for another job.

He was paid to risk his life if necessary, but that hadn't made it any less frightening when he was faced with the imminent prospect of death. If Taban hadn't got away, who knows how long it would have taken the SAS to find the compound.

And by then he might well have been tortured, or murdered, or both, by the fanatics who'd taken him captive.

He owed a lot to the African boy, whom he'd seen again on the French corvette. He had even been able to help him after explaining to the French crew that he owed his life to Taban. The Captain—was it Thibault? Some name like that—had understood at once, and when Martin Seurat had come aboard, the two of them had talked about Taban and promised Dave that they would do their best to help him stay in France, where he could get an education. Dave was glad he had done something for the boy, and he had promised to keep in touch with him through Martin Seurat.

As they sailed smoothly on down the coast of Italy he pushed the buzzer on the table in front of him. When the waiter came, he ordered a gin and tonic—a large one.

The days wore gently on. The ship called at Naples and Dave stirred himself enough to join the organised trip to Pompeii, where he listened to the guide's account of the eruption of Vesuvius, and bought some postcards in the gift shop, which he didn't send.

A few days later, as he was sitting on deck at his favourite table, he looked up and saw Mount Etna silhouetted against a deep blue sky, snow-capped and majestic, with a trail of smoke wafting from one of its volcanic cones. The waiter brought his drink, and when he'd gone Dave raised his glass. This volcano was alive; so, by the skin of his teeth, was Dave.

*   *   *

Berger went to meet Hal Stimkin at what the CIA man now referred to as their 'watering hole'. Fortunately this would be the last time Berger would have to drink with him in the bar of the Venus de Milo; the last time he'd have to come running when Hal Stimkin called. Goodbye, Athens, he thought cheerfully, and good riddance to his former employer, the CIA.

Stimkin was already there on his usual bar stool. Berger sat down next to him, ordered a beer, and came right to the point.

'I've got news for you,' he said.

'Good or bad?'

'Good for me.' He took a long swallow of his beer. 'My boss back in London's resigned.'

'Oh?'

'Yeah, and the thing is, they've offered me the post and I've accepted.'

'Congratulations,' said Stimkin matter-of-factly. Berger was slightly taken aback that he didn't seem more surprised.

'So you see, Hal, this is our valedictory session. I'll be leaving Athens next week. And it's going to be my farewell to Langley too. In my new job it just wouldn't be right for me to moonlight for you guys. I'm sure Langley will understand.'

'Oh, I don't know about that,' Stimkin said disconcertingly. 'You see, news of your appointment has already reached Langley and they've passed it on to Grosvenor Square. I had a call from the Head of Station there just this afternoon. Guy called Andy Bokus . . . he can't wait to meet you. Andy isn't everybody's cup of tea, but I'm sure you two will get along like a house on fire.'

354

Berger put his head in his hands and groaned. Stimkin patted him on the back. 'Cheer up, Mitchell. Remember what they say, don't you? You can take the boy out of Langley, but you can't take Langley out of the boy.'

63

That evening, Liz and Martin had supper in his flat in Paris. Neither of them wanted any more excitement after the stress and frantic activity of recent weeks.

They had spent several hours that afternoon at the Santé prison, talking to Amir Khan. Martin had already told him about events in Birmingham— how Malik, his old friend and comrade at the mosque, had tried to blow himself up at a pop concert. Amir had remained silent, clearly shocked. It was as though, for the first time, he'd realised what the extremist views that both he and Malik had held, actually meant. How the logical end of them was the death of people, casually chosen, when they were doing no more than enjoying themselves.

Then Seurat added something else—that at the end, Malik had done his best to kill Tahira too— and Amir's shock had turned to outrage.

With the news of his former friend's betrayal, whatever doubts he might have had about his own recent collaboration with the security authorities disappeared in an instant. It was clear that the entire belief system by which Amir had recently lived had now collapsed. He had asked Martin

Seurat how anyone could defend a cause which would slaughter the person closest to him in the world. And Martin replied that no one could.

So when Liz had arrived that afternoon, Amir Khan had listened quietly to the joint French and English proposal. He would be released from prison and would stay in France, under the protection of the security authorities there, who would give him a new identity and a place to live. In return he would help them by reporting on extremist Islamist activity. They did not spell it out in detail at that stage, but what Amir was being offered was a job as an agent, to be run by colleagues of Martin Seurat.

As Amir hesitated, trying to understand the implications of what they were saying, Liz added that there was something else she had to suggest. It was no longer safe, she said, for Tahira to live in Birmingham. She might well be suspected of having helped to prevent Malik's suicide attempt, even if she had not been seen in the park with Liz or leaving in DI Fontana's car. Tahira was longing to see her brother. Liz told Amir that she'd promised the girl she would arrange for her to come to Paris as soon as possible. But more than that, when Liz had suggested to Tahira that she might like to live in France too if Amir agreed to settle there, she had jumped at the idea. What did he think of that?

To the relief of both Liz and Martin, Amir had liked the idea. In fact he had been delighted by it, and grinned as he shook Liz's hand when she said goodbye. 'I hope we meet again—but not in a prison,' were his parting words.

Liz had been looking forward to relaxing for a few days with Martin in Paris. But now, as she cleared the dinner plates from the table in the small dining alcove overlooking the square, she realised there were unresolved issues even here.

They were both tired. Martin had been closely involved in the planning that had foiled the last attempted hijack of the *Aristides*, and had flown an hour south to the French base at Toulon as soon as he'd heard that Dave and Captain Guthrie had been taken off the ship as hostages. Though they had been freed without any losses on the French or British side, it had been a close-run thing.

Liz was tired too, but not pleasantly so. She felt on edge. It wasn't the recent operation or that afternoon's conversation with Amir that was nagging at her. It was Martin. Well, not the man himself, but what he had come to represent. Since he had asked her to come and live with him in Paris, he had started to pose a threat to the one other love of her life—her job. For Liz, her work wasn't just important to her; to a large extent it *was* her.

She sat down again at the table and Martin poured her another glass of Burgundy and offered the plate of cheeses they had carefully chosen that afternoon from Madame Lileau's little shop around the corner. He was looking at her thoughtfully. He said, 'You seem tired, *ma chérie.*'

'I suppose I am. You must be exhausted too.'

He shook his head. 'Having you here gives me energy.'

She smiled to acknowledge the compliment,

but words were forming in her head. 'Martin, you know, I've been thinking—'

But he interrupted her, reaching across the table to hold her hand. 'Let me speak first, if you don't mind. I have been thinking too. When I asked if you would consider moving to Paris and coming to live with me, I thought it was an offer you couldn't refuse.' He smiled wistfully. 'But that was very selfish of me, I see it now. Love is not always about the other person; it is all too often about one's self.'

'You're the least selfish man I know.'

'That is very kind of you to say, but sadly untrue. However, a man can make amends,' he said lightly. 'And in my case the situation can be recovered. Even an old dog like me can learn a new trick or two. And I have come to realise, my dear Miss Carlyle,' he said now, gently stroking her hand, 'that fond as you may be of me, there is another love in your life.'

'What do you mean?' she asked. Could he really think she was seeing someone else?

He shook his head. 'I don't mean another man. Much as Geoffrey Fane might like to play that role.' He smiled. 'I was thinking of your career. Only the proper word, I believe, is vocation. It is not just important to you, Liz, it is part of you. If I kept nagging at you then possibly you would be willing to give it up—we are all sometimes tempted to quit, ours are not the easiest jobs in the world. But that would not only be selfish of me, but very wrong—and I would know, however happy we were together, that I had taken you away from something you hold tremendously dear.'

He let go of her hand and leaned back in his chair, a look of wry amusement on his face. 'You know, I practised that speech a hundred times, and still it came out different from the way I'd intended.'

'It came out very well, Martin,' Liz said, touched by what he had just said. He was not the first man in her life to have understood how important her work was to her—but he was the first to swallow his disappointment, accept the way things had to be for them, and continue to offer her his love and support.

'Thank you,' she said, as his arms came around her and she rested her head against his shoulder. She remembered what her friend Elaine, an ex-researcher in the Service turned Hampstead housewife and mother, had once told her: 'Life is about love and work. If neither's right, you're in trouble. If one's right, you'll probably be okay. But for a truly fulfilled life, you need them both to be in order.'

Liz could see the truth in that. It was a difficult balance and one she hadn't so far managed to achieve. Might she be able to with this patient man who, for now at least, was prepared to put her needs ahead of his own? Martin said softly, 'I do hate having the Channel between us. But thanks to Eurostar I can just about put up with it. I only hope you can as well.'

Liz looked at Martin. 'Of course I can.'

Then, with a grin, she said, 'Tell you what: let's buy each other season tickets for Christmas.'

A NOTE ON THE AUTHOR

Dame Stella Rimington joined the Security Service (MI5) in 1968. During her career she worked in all the main fields of the Service: counter-subversion, counter-espionage and counter-terrorism. She was appointed Director General in 1992, the first woman to hold the post. She has written her autobiography and five Liz Carlyle novels. She lives in London and Norfolk.